3/06

Second Honeymoon

Second Honeymoon

A Novel

JOANNA TROLLOPE

BLOOMSBURY

Published by Bloomsbury Publishing, New York and London
Distributed to the trade by Holtzbrinck Publishers

All papers used by Bloomsbury Publishing are natural,
recyclable products made from wood grown in well-managed
forests. The manufacturing processes conform to the
environmental regulations of the country of origin.

Library of Congress Cataloging-in-Publication Data

Trollope, Joanna.
Second honeymoon : a novel / Joanna Trollope.–1st U.S. ed.
p. cm.
ISBN-13 978-1-59691-038-6
ISBN-10 1-59691-038-0
1. Adult children living with parents–Fiction. 2. Parent and adult child–Fiction.
3. England–Fiction. 4. Domestic fiction. I. Title.
PR6070.R57S43 2006
823'.914 2 22
2005057011

First U.S. Edition 2006

1 3 5 7 9 10 8 6 4 2

Typeset by Hewer Text UK Ltd, Edinburgh
Printed in the United States of America by Quebecor World Fairfield

CHAPTER ONE

Edie put her hand out, took a breath and slowly, slowly pushed open his bedroom door. The room inside looked as if he had never left it. The bed was unmade, the curtains half drawn, the carpet almost invisible under trails of clothing. There were single trainers on shelves, mugs and cereal bowls on the floor, scatterings of papers and books everywhere. On the walls the same posters hung haphazardly from nuggets of blue gum: a Shakespeare play from a long-ago school outing, Kate Moss in a mackintosh, the Stereophonics from a concert at Earls Court. It looked, at first glance, as it had looked for a large part of his twenty-two years. It looked as if he was coming back, any minute.

Edie stepped through the chaos on the floor – ah, that's where her only bone-china mug had got to – and pulled the curtains fully apart. One side, obviously accustomed to doing this, rushed headlong to the left and slid triumphantly off the pole to the floor. Edie looked up. The finial that stopped the end was missing. It had probably been missing for months, years, and Ben's solution had been simply, pragmatically really, not to touch the curtain. In fact, on reflection, he would have had to thread the curtain back on to the pole just once, when the finial first fell off, and this small sign of enterprise and efficiency on his part made Edie think that she might cry. She picked up the fallen curtain and held it hard against her, swallowing against the crying.

"He hasn't gone to Mongolia," Russell had almost shouted at her that morning. "He hasn't *died*. He's gone to Walthamstow."

Edie had said nothing. She had gone on jabbing at a hermetically sealed packet of coffee with the wrong kind of knife and said nothing.

"End of a tube line," Russell said unnecessarily. "That's all. Walthamstow."

Edie flung the coffee and the knife into the sink. She would not look at Russell, she would not speak. She hated him when he was like this, when he knew perfectly well what was the matter and refused to admit it. She didn't hate his attitude, she told herself: she hated *him*.

"Sorry," Russell said.

Edie pulled the curtain up now and covered her face with it. It smelled of dust, years and years of grimy London dust, silting in through the window frames like the fine tilth from a tea bag. She hadn't acknowledged Russell's "Sorry." She hadn't looked at him. She had remained silent, distanced by emotion, until she heard him go out of the room and down the hallway – fumble, fumble by the coat rack – and out through the front door, letting it crash behind him the way they all had, two parents, three children, for close on twenty years. Twenty years. Almost all Ben's lifetime, almost a third of hers. You come to a house, Edie thought, pressing the dusty curtain against her eye sockets, carrying almost more life, more people, than you can manage. And then, over time, almost everything you have carried in begins to leak out again, inexorably, and you are left clutching fallen curtains at ten o'clock on a Saturday morning instead of applying yourself, with all your new reserves of no longer required maternal energy, to quality leisure.

She dropped the curtain back on to the floor. If she turned, slowly, and half closed her eyes, she could persuade herself that Ben had left his room in a mess as a signal to her that he hadn't really left it. That this notion of his to put all the essentials of his life into a duffel bag and carry it off to live with Naomi, in a spare room in her mother's flat in Walthamstow, was in truth no more than a notion. That he would begin to miss things, his childhood home, the cat, his pillow, his mother, and would see that life was not to be lived so satisfactorily anywhere else. But if she made herself open her eyes wide, really wide, and looked at the caliber of things he had left, the outgrown garments, the broken shoes, the discarded or irrelevant books and disks and papers, she could see that what Ben had left behind was what he didn't want anymore. He had taken what represented the present and the future, and he had left the past, leaving it in such a way as to emphasize its irrelevance to him. Edie bent down and began, without method or enthusiasm, to pick up the cereal bowls.

It wasn't as if Ben had ever, really, been away from home. His school days had melted comfortably into his college days and then into irregular, haphazard days of assistant to a self-employed photographer who specialized in portraits. All through these years Ben had come home, more nights than not, to sleep in the bedroom across the landing from his parents' bedroom, which had been allotted to him when he was two. His bedroom had been by turns pale yellow, purple, papered with airplanes, and almost black. The detritus of his life, from *Thomas the Tank Engine* to trailing computer cables, had spilled out of his room and across the landing, symbols of his changing taste, his changing world. The thought of the order – no, not order, the absence of chaos – that might follow his departure for Walthamstow brought Edie close to panic. It was like – like having an artery shut off, a light extinguished. It was far, far worse than when Matt had gone. Or Rosa. It was far, far worse than she expected.

She began to pile mugs and bowls without method on Ben's table. He had done homework at that table, made models, hacked with blades at the edges. She sat down by it, on the chair with the broken cane seat, filled in by a gaudy

3

Indian cushion embroidered with mirrors. She looked at the mess on the table. Ben was her youngest, her last. When the others went, she had felt a pang, but there had always been Ben, there had always been the untidy, demanding, gratifying, living proof that she was doing what she was meant to do, that she was doing something no one else could do. And, if Ben wasn't there to confirm her proper perception of herself in that way, what was she going to do about the future? What was she going to do about herself?

"It's awful," her sister Vivien had said on the telephone. "It's just awful. You spend all these years and years developing this great supporting muscle for your children and then they just whip round, don't they, and hack it through." She'd paused, and then she'd said, in a cooler tone, "Actually, it's not so bad for you because you've always got the theater."

"I haven't," Edie said, "I –"

"Well, I know you aren't working at this precise moment. But you always *could* be, couldn't you? You're always going for auditions and things."

"That," Edie said, her voice rising, "has nothing to do with Ben going, nothing to do with *motherhood*."

There was another pause and then Vivien said, in the slightly victim voice Edie had known since their childhoods, "Eliot's gone too, Edie. And he's my only child. He's all I've got."

Eliot had gone to Australia. He had found a job on a local radio station in Cairns, and within six months had a flat and a girlfriend there. Ben had gone five stops up the Victoria line to Walthamstow.

"Okay," Edie said to Vivien, conceding.

"I do know –"

"Yes."

"Lovely," Vivien said, "for Russell."

"Mmm."

"Having you back –"

Edie felt a flash of temper. Eliot's father, Max, had drifted

4

in and out of his wife and son's life in a way that made sure that the only thing about him that was predictable was his unreliability. Vivien might be able to trump her over the pain caused by distances, but she wasn't going to trump her over the pain caused by husbands.

"Enough," Edie said, and put the telephone down.

"Enough," she said to herself now, her elbows on Ben's table. She twisted round. Against the wall, Ben's bed stood exactly as he had left it, the duvet slewed toward the floor, the pillow dented, a magazine here, a pair of underpants there. It was tempting, she thought, holding hard to the chairback as an anchor, to spring up and fling herself down on Ben's bed and push her face into his pillow and breathe and breathe. It was very tempting.

Downstairs the front door crashed again. She heard Russell's feet on the tiles of the hall, heard him say something companionable to the cat.

"Edie?"

She went on staring at Ben's pillows.

"I've got the newspapers," Russell called. "An orgy of them –"

Edie looked up at Ben's bookshelves, at the space at the end where his teddy bear always sat, wearing Russell's old school tie from over forty years ago. The bear had gone. She stood up, holding an awkward stack of crockery.

"Coming," she said.

The garden was one of the reasons they had bought the house twenty years ago. It was only the width of the house, but it was seventy-five feet long, long enough for Matt, then eight, to kick a ball in. It also had a shed. Russell had loved the idea of a shed, the idea of paraffin heaters and fingerless gloves and listening to the soccer results on an old battery-operated radio. He saw seclusion in that shed, somewhere set apart from his family life and his working life because both were, by their very nature, all talk. He had a vision of being in the shed on winter weekend afternoons, probably wrapped in a sleeping bag, and looking back down the garden to the house, a dark shape with lit windows, and knowing that all that life and clamor was there for him to step back into, when he chose. It was a very luxurious vision, in that it encompassed both privacy and participation, and he clung to it during the years while the shed filled up with bikes and paint tins and broken garden chairs, leaving no space for him. It was even called "Dad's shed."

This Saturday afternoon, he told Edie, he was going to clear it out.

"Why?"

"Because it's full of useless junk."

She was chopping things, making one of her highly colored, rough-hewn salads.

"And then?"

"Then what?"

"When you have cleared out the shed, what will you do with it?"

"Use it."

Edie threw a handful of tomato pieces into the salad bowl.

"What for?"

Russell considered saying for reading pornography in, and decided against it.

He said, "The purpose will become plain as I clear it."

Edie picked up a yellow pepper. She had gathered her hair on top of her head and secured it with a purple plastic comb. She looked, in some ways, about thirty. She also looked small and defiant.

"You were clearing Ben's room this morning," Russell said gently.

"No," Edie said.

He went over to the fridge and took out a bottle of Belgian beer. The boys would drink it straight out of the bottle. Russell went across the kitchen, behind Edie, to the cupboard where the glasses were kept.

He said, his back to her, "What were you doing then?"

"Nothing," Edie said. "Thinking."

Russell took a glass out of the cupboard.

He said, his back still turned, holding the glass and the bottle, "They just do grow up. It's what happens."

"Yes," Edie said.

"It's what's *meant* to happen."

"Yes."

Russell turned. He put down the glass and the bottle and came to stand behind her.

"He's doing what he wants to do."

Edie sliced through the pepper.

"I know."

"You can't –"

"I know!" Edie shouted. She flung the knife across the table.

Russell moved to retrieve it. He held it out to her.

"Stop chucking things. It's so childish."

Edie took the knife and laid it down on the chopping board with elaborate care. Then she leaned on her hands and looked down into her salad.

"I love Ben as much as you do," Russell said. "But he's twenty-two. He's a man. When I –"

"Please don't," Edie said.

"I met you when I was twenty-two."

"Twenty-three."

"All right, then. Twenty-three. And you were twenty-one."

"Just," Edie said.

"I seem to remember us thinking we were quite old enough to get married."

Edie straightened up and folded her arms.

"We'd left home. We wanted to leave home. I left home at seventeen."

"Ben didn't."

"He liked it here, he loved it –"

And now he loves Naomi."

die gave a little snort.

.ussell went back to his beer.

He said, pouring it, "This happens to everyone. Everyone with children. It started with Matt, remember. Matt left at twenty-two."

Edie moved away from the table and leaned instead against the sink, staring out into the garden.

"You just don't think," she said, "that it's going to end."

"God!" Russell said. He tried a little yelp of laughter. "End! Does parenthood ever, *ever* end?"

Edie turned round and looked at the table.

"If you want any lunch," she said, "you finish that."

"Okay."

"I'm going out."

"Are you? Where are you going?"

"A film maybe. Sit in a café. Buy a forty-watt lightbulb."

"Edie –"

She began to walk toward the door to the hall.

"Better practice, hadn't I? For the next chapter?"

Outside the shed, Russell made a pile of things to keep, a pile of things to throw away, and a pile to ask Edie about. He had made a cheese-and-pickle sandwich from the last of the white sliced loaf – there would presumably be no more of those, without Ben around to indulge with them – and had eaten it sitting in a moldy Lloyd Loom chair that had belonged to his mother, in the pale April sunshine. He would also have added a newspaper or two if the sunshine hadn't been qualified by a sharp breeze blowing intermittently through the gap between the semidetached houses that backed onto his own. They were much grander houses than his – broad steps to the front doors, generous windows to the floor, graveled car-parking spaces – in a much grander road, but they faced east, rather than west, so they got the wind before he did, and only early sun.

Edie wasn't back. She had returned briefly to the kitchen, wearing a cast-off denim jacket of Rosa's, and kissed his cheek. He had wanted to say something, to hold her for a moment, but had decided against it. Instead, he let her bump her face against his, fleetingly, and watched her go. The cat watched her too, from a place on the crowded dresser where he was not supposed to sit, next to the fruit bowl. When the front door slammed, the cat gave Russell a quick glance and then went back to washing. He waited half an hour after Russell went out to the garden and then he came out to see what was happening, stepping fastidiously over the damp grass. As soon as Russell left the Lloyd Loom chair, he leaped into it and sat there, watching, his tail curled trimly round his paws and his expression inscrutable.

He was really Ben's cat. Ben had been the only one of their children who had longed for an animal, who had gone badgering on about everything from a hippo to a hamster until, on his tenth birthday, Russell had gone to a dingy pet shop somewhere in Finsbury Park, and come home with a tabby kitten in a wire basket. Ben called the kitten Arsenal, after his chosen soccer club, and remained indifferent to the implications of this being inevitably shortened to Arsie. Arsie was now twelve and as cool as a tulip.

"Look," Russell said to Arsie, "Rosa's tricycle. She loved that."

Arsie looked unmoved. Rosa's tricycle, once metallic lilac with a white plastic basket on the front, was now mostly rust.

"Keep or chuck?" Russell said.

Arsie yawned.

"Chuck," Russell said. "Chuck, but inform Rosa."

He crouched and inspected the tricycle. Rosa had stuck stickers everywhere, glitter stickers of cartoon animals and fairies. She had looked sweet on that tricycle, pedaling furiously, straight red hair flapping, the white plastic basket crammed with all the stuffed animals she carried everywhere,

9

lining them up at meals round her place, putting them in a circle round her pillow. Sometimes when he looked at her now, twenty-six years old and working for a public relations company, he caught a glimpse of the child on the tricycle, like a ghost in a mirror. She had been a turbulent little girl full of noise and purpose. Some of the noise and purpose were still there, but the turbulence had translated itself into something closer to emotional volatility, a propensity to swerve crazily in and out of relationships. At least one had to be thankful that she did swerve out again, particularly in the case of the appalling Josh.

Russell straightened up and looked at the house. Rosa's window was on the top floor, on the left. Since Rosa had left home, they'd had the odd lodger in that room, and in Matt's, next to it: drama students Edie was teaching or impoverished actors she'd once been in repertory with who had small parts in plays in little North London theaters. They were good lodgers on the whole, never awake too early, never short of something to say, and they provided, unconsciously, the perfect excuse to postpone any decision about moving to something smaller. The house might be shabby, in places very shabby, but it was not something Russell could imagine being without. It was, quite simply, a given in his life, in their lives, the result of being left a miraculous small legacy in his twenties, when he and Edie were living in a dank flat, with two children and a baby, above a hardware store off the Balls Pond Road.

"Four bedrooms," Edie had said, whispering as if the house could hear her. "What'll we ever do with four bedrooms?"

It had been in a terrible state, of course, damp and neglected, with mushrooms up the stairwell and a hole in the roof you could see the stars through. But somehow, then, with Edie enjoying a steady spell of television work, and the agency getting going, the house had seemed to them needy rather than daunting, more theirs, somehow, because it was crying out for rescue. They had no kitchen for a year, no finished bathroom for two, no carpets for five. Matt wore gumboots all his childhood, from the moment he got out of bed. It was perhaps no surprise that Matt should turn out to be the most orthodox of their children, the one with an electronic diary and polished shoes. When he came home, he was inclined to point out that the crack in the sitting-room ceiling was lengthening, that the smell of damp in the down-stairs lavatory was not just a smell, that regular outside painting was a sound investment.

"It's hard," Russell said, "for us old bohemians to get worked up about such things."

"Then listen to me," Matt said.

He said that often, now. He had started saying it after he left home, and returned, just for occasional meals, with a newly critical eye. "Listen to me," he'd say to Edie about a part she was reading for, to Russell about some new direction the agency might take, to Ben about his A-level choices.

"You're so adult," Edie would say, looking at him fondly. "I love it."

She loved it, of course, because she didn't listen to him. She loved it the way she loved his regular haircuts and well-mannered clothes and competence with technology. It was amusing to her, and endearing, to see this well-put-together grown man in her kitchen, explaining to her how to send text messages on her mobile phone, and visualize him, simul-taneously, once asleep in his cot or sitting, reading earnestly, on his potty. She could play games like that, Russell thought, because she still had Ben; the security of Ben gave her the license not to take Matt seriously, not to see his maturity as anything other than sweet play-acting.

If Matt was irritated by her attitude, he gave no sign. He treated her as he had always treated both his parents, as very well-meaning people of whom he was fond and who he needed to take practical care of because they seemed to decline to do it for themselves. It was plain he thought Edie indulged Ben, just as it was plain he thought Rosa indulged herself, but he kept these opinions to their proper place, on the edges of his own rightly preoccupying life. He worked for a mobile-telephone company, had a girlfriend with a job in the City, and with whom he shared a flat. He was entitled, Russell thought, inspecting a neat stack of broken lamp-shades and wondering why they had ever been considered worthy of salvage, to say, every so often, and to a family who lived so much more carelessly than he did, "Listen to me."

Russell did listen. He might not often take advice, but he listened. He had listened while Matt had explained, at tremendous length one evening in a cramped bar in Covent Garden, that Russell should specialize. Matt described his father's agency, which represented actors who were parti-cularly interested in film and television work, as "limping along." Russell, nursing a glass of red wine, had been mildly affronted. After the next glass, he had felt less affronted. After the third glass, Matt's proposal that Russell should specialize in providing actors for advertising voice-over work seemed less alien, less unattractively practical than it had an hour before.

"I know it's not theater," Matt had said, "but it's money."

"It's *all* about money!" Edie had cried, two hours later, brushing her teeth. "Isn't it? That's all it's about!"

"Possibly," Russell said carefully, "it has to be."

"It's sordid. It's squalid. Where's the acting in bouncing on sofas?"

"Not bouncing on them. Talking about them."

Edie spat into the basin.

"Well, if you can *bring* yourself –"

"I rather think I can."

"Well, just don't ask *me*."

Russell let a pause fall. He climbed into bed and picked up his book, a biography of Alexander the Great. He put his spectacles on.

"No," he said. "No. I rather think I shan't."

Since 1975, Russell Boyd Associates (there were none) had

occupied three attic rooms behind Shaftesbury Avenue. For almost thirty years, Russell had worked in a room that had undoubtedly once been a maid's bedroom. It had a dormer window and sloping ceilings and was carpeted with the Turkish carpet that had once been in Russell's grandparents' dining room in Hull, now worn to a gray blur of weft cotton threads, garnished here and there with a few brave remaining tufts of red and blue and green. Matt, encouraged by Russell's acceptance of his advice about the agency, then tried to persuade him to modernize the office, to put down a wooden floor and install halogen lights on gleaming metal tracks.

"No," Russell said.

"But, Dad –"

"I like it. I like it just as it is. So do my clients."

Matt had kicked at several straining cardboard folders piled like old bolsters against the bookshelves.

"It's awful. It's like your old shed."

Russell looked now, at his shed. It was half empty, but what remained looked intractable, as if prepared to resist movement. Arsie had left the chair and returned to the house and the sun had sunk behind the houses leaving a raw dankness instead. He glanced down at Rosa's tricycle, on its side in the stack to be discarded.

"Rosa's bike," she had always called it. Not "mine" but "Rosa's."

"Russell!" Edie called.

He raised his head.

She was standing at the corner of the house, where the side door to the kitchen was. She had Arsie in her arms.

"Tea!" Edie shouted.

"Look," Edie said, "I'm sorry."

She had made tea in the big pot with cabbage roses on it. It was extremely vulgar but it had intense associations for Edie, as everything in her life did, everything that reminded her of a place, a person, a happening.

She said, "I was fed up with you because you wouldn't understand."

"I do understand," Russell said.

"Do you?"

He nodded, tensing slightly.

"Then tell me," Edie demanded. "Explain what is the matter."

Russell paused.

Then he said, "It's the end of a particularly compelling – and urgent – phase of motherhood. And it's very hard to adjust to."

"I don't want to adjust," Edie said. She poured tea into the huge cracked blue cups she had found in a junk shop in Scarborough, touring with – what was it? A Priestley play, perhaps.

"I want Ben back," Edie said.

Russell poured milk into his tea.

"I want him back," Edie said fiercely. "I want him back to make me laugh and infuriate me and exploit me and make me feel *necessary*."

Russell picked up his teacup and held it, cradling it in his palms. The aroma of the tea rose up to him, making him think of his grandmother. She had saved Darjeeling tea for Sundays. "The champagne of teas," she said, every time she drank it.

"Are you listening?" Edie said.

"Yes," he said, "but you forget I know."

She leaned forward.

She said, "How do I make you *mind*?"

"Good question."

"What?"

He put his cup down.

He said, seriously, not looking at her, "How do I make *you* mind?"

She stared.

"What?" she said again.

"I've been out there," Russell said, "for about three hours. I've been sifting through all sorts of rubbish, things that mattered once and don't anymore. And that's quite painful, knowing things won't come again, knowing things are over forever."

"But –"

"Wait," Russell said, "just *wait*. Rosa's not going to ride that trike again, Matt's not going to hit with that bat, you're not going to read under that lampshade. That's not comfortable, that's not easy to know, to have to accept. But we have to, because we have no choice. And we also have something left."

Edie took a long swallow of tea and looked at him over the rim of her cup.

"Yes?"

"You talk about wanting Ben back. You talk about his energy and neediness and that way it makes you feel. Well, just think for a moment about how *I* feel. I didn't marry you in order to have Matt and Rosa and Ben, though I'm thankful we did. I married you because I wanted to be with you, because you somehow make things shine for me, even when you're horrible. You want Ben back. Well, you'll have to deal with that as best you can. And while you're dealing with it, I'll give you something else to think about, something that isn't going to go away. Edie – I want you back. I was here before the children and I'm here now.' He put his cup down with finality. "And I'm not going away."

CHAPTER TWO

W hen it came to business, Bill Moreton prided himself
on his firing technique. His father, who had died
before Bill was twenty, thereby bequeathing his son the
luxury of mythologizing him, had been a general surgeon.
His basic belief had been "Cut deeply, but only once," and
Bill had adopted this mantra as his own, and had carried it,
grandiosely, into the world of public relations where, in the
process of building up a company, there had been a good
deal of hiring and firing to do.

Because many of Bill's hiring choices were disastrous, he
got in plenty of practice at subsequently firing them. He was
impervious to any suggestions, however diplomatically put,
about his judgment, and equally resistant to criticism about
the manner in which he eradicated his own errors. The sight
of an inadequate employee was a living reminder of Bill's
own inadequacies, and he could not endure it. The only way,
he had discovered, to avoid confronting his mistakes was to
summon the employee in question to his office – paperwork
already in place – smile, sack them, smile again and show
them the door.

Which was exactly what he planned to do, this cool April
day, to Rosa Boyd. Rosa was twenty-six, perfectly capable at
her job, and a good-looking redhead if you liked your
women on the big side and redheaded into the bargain.
The reason for sacking Rosa was not the one Bill planned to

give her, smilingly and briefly. He was going to tell her that she was not, he regretted, suited to public relations work because she lacked the patience to build up a relationship with a client that could take, oh, five or six years in some cases, with the client behaving most capriciously from the outset. What he was not going to tell her was that the company's figures, drawn up as they always were in anticipation of the end of a tax year, were alarmingly poor, and that he had decided – against his accountant's advice – to sack two members of staff because to sack one would have looked like victimization. And so, Victor Basinger was to take early retirement – fifty-four was too old, anyway, for the PR game – and Rosa Boyd was to go.

Bill stood by the window of his office, contemplating the blank view of the adjoining building it afforded, and rehearsed what he would say to Rosa. He had to be careful to adjust his tone to precisely the right pitch because even a hint of too much of anything might betray his uncomfortable knowledge that, for all professional and practical reasons, it should not be Rosa Boyd walking into his office to be sacked, but Heidi Kingsmill. The difficulty was that Heidi was an aggressive and volatile personality who had, five years before and by sheer fluke, brought the company one of its most reliably lucrative accounts. The fact that Heidi had done absolutely nothing constructive since, and was an emotional liability, could not be admitted. Nor could the fact that Bill had spent an energetic night with Heidi after an office Christmas party four years before and, although Heidi had not as yet exploited this fact, she made it perfectly plain that she always – if pushed – could. Bill's wife had invested some of her private money in his company, and might be required, shortly, to invest more, and she was a woman who set a great, even hysterical, store by fidelity. So, all in all, it was Rosa Boyd who had to go, in order to keep a space of clear blue water between Heidi Kingsmill and Mrs. Moreton.

Bill heard a sound behind him. Rosa Boyd was standing in his office doorway, her right hand resting on the doorknob. She wore jeans and an orange tweed jacket and boots with immensely high heels. Her hair was loose. She looked to Bill about eight feet tall and mildly alarming.

"Rosa!" Bill said. He smiled. "Hello."

Rosa said nothing.

Bill moved round his desk and patted the chair nearest to Rosa invitingly.

"Sit down."

Rosa didn't move.

"Sit, Rosa," Bill said, still smiling. "This won't take a minute."

Rosa gave a small sigh, and relaxed on to one leg.

"Come in," Bill said. "Come in and shut the door. This is just between you and me. We don't want the office hearing, do we?"

"They know," Rosa said.

Bill swallowed. He patted the chair again.

He opened his mouth to speak, but Rosa said, before he could begin, "They're taking bets. On how quickly you'll do it."

Bill looked at the opposite wall.

"I'm going to win," Rosa said. "I said it'd be under a minute. And I'm right."

And then she stepped backward and pulled the door shut behind her with a slam.

Kate Ferguson lay on the bathroom floor waiting to be sick again. She had been well prepared, she thought, for morning sickness in early pregnancy to afflict her in the mornings when Barney could bring her tea and a biscuit (Kate's mother had sworn by Rich Tea) and hover round her in a clumsy, husbandly way. But she was not at all prepared to feel sick all day, every day, too sick to go to work, too sick to allow brown bread or coffee to tiptoe anywhere near her mind, let alone her kitchen cupboard, too sick to be even remotely civil to people who wanted to congratulate her, soppily, on being pregnant so soon after getting married.

"So lovely," her mother's best friend had said, "to see someone doing it *properly*. None of this heartless career-girl stuff, leaving having babies until you're practically old enough to be a granny."

At this rate, Kate thought, moaning faintly against the floor tiles, she'd never be a granny because she'd never even be a mother if this is what it took to get there. It was such a terrible kind of nausea too, so engulfing, so endless, so devoid of any possibility of relief. The baby, down somewhere in those tortured realms, felt like an enemy, a malevolent walnut-sized goblin, remorselessly pursuing its own determined path of development. Barney had the photograph from the first ultrasound scan in his wallet but Kate didn't really even want to look at it, didn't want to give herself the chance to visualize this tiny thing that was making itself so violently unlovable. One minute, it seemed, she and Barney had been honeymooning in Malaysia and planning their excited newly married lives back in London, and the next she was lying on the bathroom floor, clammy and ashen, whining and sniveling to herself without even a tissue for comfort.

The phone rang.

"Sod off!" Kate shouted.

The phone rang four times, and then stopped. Then it started again. It would be Rosa. Kate and Rosa had started a four-ring pattern as a kind of signal to one another, at university, first as a let-out for dates that were either dull or dangerous and then simply as a demonstration of consciousness of the other. Kate began to pull herself, whimpering, across the bathroom floor and into the bedroom next door where her phone lay, muffled in the duvet.

"I want to die," Kate said into it.

"Still? Poor babe."

"Four weeks, nearly five. I hate this baby."

"Try hating your hormones instead."

"I can't picture them. I can't hate something I can't picture."

"I'll give you something to picture," Rosa said, "and you can hate him all you like. Bill Moreton."

Kate crawled up onto the bed and fell into the folds of the duvet.

"What's he done?"

"Sacked me," Rosa said.

Kate groaned.

"Rosa –"

"I know."

"What did you *do*?"

"Nothing."

"People don't get sacked for nothing –"

"In Bill Moreton's skin-saving world they do. He can't sack Heidi because he screwed her and she'd squeal. And the business isn't doing well enough to support us all."

Kate rolled on to her side and crushed a pillow against her stomach.

"Rosa, you *needed* that job."

"Yes."

"What did you say, five thousand on your credit cards?"

"Nearer six."

"You'd better come and live with us –"

"No."

"Barney wouldn't mind –"

"He would. So would you. So would I."

"But thank you, Kate, all the same."

"Thank you, Kate."

"How soon," Kate said, "are you going?"

"I've gone. I cleared my desk, mostly into a black bag, and dumped it outside his office."

"So you won't get any kind of reference –"

"I don't *want* a reference –"

Kate sighed heavily.

"Rosa –"

"I'll think of something."

"Like what?"

"Telemarketing, maybe –"

"I feel too awful," Kate said, "to cheer you up."

"I'm still in a rage," Rosa said. "I'm fine as long as I'm furious."

"Aren't you worried?"

There was a long pause. Kate released the pillow a little. "Rosa?"

"Of course I'm worried," Rosa said. "I can't remember when I wasn't worried. About money."

"But all that *spending* –"

"Yes," Rosa said. "It frightens me and I can't stop doing it. When I was with Josh –" She stopped.

"Yes?"

"Well, there was a reason then. Meals, holidays –"

"He exploited you."

"So you always said."

"Well, at least I was right."

"Mmm," Rosa said.

"What are you going to do?"

Rosa said slowly, pacing out the words, "Don't know. Haven't thought. Yet."

"I wish –"

"You can't do anything. I had to tell you but I didn't tell you so's you'd feel you had to do anything."

"I'll be more use when I can think about something other than dying."

"You ought to be so happy –"

"Because I've got everything?" Kate said sharply.

"I wasn't going to say that –"

"But you thought it."

Rosa said crossly, "Of course I did. What do you expect?"

Kate closed her eyes.

"Go away."

"I'm going. To find a begging pitch under a cash machine."

"I meant it. I meant it about coming here."

"I know. Thank you."

Kate's stomach heaved and turned. She flung the phone into the dented pillows and scrambled off the bed. "Bye!" she shouted after it and fled toward the bathroom.

Rosa bought a Mexican bean wrap from the sandwich bar and took it to a bench in Soho Square. At the other end of the bench a hunched girl in a long gray overcoat and tinted glasses was speaking in a low monotone into a mobile phone. She wasn't speaking English and in a strange, almost undefinable way, she didn't look English, either. Perhaps, Rosa thought, she was Latvian or Romanian or even Chechen. Perhaps she was a refugee, or on the run; perhaps someone had kept her as a sex slave, sharing a windowless room with five other girls and made to service twenty men a day. Perhaps, Rosa thought, inspecting her wrap and regretting the choice of filling – unfortunate color, somehow – she led the kind of life that would make Rosa's current situation seem no more than a temporary and trivial blip in an otherwise indulged and comparatively prosperous one. Maybe the trouble with Rosa was not her circumstances, but her eternal expectations, her conviction that, with enough energy on her part, enough desire, enough – *focus*, she could bring about the kind of satisfaction that she was sure lay out there, the reward for the brave.

She peeled back the plastic film from the wrap and took an awkward bite. Three red beans immediately fell wetly onto the knee of her jeans – clean that morning – and thence to the path where they lay, bright, exotic and faintly sinister. Glancing at them, Rosa reflected how odd it was that one hardly noticed details in life – or at least, didn't dignify them with significance – until one was forced into some heightened state of consciousness by joy or grief or disappointment or fear, at which point the whole of existence, from the largest things to the smallest, seemed to take on a kind of meaningful drama. Three red beans on a path, a girl in a gray coat speaking another language softly into a phone – suddenly, both seemed emblematic, important. And yet both were probably no more than irrelevant objects that happened to accompany a moment in Rosa's life, which she ardently, fervently wished she wasn't having.

She laid the wrap on the seat beside her. In these circumstances, it didn't manage to taste exotic and foreign, only alien. Rosa leaned back and looked up at the steady gray sky and the spidery branches of the trees already lumpy with incipient leaves, and thought that one of the hardest aspects of what had just happened was that she had not reckoned on it. Any of it. She had not supposed, for one moment, that five years after leaving university she would have failed to find absorbing employment, failed to sustain a romantic relationship, and failed to gain exactly the kind of control over her life that she had assumed to be an automatic part of growing up.

Education had, by contrast, been easy. Rosa had been good at education, good at friendships, comfortable with achievement. She had negotiated, from the age of eleven, a subversive but successful pathway between intelligence and rebelliousness, a pathway that her elder brother admired and her younger brother emulated. She had cultivated, all those long, busy, channeled educational years, a subtle flamboyance, which she had believed would carry her through both dullness and difficulty. And, almost, it had, until falling for a man who preferred to believe her publicity rather than what lay beneath it in more vulnerable reality exposed her in a way that seemed to have deconstructed all those assiduously built years of showy confidence in an instant.

Everyone had taken pains to tell her how much they disliked Josh. Under the conventional but false banner of telling her that everything they were about to say was because they had her welfare at heart, family and friends told her that Josh was spoiled, unreliable, immature and selfish. In reply, she would simply say, "I know." She did know. She knew from the first few exciting but unnerving dates that Josh was neither able nor prepared to give her the steady glow of supportive love that women's magazines assured her was every girl's absolute right. But the relationship with Josh was not about anything steady or supportive. It was about being, in every sense, bowled over – bowled over by the electricity of his unpredictable com-pany, bowled over by desire. Falling for Josh had been the heady, unbidden moment when Rosa, up to now counting herself serenely as one of life's adoreds, turned into a helpless adorer. Josh could have anything he wanted as long as he didn't go.

He didn't go for almost two years. He moved into Rosa's flat and spent hours playing poker on her computer or ringing long-distance on her telephone. He booked seats at ballets and theaters, nights in hotels, tables in restaurants without ever, mysteriously, managing to pay for them. He left roses on her pillow and messages on the bathroom mirror and tiny, beguiling presents wrapped in tissue paper in her shoes. She was driven to every extreme of emotion and temper by his presence and, when he finally left, she was convinced for months that not only had he left her with a frightening amount of debt, but also without any capacity to feel alive to the full ever again.

"He wasn't *drama*," Kate said to Rosa, "he was *melodrama*."

Rosa had looked at the list in Kate's hand. It was the beginning of her wedding-present list and it featured saucepans and bath mats and an espresso machine.

"Give me melodrama any day," Rosa had said.

She wouldn't, she thought, sitting on her bench beside her unwanted lunch, say that now. Josh had been an addiction and, when he had gone, she missed the dark glamour of that addiction, the tension and the sense that her adrenaline was always racing. And then, hour by hour, day by day, the enthralling substance Josh had represented drained out of her veins and left her, not exactly regretful, but certainly disorientated, lost, as if she had entirely abandoned the person she grew up with and was too altered now by experience to go back and retrieve it.

She glanced along the bench. The girl in the gray coat had stopped talking into her telephone and was now reading a Greek newspaper. Rosa picked up the remains of her wrap gingerly and rose from the bench. She carried the wrap over to the nearest litter bin, dropped it in, and then set off purposefully southward, toward Shaftesbury Avenue.

Russell was on the telephone. An actor, who possessed a wonderfully flexible speaking voice and no sense of obligation to any work he considered beneath him, however lucrative, was explaining at length why he had failed, for the second time, to turn up for a studio appointment to record the voice of a cartoon tiger representing a major insurance company.

"Sorry," Russell said at intervals. "It's no good. It's no good my putting in effort if you won't match it."

The door of Russell's office stood open. Beyond, in the small reception area, furnished with wicker sofas and copies of *Spotlight* and *The Stage*, Russell's assistant, Maeve, who had been with him almost all his working life, administered the agency with the assistance of a computer she always referred to as the Prototype, on account of its age. Russell liked Maeve to hear most of his conversations. He liked her to be a witness to his reasonableness in the face of often great provocation.

"I'm sorry, Gregory," Russell said, "but I shall have to send them someone else. It's very nice of them, actually, even to agree to that."

The doorbell to the street door rang, a peculiar vibrating growl, which, like his carpet, he refused to let anyone change.

"Sorry," Russell said, "but you've blown it."

"Oh!" Maeve said into the intercom with pleasure. "Oh, it's you! Come up!"

Russell put his hand over the mouthpiece of his telephone. His heart had lifted a little.

"Who, Maeve? Edie?"

Maeve's face appeared briefly round the door.

"No," she mouthed, "Rosa."

Russell took his hand away.

"Go away and think about it, Greg. Go away and think about how you are going to live until you are noticed by Anthony Minghella. Then we might have another conversation." He took the telephone away from his ear, listened for a few more seconds to Gregory's aggrieved voice, and replaced it softly on his desk.

There were footsteps running up the last flight of stairs.

He heard Maeve open the door.

"Well, there's a cheerful sight. What a wonderful color, *nobody* but you –"

"Nobody but me," Rosa said. "Anybody else would have had more sense and bought black."

"I'm sick to death of black," Maeve said. "Leave it to the beetles, I say –"

Rosa appeared in the doorway of Russell's office.

"Dad?"

He got up and leaned across the desk to kiss her.

"Lovely surprise –"

"Well," she said, "passing –"

"At lunchtime."

"Well . . . Actually I'm not hungry."

"Even," Russell said, "if I'm paying?"

She glanced down. Her shoulders drooped a little. Then she straightened up, shook her hair back and gave him a familiarly full-on smile.

"That would be great. Because – well, because there's something I'd like to ask you."

Russell looked at her over his reading spectacles.

"Is there?"

"Yes," she said. "Please." And then she smiled again, "Daddy."

Rosa looked at her father's plate. Hers was empty, but his still bore a good half of his order of gnocchi.

She raised her fork, questioningly.

"Can I?"

Russell gave his plate a little nudge.

"Help yourself."

Rosa speared two gnocchi and put them in her mouth.

Then she said, round them, "I mean, I'm not worried about finding another job. And I'm not at all concerned by what Bill Moreton thinks of me. I know I was doing a good job. I know it."

"Hmm," Russell said. He had ordered a bottle of wine and was now wondering if Rosa's share was giving her a fleeting and unreliable confidence.

"It wasn't as if I was earning a fortune there anyway," Rosa said, spearing more gnocchi. "Lots of my friends are earning well over twenty by now."

"Have you ever worked out," Russell said, "what you *need* to earn?"

Rosa stopped chewing. She gave him a quick, direct look and dropped her gaze.

"No."

"Don't you think –"

"Did you?" Rosa demanded. "Did you? At my age?"

"I was married –"

"So?"

"Two incomes –"

"And a baby." Rosa gave a little snort. "I'd love a baby."

Russell picked his plate up and exchanged it for Rosa's empty one. Rosa looked down.

"I couldn't eat all that –"

"Rosa," Russell said, "I've listened to you. I've listened to you very patiently and I quite agree with you that Bill Moreton was a second-rate boss who behaved accordingly. But you'd been in that job eight months. He didn't exactly owe you a pension and a gold watch."

Rosa said nothing. It seemed to her that she was behaving exactly as she always vowed she would never behave again when with a parent. She could hear in her voice an undertone of whining and cajoling that reminded her of raging nights, when she was seven, or nine, or eleven, and had prayed fervently to be an orphan. She swallowed hard, against the plaintiveness.

"It's a very nasty thing to have done to you," Russell said, visualizing Edie listening to him, "especially when it so plainly wasn't justified and you were made a scapegoat. But it was just a job, wasn't it? Not a vocation. Not even a career."

Rosa pushed her father's plate aside.

"It isn't that."

Russell sighed.

"No."

"You see," Rosa said, "I'm in debt."

"Ah."

"I owe nearly six thousand on my credit cards."

Russell leaned back. It occurred to him to ask how the situation had arisen, but then it struck him forcibly that he did not, somehow, want to become involved in the reasons because that would mean reaction and, even, responsibility. He loved Rosa. He loved her dearly, but she was twenty-six.

He said, as gently as he could, "That will take a while to pay back."

She nodded.

"Have you thought of that?" Russell said. "Have you made any plans?"

She said, in a small voice, "I'm beginning to."

"Economies," Russell said. He picked up his wineglass and put it down again. "My mother loved economies. If she could make one haddock fillet feed four she was triumphant. She thrived on economies."

Rosa said sadly, "Then I don't take after her."

"Frugality was rather encouraged in the fifties," Russell said. "Postwar and all that. Now, it just looks as if you are crabbed of spirit and letting life pass you by."

Rosa leaned forward.

"I think it was trying not to let it pass me by that got me into this mess."

"Josh," Russell said, without meaning to.

"Oh, Dad –"

"No," he said, hastily. "No. I shouldn't have mentioned him. We must focus on what is rather than what was."

She gave a faint smile.

"I knew you'd help –"

"It depends –"

"On what?"

"On what form you see that help taking."

Rosa said quickly, "I'm not asking for money."

Russell gave a little sigh.

"I don't want money," Rosa said, "I want to straighten myself out. I want to find another job and work hard and meet new people and make a plan and change the way I do things."

"Mmm."

"Don't you think that's right? Don't you think I sound like you'd like me to sound?"

"Oh I do –"

"Well, then?"

"I'm just waiting," Russell said. "Patiently, fondly even, but wearily and warily, to see what it is you are working up to say."

Rosa fiddled a bit with the cutlery left on the table.

"I'm not very proud of myself."

"No."

"I hate having to ask this –"

"Yes."

"But can I come home?"

Russell closed his eyes for a fleeting second.

"I know it's not what you want," Rosa said. "I don't want it either, really, if you see what I mean, but it wouldn't be for long, probably only a few months, but if I'm not paying rent, the rent money can go toward the credit-card debt, and it would make such a difference, it would make all the difference –" She stopped. Then she said, much more slowly, "Please, Dad."

Russell looked at her.

He said sadly, "I'm so sorry, darling, but no."

She stared at him.

"No!"

"I want to help you," Russell said. "I *will* help you. But you can't come back home to live."

Rosa said, stunned, "But it's my home!"

"Well, yes, in a way. It was your childhood home, your growing-up home. But you're grown-up now. You need your own home."

"Of course!" Rosa cried. "In an ideal world, that's exactly what I'd have by now! But I can't, can I? I can't have what I ought to have because of what's happened!" She glared at him. "I cannot believe you said no."

Russell sighed.

"It isn't about you. It's about us, Mum and me. It's – well, it's *our* home."

"Your *family* home."

"Yes, when children are dependent –"

"Ben was allowed to stay, Ben was always –"

"Ben has gone," Russell said.

"So there's room for me."

"Rosa," Russell said with sudden force, "it's not about room, it's about distraction. It's about Mum and me having time to be married again, it's about us, having time and space for that."

"What?"

"You heard me."

"But," Rosa said, gesturing wildly, "I'm not going to stop you! I'm not going to get in the way of your – rediscovering each other, if that's what you want –"

Russell said carefully, "You may not *mean* to."

There was a pause.

Then Rosa said, in a quite different voice, "I see."

"Good."

"I see that you don't want Mum's attention diverted from you for one little single, baby *instant*."

"No –"

Rosa stood up clumsily, shaking the table.

"Fool yourself if you like, Dad," she said, "but don't try fooling *me*."

"Rosa. Rosa, I really would like to help you, I really want –"

"Don't bother," Rosa said. She gathered up her bag and scarf and telephone. "Just forget I said anything. Just forget I even *asked*." She twitched her bag on to her shoulder and glared at him again. "Luckily for me, I have *friends* who care."

CHAPTER THREE

E die watched the cat make a nest for himself in a basket of clean laundry. It wasn't ironed – Edie had never been able to see ironing as other than faintly neurotic – but it was clean, or had been. The cat had dug about in the basket, tossing small items contemptuously aside, and rearranged pillowcases and shirts until there was a deep well in the center, with comfortable, cushioned edges to rest his chin upon. Then he sank down fluidly into it and closed his eyes.

"Arsie's missing you," Edie said to Ben on the telephone.

"Yeah," he said, "poor old Arse. But I can't have him here."

"No, I wasn't suggesting that."

"Naomi's mum has allergies."

"Does she?"

"And our room is only about big enough for the bed."

"It doesn't," Edie said lightly, "sound very comfortable –"

"It's ace," Ben said. "It's fine. Brilliant. Look, I've got to go."

"Why don't you come to supper one night?"

"Well –"

"Bring Naomi, of course. And her mother, if you'd like to –"

"Mum," Ben said, "I'm late."

"Just supper."

"Going!" Ben called. He'd taken the phone from his ear. "Going. Take care, Mum. Gone!"

Edie stepped over the washing basket and began to sift restlessly through papers on the kitchen table. Russell had produced catalogs in an uncharacteristic manner, catalogs about garden furniture and modern lighting and city-weekend breaks in Europe. He'd also brought flowers, a bunch of anemones that drank a jug of water a day, and a novel that had won a literary prize, and a bottle of oil to put in her bath scented with something she'd never heard of called neroli. It was touching, all this, Edie thought, shuffling items about, but it was also mildly irritating. As conduct, it reminded her of a dog her sister, Vivien, had once had, a small spaniel-ish dog, which always wanted to sit on your knee and gaze into your face with an intensity that required you to give something in return. Not only did Edie not want, particularly, to be given flowers and bath oil and weekends in Ghent, but she also, most particularly, did not want the accompanying obligation.

"It isn't very grateful of you," Vivi said, on the telephone.

"I'd be able to be grateful," Edie said, "if there weren't strings attached. But I can't go from longing for Ben to be back to playing being just married all over again in a single seamless movement."

"Poor Russell —"

"*Poor?*"

"Perhaps he's been waiting, all these years, to be other than on the edge of your peripheral vision."

"He liked family life, you know. He liked the children. He adores Rosa."

"Men love women," Vivi said. "Women love children. Children love hamsters."

"Oh, I know. I *know.*"

"You just don't know how lucky you are."

"Don't start —"

"I have to remind you sometimes."

Edie leaned against the wall.

"Rosa's lost her job."

"No! Poor girl —"

33

"She sounded completely matter of fact. Wouldn't let me sympathize, really. I said come back home –"

"I bet you did –"

"And she said no, no, she was fine, she'd got friends who were helping." Edie paused, and then she said, "I do find that hard. Friends, not family."

"Friends are the new family."

"Sometimes I wonder why I bother to turn to you for consolation."

"I know," Vivi said. "I won't do drama, will I? I won't do it because, compared to mine, your life isn't drama. Speaking of which –"

"Yes?"

"What *about* drama? What about work?"

Edie sighed.

"Nothing much. I must be turned down twenty times for every part I get. There's a casting for an Ibsen next week –"

"Yes?"

"Mrs. Alving. In *Ghosts*. I won't get it."

"*Edie*. Why not?"

"Because I won't. Because I can't *feel* about it at the moment. Because I'm all jangled up and raw –"

"And cross with Russell for being romantic."

"Yes."

"Edie," Vivi said, "I'll ring you again when you have the manners, never mind the empathy, to remember to ask me a single question about *me*."

Edie sat down at the kitchen table now and made space for her elbows among the papers. It was not like her, she told herself, to be so hopeless, to feel herself drifting, to be miserable and – Ben's favorite word when he was small – grumpy. He'd say stressy, now, Edie thought, if he was still seven, and Rosa was eleven and Matt was thirteen, and there were still school mornings, with their inevitable chaos of uneaten things and forgotten things and unbrushed things. She'd imagined those times were timeless somehow, that either they would never end, or that she would change, gradually and peacefully, as they changed, so that she would be ready for the difference, ready to face a new chapter, ready, even, to confront herself.

She brought her hands up to her face and held it. That was the problem, really, that was the element that was proving so difficult, this business of knowing how to arrange oneself. For years, almost thirty of them, she had known what she was for, what she was supposed to do. Sure, she'd been passionate about the theater at school – still couldn't, with complete equanimity, replay those scenes with her parents in which she had insisted on applying for drama school rather than university – passionate enough to appear unmoved at being turned down by the National Youth Theatre, and to persist until she gained a place at RADA. But, if she was honest, it had all been a bit sketchy since: stints in regional repertory companies, stand-in presenter on children's television, advertisements, short runs in strange plays in tiny theaters. Nothing – nothing to boast about exactly.

"I'm a jobbing actress," she'd said for years, holding a child, carrying groceries, clutching dirty bed-linen. "I'm up for anything. As long as it'll fit round the children."

Secure in the essentialness of motherhood, she'd even, she recalled, been able to lecture herself. There'll come a time, she'd told herself, when you'll have to identify yourself *without* your children. They will simply shed you, like a snakeskin, and your support for them will become a need, your need. Motherhood, she'd declared grandly, will not be a proud, public banner anymore, but a quiet, private admission. Rosa will take motherhood over and you, Edie, will have to submit to her supremacy. Well, the time had now come. And, like most anticipated things, the reality did not match the imagining. Rosa was years away in both circumstances and ambition from having a baby, and she, Edie, was as unprepared to surrender positive support for negative need as she possibly could be. Motherhood had been such a solace, had acceptably papered over so many cracks, had given her, if she was honest, such a seemly excuse for not risking failure or disappointment or loss of confidence, that she could not for the moment think what she was going to do, without it.

She took her hands away from her face and laid them in front of her, palms down on the table. On top of the pile about two feet away lay the copy of Ibsen's plays that Russell had brought down from the bookcase on the first-floor landing when he heard about the casting for *Ghosts*, the student copy that she had had at RADA, full of her energetic underlinings. Ibsen had been obsessed by the past. He'd written once that "we sail with a corpse in the cargo." Ibsen was, Edie decided, the very last thing she needed at the moment. She picked up a copy of the *Islington Gazette* that was lying close to her elbow, and covered the book with it. Out of sight: out of troubled mind.

Holding a telephone between his hunched shoulder and his ear, Matthew Boyd was writing down some information.

"Open plan. Interior walls of glass brick. View of Tate Modern and Millennium Bridge. Four hundred thou – wow," Matthew said. "Four hundred thousand?"

"That was what Ruth told me," the agent said.

Matthew made a face. What was an estate agent, who hardly knew her, doing calling Ruth Ruth? He said, "I don't think –" and the agent said, "Admittedly, top whack. But she said she could consider that if the place was right."

"She –"

"And the value of lofts in Bankside have almost tripled since the mid-nineties."

Matthew drew an angry line under his jottings. He and Ruth had not, as far as he could remember – and he was good at remembering – discussed Bankside. They had discussed Docklands and Hoxton and Clerkenwell, but not

Bankside. Bankside was much more central and therefore much more expensive. The budget – putative, but shared, obviously – had been three hundred. Tops. Matthew added teeth to his line.

"I've made an appointment for Ruth to see it," the agent said.

"You –"

"She asked for Saturday morning, so this is a courtesy call."

"A –"

"Saturday morning at ten-thirty. It's about three hundred square meters, by the way. Shall I tell Ruth or will you?"

Matthew wrote "Sod off" in capital letters above the teeth.

"I will," he said, and rang off.

He dropped the phone on his desk and shoved his chair back so violently that it cannoned into Blaise's desk behind him. Blaise was on the telephone, hands-free. He put his hand over the mouthpiece.

"Oy!"

Matthew stood up. He mouthed "Sorry" in Blaise's direction. Then he bent over his desk and retrieved his phone. Ruth's was the first number in his speed-dial address book.

"Hello," her voice mail said, cool and friendly. "This is Ruth Munro's telephone. I'm away from my desk just now so please leave me a message."

"Ring me," Matthew said. He took a breath. "Please, I mean. Please ring me."

He dropped the phone in his pocket and turned to make coffee-drinking gestures at Blaise. Blaise nodded. Matthew went quickly across the office, threading his way between the gray plastic desks, and made for the lifts. They had all, as usual, collected on the top floor. He made a face at himself in the brass panel that lined the wall between the lifts.

"Cross," Ruth had said to him at the weekend, tapping away at her laptop and not looking up. "You look so cross."

He looked at himself now, stretched and blobbed by the

soft reflections in the brass. Cross might be how he looked: frightened was how he felt. And frightened was how he had always hated feeling, ever since those first unnerving nights in that new ramshackle house when he was a child and they expected him to sleep, knowing that there were holes in the roof, real holes through which anything might swoop, anything clawed and fanged and malevolent. His gum boots, Matthew remembered, had been his salvation. Solid and reassuring and rubber, he had worn them in the uncarpeted house all day for years, and slept with them by his bed. When they began to cramp his toes, he would pester Edie for new ones, so great was the terror of being without a pair, without their simple reassurance. They seemed to be able to insulate him from fear, from the unknown, to protect him while still letting him see what lay ahead. When he finally had to trade them in for trainers, he'd known he'd never have such a straightforward mechanism for consolation ever again. And he'd been right.

The lift doors slid open, revealing walls and floor made of stamped silvery metal. Matthew rode down to the ground floor with his eyes shut and emerged into the immense glass foyer that in turn gave on to a vast pale outdoor concourse where architectural trees planted in concrete drums blew stiffly about in the wind from the river. Matthew buttoned up his jacket to stop his tie whipping across his face, and plunged out toward the coffee shop on a distant corner. A large latte – a girl's drink, but sometimes it offered just the right kind of unremarkable comfort – and half an hour nudging figures about would restore him, he was sure, to a place where anxiety resolved itself into being nothing more than a very temporary state of not quite understanding.

He carried his tall white mug to a table by the window. Across the square, even though the river itself was hidden, he could see a huge, clear sweep of sky, hurrying spring sky full of racing clouds and the sharp white trails of airplanes. He had never liked weather much, had always seen its unpredictability as vaguely threatening, but it was a pleasure to look at from behind the safety of glass, like looking at a turbulent painting, a Turner maybe, or a Goya, securely confined within a frame. He had once confessed to Ruth, in the early days when they were still entrancedly exploring one another, that he enjoyed the idea of the presence of chaos, somewhere out there, whirling away with all its arbitrary energies, but he couldn't actually handle it if it came too close to him.

"Oh, I know!" she'd said, her eyes shining. "We couldn't have a world without perfect control, but please may we be allowed to control our own bit of it, forever and ever, Amen!"

After Edie, Matthew could not believe Ruth's sense of order: her makeup in Perspex boxes, her T-shirts in piles of three, her papers filed in translucent plastic folders made meticulously – and cheaply – in Japan. There were no leftovers in her fridge, no scattered newspapers on her sofa, no jumble of tired shoes in the bottom of her cupboard. Ruth had been a business consultant when he met her, and was now, at thirty-two, a junior head hunter for a firm that specialized in finance directors. When they met, she was earning a third again as much as he was; now, her income was closer to twice his. For the sake of his dignity – undefined as a danger area, but well understood by both of them – they had shared everything as an equal financial commitment on both sides: rent, bills, entertainment, travel. To create flexibility within this equable arrangement, a further understanding grew up that if Ruth contributed more money (a cashmere sweater for Matthew, Eurostar tickets to see an exhibition in Paris), Matthew would repay, without being asked, in kind (replant the window boxes, breakfast for Ruth in bed). It was a system, Matthew thought, that had worked very well for two and a half years and that his parents would consider not just barmy, but overcontrolled to a point of inhumanity.

His parents' opinion on most things was, in fact, something Matthew never sought. He loved them in a suspended, un-examined way, and while he found their way of life hopelessly dated, it was something that was as much part of them as their personalities. When he saw Ruth – these occasions were very seldom – seated at his parents' kitchen table in her considered weekend clothes and forming such a contrast to the evolved disorder of her surroundings, he felt an unmistakable affection for the way he had been brought up, and a profound pride in the way he was living now. It was made easier, of course, by the fact that Edie and Ruth liked each other, that each fulfilled the expectations of how the other should be.

"Ghastly cat," Edie would say, snatching Arsie off Ruth's black cashmere.

"Bliss," Ruth would say, sinking into one of the deep, battered armchairs in the sitting room, full of the kind of food she would never buy herself. "Instant destress."

Periodically, Matthew would urge his parents to mend the house, update their wills, reconsider their futures. Encour-aged by the success of persuading his father to specialize more, he had hoped to nudge his mother toward more commitment to work and thereby – though he bore his brother no grudge – detach her from the long, long nurturing of Ben. He was actually slightly congratulating himself on the success – or rather, lack of fireworks – in initial conver-sations with Edie about how life might be after Ben, when Ben confounded them all by announcing he was off to live with a girl none of them really knew, in her mother's flat in Walthamstow. When told this news by Matthew, Ruth said, "Heavens. Where's Walthamstow?"

Matthew was, he supposed, glad of Ben's initiative. But it had been impulsively done and had left all kinds of ragged ends behind, which Matthew was only just beginning to collect his thoughts about when Ruth announced, quite suddenly, that it was time they were thinking of buying somewhere to live.

"Actually," she said, "it's not just time. It's overdue. I should have bought five years ago."

Matthew was in the middle of assembling a flat-pack cabinet to house the television and DVD player. At the moment Ruth spoke, he was counting the screws supplied for the door hinges, and hoping that there would be sixteen as promised and not fifteen as seemed likely.

He said stupidly, "You didn't know me five years ago."

"I'm not talking relationships," Ruth said. She was sorting gym kit. "I'm talking property investment."

Matthew looked down at the screws in his hand. It would be so bloody annoying to have to go shopping for one single screw. His father, of course, would have screws of every type, mostly paint-stained and kept unsorted in old coffee jars, but at least he would *have* them.

"Matt?"

"Yes."

"Did you hear me?"

"Yes. You need four screws a hinge for this and they have given me fifteen."

Ruth put the gym kit down and came across to where Matthew was standing. She put her hand into his and scooped up the screws.

"Just concentrate on what I'm saying."

He looked at her.

"It's time we bought a flat of our own," Ruth said.

That was a week ago. One week. In the course of that week they had talked endlessly about the subject and Ruth had given Matthew a number of things to read. One of these was a newspaper article that asserted that there were now over three hundred thousand professional young women working in the City with liquid assets of at least two hundred thousand pounds each.

"I'm not there yet," Ruth said, "but I'm getting there. It's time to start buying property for the long term."

Holding his latte mug in both hands and gazing over it

now at the flying clouds, Matthew knew she was right. What Ruth was proposing was not only shrewd and sensible but also indicated, from her use of the word "we" in so many of these conversations, that she saw their future as something that they would unquestionably do together. All that, her rightness, her evident commitment, should have heartened him, should have enabled him to catch her enthusiasm for this great step she was proposing, and fling himself into the process with the eagerness that she clearly – naturally even – expected to match hers. And he would have, if he could. He longed to be able to seize upon this project as the exciting next stage of their relationship. But he couldn't. He couldn't because – he shut his eyes and took a swallow of coffee – he couldn't afford it.

He had been over the figures twenty times. He had rearranged them, looked at them in the short term and in the long term, and come to a point that there was no escaping from, a point that made it plain, in black and white, that in order to match Ruth's present expenditure in their lives and therefore preserve the fragile equilibrium of modern partnership, every penny he earned was already committed. He was not, baldly, in a position to finance any borrowing whatever, and such assets as he had were so small by comparison with Ruth's that they were hardly worth mentioning. What crowned it all was that Ruth had little or no idea of how stretched he was for the simple reason that he had preferred her not to know. And as a result, here she was proposing to embark on something she assumed, because she had no reason not to, that he could comfortably join her in.

He glanced over his shoulder. The coffee shop was filling up, filling with people in his kind of suit, his kind of haircut. They looked, as people always looked when you yourself felt out of step with humanity, painfully secure and confident. Money should not be like this, Matthew told himself, swirling the tepid last inch of his coffee round the mug, money should not dictate or stifle or divide, money should never take precedence over loyalty or love. He gave a huge sigh and thumped the coffee mug down. Money should simply not matter this much. But the trouble was, it did.

"I would have paid," Rosa said. "I wasn't suggesting I go home for free. I was going to offer to pay but he never gave me the chance."

Ben, lighting a cigarette, said indistinctly, "I give Naomi's mum fifty quid a week."

"Do you?"

"She pays all the bills. Says she'd rather have it that way."

Rosa examined her brother. He looked – well, more sorted, somehow, even in the dim lighting of a pub, less flung together.

She said, "She also plainly likes ironing –"

"Nope."

"Well, you look distinctly less scruffy."

Ben drew on his cigarette and said, with elaborate modesty, "*I* iron."

Rosa gaped.

"Didn't know you knew how."

He grinned, not looking at her.

"Lot of things you don't know."

"Clearly." Rosa picked up her drink. "So you're now playing happy families with Naomi's mum."

"Hardly ever see her. She's a caller at the bingo hall."

"I thought she worked in a supermarket."

"She does. And cleans offices."

"Heavens. Poor woman."

Ben glanced at her.

"No, she isn't. She likes it. She says she likes being independent."

Rosa flushed.

"Thanks a –"

"Don't patronize Naomi's mum, then."

"I wasn't –"

"Your voice was," Ben said. "Your *tone*."

"Sorry."

"And I'm sorry about Dad. What's going on?"

"I think," Rosa said, taking a swallow of vodka, "that he doesn't want any competition for Mum's attention."

Ben gave a snort.

"I only meant for a few months," Rosa said. "Till the summer. September at the latest. I'd pay rent, I'd be out all the time, I'd feed the cat –"

"I kind of miss the cat."

"I was just assuming in my naïve way that home is home until you have one of your own."

Ben blew smoke out in a soft plume.

"Have you told Matt?"

"No point."

"Why?"

"Because he and Ruth are thinking of buying a trendy loft."

"Room for you then."

"No *thank* you," Rosa said. "Ruth is great but she's so organized and professional that I don't feel I could begin to lay the mess of my life out in front of her."

"She might clear it up."

Rosa made a face.

"Pride," she said.

"So," Ben said, holding his beer bottle poised, "what are you going to do?"

"Not sure."

"Have you asked Mum?"

Rosa looked full at him, as was her wont when skimping on the truth.

"I can't. I can't be turned down by Dad and go straight to Mum."

Ben grinned again.

"Why not? You always used to."

"No," Rosa said, "I got turned down by Mum and went straight to Dad."

Ben tilted his beer bottle.

"Mum'd have you back."

"How do you know?"

"Just do."

"Ben," Rosa said again, "I can't."

He shrugged.

Rosa said slowly, "Kate said I could stay there."

"Fine, then."

"Well, no, not really. She's pregnant and they've only been married five months and Barney's lovely, really lovely, but he wants Kate to himself, he doesn't want –"

"Just like Dad," Ben said. He looked at the clock over the bar. "Gotta go, Rose. Meeting Naomi."

"What are you going to do?"

"Catch a movie, maybe. Don't know."

He bent sideways and retrieved from a canvas bag at his feet a black knitted hat, which he jammed down well over his hairline.

"You look like a peanut," Rosa said. "That hat does *nothing* for you."

Ben upended his beer bottle.

"Naomi thinks it's cool."

He slid off his bar stool.

"Hope things work out, Rose."

"Thanks."

He winked.

"You'll find another job."

"And a flat. And a man."

Ben leaned forward and grazed her cheek with his unshaven one.

He said, in an Irish accent, "Keep the faith," and then he shouldered his bag and pushed his way through the happy-hour drinkers to the door.

Rosa looked down at her own drink. Before seven o'clock, if you paid for one, you got the next one free. Two vodkas might provide her with enough brief courage to ring Katie and ask if, after all, for just a short while and paying rent of course, she might sleep in the tiny room beside the front door that Barney was intending to decorate ready for the baby. She raised a hand and signaled, smiling, at the barman.

CHAPTER FOUR

V ivien Marshall worked part-time in a bookshop. She
would have liked to have worked more, but if she did
her husband Max, from whom she had been separated for
four years, might notice and stop paying her the maintenance
that he was perfectly entitled not to pay now that Eliot really
had left home definitively, and gone to Australia. It wasn't
the money in itself that Vivien wanted, useful though it was
in maintaining the cottage in Richmond, and the car, but the
contact it provided with Max. When he had suggested that
they separate – she had known it was coming but had chosen
to shut her eyes to it, like someone in an impending car crash
– she had agreed in order to prevent him reacting to any
objection by insisting that they divorce.

Vivien did not want to divorce Max. She didn't even,
maddening and undependable as he had always been, much
want to be separated from him. Not only was he Eliot's
father but he was also, for Vivien, an exciting and energizing
presence whose absence had rather drained the color out of
things, particularly other men.

"You'd think," she said to Alison who managed the
bookshop, "that you'd be thankful not to live on tenterhooks anymore, whatever tenterhooks are. But actually, I
rather miss them."

Alison, who was not attracted to men of Max's type who
wore leather and denim well into middle age, said she

thought they had something to do with stretched damp cloth in the dyeing trade.

"What do?" Vivien said.

Alison sighed. Max might not, as a type, be to her taste but there were times when she felt a sympathy for him. Vivien was someone who couldn't help, it seemed, being a permanent small test of patience.

"Tenterhooks," Alison said, and put her glasses on.

Vivien went back to dusting. When Alison had offered her the job, years ago when Eliot was still young enough to let her kiss him at the school gates, she had made it very plain that bookselling was not a white-handed occupation involving delightful literary conversations with cultivated customers.

"It's more like always moving house. Endless heavy boxes and books parceled up in shrink wrap. Nonstop tidying and cleaning. Lists. Difficult people."

Vivien had looked round the shop. Alison's predilection for all things South American was very obvious: brilliantly colored wool hangings, posters of Frida Kahlo and Christ of the Andes, a shelf of Chilean poets.

"I like housework," Vivien said.

She always had, if she thought about it. When she and Edie had shared a bedroom as children, her side of the room – fiercely marked out by a strip of pink bias binding drawing-pinned to the carpet – had been both tidy and clean. On Saturday mornings she had dusted her ornaments with lengths of lavatory paper, and was apt to cover her favorite books in library film. It was this fondness for keeping house that she supposed drew her toward Max, toward a man who, although outwardly organized, was inwardly chaotic. He gave her the excited feeling that she was breaking rules to be with him, that she had kicked over the tidy traces of her upbringing and embarked on a heady and abandoned adventure. The trouble was that, in time, the tidiness reasserted itself and Max said he couldn't breathe. He began to set her challenges – champagne in the middle of the night, impulse trips to New York, having sex in the car in sight of neighbors' front windows – and, when she couldn't rise to them, he looked at her sadly, and sighed, and told her motherhood had changed her, had made her into someone he no longer recognized.

Working her way along the travel section with a new synthetic duster that was supposed to attract dirt to it like a magnet, Vivien thought that it wasn't motherhood that had changed her: it was Max. Motherhood had been something she felt very comfortable with, something, indeed, that she would have liked to extend to brothers and sisters for Eliot if she had not been so preoccupied with not giving Max the opportunity for straying. Max had, in truth, given her a brief and glorious holiday from herself, but he hadn't changed her. He had tried, and part of her had hoped he would succeed, but the basic Vivien stayed the same and preferred, if she was honest, filling the freezer with puréed carrot cubes for baby Eliot to suddenly dropping everything domestic in favor of some scheme of Max's that meant packing for an unknown destination without any certain timetable or sartorial guidelines.

Eliot, Vivien couldn't help noticing, was not like his father. Nor was he much like her. Eliot wanted life to be as simple as possible, which meant as little pressure in it, and discussion about it, as possible. His Australian girlfriend, as far as Vivien could detect from conversations on the telephone, made laconic seem an urgent word. They had a flat five minutes from the beach, they worked lightly, played water sports, and drank beer. The latest photograph Eliot had e-mailed back showed them both on the beach, thin and brown, with similar bleached spiky hair and bead bracelets. The girlfriend was called Ro.

"Short for Rosemary?" Vivien had asked.

"No," Eliot said, after a pause. His voice already had a faint Australian edge to it, making every statement a question. "Not short for anything. Just Ro."

When he had rung off – "Gotta go, Mum. Take care" – Vivien had cried a little. Then she had got up from the kitchen table where she had been crying, blown her nose, and assembled the clothes for drycleaning – folded, not dumped – in a carrier bag. An hour later, she had managed to recount her conversation with Eliot to his father on the telephone without crying at all.

"That's good," Max said. She could hear the faint tap of laptop keys as he spoke. "Good for you, Vivi. You're getting used to him being grown-up." He paused and the tapping stopped. Then he said, in the voice he had always used to indicate he knew he'd chosen the right sister, "Not like Edie."

Vivien leaned against the section on Eastern Europe. She rested the duster on top of several city guides to Prague. Maybe Max was right. Maybe what made her cry after talking to Eliot was not that he was twenty-two and had chosen to live in Cairns, Queensland, Australia, but that he wasn't eight or ten anymore, with a life that she had both detailed knowledge of and control over. And maybe that knowledge and control had, for a few years only, been absorbing enough for her not to fret about Max, about what he wanted and what she could – and more importantly, couldn't – provide. Crying for Eliot was crying for a lost small boy, not crying for a lost role, like Edie.

Vivien put a hand up and pushed her duster to the back of the Prague guides. Edie was distraught, really, quite un-hinged by the last of her children going and pretty well indifferent to poor old Russell's feelings. Vivien liked Russell, always had, but you couldn't compare him to Max for dash and glamour, just as his children, his and Edie's children, were making, with the exception of Matt, who was the only one Max had ever had time for, a very amateurish business of leaving home. Poor Rosa: too proud to go home, too short of money to stay independent. And Ben living with a girl he'd met having his hair cut, one of the

Saturday-morning juniors. She gave the final volumes of the travel section a little triumphant flourish of the duster. Poor Edie.

"For how long?" Barney Ferguson said.

He was standing at the foot of the bed wearing a bath towel wrapped around his hips. His hair was wet. Kate lay against the pillows with the tea he'd brought her, and the biscuit halves of a custard cream that she had peeled away from the filling.

"I did ask for *plain* biscuits."

Barney shook his wet head.

"They were all I could see. Except for pink wafer things. How long is she staying?"

Kate shut her eyes.

"A month?"

"A *month*!"

Kate bit a tiny piece out of one of the biscuits.

"Four weeks. Only."

"Four weeks isn't only," Barney said. "That's a fifth of the time we've been married."

Kate opened her eyes.

"Barn, I couldn't not ask her."

"Why?"

"Because she's my best friend and she's on her absolute uppers."

"I'm your best friend."

"My best woman friend."

"Suppose she doesn't get a job —"

"She will. She's got to."

"And supper, us having supper together —"

"She'll go out."

"You said," Barney pointed out, "that she's got no money."

Kate shut her eyes again.

"Please, Barn."

He moved round the bed so that he could sit close to her on the edge.

"I just want you to myself."

"I know."

"And although I like Rosa, I *do*, I don't quite like her enough to want to live with her."

Kate sighed.

"I wanted to paint that bedroom," Barney said. "Yellow, with elephants."

"Why elephants?"

"I loved elephants, when I was little."

Kate looked at him.

"Suppose this baby likes bears?"

"It can have bears."

"Rosa can draw," Kate said. "Rosa could do bears, by way of rent."

"You mean you haven't asked her for *any* rent?"

Kate said in a small voice, "Just bills. Sorry."

Barney stood up.

"I can't be cross with you. You look too pathetic."

"What a relief –"

"But I might be cross with Miss Rosa Boyd if she doesn't prove herself the *model* lodger."

"Guest."

"Guest. Too right."

Kate gave him the half-smile he said had been the first thing he noticed about her apart from the backs of her knees.

"Promise I won't ask anyone else."

"You bloody *will* promise."

He looked down at her in mock exasperation. Then he walked toward the bedroom door.

"Barney –"

He turned.

Kate smiled again.

"Thank you."

Barney smiled back. Neither of his married sisters had

produced any children yet, and his parents were treating him as a miracle of potency.

He wagged a finger at Kate.

"Strictly on sufferance," he said, still smiling.

The readings for *Ghosts* were held in an upstairs room above a pub on the Canonbury Road. The room was used for all kinds of purposes, including ballet classes, and along one wall ran a bar screwed into a series of huge dim mirrors, which gave an eerie effect of plunging the place underwater. At one end, sharing a littered card table, the director and producer of the play – both, Edie thought, about half her age – were sitting on gray plastic chairs with tin pub ashtrays on the floor at their feet. There was also a thin girl in black sitting by an upright piano and another man, in a gray ski jacket, reading a newspaper.

Edie had decided that, as she was doing this reading to placate her agent, who had complained that Edie was not, repeat not, in a position to be choosy, she was not going to prepare meticulously. She had read the play once, quite fast, and had determinedly not decided to dress in any particular way, not to think herself, with any depth, into the mind of Mrs. Alving.

She had also seen Russell look at her that morning, wondering.

"I'm not in the mood," she'd said, pouring coffee.

"Oh?"

"I can't apply myself. I feel too – too *scattered*."

"Pity," Russell said. He was putting on his mackintosh. "It's a wonderful part."

"This is a wonderful part," the director said now. He had a narrow dark face and a goatee beard.

"Oh, yes."

"Have you played Ibsen before?"

Edie shook her head. She'd been a nonspeaking visitor once, at the spa in *When We Dead Awaken*, but that didn't seem worth mentioning.

The producer looked at her.

He said, in a voice she regarded as unhelpful, "What do you know about Ibsen?"

Edie looked back.

"He was Norwegian. And short. Very short."

"I see."

The director turned to the man reading the newspaper.

"Ivor will read Pastor Manders for you. Act One. The scene revealing her husband's conduct."

"Okay," Edie said. She walked to a chair by one of the huge mirrors and dumped her bag on it, before rummaging in it for her book.

"From this copy," the director said. "If you would."

Edie turned. He was holding out a sheaf of papers.

"We have slightly annotated the Peter Watts translation." He glanced at the man with the newspaper. "Ivor speaks Norwegian."

Edie came slowly forward.

"We'll hear you read," the producer said. "But, personally, I think Mrs. Alving should be taller."

The man with the newspaper looked up for the first time.

He said, in accented English, "Good face."

"But height," the producer said. "So important for dignity. This is a woman who has *suffered*."

"How do you know I haven't?" Edie said.

Nobody answered her. She took the sheaf of papers from the director's hand.

"Are you sure you want me to do this?"

He gave her a fleeting smile.

"Now you're here."

"Is that enough reason?"

"Miss Allen, you *applied* for this casting –"

Edie swallowed.

"Sorry."

The girl by the piano said, "Clare was a good height."

They all turned to look at her.

"Yes."

"And she'd prepared meticulously. She understood that this was a progression from the heroine of *A Doll's House*. What might have happened if Nora had stayed."

Edie waited. She had begun to feel faintly sick, sick in the way you feel when you have told yourself that, as you don't want something, you will make no effort to secure it, and then discover that your indifference is not as deep as you had supposed.

The producer turned back and looked at Edie.

"Did you make that connection, Miss Allen?"

"I do now –"

The man with the newspaper put it down and stood up. He was burly, even allowing for the ski jacket, and had light, blank blue eyes.

He said to Edie, "This will be the seventh time I have played Pastor Manders."

"Heavens."

"Three times in Oslo, once in Edinburgh, once in Scarborough and once in London already."

She gave him a nervous smile.

"Are you Norwegian?"

"Half."

"Your father –"

"My mother."

Edie nodded.

"You have," Ivor said, "a wonderful line to read."

"I do?"

"The line, 'There you see the power of a bad conscience.'"

"Well," Edie said, making an effort, "I at least ought to know about *that*."

The director leaned forward.

"We should start. There are other appointments."

Edie looked at the script in her hand.

"Where would you like –"

"I will start," Ivor said, "I will start with the line: 'It almost makes my head reel.'"

Edie looked at him.

"No script?"

He smiled.

"No need."

Edie gave a little laugh.

"How very disconcerting –"

"Not at all. Quite the reverse. Reassuring for you."

"Oh?"

"Like," Ivor said, smiling, "playing tennis with someone much better than you are."

Edie swallowed. A rising tide of temper was beginning to eliminate the sensation of sickness.

"Of course."

"We will begin."

"Very well."

"And I will indicate when we will stop."

Edie glanced at the director. He was looking neither at her nor at his own copy of the script. She cleared her throat.

"Sorry," he said, without moving. "Sorry, Ivor. *I'll* tell you when to stop." His gaze traveled slowly across the room and came to rest on some object outside the window. The producer was looking at his fingernails.

"Fire away," the director said.

Ruth Munro was, as was her wont, one of the last to leave her office. She felt that, not only did her conscientiousness set a good example, but it also gave her the chance to leave everything in the state she would like to find it in the following morning: desk orderly, as many e-mails from the U.S. cleared as possible, work-to-do papers assembled in a pile weighted with a large, smooth gray-and-white pebble, picked up on a north Devon beach during the first weekend that she and Matthew Boyd had ever spent away together. Being alone in the room also gave her the chance to slow the pace, to be reflective, to take advantage of that brief no-man's-land of time between the working day and the evening ahead. It also gave her time to stay in touch.

Ruth's closest friend, Laura, had gone to Leeds two years previously, to join a law firm. In those two years, Laura had become engaged to a fellow lawyer and had bought an apartment on Leeds' regenerated waterfront that had two bathrooms, a balcony and a basement laundry on the Swiss model. It was Laura, now owner of a Tiffany engagement diamond and with plans for Vera Wang shoes for her wedding day, who had intimated to Ruth, with the effect that only close friends can have, that if she did not buy a flat of her own soon she would be making a grave mistake.

Ruth had e-mailed Laura photographs of the loft on Bankside. Laura had been most approving, especially of the glass brick walls and double-height ceilings.

"Go for it!" she'd written.

Ruth had waited three days while she adjusted her need to confide against her loyalty to Matthew, and then she'd written, "I really want to. But there's Matt."

"Doesn't he like it?"

Another two days elapsed.

"Yes," Ruth wrote reluctantly, "I think he does. But he's worried about the money."

Laura was marrying a lawyer who earned more than she did. Ruth sometimes thought it made her a little callous.

"You mean he can't afford it?"

"Yes."

"Can you?"

"Yes," Ruth wrote.

"Well?"

Ruth looked up from the screen. With no one in the office, she could hear the faint purring hum of the air-conditioning system and, beyond the immediate silence of the office, the bigger hum of Liverpool Street outside. If the truth were told, Matthew had not actually said he could not afford to share equally in the loft on Bankside: he had, instead, made it very plain that he would – could? – not talk about it. He had been very busy in their present flat, fixing all kinds of things that Ruth regarded as the future tenants' responsibility, but he had eluded any attempt at the kind of conversation Ruth was trying to have. She looked back at the screen.

"The thing is," she wrote, "that we have never had an I-have-this and you-have-that conversation. I suppose neither of us wanted to spell out the difference. And the difference hasn't been a factor, really, up to now. We've managed rather well." She paused. Laura was bound to challenge that. "Don't ask why we didn't sort it at the beginning. You know what beginnings are like. You don't care who earns what as long as you can be together and, by the time you start caring, it's too late, the patterns of behavior are in place." She stopped and then she typed, "I love Matt."

She lifted her hands off the keyboard and put them in her lap. Laura would tell her that everybody loved Matt, that Matt was the kind of thoughtful, decent, straightforward man who it would be perverse not to love. What Laura would also imply, from the current safety of her shiny new engaged situation, was that love might be about more than simply lovableness, it might include more stimulating elements like shared ambition and respect for professional achievement. She might also say – and she would be right – that Ruth and Matthew should have worked out this inequity early on in their relationship, that no amount of rapturous hand-holding on Devon beaches should have blinded Ruth to the fact that they had driven there in Ruth's car, Matthew not possessing one, and were staying in the kind of hotel he quite candidly would not have considered.

It wasn't, Ruth reflected, that he didn't pay his way because he did, with sometimes almost painful eagerness, but she couldn't help noticing that a tension about money had grown in him in the last year and, while she was genuinely sympathetic to that, she also felt that his concerns couldn't take precedence over her ambitions, that what held him back shouldn't hold her back too. If you made too many personal sacrifices, she and Laura had often agreed during late-night talking sessions with bottles of wine and Diane Krall on the stereo, you only ended up resenting the person you'd made the sacrifices for. Those old words, like "duty" and "honor," belonged to the history books, to an ancient imperial vocabulary that didn't belong in anyone's hearts or minds anymore. You couldn't, as a woman, make yourself into someone lesser in order to accommodate a man's weaknesses. You couldn't agree not to want, not to strive for, a very desirable flat on Bankside because the man you were sharing your life with quite simply couldn't afford to match your input. She picked up a ballpoint pen.

"Does that mean," she wrote across her jotting pad, "that I don't love him enough?"

She tore the page off the pad and screwed it into a ball.

"Or," she wrote, "are my values so skewed that at this moment I almost want a flat more than a man? And why do I want this particular flat so much? What is it about *this* one?"

She looked across her desk. There was a photograph of Matthew there, in a black bamboo frame, taken on holiday in the Maldives, a holiday he had suggested and had then – she could see it – had anxieties about paying for. He looked quite without anxiety in the photograph. He was wearing a white T-shirt and a wide smile and his hair was ruffled against a sky as blue as delphiniums.

Ruth ripped the second sheet off the jotting pad and tore it across. She glanced at her e-mail to Laura. What possibilities it opened up for Laura to implore her – or instruct her – not to let herself down. She ran the cursor up the screen to cancel the message.

"Do you," her computer asked politely, "wish to save the changes to this message?"

"No," Ruth clicked. She looked at Matthew, laughing on his tropical beach.

"Sorry," she said.

She could see, from the pavement below their building, that Matthew was home before her. She could also see, from the way the light fell, which lamps he had switched on and, from that, what sort of ambience there would be when she reached the second floor and even what kind of atmosphere. Sometimes, she wished she didn't notice so much. Sometimes, she thought how peaceful it would be to be someone who didn't observe so minutely and deduce so analytically. It meant, as Matthew had sometimes affectionately pointed out, that she lived her life twice, exhaustingly, once in preview, once in actuality.

"What will you do," he'd said, holding her, his face against hers, "with the three spare days at the end of your life that you've lived already?"

She put her key into the main door. The communal hallway, solidly decorated in the style of a decade earlier, contained only a small reproduction side table on which all the mail for the building was piled. Matthew would already have sifted through the pile for their own mail, but something in Ruth needed to recheck it, every time she came in. Her father had been the same, she told herself consolingly, perpetually reassuring himself that everything was in order, even down to counting the change from his trouser pockets every evening before piling the coins, in precise order of size, on the chest of drawers in her parents' bedroom. No wonder, she thought now, forcing herself past the side table without pausing, that she'd chosen someone like Matthew, someone who'd come from a family who regarded orderliness as a sadly psychotic condition. Two people like her in one relationship would simply have fossilized in their own methodicalness.

She ran up the two flights of stairs to their landing. The

front door was slightly open and there was the sound of music, some of the dance-rock stuff Matthew liked.

She pushed the door wider open.

"Hi there!"

Matthew appeared from the bedroom, feet bare on the wooden floor, but still in the shirt and trousers of his business suit. He bent to kiss her.

"I like it," she said, "when you're back first."

He straightened.

He said, "I haven't done anything, though, except take my jacket off –"

"I didn't mean –"

"I know," he said.

She went past him into the sitting room.

"Any mail?"

"Only dull things."

She picked up the envelopes and glanced back at him.

"Good day?"

"So-so."

She put the envelopes down.

She said, "I thought I'd go to the gym –"

Matthew leaned against the sitting-room door frame.

"I thought you might."

"Want to come?"

Matthew shifted his shoulder.

"No thanks."

"Then I –"

"Ruth," Matthew said.

She looked down at the envelopes. Notifications of payment by direct debit every one, evidence of system and organization, evidence of knowing that vital energies should not be dissipated in muddle and inefficiency, evidence –

"Ruth," Matthew said again.

She looked at him.

"Sit down."

"What are you going to say –"

"Sit down," Matthew said. "Please."

Ruth moved to the leather sofa – joint purchase, half-price in a January sale, excellent value – and sat down, her knees together, her back straight, as if in a business meeting.

Matthew padded past her and sat down at her side. He took her nearest hand.

"Look," he said, "this isn't very easy to say –"

"Does it have to be now?"

"Yes. There isn't a right time or, if there is, it mightn't occur for weeks and I have to say this thing, I have to tell you."

She gripped his hand.

"What?"

He said, looking at the floor, "I'm really sorry."

"Matt –"

"I wish it wasn't like this. I wish I could match you in everything. You're quite right to want to buy the flat. You're quite right to want to climb the property ladder and I'm sure you're right about not leaving it any later. And it's a great flat." He stopped and gently took his hand away. "It's just," he said, "that I can't manage it. I've tried and tried to see how, but I can't afford it. I can't, actually, afford how we're living now and I haven't faced up to that. Until now. I'm having to, now, because I'm having to face the fact that I can't even think about buying the flat on Bankside with you." He looked up from the floor and gave her a small smile. "So if you want to go ahead, go ahead without me."

CHAPTER FIVE

"Aren't you going to get up?" Kate said. She was dressed in a velour tracksuit and had pulled her hair back tightly so that she looked about thirteen and far too young to be pregnant.

"No," Rosa said.

"It's twenty to eleven –"

"Yesterday," Rosa said, "I went to four crappy interviews and was turned down at every one. This afternoon I have three more. This morning I have decided not to punish myself any more than life seems to be doing anyway."

Kate kicked at a pile of clothes and bags on the floor.

"You could clear all this up a bit –"

Rosa looked.

"Yes, I could."

"You'd feel better if you didn't keep telling yourself that life's got it in for you."

"Shall I," Rosa said, sitting up in bed and pushing her hair back, "talk to you when you're feeling less priggish?"

"You know," Kate said, "none of this is very easy for me. I want to help you, I want to make things nice for Barney, I want to stop feeling so awful and start feeling pleased about this baby, but it doesn't *help*, Rosa, if you lie in bed in all this mess having the mean reds and not even *trying*."

There was a pause. Rosa twisted her hair into a rope and held it against the back of her head.

"How do you know I'm not trying?"

Kate kicked at the bags again.

"Look at this –"

"No cupboards," Rosa said, "no drawers. Floor last resort. Floor it is."

"There's floor and floor. There's attempt-at-tidy floor or there's throw-everything-about-like-a-sulky-teenager floor."

Rosa let her hair go.

"I can't believe we're having this conversation. This is like talking to my *mother*."

"Not your mother, surely –"

"No. Quite right. Not my mother. *Your* mother."

"Don't take your spite out on my mother –"

"Oh Kate," Rosa said wearily, pushing back the duvet and swinging her legs slowly out of bed, "don't let's do this."

"Then tidy *up*," Kate said shrilly. "Stop abusing my hospitality and make an *effort*."

Rosa stood up. She looked down at Kate.

"What would you like me to do?"

"I would like you," Kate said, "to clear up this room. I would like you not to put washing in the machine and then just leave it there. I would like you not to finish the milk or the yogurt or the bananas and then not replace them."

"Do you know," Rosa said, "you were never like this when we were students. You didn't, as I recall, give a stuff about washing or bananas."

Kate sighed.

"I was thinking about Rimbaud then. And Balzac. And the practicalities behind the traditions of courtly love."

"And Ed Moffat."

"Well, yes."

"Ed Moffat didn't make you want to count bananas –"

"I didn't marry Ed Moffat," Kate said. "I wasn't *obliged* to Ed Moffat."

Rosa stooped for her clothes.

"Does Barney mind about bananas?"

"He minds about me minding."

Rosa looked at her.

"But *why* do you mind?"

Kate rubbed her eyes.

"Because being married changes things. It puts you in a different place, somewhere where it just suddenly seems childish to live in a student mess."

"Childish."

"Yes," Kate said.

Rosa found a pair of blue lace knickers on the floor and stood on one leg to put them on.

"I've had a flat, you know. I've bought milk and paid bills and taken washing out of machines. I've done all that."

"Then why –"

"Because I've lost control of things," Rosa said. She pulled the knickers up under her nightshirt. "It's all kind of got away for the moment, like something big and slippery, just sliding off the edge. I'd love, frankly, to be back in charge of my own fridge."

There was a small silence. Then Kate shuffled through the bags on the floor and put her arm round Rosa.

"Sorry."

"Me too."

"But you see –"

"Yes," Rosa said, "I see. Of course I see."

"I can't share my life with you the way I once did –"

"I know."

"But I want to be there for you –"

"Please," Rosa said, pulling off her nightshirt. "Please don't say that."

"Why not?"

"Because it's such an awful, meaningless phrase."

"But Rose, I'm your friend, I want to –"

Rosa looked at her.

"You are."

"What?"

65

"Helping. You've given me a roof and a bed and I'm grateful. I am also sorry about the bananas." She bent and picked up a black bra. "I will sort this room."

Kate watched her.

"You're so lucky," she said, "to have *normal*-sized breasts still. Seen mine?"

There had been no word from the director of *Ghosts*. From past experience, Edie knew that this meant she hadn't got the part, but then, she told herself, she'd known that the moment she'd walked into the room for her casting and sensed the profound boredom her presence aroused. Just after the casting, she had been buoyed up by a kind of righteous indignation – how dare they be so rude, so dismissive, so unprofessional? – and then she had sunk slowly down, as she had done hundreds of times over the years, through disappointment and discouragement, to the kind of weary resignation that made her agent's consoling platitudes sound more clichéd every time they were uttered.

"They are a good outfit, Edie, they do pull off some marvelously fresh interpretations, but *every*one complains about the way they behave and I know really distinguished people, if you'll forgive the comparison, dear, who've been simply treated like dirt and it just isn't right or reasonable that they can fill theaters the way they do after treating people like that, but the fact is they do and that's why I put you up in the first place because it would have been such a step up for you, but there we are. *Sorry*, dear, *sorry*. But don't take it personally. We'll get you there, promise. You're just about right now for one of Shakespeare's mad old queens. Don't you think?"

Yes, Edie thought, lying on Ben's bed in the middle of a Thursday afternoon, still clasping the clean towels she'd been bringing upstairs to the airing cupboard when she had spied his bed through the open door of his room and been irresistibly drawn toward it, yes, mad certainly, and

66

old any minute and why not a queen since being anything more realistic seemed to be, at the moment, out of the question? Why not point out, to the Royal Shakespeare Company, what they'd been missing in Edie Allen all these years and watch them throw crowns at her in an agony of remorseful recompense? Why not continue pretending that the world, as she knew it, hadn't fallen to pieces and left her washed up somewhere alien and empty with no notion of how to proceed? Why not keep saying, as Russell kept saying, that this is a rite of passage that all mothers go through, and do not all go off their heads forever in the process?

Edie shut her eyes. It would be luxurious, in a way, to be truly off her head, to be so much in another place mentally and emotionally that any requirement to behave conventionally was neither demanded nor expected. The difficulty for her was that she could see how much easier it would be for Russell, for herself even, if she could slide seamlessly from one stage to another, from something almost all-consuming to something still supportive but more detached, but the trouble was that these states of mind and heart did not seem to be a matter of will but more a matter of chance. There were women who could manage to be both kind and somehow still cool; and there were fierce women, women whose feelings tossed them about like corks in a storm. If you were fierce, Edie thought, you couldn't fake cool. Nor could you think where on earth to put, let alone use up, all that *energy*.

She sat up, hugging the towels. Two towels, two adult-size bath towels, which had washed over time from sage green to pale gray. Once there would have been five towels, plus swimming towels and – stop this, Edie said to herself, stop this *nonsense*, stop indulging yourself. She turned to look out of the window. The sun had come out, a light hard spring sun that only managed to show up just how dirty the glass was.

From downstairs, she heard the telephone ring. It was never plugged in, in her and Russell's bedroom, unless the children were out late, and as they were no longer there to be out late, it remained unplugged. She sat where she was, her chin on the towels, listening to the cadences of Russell's polite, easy answer-phone message and then the same cadences saying something quite brief, like he'd be having a drink with someone after work or he'd be bringing something back for supper that had caught his fancy. He rang a lot now, little inconsequential messages about this or that, sometimes just to say he was thinking about her. Which was lovely of him, sweet, attentive, thoughtful. And which left her strangely, disconcertingly, guiltily unmoved.

She stood up. Vivien had said, in a rare moment of not needing to score a point, that Edie should just wait, that this was a kind of grief, and that griefs of all kinds were susceptible to time and that, even if time didn't heal them, it made them possible to accommodate to.

"Just wait," Vivien said, shouting into her mobile against traffic noise. "That's what I'm doing, just waiting."

"What do I do," Edie said, "while I'm waiting?"

"Be nice to Russell!" Vivien shouted. "Try that, why don't you?"

There was a pause and then Vivien said, "Why do you have to make such a *drama* out of it, Edie? People leave home all the time! They're supposed to!"

Edie moved slowly out of Ben's bedroom and across the landing to the airing cupboard. There was a trick to opening the door, a trick involving lifting the handle slightly as one pulled, while pulling slowly in order not to precipitate an avalanche of towels and duvet covers, which had been stacked, for twenty years now, on slatted shelves that were neither level nor deep enough. Holding a bulging pile back with one hand, Edie half threw the clean towels up toward a space near the top of the cupboard, shut the door hastily and leaned against it. Then she peeled herself gingerly away, waited for ten seconds to make sure the catch would hold, and went downstairs to the kitchen. She glanced at the telephone. There was something slightly pressured about being thought about by the wrong person. Sweet though it was, imaginative, loving, kind – Russell's message could wait.

Russell decided he would go home early. He had been invited, with Edie, to the preview of a remake of a classic Hitchcock film, starring a hot new young Hollywood actor, who thought, as hot new young actors had probably thought since Sophocles, that they had invented bad behavior as a statement of wild independence. Russell had not mentioned the preview to Edie simply because she had never liked Hitchcock much and because the number of invitations he now received each month was so great that it had bred, even in Russell, brought up to standards of meticulous courtesy in that terraced house in Hull, a correspondingly great casualness in both responding and attending. He dropped the invitation on Maeve's desk.

She gave it the merest glance.

"It's a bit last-minute –"

"Now, there's grateful –"

"I'd be grateful if I needed to be," Maeve said. "As well you know." She looked up. "Why aren't you going?"

Russell unhooked his jacket from the bamboo hat stand behind the door.

"I'm away to my wife."

Maeve stopped typing but didn't look up.

"Is she okay?"

"To be truthful," Russell said, "not very."

"There's no dress rehearsal for these stages of life –"

"No."

"And no way that I can see of knowing how you'll conduct yourself –"

"No."

Maeve began typing again.

"How's Rosa?"

"Don't know," Russell said.

"Only asking. Pretty girl. Striking, even. And clever. Now, if Rosa was mine –"

"Good night, Maeve," Russell said. He opened the door. "See you in the morning."

She gave a tiny smile to her keyboard.

"Enjoy your evening."

Descending to the underground, Russell wondered when he had last attempted to travel not in the rush hour. At four in the afternoon, the underground was strangely easy and accessible, and the people using it looked altogether less driven and self-absorbed. He even found a seat, and extracted the books section of the previous weekend's newspaper for a leisurely read about books he would never read himself only to discover that he couldn't somehow concentrate. It wasn't leaving work early that was troubling – although he couldn't remember when he had last done that – nor even some residual nagging consciousness that he should be going to the preview because you never knew who else might be in the audience. It was Edie, really. However unresponsive she was being, however unhelpful both to herself and to him, however – well, exasperating was the word that came to mind – she was, one way and another, worrying to Russell. It was natural, perhaps, to feel the final departure of your youngest child as keenly as she felt Ben's, but was it natural to go on feeling it so keenly, to sink so deeply into the effects of loss that you couldn't see the point of, or color in, anything else? And, equally, was it fair to have to restrain oneself from telling one's wife that she was overreacting, on a daily basis, because one feared the inevitable subsequent explosion?

She hadn't, it was perfectly obvious, made any effort for the Ibsen casting. She had only gone in the end because Russell and her agent had almost forced her to, and this in itself was worrying because, in the past, however busy, however preoccupied with family life, Edie had displayed an eagerness about every chance that came her way, a kind of optimistic determination that Russell had marveled at, admired, especially in the face of so much inevitable rejection. She had even said every so often while yanking clothes out of the dryer or dumping mountains of groceries on the kitchen table, "Just *think* what it'll be like when I can think about lines and not lavatory paper!" And now that time had come, and she seemed utterly indifferent to it, indifferent indeed to almost everything except tending to this furious small flame of longing for Ben – metaphor for the children's childhoods – to be back again.

Perhaps, Russell thought, it was just a matter of time. Perhaps – more disconcertingly – it was a kind of depression. Perhaps – more disconcertingly still – Edie had been so changed by all those years of nurture that she couldn't now remember how it was to be just married, how it was to *want* to be still married. He shook his paper a little. So many books on the best-seller lists, on the review pages, were about love. Well, of course. In all its myriad forms. What else mattered, really? If it wasn't for love, indeed, why was he sitting on an afternoon train going home to someone whose current unhappiness he would gladly have shouldered himself? The train pulled into his station and stopped with a jerk. Russell helped a pregnant black girl get herself and a buggy and a sleepy toddler dressed as Spiderman off the train and on to the platform.

She looked at him. Her eyes were as dark and round as her Spiderman child's.

"Thank you," she said.

He badly wanted to say something back. He opened his mouth and then realized that what he hopelessly wanted to say was whole paragraphs of confused thinking about parenthood and letting go and not being able to and having to. He closed his mouth again and smiled. She looked at him for a moment longer and then bent and lifted the child into the buggy.

"Bye, Spiderman," Russell said.

He let the front door fall shut behind him with a bang. The hall inside was very quiet and the cat, who had been washing in a small patch of sunlight on the stairs, stopped to look at him.

"Edie?"

She came slowly out of the kitchen holding a mug.

"Edie –"

"Sorry," she said. "Oh my God, sorry. I didn't listen to it."

Russell put his bag down.

"Didn't listen to what?"

"Your message. I was fiddling about upstairs and I heard the telephone and I didn't do anything about it. And then I got deflected. As you do."

Russell came closer and gave her a brief kiss on the cheek.

"I didn't leave you a message. I came home on impulse."

Edie looked suspicious.

"What impulse?"

"Uneasiness," Russell said. He looked into her mug. "Can I have some of that?"

"It's green tea," Edie said. "It is supposed to be invigorating and it's filthy."

"Brown tea, then."

Edie turned.

"What are you uneasy about?"

Russell went past her and crossed the kitchen toward the kettle.

"You know perfectly well."

"I am waiting for it to pass," Edie said. "Like glandular fever."

"Ben left a month ago."

"What's a month?"

Russell ran water into the kettle.

"Quite a long time."

"What do you *want* of me?" Edie demanded.

Russell plugged the kettle into the wall and switched it on.

"When Ben left, I wanted you to look my way again. Now I would settle for you being able just to rouse yourself, climb out of this – this *inertia*."

"Inertia," Edie repeated calmly.

"Yes."

"Like – like not jumping up and down, every time you come home –"

"No!" Russell shouted.

"Then –"

"Like," he said more calmly, "not even bothering to listen to your telephone messages."

He went back past her out of the kitchen to the answer-phone in the hall. Edie drifted to the window and thought, without any urgency, that, if anything, the glass downstairs was even dirtier than the glass upstairs.

"It was Freddie Cass," Russell said, from the doorway.

Edie said, not turning round, "I don't know anyone called Freddie Cass."

"Freddie Cass, the director," Russell said. His voice was excited. "The director of *Ghosts*."

Edie turned.

"He wants you to ring him. He wants you to ring him *now*."

Ben had been on an assignment as assistant photographer taking pictures of a major newspaper editor at Canary Wharf. The editor was being photographed for a feature piece in a business magazine that had wanted independent pictures, which was something of a coup for Ben's boss, and one he had taken very seriously. The editor had been polite but had clearly had a thousand other things on his mind beyond being photographed in such a way as to ensure similar future commissions for Ben's boss, so the session had had a kind of tension to it, which resulted in Ben's boss giving Ben a needlessly hard time about every last little thing. As a consequence, Ben had dropped a still-damp Polaroid, mixed up the sequence of some black-and-white film, and held a reflector at an angle which, his boss said, any amateur prat could see bounced light off the ceiling and not the subject. As the subject was still in the room, trying to look simultaneously relaxed and in charge in his double-cuffed shirtsleeves, Ben could not point out that he was only obeying instructions and, if they were wrong, they were hardly his fault.

In the midst of all of this, Ben remembered, in the slow, amazed way he often did remember things, that his brother Matthew also worked somewhere in Canary Wharf. He couldn't remember where or who for, but the idea of Matthew suddenly seemed a most attractive alternative to returning on the Docklands Light Railway with his boss, who would have been stressed out by the photographic session and consequently anxious to take his stress out on somebody else. Ben mumbled that he needed a pee, and went out into the corridor outside the newspaper boardroom, and scrolled to Matthew's number on his mobile.

"Wow," Matthew said, "Ben?"

"Mmm."

"Where are you?"

"I'm here."

"Where?"

"In your office."

"What are you doing here?"

Ben leaned against the nearest wall.

"Working. Nearly done."

"Right –"

"You free?"

"What, now?"

"Half an hour or so –"

"Well, yes. Yes, I could be."

"I need a beer," Ben said. "This afternoon has pretty well done my head in."

"Fine. Fine. It – it would be good to see you."

"You too, bruv."

"Don't do that."

"What?"

"Don't," Matthew said, "use that fake East End talk."

"'Scuse *me*."

"It's phoney crap –"

"What's eating *you*?" Ben said.

"Nothing."

Ben looked down the corridor. A girl was walking away from him, silhouetted against the light from the window at the end. She was a lovely sight, tall, high heels. Naomi was tall too, nearly as tall as Ben. He suddenly felt rather better.

"Half an hour," Ben said. "Okay?"

"Yes," Matthew said. His voice had dropped a little. He sounded, abruptly, very tired. "See you."

"We can drink in here," Matthew said.

Ben peered through the glass doors.

"Looks a bit posh –"

"It's all posh round here," Matthew said. "Artificial and posh."

He pushed the door open, leaving it to swing in Ben's face. Ben followed him and seized his arm.

"What are you *like*?"

"What?"

"What are you in such a strop about?"

Matthew sighed. He looked, Ben thought, not just tired but drained and without that air of confident togetherness that Ben had supposed, for the last five years or so, to be inbuilt. He watched Matthew order, and pay for, a couple of bottles of beer, and then he followed him to a table in a corner, under a plasma television screen showing a picture of some giant freeway interchange, photographed from directly above. Matthew put the beer bottles on the table and glanced up at the screen.

"I watched the rugby World Cup on that."

Ben grunted. He put his duffel bag down on the floor and eased himself into an Italian metal chair.

"How's things –"

Matthew went on looking at the screen.

"Okay."

Ben said, "My afternoon was shite. He just put me down the whole time over stuff he'd told me to do anyway."

Matthew glanced away.

"But apart from this afternoon, everything's okay?"

"Aren't you going to sit down?"

"Yes."

"Well, sit then. I can't talk to you if you're standing."

"Sorry," Matthew said. He sat down slowly, on the chair next to Ben's. Then he said, "Sorry to snap at you."

Ben took a swallow of beer. He pulled off his knitted hat and ruffled his hair.

"That's okay."

Matthew looked at him.

"And you really *are* okay? Apart from this afternoon."

"I'm great."

"And Naomi –"

"Great. And the flat. It's cool. I really like it."

"You look as if you do."

"Don't tell Mum," Ben said, "but I should have gone before, two years ago, three."

Matthew picked up his beer.

"We all do that."

"Do what?"

"Stay too long."

Ben eyed him.

"At home?"

"And the rest."

"Matt," Ben said, "what's happened?"

76

Matthew put the neck of the bottle in his mouth and took it out again.

"I'm not sure."

"You and Ruth –"

"I think it's over," Matthew said abruptly.

"Christ."

"It just happened. It was so sudden. And I didn't see it coming." He took a mouthful of beer and shut his eyes tightly, as if swallowing it was an effort. "And I should have."

"Hey," Ben said. He leaned toward his brother. "Hey, Matt. Mate –"

"She wants to buy a flat," Matthew said, "and I can't afford to. I can't afford to because it's been costing me every penny I earn to live the way we do and I'm a stupid bloody idiot to have got in this mess. I am twenty-eight years old, Ben, and I'm back where I was at your age. I feel – I feel –" He stopped and then he said in a furious whisper, "Oh, it doesn't *matter*."

Ben said slowly, "It's hard to say –"

Matthew looked at him.

"It's hard to say, to a woman, that you haven't got enough money."

"Yes."

"And if the woman has more than you do –"

"Yes. Does Naomi?"

"No," Ben said, "and I tell her I wouldn't mind if she did. But I'm not so sure."

"It isn't good," Matthew said. "You may not have failed, but it feels as if you have. So you don't say, and she makes assumptions. She's perfectly entitled to make assumptions, if you don't say."

Ben drank some more beer.

"Don't you want to live in her flat?"

"Not under those circumstances. I'd feel like a lodger."

"So –"

"So I've said to her that if she wants the flat – and she *should* be buying a flat, earning what she does – she should go ahead and buy it, but that I can't come with her."

"Why," Ben said, "does it have to be this flat?"

"She's set her heart on it –"

"But if you had a cheaper flat, then you could manage it, maybe."

Matthew frowned.

"I tried that."

Ben gave him a quick look.

"What did she say?"

"She said she wanted me to come too. To this flat. She wants *this* flat."

"Well then."

"But I can't. And she knows I can't."

"So you're making her choose –"

"No," Matthew said, "I'm setting her free to choose."

Ben stared ahead.

Then he said, "I'm sorry."

"Thanks."

"Will you tell the parents?"

"I'll have to."

"Why have to –"

Matthew looked down.

He said, almost bitterly, "I may need a bit of help. For a while."

Ben adjusted his gaze from the distance to his beer. This was the moment, if he was going to take it, to tell Matthew that Rosa had already asked for help from their father, and been, however reasonably, turned down. But it occurred to Ben that Matthew wasn't like Rosa and that, in any case, his older brother and sister had to do things their own way, fight their own battles. If he mentioned Rosa, it might just be one more depressing thing for Matthew to have to factor in, one more difficulty in an already difficult situation.

He picked his bottle up again.

"Talk to Mum."

Matthew turned to look at him.

"Really? I was going to talk to Dad."

Ben shook his head. He was conscious of feeling something he had never felt in his life before, a sensation of not just, at last, being the same age as his brother but also, headily, almost older. He put an arm briefly across Matthew's shoulders.

"No. Talk to Mum," Ben said. "Trust me."

CHAPTER SIX

B arney reached across Kate to buckle her car seat belt. She put a hand out.

"I can do it –"

"I like doing it," Barney said. "My wanting to will probably wear off, so I should enjoy it while you can." He pushed the buckle home. "You look better."

"I feel," Kate said, "marginally less awful. *Marginally*."

Barney turned the ignition key.

"*Or* you are relieved to be getting away from the flat for the weekend."

Kate turned her head away.

"Kate?"

"Can't hear you."

"Yes, you can. Even the prospect of being a daughter-in-law for forty-eight hours is better than trying to pretend that having Rosa in the flat isn't like trying to maneuver round an agitated double bed all the time."

Kate said nothing.

"You were in her room," said Barney, pulling the car out into the street, "until one o'clock this morning."

"She was miserable –"

"And then you can't sleep so you're miserable and then I'm miserable."

Kate beat lightly on her thighs with her fists.

"Barney, we have *had* this conversation."

"But then nothing happens."

"It does. She's got a job."

"Temping."

"It's a *job*. She's going to give us some rent."

"How much?"

"Don't be so completely vile."

Barney waited until he had negotiated a small round-about, and then he said, "Okay. That was out of order. Sorry. But we wouldn't be having this conversation, and I wouldn't be saying things like that, if it wasn't for Rosa."

"I know."

"The thing is, she doesn't know how not to be a huge presence. She's somehow all over the flat even when she's in her room with the door shut."

"Barney," Kate said, looking straight ahead, "there are two weeks to go."

"And then?"

Kate said nothing.

Barney took a hand off the steering wheel and put it on one of Kate's.

He said, more gently, "And then?"

"I don't know."

"Promise me something."

"Oh –"

"Promise me you won't ask her to stay longer."

Kate said, "I'll try –"

"No."

"Barney –"

"If you do," Barney said, "I'll un-ask her. Not for my sake particularly but for yours. And ours."

Kate put her head back against the seat and closed her eyes.

"I just feel we've got so much –"

"Look," Barney said. "*Look*. Whatever we've got we've made ourselves. We haven't taken something of Rosa's."

Kate began, very quietly, to cry.

Barney glanced at her.

"Oh darling –"

"It's nothing –"

He pulled the car quickly into the side of the road and put his arms clumsily round her.

"Oh darling, don't cry, I'm so sorry, don't cry. Oh Kate –"

"It's not you," Kate said unsteadily. "It's me. And probably this baby."

Barney loosened his arms and slid down until his cheek and ear were resting against Kate's stomach.

"This baby."

Kate sniffed. She looked down, at Barney's head in her lap, at his hair, his hand on her thigh.

She said, "It's okay. I'll tell her. If she doesn't know already –"

"She's not a fool –"

"No," Kate said. She blotted her eyes on her sleeve. "No, she's not. That's part of the trouble."

Cleaning, Rosa thought, hunting for rubber gloves under Kate's sink, wasn't something she had exactly been brought up to do. Edie had been very strict about helping, had made sure that everyone – with the frequent exception of Ben – realized that the task of keeping a house going was a communal responsibility and that, just because she was the mother, it didn't automatically follow that she was also unpaid room service. But Edie was not the kind of woman for whom crushed cushions and unscaled kettles represented the first signs of domestic anarchy; washing the kitchen floor was never, for her, going to take priority over helping Matthew make a model or dancing with Rosa in front of the landing mirror. It was only staying over in school friends' houses that had revealed to Rosa that people – some people – bought vacuum cleaners for their efficiency and not solely because they had a jolly little face painted on the cylinder. Nothing she saw, no amount of gleaming bathrooms, made her feel Edie's attitude was wrong, but she did begin to see that the relief to be found in the small satisfactions of cleaning was very real and weirdly reliable. It was, in the end, living with Josh that had driven her to find the solid, if unglamorous, consolations of exercising control where you still could, in creating domestic order.

It was her intention, that Saturday, to create exactly that order in Kate and Barney's flat. It was partly that she might find personal solace in burnishing surfaces and straightening rugs, but also because she might gain a form of unspoken forgiveness from Barney, in particular, and even – this was a long shot but desperate situations required desperate measures – prepare the way to asking if her month in the flat might be extended into two. She was keenly aware that she had not behaved well in the past fortnight, that she had conducted herself with the sort of sulky resentment associated with disaffected fourteen-year-olds, and that it looked to Kate as if she was motivated by no more than the most primitive and unattractive of envies.

If she was honest, she thought, spraying cleaning fluid lavishly across the kitchen surfaces, she *was* envious of Kate. Not envious of Kate having Barney, but envious of Kate and Barney wanting to be together, and having the unspeakable luxury of a future to look forward to. At the same time, however, she knew that this kind of envy was a bitter, destructive thing, as well as a disgrace in any commendable personality. And even, Rosa thought, scrubbing at a stain, if my personality is not commendable, and certainly hasn't been recently, I would like it to be; I would like it, really, to be in charge of itself.

She straightened up. A pleasing sort of calm was beginning to overtake the kitchen. She thought of extending her efforts to the contents of the cupboards and then it occurred to her that to move so much as a box of lentils could be construed as criticism, which was, in her present shaky state, the last thing she wanted to convey. She wanted, rather, to make the flat look, by the time Barney and Kate returned, like a humble but unmistakable token of gratitude. She wanted, she acknowledged with difficulty, to appear sorry without actually having to say so.

From the sitting room, her mobile rang. Rosa went slowly to answer it, pulling off the rubber gloves and saying to herself, under her breath, as she seemed to have been saying for years every time the phone rang, "Make it a surprise, make it something nice, make it –"

"Darling?" Edie said.

"Mum, hi –"

"Are you all right? What are you doing?"

"Actually," Rosa said, "cleaning."

"Cleaning? Why?"

"I want to. I like it. It's Saturday morning. Cleaning time."

"Not in this house," Edie said.

"I remember."

"Rosa, what's happening?"

"Happening?"

"Yes. We haven't spoken for weeks –"

"Five days."

"I want to know if you're okay."

Rosa stood a little taller.

"I am."

"Are you?"

"Yes, Mum. Thank you."

"Have you found a job?"

"Yes."

"What –"

"Not a good job. But a job. In a travel agency."

"Rosa –"

"Don't start."

"You're so bright and beautiful," Edie said, "I don't want you wasting yourself."

"Nor do I."

"Darling –"

"Mum," Rosa said, interrupting. "What's going on with you?"

"Oh, that."

"Yes, that. I can tell there's something."

"Well," Edie said, "I got the part."

"Mum! The Ibsen?"

"Yes. Isn't it odd?"

"*Odd?*"

"Yes. To get a part you don't want when you weren't trying."

"You *do* want it."

"Maybe."

"I think it's wonderful," Rosa said. Her throat hurt, as if she were about to cry. "Congratulations. It's brilliant."

"We'll see," Edie said. "Read-through on Tuesday. I get to meet my stage son. Have you heard from Matthew?"

"No –"

"What about this flat he and Ruth are buying?"

Rosa put her hand to her throat.

"It sounds all very hip young professional –"

"Darling, I wish –"

"I don't want an urban loft, Mum. Or a job in the City."

"Have you spoken to Ben?"

"I haven't spoken to anyone."

"Rose, are you all right?"

Rosa shut her eyes. She mouthed, "Don't keep asking" at the ceiling.

Then she said loudly, "Fine."

"If you're not okay –"

"I am. Ring me and tell me how Tuesday goes."

"Oh," Edie said, "okay."

"How is Dad?"

"In his shed."

"You're joking."

"Would I?"

"Give him my love," Rosa said.

85

"Darling –"

"Back to Mr. Sheen!" Rosa called. She held the phone away from her ear.

Edie's voice came faintly from it, thin and small.

"Bye, Mum!"

She went slowly into the kitchen, and leaned against the sink. Edie in her kitchen, herself in Kate's, Matt and Ruth no doubt buying Alessi-inspired kettles for theirs, Ben and Naomi blissfully not giving kitchens a thought. She sighed. She had not given her mother what she wanted, on the telephone. She knew that she hadn't given it because she couldn't, for all the tired old reasons of loyalty and disloyalty that bedevil family life, the kind of reasons that made her mother and her mother's sister ring each other and bitch about each other daily in equal measure. She leaned against the sink and folded her arms. It struck her, with a small ray of dawning hopefulness, that this thought of her aunt coming into her head might not be totally arbitrary and that, beyond fathers and mothers in the leaky support system provided by families, there could sometimes also be aunts. Rosa stood straighter and laid the rubber gloves down on the now gleaming draining board. Then she went thoughtfully back toward the sitting room, and her mobile phone.

"I'm playing Osvald," the young man said.

Edie smiled at him.

"I guessed."

He gave a small snort of laughter.

"Not difficult, with a cast of five –"

He had fine features and the slight build Edie had always somehow associated with First World War poets.

He said, "Well, we're the same coloring, anyway. Mother and son."

She gave him an appraising glance.

"I expect you got your height from your father –"

He grinned.

"Among other things."

"I *know*," Edie said. "What a play."

"Not much light relief –"

"That means rehearsals will be hilarious. They always are, if the play is dark."

The young man said, "My name's Lazlo."

"I know. Very exotic."

"My sister's called Ottolie."

"Is she an actor?"

Lazlo shook his head.

"She's almost a doctor." He made a little gesture. "I've never played Ibsen before."

"Nor me. Not really."

"I didn't think I had a hope –"

"Nor me."

"It was an awful casting –"

"Horrible."

He smiled at her.

"But here we are, Mama."

"I think," Edie said, smiling back, "you call me Mother dear. At least, in this version."

He bowed a little.

"Mother dear."

She looked across the room. A dark girl with her curls tied on top of her head with an orange scarf was standing in an extravagant dancer's pose, feet and hips sharply angled, talking to the director.

"What do you think of Regina?"

He turned his head.

"Scary."

"You get to kiss her."

"Double scary."

"In two weeks' time," Edie said, "you won't be thinking that for an instant."

He said, almost eagerly, "I've only been out of drama school a year, you see –"

She looked at him, full in the face. Then she smiled and took his hand.

"How absolutely lovely," Edie said.

Barney had insisted that Kate take a taxi to work. It was her first Monday morning, after all, after feeling too terrible to leave the flat for three weeks, and he was taking no chances. He had booked the cab himself, and left a twenty-pound note weighted with an orange on the kitchen table, to pay for it.

"Just this once," Kate said.

She had looked at the note and wished that he hadn't left it. Solicitousness was all very well but the imposition of will implied by paying for something was rather different. She was extremely grateful for the thought, but not at all grateful for the money. She was still earning, after all: she would pay for her own taxi. She had picked up the orange and replaced it in the fruit bowl, and then wedged the money against it like a flag.

Sitting in the taxi, Kate felt an unmistakable rush of relief, relief at not wishing to die with such vehemence, relief at being out of the flat, relief at the prospect of the – compared to home – impersonality of work. Work was full of complications, and intractable people, but as she didn't love them she didn't have to take responsibility for them. Nor did she have to thank them, fervently, every time they did something properly that they were paid to do properly in the first place.

It was lovely of Rosa to have made such an effort in the flat. They had returned from a weekend in Dorset with Barney's parents – too much food, Kate thought, too much kindness, too many cushions and anxious questions – to find the flat smelling strongly of bleach, and every room wearing a startled aspect, as if a violent upheaval had taken place without having, exactly, come to a settled conclusion afterward. Rosa could start things and carry them energetically part of the way forward, but finishing them, calming them, tidying up tedious, final details was something she was unable to achieve because she couldn't see that it was necessary. Her essays at university had been like that, Kate remembered, full of initial energy and enterprise and then simply stopping, some way from the end, as if a fuel supply had been cut off. Barney had looked at the sitting room.

"It's like someone left the window open, and a hurricane blew through."

Kate had been very grateful – most grateful in fact – for Rosa's not being there when they got back. She'd left a jug of pale supermarket tulips, all curved and clamped together, on the kitchen table and a note saying she'd gone away for the night. Kate, feeling treacherous, had opened Rosa's bedroom door and looked inside. The bed was made, roughly speaking, and the floor was clear because all Rosa's clothes had been mounded up in one corner, and covered, with its arms outstretched in a sort of bizarre embrace, by her orange tweed jacket. Kate swallowed. There was a mug and a glass on the upended wine carton Rosa was using as a bedside table. Kate resisted the urge to go and pick them up and closed the door again.

It was easier, the next morning, and with the unquestioned freedom of a working day ahead, to feel a simpler reaction to Rosa's efforts. Losing a job, Kate reflected, was in some ways similar to the end of a relationship, even if it was a job you hadn't exactly valued in the first place. When you were faced with rejection, in whatever situation and however deserved or undeserved, it wasn't just your confidence that suffered, it was your faith in the future, your ability to see that any effort you might make could be a tiny investment in what would happen to you thereafter. I have to remember that, Kate thought, I have to remember how pointless daily life seems when you can't see where you're going. I have to remember what it must feel like when there isn't even any wreckage to cling to.

The taxi drew into the curb. Across a broad stretch of pavement rose the eccentric glass-and-steel façade of the broadcasting company where Kate had worked as a researcher for three interesting and purposeful years. It was the sort of job she had hoped for, all the time she was at university, all the time after university when she couldn't find what she wanted, couldn't seem to settle. It was, in fact, the sort of job Rosa should have had too.

Kate leaned forward and pushed a note through the glass screen in the taxi. How astonishing it was, how pleasurable, to be going back to work. She got out of the cab and stood for a moment on the pavement, her face tilted toward the sky. Married, she said to herself, pregnant, working. Go, girl.

In the coffee shop after the read-through, Lazlo said he was starving.

"I was so nervous —"

"It didn't show."

"I kept thinking, this isn't how I'm going to play it, this is *wrong*. I made him far more petulant than I want him to be. I don't want to sound so sorry for myself. Would you like a bagel?"

"I'll get you a bagel," Edie said.

"No, really, I asked you to have a coffee with me."

"And I am your mother," Edie said. "Don't forget that."

He regarded her. He said soberly, "I thought you were wonderful."

Edie's chin went up a little.

"Not really. Don't forget I've been doing this since you were in your pram."

"I don't think so."

She took her wallet out of her bag.

"How old are you?"

"Twenty-four."

She looked satisfied.

"I've been doing this since you were in your pram. What kind of bagel?"

"Toasted, please. Would two bagels be out of the question?"

"Certainly not. And cream cheese?"

"How did you know?"

"Mother stuff," Edie said.

She threaded her way between the small metal tables to the counter. Behind it, a huge mirror reflected the room and she could see that Lazlo was watching her and that he looked as her children had looked after school examinations in subjects they were good at, exhilarated and exhausted. He was going, she thought, to be a good Osvald, just the right blend of intensity and youthful spirit, frightened enough to arouse sympathy, self-absorbed enough to be maddening. As for her – well, there was a lot to think about in Mrs. Alving and most of it about lies. Watching Lazlo in the glass made her consider how rich it was going to be making those lies form the central core of violent maternal protectiveness in the way she played Mrs. Alving. She could see, from where she was, how hungry Lazlo was. She could see he was watching her in admiration, certainly, but also he was watching because she would be returning to him with a tray of coffee and bagels, and something in the simplicity of that, the neediness of that, made her heart rejoice.

She went back to their table and put the tray down.

"Can I ask you something?" Lazlo said.

"Yes."

"I want you to be honest –"

"Oh, I am excellent at that," Edie said, unloading the tray, putting the bagels down in front of him. "I have a diploma in honest. Ask my family."

He picked up a knife.

"Your family –"

"One husband. Three children, two of them older than you are."

"I don't believe it –"

"True." She turned and put the empty tray down on a nearby table. "What do you want to ask?"

"Will I –" He stopped.

"Will you what?"

"Will I be any good?"

It was rather nice, Vivien thought, lying in the bath with a mug of valerian tea balanced on the edge, to think of Rosa settling down in her spare room. The room had been made up, of course, as it always was, in obedience to the dictates of Vivien and Edie's childhoods, where whole areas of the house had been consecrated to this mythical creature called the visitor, who would expect exaggerated standards of perfection and formality were he or she ever to put in an appearance. There had not only been a front room smelling of furniture polish, but a spare bedroom upstairs that looked as if it belonged in a provincial hotel, with two beds shrouded in green candlewick covers and a wardrobe empty of everything except extra blankets and a clatter of hangers. Edie's reaction to this arrangement had been to make sure her family lived abundantly in every corner of her house; Vivien's, to emulate her mother. Rosa, in Vivien's spare room, would find books and tissues and lamps with functioning bulbs. And if she chose, climbing into a bed where the sheets matched the pillowcases, to make comparisons, that was no affair of Vivien's.

When Rosa had telephoned and asked to come and see her, Vivien had said of course, come to supper. Then she had suggested coming on Sunday and added, "Why don't you stay the night?"

Rosa had hesitated.

"Would that be all right?"

"Of course. Wouldn't you rather stay than trail back into Central London afterward?"

"Staying," Rosa said, "would actually be very wonderful."

Vivien didn't think Rosa looked very well. She had made an effort – clean hair, ironed shirt – but there was a kind of luster missing, the kind that was turned up full wattage when you were in love but could equally be dimmed down according to varying degrees of distress, until it was almost extinguished.

It became plain, as supper progressed, and Vivien began to think that a single bottle of wine was looking both meager and unhelpful, that Rosa's current state of distress had been advancing upon her for several years. First there was the affair with Josh, and then the ending of the affair and subsequent derailment of prudence and capability, and now unemployment and debt.

"Probably," Rosa said, eating grapes with the absent-mindedness of being already full, "I shouldn't be telling you this."

"Why not? I'm your aunt –"

"I mean, I shouldn't be telling anyone. In a grown-up world, I should be sorting it. I should be waking up one morning full of resolve and vow to clear my life of clutter and make a list of priorities. I shouldn't be wandering about like some hopeless animal that's escaped from its field and can't find the way back in."

Vivien got up to make coffee.

"Nice image."

"But not nice situation."

"No." She reached up for the cafetière from a high shelf. She said, "Did you think of going back home?"

There was a pause and then Rosa said reluctantly, "I tried."

Vivien turned round.

"I can't believe your mother turned you down –"

"No –"

"Well, then."

"Dad did," Rosa said. "But nobody knows that but Ben. You're not to say."

Vivien smiled at her.

93

"Wouldn't dream of it." She spooned coffee into the cafetière. She said carefully, "Your mother couldn't think why you chose to go and live with friends. Couldn't understand it. Why you didn't go home."

"Well," Rosa said, "I can't, now."

"Can't you?"

"I can't go whining to Mum after Dad said what he did."

"Which," Vivien said, switching on the kettle, "I can imagine. Men always want their wives to see them first. Except," she added lightly, "mine."

Rosa looked up.

"Perhaps that's why you still like him."

Vivien came back to the table and sat down.

"More wine?"

"Yes, but no," Rosa said. "I'm selling bargain breaks to Lanzarote tomorrow."

"Nothing wrong with that. I sell a lot of books I wouldn't read myself." She picked up a fork and drew a line with it across her place mat. She said, "You'll get another job."

"I hope so."

"It's much easier to find a job if you've already got one."

Rosa rolled a bruised grape around the rim of her plate.

"It's not really the job that worries me so much, in a way. It's how I'm going to live. How I'm going to live so that I can start on this debt, how I –" She broke off and then she said, in a slightly choked voice, "Sorry."

Vivien drew another line to intersect with the first one. Then she said, "Come here."

"What?"

"Come here. Come and live here for a while."

Rosa stared at her.

"I couldn't –"

"Why not?"

"Well, you're my aunt –"

"Exactly."

"And Mum –"

94

"Might be very pleased."

"Might she?"

They looked at each other.

"I don't think so," Rosa said.

"Does it matter?"

"Oh God –"

"Does it really matter? Just while you get yourself sorted and start paying off these cards and find another job?"

"Maybe –"

"She'll calm down," Vivien said. "You know Edie. Big bang, smaller mutterings, acceptance. She'll be fine."

Rosa said slowly, "It would be wonderful –"

"Yes. I'd love it."

"I'd make an effort –"

Vivien got up to get the coffee.

"We both would." She looked at Rosa over her shoulder. She smiled. "It might be quite fun."

It might, she thought now, indeed be fun. It might also, dwelling upon the prospect, be both a relief and comfort to become in some way necessary again, a provider of all those things only women who had lived lives and run houses could properly provide. Vivien picked up her tea. Rosa had kissed her warmly before she had disappeared into the spare room, with a kind of brief sudden fervor people feel when they have unexpectedly been thrown a lifeline.

"I only really came to talk," Rosa said. "I never thought –"

"Nor did I," Vivien said. "One seldom does."

She smiled into her tea. There was no hurry, really, about telling Edie.

CHAPTER SEVEN

The loft on Bankside was in a vast converted Victorian warehouse. Its brick walls, newly cleaned and pierced with modern windows in matte black frames, reared up from the charmingly – and also newly – cobbled alley that separated the building from a similar one ten feet away. If you looked skyward, you could see, on the two sides that looked toward the river, that little black balconies had been hung outside some of the higher windows, and on one of those, Matthew supposed, Ruth would emerge on summer evenings, holding a glass of vodka and cranberry juice, or whatever was the drink of the moment in her circle, and admire both the view and her sense of ownership.

Thinking this was not, Matthew found, at all comfortable. In fact nothing in his mind was, at the moment, in the least comfortable, being instead a sour soup of disappointment and self-reproach and a very real and insistent sadness. It wasn't a simple matter of resenting Ruth, or even berating himself for not facing facts, because the whole situation had crept up on him – on them both – so insidiously, fueled by things that were not acknowledged or uttered even more than by things that were openly expressed. He might curse himself for getting into this tangle, but the curses were only the more vehement because he could, looking back, see exactly how he had got there.

When Matthew had announced that there was no way he

could share in the purchase of the flat, Ruth had become very still. She had looked at him for a long time, thoughtfully, and then she had said, "Will you do one thing?"

"What thing –"

"Come and see the flat. Just see it."

He shook his head.

"No."

"Matthew, please."

"I can't afford it. I don't want to have my nose rubbed in what I can't afford."

"It isn't for you, I'm afraid. It's for me. *I* want you to see the flat."

He said nothing.

She said, almost shyly, "I want you to see what I'm buying."

"Why?"

"I want you to be part of it –"

"I can't be."

"But you'll come there, you'll come and see me, *surely?*"

He hesitated. His heart smote him.

He said, not looking at her, "Of course."

"Then come."

"Ruth –"

She moved toward him and put her hands on his shoulders. She looked into his face as intently as if she were counting his eyelashes.

"Matt. *Matt.* This isn't the end of *us.*"

Now, standing uneasily on those carefully patterned cobblestones, Matthew told himself that being kind – or cowardly – once was one thing: persisting in it was quite another and could lead to desperate situations. Whatever Ruth said, however beseeching she was, he must not allow her to believe that he felt other than he did, that he could somehow cope with a situation in which he only had power in the obvious department of bed, which was not, in the end, he knew, enough.

He pushed open the heavy glass door of the warehouse and entered an immensely tall foyer, floored in granite with long windows running right up to the roof. There was an industrial steel staircase curving up behind a bank of lifts and besides that nothing, not a picture nor an ashtray nor a piece of furniture, nothing but high, quiet acres of expensively finished dark gleaming space. He stepped forward into a lift and pressed the button for the sixth floor.

When the lift doors slid open, there was a sudden flood of light.

"I saw you!" Ruth said. She was standing in an open doorway with apparently nothing behind her. "I was watching from the balcony and I saw you!"

He bent to kiss her cheek. She moved to meet his mouth and missed it. He looked past her.

"Wow."

"Isn't it wonderful?"

He nodded. The room beyond the open door was pale and high and shining, and at the end there was nothing through the huge windows but sky.

Ruth took his hand.

"You see? You see why I had to buy it?"

She towed him through the door. Then she let go and spun down the length of the room.

"Isn't it great?"

"Yes."

"All this space! All this air! And Central London! I can walk to work!"

"Yes."

"Come and see the bathroom," Ruth said. "The shower is so cool. And in the kitchen, the microwave is built into the cooker unit. It looks like a spaceship."

Matthew followed her across the wooden floor, through a doorway in a translucent wall of glass bricks. She was standing in a shower made of a cylinder of satin-finished metal, punctuated with little glass portholes in blue and green.

"Did you ever see anything like it?"

"No," Matthew said, "I never did."

Ruth stepped out of the shower.

She said, more soberly, "I wish it wasn't like this."

He nodded.

She said, "I wish it wasn't you coming to stay in my flat. I wish it was ours."

He leaned against the wall. The glass felt solid and cold through the sleeve of his jacket.

He said, too loudly, "I'm afraid I won't be coming."

She said nothing. She walked past him very quickly and went back into the big room. He followed her. She was standing by the sliding doors to the balcony looking at her view of the river.

She said, "Please don't talk like that."

He stayed standing a little behind her.

He said, "Ruth, I have to. If I come and stay here, it'll change the balance between us. It's changed already, of course, but it'd be worse. You can imagine how it would be. It'd be pitiful."

She said fiercely, turning round, "You couldn't be pitiful. I wouldn't *let* you."

He tried to smile.

"You couldn't stop me. It would just happen."

"Matt –"

"We've had a wonderful time," he said, "and it's got nothing to do with not loving you –"

She stepped forward and seized his arms.

"Suppose I don't buy it! I mind far more about you –"

He stepped back, gently extricating himself.

He said, shaking his head, "It wouldn't work –"

She dropped her arms.

She said miserably, "I didn't mean this to – be like this."

"I know you didn't."

"Are – are my values all skewed?"

"Nope."

"Please – *please* don't leave."

He looked round the table.

"It's a wonderful place. You'll be really happy here."

"Matt –"

He leaned forward and laid the palm of his hand against her cheek.

He said, "And you're doing the right thing," and then he took his hand away and walked back across the echoing floor to the landing and the lifts.

Edie took a garden chair into the angle of the house where, if you tucked yourself right into the corner, you could elude every breath of wind. She also carried a mug of coffee, her script and, somehow, two ginger biscuits, a pen and her telephone. Behind her, sensing a sedentary moment of which he might take advantage, padded Arsie.

The sun, shining out of a washed blue sky, was quite strong. It showed up unswept post-winter garden corners, and interesting patterns of blistered paintwork and lingering blackened leaves on the clematis above Edie's head. She thought, settling herself into the chair and arranging her mug and phone and biscuits on a couple of upturned flowerpots to hand, that this was the first time, the first moment, in the last five weeks, when she had felt the possibility of pleasure, a tiny chance for the future to hold something that could, in turn, hold a small candle to the past. She let Arsie spring into her lap, waited while he trampled himself down into position, and then rested her script on top of his purring tabby back. Sun, cat, acting, Edie thought. She patted the script. No, not quite that. Russell would put it differently. Sun, cat, *work*.

"I can't believe this is work," Lazlo had said to her at the first rehearsal.

She'd been looking at her lines.

Without glancing at him, she said, "By the end of this rehearsal, you'll know it is."

By the end of the rehearsal, he'd been ashen. He'd looked as if he might cry. He'd been all over the place, all the wrong emphases, no sense of timing, not listening, in panic, to what the director was saying.

"Go away," Freddie Cass said to him. "Go away and learn those lines and come back to me *empty*."

"Empty?"

"Empty. We're starting again. We're not starting from Lazlo, we're starting from the *play*."

Ivor, the Norwegian, had taken him and Edie for a consoling drink. Now that the cast was established Ivor had exchanged patronage for paternalism.

He put a hefty arm round Lazlo's shoulders.

"Drink that. Relax."

Lazlo looked like a boy in a fairy tale, rescued by a genial giant. He drank his drink and shivered a little and Edie and Ivor smiled at each other across his bent head and told him that everyone had first rehearsals like this, everyone got over-excited at one point or another, and made fools of themselves.

Lazlo looked mournfully at Edie.

"You didn't," he said.

"Not on this occasion."

"Tell me," Lazlo said miserably, "about a time when you did."

They'd ended up drinking two bottles of wine and putting their arms round each other and when Edie got home, Russell took one look at her and said, "Shall I say I told you so?"

It was true that the play was drawing her in and therefore providing a distraction from her preoccupations, but that didn't mean, Edie decided, tilting her face to the sun and closing her eyes, that she didn't notice that none of the children were telephoning, nor that she didn't feel painfully aware that she knew very little about Matthew's new flat or Rosa's living arrangements, or Ben's girlfriend, or any of their working lives. She had promised herself that she wouldn't keep ringing them, and she clung to that promise with the tenacity usually required to stick to a rigorous diet, but it didn't mean she didn't think and wonder and worry. And feel left out. Playing Mrs. Alving was wonderful because it stopped her, sometimes for hours at a time, from waiting for the telephone to ring: but it wasn't a solution, it was only a diversion.

Beside her, quivering on its upturned flowerpot, her phone began vibrating.

"It's me," Vivien said.

"Damn."

"Thank you so very much –"

"I was hoping you were Matthew. Or Ben."

"At eleven-thirty in the morning?"

"Why not?"

"People only ring their mothers in the early evening. It's a sort of tradition."

"Vivi," Edie said. "You sound very perky."

"Well, the sun's out and my new little blue clematis is flowering and Eliot has passed his first diving exam."

"How useful."

"It is, if you're living in Australia, near interesting coral reefs."

"Would you call it a career?"

"I rang," Vivi said, "to ask how you are. Actually."

"And actually, I'm very pleased to hear you. Nobody rings me now. Nobody. I've vanished. Was it Germaine Greer who said that women over fifty are invisible?"

"Probably. But I expect she was thinking of them as sex objects."

Edie shifted in her chair a little and the script slid to the ground. Arsie didn't move.

"I only want to be a mother object. I'll think about sex again when I've sorted this stage. Actually, talking of mothers, I've got a sweet new stage son. He's twenty-four and anxious and pads round after me like a puppy."

"Well," Vivien said, "there you are then. Sorted."

"I want to know how my *real* children are."

There was a tiny pause and then Vivien said, almost cautiously, "I can tell you how one of them is, I think –"

"Can you?" Edie said sharply. She sat up, pulling her knees together. Arsie dug his claws in. "Ow. What do you mean?"

"I saw Rosa –"

"Did you?"

"Yes."

"Why did you see Rosa?"

Vivien said lightly, "Oh, she came to supper."

"Did she?"

"And stayed the night."

Edie opened her mouth to say, truthfully, that she didn't know or, untruthfully, that she'd forgotten, and decided against both of them.

Instead she said, in a voice that entirely betrayed her feelings, "Good!"

"I rather thought," Vivien said unkindly, "that she'd have told you."

Edie leaned forward to detach Arsie's claws from the fabric of her trouser knees.

She said, as normally as she could, "How was she?"

"Well," Vivien said, "I thought she was putting on a bit of a brave face. I mean, this travel agency job is fine, but it isn't really stretching her, you know. She knows that, of course, but it's money, isn't it?"

"Yes –"

"The real trouble was living with Kate and Barney. They're too newly married, really, to cope with having anyone else there. She didn't actually say she didn't feel welcome, but I could tell she was having a bad time."

"Was?"

"Oh yes," Vivien said, almost airily. "We sorted the living thing at least."

Edie closed her eyes.

"She's coming to live with me, for the moment," Vivien said. "That's why I'm ringing, really. I thought you should know."

Edie opened her eyes again. She gripped the telephone.

"Let me get this straight, Vivi. Rosa is working in a travel agency, and living with Kate and Barney didn't work out so she – she has asked to live with *you*?"

"No," Vivien said, "I asked her. I could see she was desperate."

"Why," Edie cried, wishing she could restrain herself, "didn't she ask *me*? Why didn't she come *home*?"

"Ah. Now that I couldn't say. I couldn't tell you about that."

"You're a smug, manipulative cow."

"Edie," Vivien said, "I am your sister and Rosa's aunt. I'm *family*."

"I don't want to talk to you anymore."

"Oh, don't be so melodramatic and *silly*. As long as Rosa is safe and comfortable, why does it matter whose roof she's under?"

Edie scooped her free hand under Arsie and lifted him off her lap. Then she stood up.

"You know very well why it matters."

"Only if you're possessive."

"I'm not possessive!"

"Well," Vivien said, "you think of another word for it."

Edie put a hand over her eyes. "To cook up this plan behind my back –"

"I'm *ringing* you."

"Rosa didn't."

"Well," Vivien said triumphantly, "can you wonder?"

Edie looked down at the ground. The sheets of her script were scattered about and the cat was sitting, washing, on some of them.

"I must go," she said to her sister.

"You –"

"Yes," Edie said. "Can't talk anymore. Got to learn my lines."

Maeve was sorting the invoices for Russell's quarterly VAT return. In the days before VAT she had entered all receipts and outgoings in a series of black analysis books and there were many occasions, either battling with the geriatric computer, or shuffling sliding piles of paper on not enough desk space, when she longed for those uncomplicated hand-written days, those peaceful, simple columns of in and out with their satisfactorily clear totals, written in red, at the foot of each one. Modern business life wasn't just more compli-cated; there was also more of it, more paper, more checking, more duplicating, more choices. Choice, Maeve sometimes thought, accounted for far more of the current propensity for depression than stress did. Choice, if taken to extremes, could quite simply drive you mad.

The door to Russell's office stood open, as usual. Russell himself wasn't in his office, having gone to a meeting with a television production company that had secured an advert-ising contract for a major bank and was in search of both actors and actors' voices. Maeve could visualize him at the meeting, slightly rumpled amid the black T-shirts and busi-ness suits, but not to be lightly dismissed on account of having known the business, and the people in it, since before some of his competitors were born. If Russell wasn't the kind of agent who commuted to Los Angeles and had a country house for weekends, it was because he didn't want to be.

"Not blazingly ambitious," he'd said to Maeve when he first interviewed her all those years ago. "Just want to have a nice time. It's what growing up in the North does to you – you're either driven by the work ethic of your childhood, or you decide to react against it. What you see, Miss O'Leary, is my small rebellion."

All the same, he probably wouldn't come back from the

meeting entirely empty-handed. He'd taken a few photographs, a few voice tapes, and he would proffer them casually, merely saying, "You might like to consider this," in the tone of voice he used to his clients when persuading them to accept a job that paid reasonably but only required a fraction of their acting skills. The clients, having reluctantly accepted, would then lie across the wicker sofas in Maeve's office and groan to her.

"I said I'd never be a lawn mower again. I promised myself no more cartoon bears. I *swore* not to be a tea bag. Not ever again. Not ever."

Maeve had made a sign years before, which she had stuck on the back of her computer, the side that faced the sofa. It read: "Just think of the money" and it had been there so long that the edges had stiffened and curled. It was supposed to save her saying it out loud, over and over, but of course everyone needed to be told, equally over and over, that being the voice of a northern Building society was going to pay the bills until that turning-point movie role became a happening rather than a hope.

Maeve got up from her desk and went into Russell's office to collect the small receipts that he threw into an old leather collar box on the cluttered shelves behind his desk. The collar box had belonged to his grandfather, whose initials, the same as Russell's, could still be seen, faintly stamped into the leather below the fastening. What would that Russell Boyd, Maeve sometimes wondered, that hard-working, God-fearing manufacturer of fish barrels for the fleets that worked off the northern coasts, close to Hull, have made of his grandson being in a poncy job like this? And what of those framed photographs, signed by some of Russell's better-known clients, all parted lips and smoldering eyes and flourishes? Maeve took down the collar box and opened the lid. There wasn't much in it. Russell might like a nice life in some ways, but that didn't include, it seemed, taking many taxis.

From her own office, the street doorbell rang. Maeve put

down the collar box and pressed the audio button on the intercom.

"Russell Boyd Associates."

"It's Edie," Edie said.

"You come on up," Maeve said. "He's not here, but I'm expecting him."

She pushed the door release, and a second later heard its muffled crash, closing behind Edie. She opened the office door and waited for Edie's steps up the stairs, light and quick, to come closer. Edie was wearing jeans, and a green wool jacket, with her hair pushed into the kind of cap Maeve remembered people wearing in the sixties, a gamine kind of cap, with a big peak.

"I've to congratulate you," Maeve said, as Edie reached the final landing, "on getting that play."

Edie gave her a pat on the arm. They had known one another for twenty-five years and had never kissed. Edie was not the kind of woman, Maeve considered, who scattered kisses about just anyhow, actor or no actor, and in any case a mutual sense of propriety had kept them friendly but formal.

"It's good," Edie said. She was panting slightly. "I'm enjoying it. No wonder Ibsen went to Italy. You couldn't breathe, then, in Norway." She looked into Russell's office. "Where's he gone?"

"Meeting with Daydream Productions. Should be back any minute. Now, will you have a cup of coffee?"

Edie considered.

"I don't think so –"

"I make it all day," Maeve said. "It's never enough for these people just to come here and see Russell and go. They need nourishment and a sympathetic ear and I'm the pro-vider of both."

Edie walked over to the window of Russell's office.

She said, almost idly, "I suppose Rosa hasn't been in?"

"Not for a while," Maeve said. "Not for a month or so.

Looking at you, I can't see where that height of hers comes from."

Edie shrugged.

"They're all taller than me. I used to have to buy shoes in Chinatown."

"It's modern nourishment," Maeve said. "It's all this feeding. When I was growing up, in County Sligo, you could have put three children into a modern one."

The street door crashed again.

"That'll be him," Maeve said. "You're a family of slammers. Not another soul in this building slams the way he does."

Edie took her cap off and put it on Russell's desk. Then she sat down in his swivel chair and leaned back.

"If you're taking him away," Maeve said, "I've some letters for him to sign before you do."

Edie shook her head.

"I just want to ask him something."

Russell's footsteps could be heard on the landing and then crossing Maeve's office.

He appeared in the doorway.

"Well," he said. He was smiling. "How lovely."

Edie regarded him.

Maeve said, "And how did it go?"

Russell was looking at Edie.

"Good," he said. "Good. Several nibbles that might well amount to a bite or two."

He put the battered canvas bag in which he carried papers down on a chair and went round his desk, stooping to kiss Edie.

"Hello."

Edie said, "I could have rung but I was restless."

"Good," Russell said again. He perched himself on the edge of his desk. "You wouldn't be here otherwise."

Maeve moved toward her office.

"Will I shut the door?"

Russell half turned.

"Don't bother."

"Please," Edie said, past him.

He turned back.

"What's happened?"

Edie waited until Maeve, with elaborate care, had closed the connecting door.

Then she said, "Something a bit puzzling –"

"What?"

She put a half-closed hand up near her face, as if she was examining the cuticles.

"Vivi rang."

"And?"

"She said Rosa was moving in with her."

"Well," Russell said, a shade too cheerfully, "isn't that a good thing?"

"Why didn't I hear it from Rosa?"

"Well, perhaps Vivi got in first –"

"Why isn't Rosa ringing? Why don't I know what's happening to Rosa?"

"To be honest," Russell said, "I don't know what's happening to her either."

Edie took her gaze off her cuticles and directed it at Russell.

"Don't you think we *should* know?"

"Darling, she's twenty-six –"

"I don't care if she's a hundred and six. She's not settled or happy and we are her parents and we should *know*."

Russell stopped smiling.

"Yes."

Edie leaned forward so that she could look penetratingly up at Russell.

"There was a hint in something Vivi said, just a hint, that something has been going on, to do with Rosa."

"Ah –"

"And when I'd rung off and was pacing about learning my

lines, it came to me that perhaps something had been going on to do with Rosa, to do with Matt too, for that matter, something that I didn't know about, but which you possibly did."

Russell looked out of the window and waited.

"Well, I couldn't go on pacing up and down, declaiming about dissolution and debauchery, I couldn't concentrate anymore, so I got on the tube, and I came. Russell?"

"Damn Vivi," Russell said lightly.

Edie put her hand on his sleeve.

"What," Edie said, "have you and Rosa been doing?"

Russell looked down at Edie's hand on his arm. He felt a sudden uncharacteristic and complete loss of temper, and moved his arm so that Edie's hand fell from it.

"Nothing," he said furiously. "Nothing. Nothing to do with you."

"But –"

"Did you hear me?"

Edie stared at him.

She hesitated and then she said uncertainly, "If you say so –"

"I do."

"But is she okay?"

Russell turned away and bent over his desk, staring deliberately at the computer screen.

"When she isn't," he said more calmly, "I'll tell you."

There were four messages on Rosa's mobile phone, one from her mother, one from her father, one from her aunt, and one from her older brother. Only the last one did she have any inclination to return. The others – well, how depressing was it, at her age, and stuffed into the sky-blue polyester blazer with yellow plastic sunburst buttons required by the travel company, to have a string of messages on your phone that are all, but *all*, from your family? It would be all very well, of course, if there were *other* messages, messages from friends and – well, better not think about that. Better not remember how happy she had been to let Josh make her miserable, better not even start down that train of thought that began by fantasizing how it might have been if she had never met him, never fallen in love with him, never been so sure that keeping him mattered more than anything else in the world. She'd hardly taken her eyes off her phone in the Josh days.

The messages were all, except for Matt's, of a kind that she didn't much want to hear. It was evident that her aunt had rung her mother to have a small but unmistakable gloat about Rosa's living arrangements, and, in the course of conversation, had hinted that something had occurred to prevent Rosa's turning at once to her parents in time of need. Her mother had then, it appeared, gone straight to find her father, who had had to confess what had happened, and they had both subsequently left messages, her father's apologetic but brisk, her mother's imploring her to come home. Matthew's, by contrast, was completely unemotional. He just said he'd like to catch up sometime soon. He was plainly calling from the office because his call took ten seconds.

Rosa dropped her phone back in the bag at her feet. She was not going to deal with any of this just now. Despite the blue polyester blazer, today had been a reasonably good day. She had sold a weekend in Venice to a party of six, booked a stag group to Vilnius and reserved several family-holiday special-offers in Croatia. If they all came good, it was the most commission she had made so far, which might translate into the first tiny repayment of debt, the first small step back to even a vestige of independence. If you coupled that with the prospect of Vivien's spare bedroom – a bit fussy, a bit overfurnished, but comfortable and convenient and almost free – it was not, Rosa considered, quite as black an outlook as it had been a month before.

She moved the mouse for her computer to access her e-mails. It was not permitted, in the travel company, to use the e-mail service for personal messages, but who was going to check on her if she bent the rule just once? She typed in Matthew's work address.

"Tx for message," Rosa wrote, one eye on the office manager eight feet away straightening the rack of brochures. "Yes, would be good to meet. When? Where?" And then she added, pulling a booking form toward her in order to look like work, "Need to talk. Parents!!!"

The office manager turned from the brochure rack. She had ironed straight hair and favored pearlized lip-gloss.

She looked straight at Rosa.

"Checking your bookings?"

Rosa smiled broadly.

"Just checking."

CHAPTER EIGHT

"News on flat???" Laura's e-mail said. "Need update!"
Then, "We are thinking of a Smeg fridge. Would
pink be idiotic and would I get tired of it?"

Ruth sighed. The notion of a huge pink fridge even
existing, let alone being a preoccupation, was at this moment
so irrelevant as to be fantastical. And upsetting. Ruth wasn't
sure she had ever felt this sad. There was, really, no other
word for this leaden suffering, this sensation that her heart,
as a muscle, actually hurt. Every time she thought about
Matthew, which she did constantly, she was invaded by an
aching distress, which she could recognize, even while it was
happening, as one of the most *real* emotions she had ever felt.

But, at the same time, she was certain she couldn't slow
her life to accommodate his. When he had uttered the word
"pitiful" she had discovered that, even if she energetically
listed and acknowledged all his qualities, she would always
know – because *he* would always know – that in a vital area
of achievement and contribution he could not at the moment
begin to match her. He was afraid of being pitied or made
allowance for, and he was right. He knew what he could
bear, and what he couldn't, and – which made her throat
constrict with love for him – he had more resolve in that
department than she did. And not only resolve, but dignity.
He had, in a way, taken quiet charge of their last meeting in
the empty flat. He had told her that, even if she withdrew

from buying it, the dynamic of their relationship had changed in a way that could not be changed back again. She had clutched at straws and he had not joined in. When she thought of the way he had behaved, she wasn't at all sure she could stand missing him so much.

Her offer on the flat had been accepted. She had arranged a mortgage through the bank used by her company. What was extremely strange was that all the time she was involved in these transactions she had felt she was right in proceeding with them, and also she had not sensed any diminishment in her excitement over the flat. How could it be that one could feel such heartache and such hope at the same time? How was it that something could feel so right and so wrong simultaneously? And how could one ever know, in these shapeless days of moral codes being so much a matter of personal choice, if one was behaving in the way that one ought to be behaving? She put the heels of her hands up against her temples and closed her eyes. What, anyway, did "ought" mean anymore?

She clicked on "Reply" to Laura's message.

"Forget fridge," she wrote, "I need advice. No, I don't. I need *comfort*. I thought if I showed Matthew the flat – and it is stunning – it would somehow persuade him that we could work it out together in a place like that. But he was wiser than me. He saw what I didn't want to see, and he's gone. Laura, he's *gone*. And I am devastated. But I am still thrilled about the flat. Laura, am I a freak?"

"Like the blazer," Matthew said, nodding at the sunburst buttons.

"It would be kinder not to mention it."

"I can't *not* mention it."

"Yes, you can," Rosa said. "Unless you want to make even more of a point about contrasting my life with yours."

There was a tiny pause and then Matthew said, indicating the menu, "What d'you want to eat?"

"Are you paying?"

"Yes."

"Well, I'll have the courgette-and-broad-bean thing with a grilled chicken breast."

"Please."

Rosa smiled at him.

"Please."

Matthew turned and gestured for a waiter.

Rosa said, "And possibly a glass of Sauvignon?"

Matthew glanced at her.

"All right."

"Matt, one glass –"

He turned back.

"I don't begrudge you a glass, Rose. You can have a bottle if you want. It isn't that."

"What isn't what?"

A waiter appeared, in a long black apron, holding a pad. He smiled at Rosa. She held up her menu, so that he could see, pointing at what she wanted. Then she looked up at him and smiled back.

"I'll have the kedgeree," Matthew said, "and a salad. And one glass of house Sauvignon."

"Aren't you having any?"

"No."

"Why not?"

"Because," Matthew said, "I really don't feel like it."

"Why not?" Rosa said again. "Tummy? Head?"

Matthew picked up the menus and handed them to the waiter.

"Heart," he said shortly.

Rosa sat up.

"What's happened?"

Matthew picked up a basket of bread and offered it to his sister.

She ignored it.

"Matt. What's happened?"

"Well," Matthew said, putting the bread down and leaning his arms on the table, "Ruth and I are – over."

"Oh no."

"Yes."

"Not you two –"

"Yes."

"Same outlook, same interests, same ambition –"

"No."

"Has she met someone else?"

"No."

"Well, from the look of you, you haven't."

"No."

"Matt –"

"I'll tell you," Matthew said, "if you'll just shut up a minute."

The waiter put a glass of wine down in front of Rosa.

She said, "I can't believe it, I can't grasp –"

"Nor can I."

"This flat –"

"That's it really," Matthew said, "the flat. The bottom line is that she can afford it and I can't. And she should be on the property ladder. It's the right decision for her, I've told her so. But I can't join her."

Rosa said slowly, "I thought you were earning a shed of money."

Matthew made a face.

"Half what Ruth earns."

"Half?"

"Yes."

"Heavens, I always thought –"

"I know. I didn't stop anyone thinking that. But the truth is, it's been a struggle to keep up and lately – well, lately I haven't been keeping up. And I certainly can't begin on fancy flat buying."

Rosa's gaze moved, item by item, over as much of her brother as she could see above the table.

He said, "Say stupid if you want to."

"I don't want to. And I'm hardly in a position to say anything anyway." She paused and took a mouthful of wine and then she said, "Poor you."

He shrugged.

"What – what if she doesn't buy the flat?"

"Too late," Matthew said.

"You mean too late, she's bought it?"

He shook his head.

"No, too late to retrieve where we were. The flat was just the catalyst. It made us face the disparity."

"Did she throw you out?"

"No!" he said angrily.

"Sorry –"

"I threw myself."

"Oh Matt," Rosa said, "I wish I'd done that."

He said sadly, "It's awful, whatever you do."

She leaned forward.

"Do you still love her?"

The waiter appeared again, holding their plates of food. Matthew leaned back.

He waited until the kedgeree was in front of him and then he said, "Of course I do. You don't just switch that off in an instant. You should know that."

Rosa looked at her plate.

She said hesitantly, "I meant, do you still love her enough to try again?"

Matthew sighed.

"Not under present circumstances."

"But Ruth will just go on being successful. Won't she?"

"Yes. And she ought to."

"What, put work before relationships?"

"Well," Matthew said, putting his fork into the rice and taking it out again, "you've got to put something first, haven't you? Not everything can take priority."

Rosa waited a moment. She cut a strip off her chicken.

"Matt, what about you? Couldn't you have compromised?"

Matthew sighed.

"Apparently not."

"A cheaper flat –"

"Ben said that. But I couldn't afford even a cheaper flat. And she was – kind of stuck on this one. Elated."

Rosa stopped cutting chicken and looked soberly across the table at her brother.

"Matt, what about you?"

He said, not looking up, "I've still got a job."

"Do you like it?"

"I don't mind it. In fact, I do quite like it. But it feels different now, if there isn't going to be Ruth. It was just one part of life and now it's got to be almost all of it. So – well, it doesn't feel like it used to. I can't quite remember what it's *for*."

"D'you think," Rosa said, "that having Mum and Dad still together makes us feel we *ought* to be in a relationship?"

Matthew took a tiny mouthful.

"I don't think that's got anything to do with it."

"Have you told them?"

"It's only just happened," Matthew said. "Ben knows, that's all."

"Before me?"

"He just rang me," Matthew said patiently. "He just happened to be around."

Rosa picked her wineglass up.

"Where are you sleeping?"

"On the sofa."

"Ruth in the bedroom, you on the sofa –"

"Yup."

"You can't do that –"

"No. Not for long."

Rosa said, as if an idea was slowly dawning, "Maybe, if you got a flat, we could share."

Matthew put his fork down.

"Sorry, Rose."

"What?"

He looked at her.

"I just feel – a bit demoralized, I suppose. As if everything has come to a halt, as if I can't decide anything for a while. I never thought I'd say this, I mean, I left about seven years ago, for God's sake, but I think I might go home. Just for a while."

"I wonder," Freddie Cass said to Edie at the end of rehearsal, "if I could ask you something."

Edie was putting on her jacket.

"Of course."

Freddie put out an arm to hold a shoulder of the jacket.

"It's Regina."

"Ah."

Regina was being played by the defiant girl called Cheryl Smith who chain-smoked and stamped about rehearsals in slouched pirate boots.

"She's good," Freddie said. "She knows what she's doing. But Lazlo's frightened of her."

Edie shrugged her jacket round her neck.

"She's in-your-face sort of sexy –"

"Exactly. That's what I wanted. Especially for Act Three. But there's no chemistry between the two of them because she's contemptuous and he's scared."

Edie said, "Well, you're the director –"

"Well, indeed I am." He smiled at Edie. He smiled so seldom, showing long, grayish teeth, that she was startled. "But you could do something for me."

"I said of course –"

"You're mothering Lazlo so excellently."

"Don't ask me to mother Cheryl –"

"Oh no. Just have her to supper."

Edie looked across the room. Cheryl, her legs arranged in their distinct dancer's pose, was smoking and talking to Ivor.

"She'd never come."

"Oh, I think so."

"With – with Lazlo?"

"That was my idea."

"She'd certainly never come if he came."

Freddie switched his smile off. Edie felt a sense of relief.

"She'd come," Freddie said, "if you told her your husband's an agent."

Edie said indignantly, "Look, sorry, but this is *your* job!"

He leaned forward and gripped her arm.

"In a production like this, dear, it's *our* job. I'll buy the wine."

Later, on the bus going home, Edie found herself having to work hard at staying indignant. Freddie should never have asked her to help him out and she should never have agreed, but once they had both done so there was little point in nursing outrage. In any case, the energy outrage would have consumed seemed to want to be channeled into thinking about having Lazlo and Cheryl to supper and how their presence in the kitchen – both in their twenties, both in a precarious profession – might serve as a useful bait for tempting Rosa to come back, just for the evening, just for supper. And once Rosa was there, it might be possible – or, at any rate, less impossible – to discover why she had chosen to seek help from her friends and her aunt rather than her mother.

Edie looked at the script in the bag on her knee. That afternoon, she and Lazlo had made a first attempt at their final, terrible scene. She had flung out her hands and cried Mrs. Alving's words, "But I gave you your life!" and Lazlo had looked back at her and said, as if he hardly knew her, "I never asked you for life." She had burst into tears. Mrs. Alving's wail of "Help! Help!" had been no trouble at all. Freddie Cass had strolled over and looked into her face with his removed, observant gray gaze.

"Nice," he'd said.

*   *   *

Vivien had emptied all the cupboards and drawers in her spare room, for Rosa. The drawers, Rosa noted with awe, were lined with sprigged paper and the hangers were solid and purposeful, not simply a motley collection left over from chain stores and drycleaners. There were also two sizes of towel, a new cake of soap and a copy of *Glamour* magazine. It was kind, Rosa thought, bundling her sweaters onto the sprigged paper, it was really very kind, but in the context of complicated family loyalties it was also making a point, a point Rosa was going to have to ignore if she was to live with her aunt in any kind of equity. It would be perfectly acceptable to thank Vivien for making her so welcome, but it wouldn't be acceptable at all to applaud her for it. Applause would imply that a comparison with Edie had been made in which Vivien was the victor. Rosa sighed.

"How could you," Edie had demanded over the telephone, "turn to friends rather than to me? I am your *mother*!"

"That's why," Rosa had wanted to say. Instead she'd said, lamely, despising herself, "Sorry."

"And now Vivien —"

"Sorry."

"Rose," Edie said, "Rose. I just want to know *why*?"

"They didn't ask me anything."

"What?"

"They didn't keep on at me. Kate and Vivien. They didn't keep asking questions."

There'd been a long pause and then Edie had said, with much diminished energy, "Oh," and then, after another pause, "Good-bye, darling," in a voice of such pathos that for five minutes afterward Rosa wrestled with the urge to ring Vivien and say that after all, for family reasons, she couldn't come and live in her spare room. It was enough to make anyone sigh; it was enough, as she'd said to Kate, to make anyone wonder if the obligations attendant upon having family support made that support actually hardly worth the candle.

"It's like presents," Kate said, eating a *salade* Niçoise with gusto. "The way people give you what they want to give you. It's a sort of conditional generosity."

"Yes."

"But then, you have to, don't you? I mean, if you help someone, you have to do it your way. You can't give the help only the way the receiver wants it because that's asking too much of anyone, it isn't human."

Rosa watched Kate spearing anchovy fillets.

"I'm glad you're hungry."

"Starving. Every two hours. Especially salty things. Do you want your olives?"

Rosa pushed her plate forward.

"Mum sounded so forlorn."

"Isn't that better than angry? Or offended?"

"Not as far as guilt goes."

"If this baby's a girl," Kate said, "I vow not to make her feel guilty."

"I think women just do. Even when it isn't reasonable. I mean, Matt and his girlfriend have just split up and, although he's devastated, he doesn't feel guilty. But I bet she does."

Kate stopped chewing.

"How awful. Poor them."

"Yes."

"Is it this woman and ambition thing?"

Rosa sighed.

"Well, she earns twice what he does."

"And I bet," Kate said, "however successful, she's afraid that makes her unlovable."

Rosa picked a cherry tomato off her plate.

"Unsuccessful isn't very lovable, either."

Does moving into your aunt's spare bedroom count as unsuccessful? she thought now. If by successful you mean financial independence, probably yes. But if you mean still having other humans in your life who'll speak to you, probably no. She picked up an armful of shoes and boots and dumped them in the bottom of the wardrobe. They looked terrible, with the sad intimate terribleness that worn shoes always have. And in addition, if Vivien were to come into Rosa's room while she was at work – not a happy thought, but not one that could be discounted, either – she would expect to see Rosa's possessions in sufficient order to denote gratitude for housing them. Rosa bent down, her head muffled in the hanging folds of her clothes, and began to sort her shoes into pairs.

Below her, in the hallway, Vivien's telephone started to ring. Vivien still had a landline with a cord, a cream plastic handset that sat on a little table with a shelf for directories and a pad and a pot of pens. Vivien drew mouths and eyes on the pad while she talked on the telephone, curvy mouths and thick-lashed eyes, swimming about the page as if they had an eerie life of their own.

"Hello?" Rosa heard Vivien say. Her voice was perfectly clear, even from a floor below and with Rosa's door closed.

"Oh," Vivien said, her voice lifting a little. "Oh! Max –"

Rosa got up from her knees and went quietly to the door, a red canvas basketball sneaker in one hand.

"Saturday," Vivien said. "Saturday. Let me see. I'll have to look." Then she laughed. "I know. So old-fashioned. But you know me. Can't even work the video machine. I'll never get beyond paper and pencil."

There was a rustling of paper.

Then Vivien said, "I'm working in the shop on Saturday. Yes, I do have to. Alison's going to some literary festival for the weekend. Max, I – Well, the evening would be lovely. Goodness. Are you asking me out to *dinner*? What's the etiquette for that, if we're separated?" She laughed again and then she said, in a fond tone Rosa recognized, "You don't change. See you Saturday."

There was the sound of the receiver being replaced, and then a small silence, and then Vivien's heels went clicking down the wood floor of the hall with an unmistakable jauntiness. Rosa looked down at the sneaker in her hand. Josh had given her those. Or at least he'd been going to, right up to the moment of standing by the till in the shoe shop and Josh discovering, as he always discovered, that he had no means of paying for them except a crumpled five-pound note and a few coins. After she'd paid for them, he spent the five pounds on a single yellow rose for her, a rose so large and long-stemmed that people stared at her on the underground, going home. A rose as showy as that must mean that something had happened, something romantic and definitive. Rosa dropped the sneaker on the carpet. All that had actually happened was that she had paid for yet another thing she didn't want.

Her phone, lying on one of the twin beds in a slew of socks and tights, began to ring. Rosa glanced at the screen and picked it up.

"Mum."

"Darling," Edie said, "how are you getting on?"

Rosa looked round the room. It remained somehow very much Vivien's spare room.

"Fine."

"I wondered," Edie said, her voice nonchalant, "if you'd help me out?"

"In what way –"

"I have to have two members of the cast to supper. To help them bond. You know. The director asked me."

"I thought that's exactly what directors are supposed to do."

"Not this one. Will you come? Will you come for supper and help make a crowd?"

Rosa frowned down at her socks.

"When?"

"Saturday. Are you busy on Saturday?"

"No," Rosa said, shutting her eyes. "No, I'm not busy."

"Will you come?"

"Um . . ."

"No strings. No thin end of wedging. Promise."

"I've never been to an Ibsen –"

"Doesn't matter. Please."

Rosa opened her eyes again. She could always stay here, of course, sitting in front of Vivien's television watching Saturday-night rubbish while Vivien skipped out in a cloud of scent and anticipation. And how sad would *that* be?

"Okay," Rosa said.

Cheryl Smith arrived for supper wearing red satin jeans tucked into her pirate boots and a black off-the-shoulder sweater so far off her shoulders that Russell wondered if it would preoccupy him all evening. She kissed him warmly, leaving a shiny cherry-colored streak on his cheek and said he'd been wonderful to her friend, Mitch Morris, whom Russell couldn't remember ever having heard of, and maybe she could come and see him sometime.

He handed her a glass of red wine.

"Anyone with talent who is prepared to work and to pay me ten percent of their earnings is very welcome to come and see me."

She laughed and drank half her glass in a swallow.

She said to Edie, "Great house."

Edie was stirring coconut milk into a pan of curry.

"When we bought this house, houses were affordable. It wasn't surprising to have a house when you got married, it was normal."

Cheryl arranged herself in her dancer's pose.

"I can't see me ever owning anything."

Russell looked at her, strictly above the shoulders.

"What would you like to own?"

"Oh, a car. A Morgan."

Edie picked up a flat plastic box of kaffir lime leaves.

"How many of these, do you think?"

Cheryl twirled her wine.

"I never cook. At drama school I lived on vodka and cheese sandwiches. Now it's red wine and pizza slices."

"Disgusting," Russell said, smiling.

Cheryl smiled back. She held her glass out to him.

Edie said, crumbling leaves into her pot, "Your mother would be horrified."

"My mother doesn't cook either. It was my father that cooked. No wonder he left, really. Five kids refusing to eat the same thing." She looked at Edie for the first time properly. "Wasn't Lazlo supposed to be coming?"

Russell gestured toward the window.

"He's here."

"Where?"

"In the garden. Talking to my daughter, Rosa."

"Our daughter," Edie said.

Cheryl moved over to the window and leaned to look out, stretching the red satin tight over her bottom as she did so.

"He's quite good," she said.

Russell looked at Edie.

Edie said, without turning, "Then why are you making it so hard for him?"

"Because he's only just out of drama school. It's no good them thinking it's easy."

Russell hitched his leg across the corner of the table and regarded Cheryl's bottom.

"But possibly it isn't very helpful for them to think it's impossible and unpleasant either."

Cheryl turned.

She said, smiling, "Unpleasant? Oo, what a word."

"I would think," Russell said, "that you'd be rather good at unpleasant."

Cheryl winked.

"Very good."

"Can you do pleasant too?"

"Duller."

"But better," Edie said, coming across the kitchen with a wooden spoon held out for Russell to taste, "if trying to work with other people, which is, on the whole, what actors in a theater *are* trying to do. Is that rather sweet?"

Russell took the spoon from Edie's hand.

"I think," he said, "that if I were Freddie Cass I'd have told you I could find another Regina very easily."

Cheryl laughed.

"Really?"

Russell handed the spoon back to Edie.

"No. It's the right sort of sweet." He glanced at Cheryl. "Really."

She put her nose in her glass.

"Do you speak to all the people you represent like this?"

"All of them," Russell said. He got off the table. "They love it."

"Cheryl's here," Lazlo said miserably to Rosa.

Rosa was wearing a sweater of Russell's over her own clothes and had pulled the sleeves down well beyond her knuckles. She could see, in the reflection of the kitchen window, that she had a Neanderthal look, a huge body and endless arms.

"Well, you knew she was coming –"

"Look what she's wearing."

Rosa peered.

"I expect that's deliberate."

"She said to me in rehearsal the other day, 'I'm not kissing you until I absolutely have to.'"

"That wasn't very nice."

"I don't know," Lazlo said, "what I'd do without your mother."

Rosa looked at him. He was taller than she was, but as thin as a lath, with one of those sensitive handsome faces that looked somehow neither girl nor boy. Not her type. She shrugged herself down inside the sweater. Not her type at all.

"It's not just that she's so nice to me," Lazlo said, "it's that she knows what she's doing and that helps me surrender to the part. D'you know what I mean?"

"I'm not an actress."

He glanced at her quickly.

He said politely, "What do you do?"

Rosa looked away.

She said in an offhand way, "I'm in the travel business."

"You don't sound as if you like it very much."

"I don't."

"That's what's so extraordinary about acting. It isn't a choice." He stopped and then he said, apologetically, "But you know that. Because of your mother."

Rosa looked toward the kitchen window again. Edie was gesturing at them to come in. First she'd sent them out so that she could soften Cheryl up without Lazlo to persecute and now she was summoning them back again. Rosa sighed.

"She wasn't like that. She did jobs around us, we sort of knew she did it, but I suppose we didn't take it in much –"

Lazlo stared at her.

"Don't you know how good she is?"

Rosa stared back.

"Oh yes."

"Well," he said, "it just sounded as if you weren't quite aware –"

"She's my mother," Rosa said.

Lazlo said nothing.

Rosa began to move away from him across the damp grass toward the house.

She said, "That didn't come out as I meant it to."

"No."

Rosa stopped.

She said, without meaning to, "I sound spoiled –"

There was a long pause, and then Lazlo said, from behind her, in the spring dusk, "Actually, you do."

CHAPTER NINE

S itting on the underground on his way up to North
London, Matthew looked at the other people in the
carriage. It was early evening, just after work, so the train
was full, not just with tired men holding computer cases and
newspapers, but tired women with computer cases too and
handbags and supermarket shopping bags. Some of the
women were young, and reminded Matthew of Ruth, young
women with considered haircuts and business suits and the
air, which none of the men had, of having thought – or
possibly had to think – about much more all day than simply
the things at work they had to react to. They made him
remember, unhappily, the way Ruth had kept all the strands
of their life together, persistently rounding up stray aspects in
a manner that, particularly when they were first together,
made him marvel.

Blaise, at the desk behind him at work, said that personally he had marveled himself to a standstill about modern
women.

"They're too much for me," he'd said by way of commiseration over Matthew's breakup. "Girls now, I mean.
Now-girls."

He was giving up girls for a while, he said, and concentrating on getting his pilot's license. He said if Matthew
wanted flying lessons too he was sure he could arrange it.
Flying made you feel in charge of things and, at the same

time, free of demands, and people, and the business of never quite living up to others' expectations.

"I'm not even living up to my own expectations at the moment," Matthew said.

Blaise didn't take his eyes off the screen in front of him.

"Lower them, then," he said.

Matthew got out of his seat now, on the underground, and gestured toward it at a pale woman, carrying a huge professional camera case and an enormous lever-arch file clasped against her chest.

She hardly glanced at him.

"Thank you –"

An elderly black woman beside her, in a felt hat and horn-rimmed spectacles, turned to look at her.

"I shouldn't think he heard that."

The pale woman, balancing case and file with difficulty on her lap, said nothing.

"There's not many young men with the manners now –"

"It's all right," Matthew said. "It's okay."

"So why discourage the few decent ones we've got?"

An ugly color began to spread patchily up the pale woman's neck.

Matthew bent down.

"She did say thank you. I heard her."

The black woman regarded him impassively.

"She should have looked at you. She should have smiled. Why shouldn't you be as tired as she is?"

"I'm not –"

"Some woman," the black woman said loudly, "is a lucky woman to have you. Some woman is lucky to have such a gentleman."

Matthew looked away. His neck felt as miserably inflamed as the pale woman's looked. A fat man strap-hanging a foot away caught his eye and winked. Matthew made a face and briefly closed his eyes.

The train pulled into Moorgate Station and stopped. The black woman, crucifix swinging at her neck as she moved, rose to her feet and made for the door.

As she passed Matthew, she said distinctly, "You tell that lady of yours she's a lucky woman."

There was faint tittering round him and sweat was sliding in an unmistakable trickle down between his shoulder blades. He looked at the pale woman for a glance, at least, of commiseration, but she was staring rigidly at the floor.

Edie had said to meet her after rehearsals. She had described where to find her, saying he would recognize the rehearsal hall in Clerkenwell because it had a yellow poster outside advertising Pilates in Pregnancy classes. She'd said that they could go for a drink together, possibly even have supper. She'd sounded so pleased to hear him, so relieved and gratified that he'd rung, that he wondered what had happened to propel him into her personal spotlight. It was the place, after all, usually occupied by Ben, who took it, as he seemed to take most things, entirely for granted. It was also the place, Matthew realized, that he had scarcely spared a thought for, over the last couple of years, because he hadn't needed to. He rather wished he didn't need to now.

The rehearsal hall was, Edie said, about ten minutes from the underground station, and he should aim for the spire of St. James's Church. Matthew thought, gazing skyward from the Farringdon Road, that that was exactly the kind of directions his mother had always given, instructing you to look out for a memorable, preferably romantic landmark that was not actually visible until you were standing almost beside it because she hadn't taken the surroundings into consideration. When they were small, Matthew remembered, Edie would often point out of the window and ask them what they could see and they would say, tepidly, oh the grass and the shed and the back of the house where the Great Dane lived and she would say no, no, no, beyond that, through that – couldn't they see oceans and castles and deserts with camels? Edie would have no trouble, Matthew thought, standing in the Farringdon Road and seeing St. James's, Clerkenwell, far away to the north beyond the Clerkenwell Road. And perhaps, by the same token, Edie would have no trouble in seeing through the miserable thickets Matthew had got himself tangled up in, and out beyond to something altogether brighter and more hopeful. Something that would stop him feeling he had spent the last two years circling round in a huge wild loop that had merely ended in a rather lesser place than he had been in before he started.

She was waiting for him outside the hall, leaning against the Pilates poster with her arms folded, and her sunglasses on.

He bent to kiss her cheek.

"Am I late?"

Edie put both arms round his neck and pulled him down toward her.

"No. We finished early. We did a lot of the joy of living today and it wore everyone out, being joyful."

Matthew said, his face against his mother's, "I didn't think Ibsen was joyful."

"Norway wasn't. Norway was *dire*, in Ibsen's day. Work was a curse and a punishment for sin."

"Jolly –"

Edie let Matthew go. She looked up at him.

"You don't look good at *all*."

"No."

"Matt?" she said. "Matthew?" She took his hand. "What's happened?"

He glanced down the street.

"Let's find a pub."

"Are you ill?"

"No," he said, "nothing like that." He moved back toward the pavement, pulling her. "I'll tell you," he said, feeling the loosening sensation of relief flowing into his chest, into his head. "I'll tell you everything."

Russell went to the preview of a new American play at the Royal Court Theatre, left at the interval and made his way home on a number 19 bus. He had asked Edie to come to the theater with him, but she had a late rehearsal, she said, and some other commitment that she was vague about but not particularly mysterious, and certainly not mysterious in a way that might cause Russell disquiet. There *had* been disquieting moments in the past, to be sure, moments when Edie seemed suddenly overalert about an actor she was playing opposite or, once at least, a father on the parent–teacher association panel at one of the children's schools, panels that Edie made vociferous and energetic contributions to. And, if he was honest, Russell had had lunches, and some afternoons, and even a weekend once, when he had been reminded of how powerfully attractive a new personality, a new face and body, can be to even the most faithful of eyes. It wasn't anxiety about what Edie might be doing that propelled Russell onto his bus before the second half of the play, but more a resurgence of the feeling that was becoming very familiar to him now, a feeling of just wanting Edie to be there, to be with him, to give another, a vivid, dimension to what he was seeing and hearing. He supposed, if he was honest, that it was years since he had actively missed Edie when she wasn't with him. Well, if that was the case, he was certainly making up for it now. He looked out of the bus window at the thronged midevening pavements and wondered how he would arrange himself, in his mind and in his feelings, when he reached home and found that Edie wasn't there.

But she was. She was sitting at the kitchen table reading the evening paper with her glasses on and a mug of tea. Beside the paper on the table, where he was not allowed, Arsie was posed like a cat on an Egyptian frieze, elongated and very, very still.

"Bad play?" Edie said, taking her glasses off.

"Wordy," Russell said. He bent to kiss her. "Wordy without grasping the subject. You indulge that cat."

Edie looked at Arsie. He didn't trouble to look back.

"I know."

"Good rehearsal?"

"Not bad. Lazlo's very good at supersensitive but he isn't making him bright enough yet. If he makes Osvald *all* quivering introspection, it'll turn the audience off."

Russell went over to the fridge and opened the door.

"What about supper?"

"I've had it," Edie said, "but there's plenty of ham."

Russell bent to look into the fridge.

He said nonchalantly from inside it, "Supper *with* anyone?"

"Yes," Edie said, "Matthew."

There was a silence.

"Matthew," Russell said, without straightening.

"Yes."

Russell stood up, holding a plate of ham.

"Why didn't you have supper here?"

"It sort of didn't arise," Edie said. She folded the paper. "We went for a drink and then we had a plate of pasta. I am beginning to think I never want to see pasta again."

Russell put the ham on the table and went across the kitchen to the bread bin.

"How was he?"

"Russell," Edie said, sitting up straight, "it was awful. He's in a terrible state."

Russell turned round.

"Matthew?"

"Yes."

"Has he lost his job?"

"He's lost Ruth."

Russell came back to the table and sat down.

"Has she thrown him out?"

"No. It's sadder really. He's left her because she wants to buy a flat and he thinks she should and she's chosen this rather glamorous one, near Tate Modern, and he can't afford it and he hasn't been able to afford their lifestyle anyway, for ages, it turns out, and he doesn't want to hold her back, so he's gone."

Russell stared at the ham.

He said, "Matt has left Ruth because he can't afford to buy the flat she wants?"

"Basically, yes."

He raised his eyes.

"Edie, what's the *matter* with them?"

"With Matt and Ruth?"

"Yes. No. With all of them. With all these children and all they're earning and still can't manage."

"It isn't them," Edie said, "it's now. It's how things are. We got married young because people did and we didn't have any money or furniture because people didn't, but now they do, and it's different."

Russell sighed.

"Does he still love her?"

"I think so."

"And does she love him?"

"Well, she texts him most days saying so, apparently."

"I don't get it."

"It doesn't matter whether you do or not," Edie said. "It's how it *is*."

Russell folded his arms on the table and leaned on them.

"He looked launched to me."

"I expect he looked launched to himself."

Russell said, "Poor old boy. Poor Matt. So it's back to bachelor flats and sharing and squalor and nosing around clubs for women."

"Certainly not," Edie said.

Russell raised his head and looked at her.

"Oh Edie –"

"I can't watch him flounder –"

"He's twenty-eight."

"That's got nothing to do with anything. He's in trouble and miserable and lost and I can't bear to see it and I've told him he can come home."

Russell sat back in his chair and crossed his arms on his chest.

He said to the ceiling, "I thought only the royal family continued to live with their parents when adult. Oh, and Italians."

"His room is there," Edie said, "and empty. He'll give us rent."

"That's not the point, really."

"I know. You told Rosa."

Russell shut his eyes.

"You told Rosa," Edie said, "that she couldn't come home because you wanted my undivided attention."

"I didn't quite –"

"Well, that may be what you want, but it isn't what I want. I want my children to know they are wanted and supported."

"It isn't good for them," Russell said. "It isn't good for them or for us. Remember the fox in *Le Petit Prince*?"

"What fox?"

"The fox who said, 'You become responsible forever, for what you have tamed.'"

Edie brought her fist down on the table.

"I'm not *taming* them. I'm helping them. It's a rubbish old myth, this idea that you undermine someone by helping them, that it's good for people to struggle –"

"It is."

Edie stood up.

"God," she said, "it's like pushing a bloody elephant upstairs."

"You don't want to let go –"

She began to move toward the door.

She said furiously, "You can't let go of being a parent. Not ever. It's the one relationship you're stuck with, besides yourself."

"Where are you going?"

Edie turned in the doorway.

"To Matthew's room," she said. "To see what he needs. He's coming on Saturday."

The weather in Cairns, Eliot told his mother, was bloody great. Twenty-five degrees and not a cloud and Ro was going to be a Buddhist.

"A Buddhist?"

"Yeah," Eliot said. "There's a temple here. She's going to meditation classes."

"Well," Vivien said, "good for her. Are you going too?"

"Nah," Eliot said, "I'm helping a mate service his power-boat."

"You sound so Australian, darling."

"Yeah. Well."

Vivien said, "I'm having dinner with Dad on Saturday. Again."

"Yeah."

"Do you know why he's asked me a second time?"

There was a pause and then Eliot said, "Why shouldn't he?"

"Well, we're separated –"

"So?"

"If you're separated, it's usually because you don't want to see each other."

"Don't you want to see Dad?"

"Yes, darling, I do, but –"

"That's fine, then," Eliot said.

Vivien gripped the telephone.

"I don't want to ask you anything unfair, darling, but – but do you know if Dad has a girlfriend just now?"

There was another pause and then Eliot said, "I've no idea."

"So he hasn't said anything to you? Named any names?"

"We don't talk about that," Eliot said. "We talk about soccer."

"Of course –"

"Ma," Eliot said, "I have to go. I'm meeting someone."

Vivien looked at her watch.

"How nice. Are you having supper with someone?"

"A few beers," Eliot said, "till Ro finishes her class."

"Lovely to hear you, darling. Give my love to Ro."

"Cheers," Eliot said. "Take care."

Vivien put the telephone down. While talking to Eliot she had drawn a huge pair of parted Roy Lichtenstein lips, with teeth just glimpsed, and a high shine. It was the biggest mouth she'd drawn for ages, taking up half a page. She wondered briefly if it meant anything, and if so, what. Possibly something a bit excitable, louche even, the same sort of thing that had propelled her into buying some suede sandals, on impulse, in a color the girl in the shop described as watermelon. They were rather high, higher than Vivien was used to, and would need a little practice. Before Saturday. Vivien put out a hand and tore the drawing of the big lips hastily off the pad.

Rosa had left a note propped up against the kettle that morning. She had also remembered to put the box of Grape-nuts back in the cupboard. The note said she was meeting a friend for a drink after work and she wasn't sure when she'd be back so not to bother about supper. Then she'd drawn a small sunflower with a smile and added, "Hope you hadn't planned anything?" Well, Vivien had, of course, because she couldn't help planning. It was one of the elements that Max always wanted to loosen up in her, this propensity to live life in detail before she actually got to it. There were two tuna steaks in the fridge, and some borlotti beans soaking, and a bag of salad leaves. Well, they could all probably wait another day, and if they didn't, she could freeze the tuna and cook up the beans and – oh, stop this, Vivien said to herself, stop this and focus on the fact that you had a lovely time last Saturday having dinner with Max and that he plainly did too because he's asked you again.

She went out of the kitchen and up the stairs to the landing. Rosa's bedroom door was shut. Do *not* open it, Vivien told herself, just do *not* because a) it is her room for the moment and b) you won't like what you see if you do. She walked on down the landing and into her own bedroom, decorated entirely in white during a moment of feeling I-am-a-strong-woman in the aftermath of Max's departure, a feeling that hadn't lasted. The pink suede sandals were sitting neatly at the end of the bed. Vivien sat down beside them, kicked off her shoes, and bent to buckle them on.

Beside her bed, next to a china tray of all her manicure things, the telephone began to ring.

"Are you hoovering?" Edie asked.

"No."

"In white cotton gloves?"

"Naked, actually," Vivien said. She lay back on the bed, the telephone to her ear, and thrust one leg upward to admire her pink sandal.

"You sound happy –"

"I've just spoken to Eliot."

"Not that kind of happy," Edie said. "Who is he?"

Vivien hesitated a moment, turning her foot this way and that.

Then she said, "Max."

"No change there then."

"We had a really good time on Saturday –"

"Did he kiss you?"

"Edie!"

"Did he?"

"No," Vivien said. "I haven't been kissed for years."

"Nor have I."

"Yes, you have. On stage."

"That doesn't count and it isn't usually what you'd choose, anyway."

"Russell kisses you –"

"Yes. But . . ."

"Did you ring," Vivien said, lowering her leg and raising the other, "to talk about kissing?"

"No. But I do rather wonder why you're seeing Max again."

"So do I."

"But you like it –"

"Yes."

"Well, do it," Edie said, and then, without a pause, "Matt's coming home."

"What?"

"He's broken up with Ruth and he's miserable and he's coming home."

Vivien let her leg fall.

"Poor boy. Was it about a flat? Rosa said something –"

"I had to shout at Russell," Edie said. "He thinks you spoil children if you help them. Or at least, that's what he says he thinks."

"Thirty percent of people between twenty-four and thirty still live at home –"

"How do you know?"

"I read it somewhere."

"Excellent," Edie said, "I'll tell Russell. If he goes on like he's going on, he'll make Matt feel a freak. Do you think I should buy a double bed?"

"Don't you have one?"

"For Matthew!" Edie shouted.

"Why?"

"Well, they all sleep in big beds now. Everyone. Nobody over ten has a single bed."

"But if Matthew hasn't got Ruth," Vivien said, "who will he put in it?"

"Someone else, I hope. Someone who doesn't put her ambition first."

"I thought you liked Ruth –"

"I did. I do. We got on famously. But I want to kill her for hurting Matthew."

Vivien turned on her side. She could, from this angle, see herself in the full-length mirror on the back of the door to her bathroom. It wasn't a bad angle, in fact, nice curves of hip and shoulder, good ankles, far enough away not to see what happened to bosoms when collapsed sideways.

She said, "Shall I tell Rosa?"

"No thank you," Edie said. "I'll tell Rosa. I'll ring her at work."

"She's going out with someone after work –"

"Who?"

"I do not know," Vivien said in a voice that implied the opposite.

"Vivi –"

"Rosa here," Vivien said, "Matt back with you. At least Ben's holding out."

"Trust you."

Vivien rearranged her legs at a better angle.

"Poor old Russell," she said.

Rosa much regretted having asked Lazlo to have a drink with her. She knew she shouldn't have, for the simple reason that she didn't really want to, but there was something about supper the other night, and the Cheryl Smith person flirting with her father, and excluding her from conversations with her mother and Lazlo by constantly referring to their rehearsals together, that had compelled her to say, in Cheryl's hearing at the end of the evening, to Lazlo, "What about a drink on Wednesday?"

He'd hesitated.

"Wednesday –"

"I'm afraid," Rosa said, "it's the only night I can manage."

"You aren't rehearsing," Cheryl said to Lazlo. "Not

Wednesday." She glanced at Rosa. "You could go wild on Wednesday."

Lazlo nodded.

"Thank you. I'd like it."

So here she was, in the refurbished bar of a central hotel, sitting on a black leather stool with her elbows on a tall metal table, waiting for Lazlo. Edie had not heard them make the arrangements, and Rosa had said nothing on the subject. She hoped that Lazlo, despite his puppy-like devotion to Edie, hadn't said anything, either. She wanted to have one drink, and leave, and somehow make it not at all possible for him to suggest either another one, or another meeting. After he'd told her he thought she was spoiled, it was difficult to think of him without dislike, but also, rather disconcertingly, without feeling distinctly interested. It was awful, really, what flashes of temper compelled you to do, flashes of temper induced by seeing other people apparently more at home with your parents than you were yourself.

She saw Lazlo before he saw her. He was in black, with a brilliant turquoise-blue scarf looped round his neck, and for a moment, she thought – indignantly, as if he had no business to be so – that he looked almost attractive. She waved. It took him some time to see her and when he did, he only gave the smallest of smiles.

"I hope you haven't been waiting –"

She indicated her glass.

"I needed a drink."

He dropped a black canvas rucksack under the metal table.

"Can I get you another?"

"Thanks," Rosa said. "Vodka and tonic."

He nodded and went off to the bar. She wondered if he had enough money to pay for their drinks and then reflected, rather grimly, that she hardly had, either. But Lazlo would be on the minimum Equity wage, and as he wouldn't, like everyone else, be legally entitled to an adult wage until he was twenty-five, that would be the barest minimum.

When he came back with her vodka and a bottle of beer, she said, rather shortly, "Sorry. I should have paid for those."

"No, you shouldn't."

"I asked you for a drink."

He shrugged.

She added, "And now you'll think I'm even more spoiled."

He hitched himself on to the stool opposite her.

He said quietly, "It wasn't about that. I shouldn't have said it anyway."

"Why not, if it's true?"

He picked up his beer bottle.

"It isn't the kind of thing you ought to say to anyone twenty minutes after meeting them."

"Okay," Rosa said. She raised her glass. "Cheers."

He tipped his bottle toward her.

She said, "Well, what did you mean?"

"Please forget it –"

"I meant not to mention it but now I have and I'd like an answer. What did you mean?"

He hunched forward over the table. He looked weirdly glamorous. Perhaps it was the exoticism of the scarf. It was made of silk, the kind of rough silk that came from somewhere in the Far East.

"I'd really rather –"

"Lazlo," Rosa said, "please."

He gave her a quick glance.

"Well, I suppose I just thought you – you gave the impression of taking things for granted."

"What things?"

He shrugged.

"Your mother. Your parents. Having a home, somewhere to go to."

Rosa put her hands in her lap. She looked directly at him.

"Haven't you?"

"Not really. Not like that."

"Haven't you got parents?"

"My father lives in Arizona. My mother married a Russian and they have two children and live in Paris. My sister is a medical student, nearly a doctor, and she lives in hospital accommodation."

"And you?"

Lazlo looked sheepish.

"This is turning into a sort of pathetic Dickens-style sob story –"

"Where do you live?" Rosa said.

"In a room –"

"Where?"

"Maida Vale."

"Well, that's –"

"Kilburn, actually," Lazlo said. "In a room in a house belonging to my sister's ex-boyfriend's grandmother."

Rosa leaned forward.

"Why?"

"Because she charges me almost nothing because she likes having a man in the house. She's panicked about security."

"Is it awful?"

Lazlo was silent.

"Depressing?" Rosa said.

"Well," Lazlo said, "I don't have hang-ups about old people, but this is pretty extreme. She won't ever open the windows."

Rosa took a swallow of her drink.

"Does it smell?"

Lazlo nodded.

"So when this play is on, you'll be traveling from Kilburn to Islington?"

"Lots of people do," Lazlo said. "Theater people all have to live in awkward places."

"Theater people," Rosa said mockingly.

He flushed.

"I *am* one," he said, "I'm an actor. So is your mother. I don't know why you feel the need to sneer."

"I'm not sneering –"

"Well, that's what it sounds like."

"Sorry."

"Okay."

"I am sorry," Rosa said. "Truly."

Lazlo said nothing.

"Please," Rosa said, "I am truly sorry."

He looked up slowly.

"I believe in it," he said.

"The theater?"

"In acting," Lazlo said seriously. "In – in its radiant energy. In being possessed, and passionate, yet still yourself after a performance. I like having to concentrate this way, I like having chosen something so difficult it makes me display fortitude."

"Well," Rosa said, "I certainly hadn't thought of any of that."

"You didn't listen to your mother."

"My mother never said anything like that in all her life."

"She didn't need to," Lazlo said vehemently. "She didn't need to *say* it. If you'd ever taken her acting seriously, you'd have *seen* it."

Rosa said nothing. She fidgeted with her glass. Rising up in her, unwanted but not to be denied, was a peculiar wish to say sorry again somehow, to show herself in a better light.

She said slowly, "Your room. Your room in Kilburn –"

He looked irritated, as if dragged back to banality from something much more compelling and important.

"What about it?"

"Have you told my mother?"

"What?"

"Have you told my mother," Rosa said, "about how you have to live?"

CHAPTER TEN

"I hope you'll be comfortable," Russell said from the doorway.

Matthew was standing by the window of his old bedroom, looking down into the garden. His cases, all very orderly, were on the floor. He had his hands in his pockets and the set of his shoulders from behind was not one that Russell could deduce anything from.

He looked at the walls. Edie had not removed a single childhood picture.

"Of course," Russell said, "you can change anything you want to. No need to live with Manchester United 1990."

Matthew said, without turning, "I don't mind."

Russell said, "I am so very sorry about what's happened."

"Thanks."

"Anything we can –"

"It's much harder than I thought it'd be," Matthew said. "Emptier."

"Yes."

Matthew turned. He looked as if he hadn't slept for days.

"When you go back somewhere, it's not the same –"

"Or perhaps," Russell said, "you aren't."

Matthew looked at the bed.

"I haven't slept in that for nearly seven years."

Russell moved into the room and put his hands on Matthew's shoulders.

"Poor Matthew. Poor old man –"

Matthew shook his head.

"It's not that I'm not grateful –"

"I know."

"I just feel – such a bloody *failure* –"

"Try not to. Things are much harder now."

"Are they?"

"I think so. We were stifled by too little choice, you are panicked by too much."

Matthew looked round the room.

Russell said gently, "You don't want to be here –"

"I thought I did."

"Maybe it won't be for long. You have a job, after all."

Matthew nodded. He pulled a face.

"Flat sharing –"

"Perhaps."

"Hard," Matthew said, "to go back to."

"Harder than this?"

Matthew nodded.

"For the moment."

Russell took his hands away. He said, "Sorry, old son, but we do have to talk about money."

Matthew looked puzzled.

"Money."

"Well," Russell said, "as you say, coming back somewhere is never the same as when you were first there. Coming back home as a salaried twenty-eight-year-old isn't the same as living at home as a student."

Matthew took a step backward.

"I thought," Russell said, "that you and Mum had discussed it."

"No."

"Well –"

"I see," Matthew said, "I see. Of course I do. I was just a bit taken aback –"

"To have me mention it?"

"Well," Matthew said uncomfortably, "maybe mention it even before I'd opened a suitcase."

Russell sighed.

"Like all awkward topics, I want to get it over with."

"You do –"

"Yes."

"Couldn't you have waited," Matthew said, slightly desperately, "until we were having a beer or something?"

Russell sighed again.

"All right," he said, "let's postpone the topic until later. Stupid me. As usual."

Matthew bent to retrieve a checkbook from his briefcase.

"No, Dad. The subject's broached now. Why don't I write you a check for the first month?"

"Matt, I really didn't –"

"What d'you want?" Matthew demanded. He looked suddenly rather feverish. "Two hundred pounds a month? Two hundred and fifty? Three hundred?"

"Don't be –"

"All in?" Matthew almost shouted. "Two hundred and fifty all in and do my own ironing?"

Russell shut his eyes.

"Stop it."

"Stop what?"

"Stop being so melodramatic and putting me in the wrong."

"Melodramatic? Couldn't you have waited, knowing how I was feeling, *seeing* how I was feeling? Couldn't you just have exercised a bit of bloody *tact*?"

Russell opened his eyes.

"Probably," he said tiredly.

Matthew stooped to find a pen in his briefcase.

"How much do you want?"

"It really doesn't –"

"Look," Matthew said, "you started this, and it's all gone wrong, so let's finish it and get it over with. How much?"

148

"I haven't talked to Mum –"

"Mum probably wouldn't talk about it anyway. This can be between you and me."

"You manage," Russell said, "to make a perfectly reasonable adult request sound very sordid."

Matthew sat down on the edge of the bed and opened his checkbook and looked up at his father.

"Dad?"

Russell didn't look at him.

"Two fifty all in, and as you know no ironing is done in this house unless you do it yourself."

Matthew wrote rapidly and then tore the check out of the book. He held it out.

"Here."

"I do not want to take this –"

"You asked for it."

"But not this way. I didn't want it now. I just wanted to talk about it, raise the subject. I never meant it to get out of hand –"

"In my experience," Matthew said, "the danger of things getting out of hand is there whenever anyone opens their mouths."

Russell folded the check into his hand.

"Thank you."

Matthew said nothing. He stood up and watched his father slowly turn and walk out of the room. Then he moved forward and closed the door firmly behind him.

"It's Ruth, isn't it?" Kate Ferguson said.

Ruth turned round. She was holding a small melon she had just taken from a pyramid on a market stall.

"I'm Kate," Kate said. "You probably don't remember. I'm a friend of Rosa's, Matthew's sister. We met once, ages ago, at that concert in Brixton, we –"

"Oh," Ruth said. She transferred the melon to her other hand. "Oh yes. Kate. Sorry, I was sort of concentrating –"

"What are you doing here?" Kate asked. "I thought you worked in the City –"

Ruth put the melon back in its place on the pyramid.

"I do. But I live here now." She gestured out toward the edge of the market. She said, with a complicated kind of pride, "I've got a flat on Bankside."

Kate hesitated. Something in Ruth's expression and tone was half expecting her to say, "Wow. Lucky you." But something else, at the same time, suggested that, even if Ruth would have loved such a straightforward reaction, she knew it was too luxurious to hope for.

Kate put out a hand and briefly touched Ruth's sleeve.

"Actually," she said, "Rosa told me. Just a bit."

Ruth said quickly, "It's so brilliant here, all this air and views and location. And then, Borough Market on my doorstep –"

"I always shop here on Fridays," Kate said. "I leave work early and come here."

"Yes."

"Goodness knows what I'll do when I can't."

"Can't?"

"After the baby."

Ruth looked at the swell under Kate's jacket.

"Oh, congratulations –"

"It's a bit of a surprise," Kate said. "We've only been married a minute. I'm still rather shell-shocked. I keep thinking about being away from work, not coming here, not zipping out to the movies –" She looked at Ruth's black briefcase bag. "Sorry –"

"Why sorry?"

"Not very tactful."

Ruth said, "Rosa told you about Matthew and me?"

"Yes."

"We'll have to see how things work out –"

Kate nodded.

"It's just," Ruth said in a rush, "that however enlightened you are, you *both* are, you still seem to be swimming against the norm. If you're a woman earning more than a man." She glanced at Kate. "Sorry. I don't know why I said that." She looked round, at the fruit-and-vegetable stalls, at the surging crowds of people. "You must think I'm mad –"

"It's on your mind," Kate said, "like being pregnant's on mine."

"Will you go back to work?"

"Yes," Kate said, and then, in a different tone, "probably."

"I hope it's easy," Ruth said earnestly.

"So do I. I'm hopeless at being uncomfortable, never mind in pain –"

"No, I didn't mean that. I didn't mean having the baby. I meant afterward. I meant I hope it's easy deciding what to do after the baby."

Kate gave her a smile.

"Thank you."

"I mean it."

"I know –"

"I never knew," Ruth said, "that deciding was going to throw up such problems. I always thought decisions meant the end of something difficult, not the beginning." She put a hand out and picked up the melon again. "Why is the only way you learn something the hard way?"

Edie was sitting sideways on a molded plastic chair in the dimness at the edge of the hall. She had her arms along the back of the chair, and had leaned forward to rest her chin on them. About ten feet away, on the small bare stage illuminated by clumsy lights that had plainly been installed a very long time ago, Pastor Manders and the carpenter, Engstrand, were rehearsing the opening of Act Three. Engstrand was being played by an actor called Jim Driscoll who had, decades before, played Edie's comedy sidekick when she was presenting a children's television program. He had been young and wiry and gingery then. He was older and skinny and grayish now, standing in front of Pastor Manders with a kind of obsequious malevolence that he seemed able to convey without uttering a syllable. He had his hands clasped in front of him, swinging slightly away from his stooped body, and his face was raised toward Ivor with a stretched and ingratiating smile. He managed to look, Edie thought, both simian and sophisticated. He managed, too, to look a very subtle kind of threat. She shifted a little in her uncompromising plastic chair. In a minute, she would have to go and join them. In a minute, Mrs. Alving would come in from the garden, dazed by calamity, and say, in a voice Edie hadn't quite decided upon yet, "I can't get him away from the fire."

The fire, Freddie Cass had explained to Lazlo, was metaphorical as well as actual. The fire that burned the orphanage built in his dead father's name was also the fire that was consuming all the lies that had been told to protect him and, in the process, his own life as his inherited malady began to possess and then devour him. Edie could see that Lazlo loved this kind of direction, loved falling under the spell of such fatalism. He'd come to find Edie afterward, eyes shining.

"I know what it's about now, it's not just something that's happening, it's something that had to happen, and you don't know it yet, as my mother, because you've always thought you could protect me, by telling lies, by keeping the truth from me." He gave Edie a quick, fervent hug. "This is amazing."

He was sitting on the floor at the side of the stage now, in jeans and a shrunken gray T-shirt, hugging his knees and watching the others. His arms, wound round his knees, looked to Edie like a boy's arms, rather than a man's, not just because they were thin, but because they were slightly unformed, slightly tentative. Whether they were the result of Lazlo's genetic makeup, or the result of the haphazard way he lived, was uncertain, but they lent a pathos to his absorption, a pathos that had been uppermost in Edie's mind ever since Rosa had telephoned and said, in the throw-away way she had, at the end of a conversation, "D'you know where Lazlo's living?"

"No," Edie said, "why should I? He's rather private about all of that. Somewhere in West London –"

"Kilburn," Rosa said.

"Well," Edie said, "not the perfect journey to work but not impossible –"

"He lives," Rosa said, "in a room in someone's granny's house and she won't open the windows because she's panicked about burglars and it smells like a cat's lavatory."

"Poor boy. Why is he living there?"

"It's all he can afford –"

"What about family –"

"All over the place," Rosa said, "and they don't care."

"Surely –"

"Mum," Rosa said, "he didn't tell me all of this. I had to get it out of him."

"And why are you telling me?"

"Because," Rosa said casually, "it's the sort of thing you like to know."

Edie sat up a little straighter and took her gaze off Lazlo's arms. Then she put it back again. She thought of the house in Kilburn. She thought of Lazlo ravenously eating bagels after the first rehearsal. She thought of Lazlo taking off that T-shirt and devising some forlorn and unsatisfactory way to launder it. She thought of Matthew – unhappy but somehow safe – back in his own bedroom. She thought of Rosa's empty bedroom next to it, and Ben's, on the floor below.

Freddie Cass turned toward her from the stage. He didn't, as was his custom, raise his voice.

"Stage left, Edie, please," he said.

"Dear Laura," Ruth wrote via e-mail, "I need someone to talk to. Or someone to think aloud to. Please read this through to the end. Please."

She paused and took her hands off the keyboard. She had set up a table – trestle, black, very expensive considering its construction hardly differed from the table her father used for one of his meticulous wallpapering sessions – in the window of her new sitting room so that she could glance up from her laptop and look out at her amazing view. There was nothing else much in her sitting room except the leather sofa – which Matthew had insisted she take – and a television and two tall metal lamps that threw their light modishly on to the ceiling.

"It isn't that I don't want things," she'd written to Laura. "It's more a case of adjusting to buying them on my own. It feels as if everything in my life has suddenly sort of liquefied – it's quite exciting but it's unnerving too. Perhaps I should just wait until I've calmed down a bit."

Laura hadn't replied to that message for four days. Ruth knew she was writing a lot and had even explained, slightly mortifying though it was to have to do so, that without Matthew to talk to, and being in a very preoccupying and distressing situation, which required a lot of talk in order to attempt to get her thoughts in some kind of sequence, she needed both a listening ear and a response. Laura, mindful of the fact that Ruth had nursed her steadily through a variety of affairs and a broken engagement prior to the lawyer in Leeds, said that of course she was always there when needed. The trouble was, Ruth thought, staring at some gulls riding the wind above the river, that even if people were there, as it were, they weren't always there in the right spirit. Laura, however well-intentioned, inevitably had her spirit diverted by the prospect of her future, by the right fridge in her kitchen, the right music at her wedding. And I can't blame her, Ruth thought, I certainly can't resent her, but I haven't yet got to the point where I can work through my thinking by myself. If, indeed, I ever get there.

She looked back at the screen. "Please," she'd written pleadingly. She could hear herself saying it.

"What I mean is," she typed rapidly, "I need to get all this stuff out – issues, as human resources at work call them – and it would be very kind of you to read through to the end and even kinder to tell me if I'm mad or what passes for normal.

"Laura, three people now have accused me of being ambitious and I mean accused, not described (no, one of them isn't Matthew, but I think his mother is). A colleague (male) says he thinks of ambition as both a necessary and desirable part of his life, but when I think about it in relation to myself it seems to imply things I don't like at all, like egotism and selfishness and the manipulation of other people for my own ends. I want to tell people that being good at work isn't about me, it's about the work. But why do I want to? And why do I feel especially compelled to, now, because I have achieved this flat and lost Matthew in the process?

"And it gets worse. I don't just feel guilty about what's happened, I feel resentful about feeling guilty. Nobody, Laura, not my colleagues, not my family, not even Matthew before all this happened, said well done about getting to this level at your age. Or even well done about getting to this level. We praise children now until they can't take failure of the smallest kind, so why can't we praise women for being good at things that aren't traditionally female? Why do women always, always have to be the givers? And if they stop giving, even for a minute, why is there this unspoken accusation that they have somehow surrendered on being truly female?

"Laura, I don't want to give up what I'm doing, I don't want to give up my opportunities. I can't believe that being accepted has to mean being frustrated too, but nor can I bear the thought that, if I make choices the way I just have, I'll end up without a man and without a family because I'm not, somehow, *allowed* to have both.

I don't want to downsize my ambition.

I want to live in this flat.

I want Matthew back.
Love, Ruth."

The restaurant Max had chosen to take Vivien to, for dinner, was one she had never been to before. It had a conservatory at the back, which, Max said, was opened up in summer to the paved garden behind and they put up big white Italian market umbrellas, and candle lamps in the trees, and it was really a very, very nice ambience indeed.

Vivien, walking carefully to the table in her new sandals, decided not to ask how Max knew so much about this restaurant, particularly by candlelight. In the four years they had lived apart, Vivien had been out with two men, neither of whom became more than perfunctory lovers, and Max had had, to her certain knowledge three, and to her sharp suspicion five girlfriends, all younger, all long-haired and all sexually available and active. Max had never mentioned any of them by name, but Vivien knew that one was called Carly and one was called Emma and one was an air hostess whom Max had met on a flight back from Chicago and who had subsequently, and annoyingly, engineered a very cheap flight for Eliot to get to Australia. Maybe Emma and Carly and the air hostess had all been to the restaurant with the conservatory, with Max. And maybe, even if they had, sitting down with him as still her legal husband gave Vivien a trump card that no amount of long hair and sexual ingenuity could deprive her of.

She sank into her chair and looked at Max across the candles.

"Lovely."

He indicated the menu.

"Take a look at that. Have what you want. Have lobster."

She smiled at him. He wore a pale suit and a strong blue shirt and he looked, Vivien thought, very distinguished. It was always a pleasure to see a man who looked after himself.

"I don't like lobster, Max."

He smiled back.

"Nor you do."

"What else don't I like?"

He closed his eyes.

"Let me think –"

"Green peppers," Vivien said. "Rhubarb. Coriander."

He opened his eyes.

"Battenberg cake."

"Battenberg *cake*?"

"Yes," he said.

"You don't even know what it is –"

"I do," Max said. "Pink and yellow squares. I bought you some once, at a motorway place, on the way up to Scotland. You threw it out of the car window."

Vivien smiled delightedly.

"You made that up."

"Never. I remember it as if it was yesterday. I've ordered champagne."

"Champagne!"

"Why not? We're celebrating, aren't we?"

She turned her head a little and looked at him coquettishly.

"Are we? What are we celebrating?"

He winked.

"A little – rapprochement, Vivi."

"*Oh*," she said, "is *that* what this is?"

A waiter put a small metal champagne bucket on the table between them.

"Goodness –"

"When did you last drink champagne?"

"Can't remember."

"Well, it's time you did. It's time you *lived* again a little, Vivi."

The waiter poured champagne slowly into a tall, thin glass flute and set it ceremoniously in front of Vivien. "I bet he gives you champagne," Rosa had said, waving Vivi off from the sofa, in her tracksuit. "I bet you get the works tonight."

Max raised his glass.

"To –" he said, and stopped.

Vivien waited.

"To Eliot," Max said.

"Of course," Vivien said, a fraction too eagerly. She raised her glass, too, and touched Max's with it. "To Eliot."

"What about this Ro?"

Vivien made a small face.

"Well, you have to remember that what suits an Australian beach wouldn't suit Richmond."

"Come on," Max said, "this isn't like you. Come on, Vivi."

Vivien looked up.

"I've never spoken to her."

"Nor me."

"She's learning to be a Buddhist."

"A Buddhist," Max said. "Oh please."

"But she surfs and drinks beer –"

"All you could ask, really."

"Now, Max –"

"We'll let it go, shall we," Max said. "For now?"

"We?"

"Yes, we. He's our son, remember."

Vivien took a small sip of her champagne.

"And the diving?"

"My feeling is," Max said, "to let that go for now too. If he's still doing it, and only it, when he's thirty, we'll fly out and give him a rocket."

"Aren't you going to see him before he's thirty?"

Max looked straight at her.

"Anytime you're ready, we'll go out and see him."

Vivien smiled at her champagne glass.

"Oh."

"Say the word," Max said.

Vivien leaned back in her chair.

She said, looking away across the restaurant, "What happened to the air hostess?"

"She went back to her airline."

"And," Vivien said, feeling a small and happy surge of confidence, "you didn't replace her?"

"Oh, I tried," Max said, "I tried like anything."

"Should I know about this?"

He put his head on one side.

"Only if you want to be very bored. As bored as I got. What are you going to eat?"

"Guess."

He looked down at the menu.

"Avocado and red mullet."

"There," she said, "you haven't forgotten."

"No," he said, "I haven't."

"And you'll have wild mushrooms and guinea fowl."

"Or duck."

"Oh yes, duck. I haven't cooked a duck for four years."

Max glanced at her over the menu.

"We should rectify that."

"I cook girls' food now," Vivien said. "Fish and salads and pasta. Rosa's on a diet."

"I hope you aren't joining her."

"Well, I thought of it –"

"Don't," Max said, "you don't need to. You're –" He stopped and grinned. Then he said, "What was I going to say, Vivi?"

"I have no idea."

"What did you *hope* I'd say?"

"Stop it," Vivien said.

"But you like it."

She lifted her chin.

"Not any more."

"We'll see."

"No, we won't."

Max leaned forward.

He said, "Actually I am going to say something."

"Oh?"

"I was going to say it later, but I think I'll say it now."

He put the menu down and leaned toward Vivien across the table.

"We had a good time last week, didn't we?"

"Yes –"

"And you aren't exactly miserable now –"

"Not exactly."

"Look," Max said, "look, Vivi. Things have changed, haven't they? I've had a bit of freedom, you've had a bit of time to sort yourself out, Eliot's grown up and gone –" He paused and looked at her. "I was just wondering, Vivi, if you'd let me try again?"

While she was in the shower, Ruth played Mozart. It was a recording of *Don Giovanni*, and she turned it up very loud, so that she could hear it above the water, and the music and the water could combine in a way that would be briefly overwhelming and stop her thinking. Her mother had once said to her, when she was about fourteen, that it didn't do to think too much, that you could think yourself out of being able to cope with ordinary life, which Ruth had then considered to be her mother's excuse for ceaseless practical activity. She now thought her mother's theory had possibly a certain truth to it, and that her mother's passion for organization and committees and busyness had been a way of dealing with not being able to use her capacities to the full. It was a case, perhaps, of accommodating yourself to what was permitted, as long as – crucial, this – you didn't start raging against whoever did the permitting in the first place and why they'd got the power.

Ruth turned off the shower and stepped out into the bathroom and a wall of singing. She'd keep it that loud, she thought, until somebody from a neighboring flat either complained or played something she hated at equal volume. She picked up a towel and wound herself into it, like a sarong, then went barefoot across the smooth, pale wood floor of her sitting room to her desk. She bent over her computer. There would be nothing in her inbox, just as there were no messages on her answerphone, no texts on her mobile. Apart from work, there'd been a sudden cessation of all communication, as if someone had shut a soundproof door on a party.

There was one new message on her e-mail. She sat down in her bath towel and clicked her mouse.

The message was from Laura.

"Dear Ruth," it said. "Just ring him!"

Ruth looked up at the ceiling high above her and closed her eyes. There was a lump in her throat.

"Just ring him!"

CHAPTER ELEVEN

"Are you sure?" Lazlo said.

Edie pushed the sugar toward him across the café table.

"Oh yes."

"But it would be your son's room —"

"Or my daughter's. We've had lots of actors there, over the last few years, on and off —"

"Really?"

"Oh yes."

"What about," Lazlo said, taking two packets of white sugar, "your husband?"

"He's called Russell."

"I know," Lazlo said. "I just felt a bit shy."

"*Shy?*"

"I don't know my own father very well."

"Russell isn't at all alarming. Russell is very used to actor lodgers."

"Have you told him?"

"What?"

"That," Lazlo said, "you were going to offer a room to me."

Edie watched him tear the sugar packets across and pour the contents into the cushion of milky foam on the top of his coffee.

"Lazlo dear, I don't need to ask him."

"I said tell —"

"I don't need to tell him either. He likes having the house full. He likes having it *used*."

Lazlo began to stir his coffee.

"I must say, it would be wonderful. It would make me feel –" He stopped, and then he said, "Different."

"Good."

He looked at her and then he looked away.

"I would try – not to be a nuisance."

"If you were," Edie said, "I probably wouldn't notice. My children, with the possible exception of Matthew, are usually a nuisance. If you don't have any nuisance in your life, I've discovered, something dies in you. It all gets very bland and boring." She leaned across the table. "When I was a child, I shared a bedroom with my sister Vivien and we fought all the time because she was very tidy and I was very messy, extra messy, probably, to annoy her, and when our mother said we could have separate rooms, I was miserable. There was no point in being messy on my own." She looked across at Lazlo and smiled at him. "There still isn't."

He said, "Is that the sister that Rosa lives with?"

"Yes."

"Are you still fighting?"

"Certainly," Edie said.

"I never fight with my sister. I wouldn't risk it. You have to have enough family to take that kind of risk."

"Goodness," Edie said, "what a dramatic view of family. You sound like a Russian novel. If that's what you're expecting, you'll find us very dull."

"I don't think so."

She reached across the table and grasped his wrist.

"We'll like having you. Really."

He shook his head and gave her a quick glance, and in the course of it, she saw he had tears in his eyes.

"Heavens, Lazlo," Edie said, laughing. "Heavens, it's only a *room*."

*   *   *

The evening paper had two columns advertising rooms and flats to let. They varied in monthly price by several hundred pounds and also in tone of advertisement, some being baldly commercial and some more haphazard, personal offers of flat sharing. Ben was certain that Naomi, even if she could be persuaded to leave her mother's flat, would be adamant about not sharing any accommodation with anyone other than Ben. It had been an eye-opener for Ben, living with Naomi and her mother, to see the fierceness with which privacy and possessions were not just owned, but guarded. Naomi's mother didn't refer to "the" kettle or "the" bathroom: both were "my." For Ben, growing up in a house where ownership of anything that wasn't intensely personal seemed comfortably communal, this domestic demarcation and pride had been very surprising.

"Feet off my coffee table," Naomi's mother had said to him on his first evening. "And the way I like my toilet seat is down."

Ben had felt little resentment about this. Faced with a rigidly organized kitchen and a tremendous expectation of conformity, he had, rather to his surprise, felt more an awed respect. Naomi's mother spoke to him in exactly the same way that she spoke to Naomi after all, and as Naomi plainly thought her mother's standards and requirements were as natural as breathing, Ben was, at least for a while, prepared to pick up his bath towel and replace the ironing board – ironing was a bit of a revelation – on its specially designated hooks behind the kitchen door. Only once, in his first few weeks, did he say to Naomi, watching her while she made an extremely neat cheese sandwich, "Has your Mum always been like this?"

Naomi didn't even glance at him.

She shook her long blonde hair back over her shoulders and said evenly, "It's how she likes it.'

Living the way you liked, even Ben could see, was what you were entitled to if you owned a house or paid the rent.

Indeed, one of the reasons he had left home, besides the consuming desire to spend the nights in the same bed as Naomi, was a strong, if unarticulated, understanding that he wanted to live in a way that didn't coincide with the way his parents were living but, as it was their house, their entitlement in the matter came before his. Living with Naomi's mother was, especially at the beginning, no problem at all because of Naomi herself and because her mother, for all her insistence on her own particular rule of law, was someone whose palpable industry and independence required – and got – Ben's deference. In addition, and to Ben's abiding and grateful amazement, she seemed to find his presence in her flat and her daughter's bed perfectly natural. There hadn't been a syllable uttered, or even implied, that Ben could construe as an inquiry about their relationship, let alone a criticism.

All this, for some time, made Ben amenable to making his large male presence in a small female flat as invisible as possible. Indeed, it was only gradually, and not in any way triggered by a particular incident, that he began to feel a sense of being both watched and stifled. The setting down of his coffee mug or beer can, once a matter of discovery and trial and error, became insidiously more of an issue, as did the placing – or even presence – of his boots in the narrow hallway. Naomi's mother didn't operate by correcting her daughter or her daughter's boyfriend more than once. After that, she took matters into her own hands and effected the changes she wanted, in silence, but in the kind of silence that made Ben, rather to his surprise, think wistfully of his own mother's approach to domestic management. He had absolutely no desire to confront or displease Naomi's mother, but it had begun to occur to him, several times a day, that he was on a hiding to nothing because she was, in fact, constantly changing the goalposts. That morning, the hunt for his boots had ended in discovering them in a plastic carrier bag hanging on a hook under his overcoat.

He'd said nothing to Naomi about moving out with him. With the newly hatched confidence of having had his older brother recently take his advice, he had decided that the best course of action was to identify some flats, or even rooms in flats, and choose one or two to show her so that she would have something to visualize and also have to make a choice. If he just said to her, "What about a place of our own?" she'd look at him as if he wasn't in his right mind and say, "What for?" But if he had a key to a door, and opened it, and showed her the possibilities of a way of living that lay beyond it, she might be persuaded. Or at least, he thought, staring hard at a photograph in the window in front of him, she might hesitate a little before she said, "What for?"

"I'll have tomato juice," Kate said.

Rosa paused on her way to the bar.

"Are you sure? I'm paying –"

"I only half feel like 'drink' drink," Kate said, "and I don't like the way people look at me when I drink it."

"Do they?"

"Well, I think they do."

"Right," Rosa said, "tomato juice it is."

"Should you be paying?"

"Yes."

"Can you –"

"I got a bonus this month," Rosa said. "Slovenia will be overflowing this summer, thanks to me."

Kate said, smiling, "So you're making headway on the money?"

Rosa shook her hair back.

"Well, I can afford the interest on the interest."

"*Rosa* –"

"I can afford to buy you a tomato juice."

"I don't want you –"

"I do," Rosa said and went away to the bar.

Kate shrugged off her jacket and pushed her shoes off, under the table. She hadn't told Barney she was meeting Rosa for a drink because, for some reason, Barney had assumed that not having Rosa in their flat meant not having Rosa in their life, either. He maintained that this was not because he didn't like Rosa, but only that he didn't think Rosa was good for Kate: too demanding, he said, too exhausting, too needy. Kate, who had declined, in the course of their lavish and traditional wedding, to promise to obey him, wondered if that was, in fact, exactly what she was doing. What was it, in an emotional relationship, that constituted a loving and generous action, and what – only apparently differentiated by a whisker – an act of submission instead?

Rosa came back and put two glasses on the table. Kate's tomato juice had a stick of celery planted in it and a wedge of lemon balanced on the rim. She took the celery out and laid it, dripping, across the ashtray on the table.

Then she said, licking tomato juice off her fingers, "I saw Ruth."

Rosa looked up from her drink.

"Why did you?"

"It was chance," Kate said. "We were both buying fruit in Borough Market."

"And?"

"She looked awful. And was sort of agitated. I think she thinks everyone disapproves of her."

"I do," Rosa said.

Kate leaned back, adjusting her T-shirt round her belly.

"Do you now?"

"Uh-huh."

"For hurting Matthew? Or for being very good at what she does and earning a lot of money?"

Rosa eyed her.

"For hurting Matthew, of course."

"Really."

"Yes, really."

"I don't believe you," Kate said. "I think you can't handle her being ambitious."

"Well, *you* aren't ambitious –"

"Yes, I am," Kate said. "I didn't think about it before I got pregnant, but I think about it a lot now and I know that I don't just like my job, I want it."

Rosa picked up her drink.

"I don't think I am –"

"Maybe not. And that's fine. What's not fine is thinking badly of poor Ruth because she is."

"Poor Ruth, is it?"

"Yes," Kate said, "poor Ruth. She looked to me like she misses Matthew like anything."

"Well, she chose to go ahead with this flat –"

"And he chose –"

"He had to," Rosa said.

"Oh, *Rosa* –"

"It was humiliation or get out."

"But *she* wasn't doing the humiliating," Kate said. "Or do you think she should have taken a lesser job and earned less just to make him feel better? How humiliating is that?"

Rosa closed her eyes.

"He's my brother."

"About whom," Kate said, "you are often very rude. Of course you should be sorry for him but don't load all the blame on Ruth just because she's doing what a man would be praised for doing." She leaned forward again and said, "What does your mother say?"

"She's thrilled Matt's gone home."

"Is that all?"

"What d'you mean?"

"Is your mother's only reaction being pleased to have Matthew back again?"

Rosa sighed.

"Of course not. She likes Ruth but she doesn't understand

why she's done what she's done. It wasn't the way she did things, it was always family first with Mum."

"That's generational."

"Kate," Rosa said, "I thought we were going to have a quiet drink and be pleased to see each other, but all you want to do is argue."

Kate took a swallow of tomato juice.

She said, "You *need* arguing with."

"Why, thank you –"

"You need jolting and galvanizing. You need to use that brain of yours, you need to stop just drifting along –"

"Oh, shut up," Rosa said.

"Rose, I'm your *friend*, I'm –"

"Sorted and organized and married and interestingly employed and pregnant and insufferable."

Kate picked up the stick of celery and jabbed it into the ashtray for emphasis.

"When did you last do anything decisive?"

Rosa said, without looking at her, "Last week."

"And what was it, precisely?"

"I helped," Rosa said deliberately, "someone I don't really like find somewhere to live."

"Oh?"

"An actor. In Mum's company. He's going to rent my room."

"What?"

"He's going to rent my bedroom. Mum offered it to him. So she's got two bedrooms full now and Dad is not happy."

Kate stared at her.

"This is *bizarre*."

"Isn't it just."

"And you living with your aunt –"

"Yes. So don't go on at me about drifting and being hopeless."

Kate put the celery down and reached across to grasp Rosa's hand.

"Sorry."

"That's okay."

"It's probably hormones," Kate said. "Everything I do at the moment seems to be hormones. I have this enormous urge to get everything sorted."

Rosa turned her hand over to give Kate's a squeeze, and then took it away.

"I hope it's catching –"

Kate grinned at her.

"What's it like, living with your aunt?"

"Very comfortable and very restricting. It's so funny, she's dating –"

"She isn't!"

"Well, it's only my uncle, who she's separated from. She keeps skipping out on Saturday nights, all kitten heels and chandelier earrings."

"Sweet or sickening?"

"Oh, sweet mostly," Rosa said. "It'd only be sickening if Uncle Max was anything other than a joke."

"Does she come into your room and sit on your bed and tell you all about it?"

"No, thank you."

Kate reached awkwardly behind her, for her jacket.

"I ought to go –"

"Supper –"

"Well, Barney's cooking," Kate said, "but he does quite like to be admired."

Rosa leaned back, holding her glass.

"There you go," she said with satisfaction. "There's always a price to pay."

The door to Ben's bedroom on the first-floor landing was open. Through it, on the bed, Russell could see a pile of cushions that looked familiar but out of context and a mauve felt elephant and a lampshade made of strings of pink glass beads. He moved closer. On the floor by Ben's bed was an old white numdah rug, appliquéd with naïve animals and flowers, which he recognized as the rug he and Edie had given Rosa when she was five, as a reward for stopping sucking her thumb. Now that he looked at them with more attention, he saw that the cushions – Indian brocade, Thai spangles – and the lampshade were also familiar from Rosa's room, as was the elephant and a mirror edged with pearly shells and a gauze sari which, at one point, Rosa had pinned clumsily to the ceiling over her bed to try and create some kind of exotic canopy.

Russell went out of Ben's room and up the stairs to the top floor. The door to Matthew's room was closed but the one to Rosa's room, next door, was open, almost defiantly wide open, Russell thought, as if to make an emphatic point. Through it, he could see that although the furniture in Rosa's room hadn't been moved, the atmosphere had been definitely changed. There was a plaid rug on the bed, new dark-blue shades on the lamps, and the chest of drawers, which had always displayed Rosa's childhood collection of china shoes and thimbles, was empty except for a black-framed mirror propped against the wall. Edie had taken all the girl she could find out of the room and replaced it with boy. And she had done this for the benefit of someone Russell hardly knew, who appeared quite homeless and therefore liable to stay indefinitely, and who was not just homeless but penniless also, so Edie was only asking him to pay forty pounds a week, which had infuriated Matthew – who was their own son and paying almost twice that – as well it might.

Russell walked into Rosa's room and sat down on the edge of the bed. He put his elbows on his knees and leaned forward to stare at the carpet and a new, modern, striped cotton rug that had been laid on it. He had always, he told himself, liked the challenging quality in Edie's nature, he enjoyed the way she wouldn't take any form of rubbish lying down, the way she rose up to argue and rebel. But what was likable, lovable even, in someone as a spectator sport wasn't always as pleasurable, or even bearable, when one's own feelings were involved. He couldn't, in principle, object to her offering shelter to her own, or anyone else's, child in trouble, but the difficulty was that he couldn't be sure that filling the house up with young men, at this precise moment in time, was actually an act of altruism. The more he thought about it, the more he felt that not only was Edie asserting a right to use her house as she pleased, but that she was also making it painfully plain that the last thing she wanted was to be left alone in it with him.

Russell shifted his feet. He couldn't remember when he had started looking forward to being alone with Edie, but it seemed to be a very long time ago. As each of his children left, he had felt an unmistakable pang, and he had also missed them, missed them, sometimes, quite keenly. But at the same time as those doors were closing, he had had a happy, anticipatory feeling about another one opening, one that led back, or perhaps led on to the relationship that had started it all, the relationship with the short, excitable girl in a cherry-colored beret who he'd first seen queuing for cinema tickets to see *High Society* with Bing Crosby and Frank Sinatra and Grace Kelly in a chignon.

And if that feeling wasn't reciprocated, if Edie could no longer quite stand the thought of being left alone with him, then at best he was very disappointed and at worst he was very hurt. He also felt, looking round at the walls denuded of Rosa's posters and pictures, peculiarly powerless. Edie had set something firmly in train, which, if he disrupted it, would only make him look an unpleasant and heartless person.

He got up, sighing, and went over to the window. The garden, from up here, looked pleasingly controlled and almost cared for. Neither he nor Edie had ever been en-thusiastic gardeners but it was odd how, over the years, if you owned a garden you somehow acquired some know-ledge about it by osmosis, and fell into the annual rituals of sowing and pruning and clipping. If he was honest, he'd actually indulged in a little fantasy or two about Edie and him being out in the garden together that summer, companionably trimming things or drinking wine under the torn garden umbrella. Like all fantasies, he supposed, that one owed its only existence to impossibility, but it had been nice to contemplate, even more than nice, when the reality was that Edie would now be too preoccupied even to consider tranquil moments, glass in hand, admiring the roses. He shook his head. What was he thinking of, sad old fool that he was? When the play's run began, Edie wouldn't be looking to right or to left, let alone at the roses.

He moved slowly back, past Rosa's bed all ready for Lazlo, and out onto the landing. The brown stain left by a long-ago wasp's nest under the roof tiles was still there on the once-white ceiling, as was the split in the top step of the stair carpet and the missing knob to the newel post at the turn of the banisters. Doubtless, Russell thought, there were people who made lists of things to be repaired in their houses, and then attended to those lists with efficient toolboxes filled with the right tools for every job in special compartments, but if so he definitely wasn't one of them. His mother had always told him, finding him reading as a child yet again, that he was lazy. Possibly she was right and would therefore be amazed to know that at the age of fifty-six and faced with a situation in his personal life he could neither control nor adjust to he was resolving to devote all the energies he had planned to use for a renewed life with Edie to his work.

When Max finally kissed Vivien, she had been ready for both him and it. The steady succession of dates, the careful way in which he had refrained from startling her, the new gravity of his goodbyes had made it absolutely plain to her that when he kissed her it would not be on impulse and therefore, if she had a single wit about her, she could see it coming. And so, when he stopped the car outside her house, and switched off the ignition and turned toward her, she was very excited and quite prepared. The kiss itself was possibly one of the best he had ever given her, being both familiar because of the past and unfamiliar because it hadn't happened for well over four years. She received it with skill and just enough response to engage him. Then she got out of the car.

He got out too.

"Can I come in?"

Vivien looked up at her house. Rosa's bedroom window, above the front door, was still lit.

"No, Max."

Max looked up too.

"Vivi –"

She reached out a hand and laid it flat on his chest.

"No, Max. Not now."

He seized her hand in both his.

"But will you think about it?"

"Yes."

"Promise, Vivi, promise. And I promise it'll be different."

She disengaged her hand and took a step away.

"I said I'd think about it, Max," she said, "and I will. Thank you for a lovely evening," and then she stepped away from him in her heels and crossed her little front garden to the door. When she turned to wave good night he was standing staring after her in a way she had never dared to hope he would again.

Inside the house, Rosa had left the hall light on and a note by the telephone that said, "Alison rang. Can you do Tues p.m., not Wed, this week?" and underneath, "Will take washing out of machine first thing, promise. X" Vivien went past the telephone table and down the hall to the kitchen, which Rosa had left approximately tidy in the way Edie always left things tidy, with none of the finishing details attended to and no air of conclusion. Most nights, she would have spent ten minutes brushing up crumbs and putting stray mugs in the dishwasher, but tonight, in her mood of command and composure, she merely filled a glass with water, switched off the lights and made her way carefully upstairs.

There was a line of light still, under Rosa's door. Vivien hesitated a moment and then knocked.

"Come!" Rosa called.

She was sitting up in bed in a pink camisole, reading *Hello!* magazine. Her hair, newly washed, was fanned out over her shoulders.

"You do have lovely hair," Vivien said.

Rosa smiled at her over the magazine.

"And you plainly had a lovely evening."

Vivien hitched her cream wrap over her shoulders and settled on the edge of Rosa's bed, cradling her glass of water.

"Fusion tonight. Sea bass and curried lentils."

"And champagne?"

"Oh yes," Vivien said smiling, "always champagne."

Rosa put down the magazine.

"You're costing him a fortune."

Vivien nodded.

"Oh, I should hope so –"

"Is this payback time now, then?"

"Oh no," Vivien said, "it's just that a man like Max only understands value for money as exactly that. That's why he never minded me being so literal." She looked at the magazine. "Have you had a nice evening?"

"No," Rosa said, "but that's not what I want to talk about. I want to hear about yours."

Vivien took a savoring swallow of water.

She said, artlessly, "Well, it was just dinner, you know –"

"Just dinner," Rosa said. "So why come and tell me about it? You don't usually."

Vivien looked away across the room as if she were either visualizing or remembering something particularly satisfying.

"I think," she said, still gazing, "that Max hasn't found the bachelor life all he thought it would be."

Rosa waited. Vivien slowly retrieved her gaze and transferred it to her glass of water.

"All those girls of his, even the working ones, well they do seem very interested in what he earns –"

Rosa said nothing.

"Max says that none of them was prepared to look after him in any way, but at the same time they wanted him to look after them; oh yes, holidays and meals out and Center Court tickets at Wimbledon. He said they almost made it sound like they were *entitled* to be treated like that."

Rosa leaned back against her pillows.

She murmured, "How *very* shocking –"

"Well," Vivien said, "it's not the way your mother and I were brought up. You never expected a man to treat you like a princess and then all he expected really was to be allowed a bit of sex in return."

"Really?"

"It wasn't take, take, take, with us," Vivien said. "We were brought up to keep house and put food on the table."

"I thought," Rosa said slowly, "that one of the troubles with Max was that he never came home to eat the food you'd put on the table."

Vivien raised her eyes and looked seriously at Rosa.

"He's changed," she said.

"I saw him out of the window when he came to collect you, and he looked exactly the same –"

"He's changed," Vivien said. "*Inside.*"

"Oh."

"He knows how badly he behaved. He knows he exploited me. He knows that almost nobody would have put up with him the way I did."

Rosa sat up suddenly.

"Oh Vivi. Oh Vivi, do be careful –"

Vivien smiled at her.

176

"He's learned so much in the last four years," she said. "He's been so unhappy and he's missed me so badly and our life together." She let a small, eloquent pause elapse and then she said, "That's why he wants to come and live with me, and try again."

CHAPTER TWELVE

L azlo was being very quiet. Lying on his bed against the
wall between their bedrooms, Matthew wondered if he
was sitting staring into space like a petrified rabbit or
earnestly reading the Theban plays in his pursuit of true
professionalism. He was a nice enough guy, Matthew
thought, even if slightly geeky, and obviously pathetically
grateful to be in Rosa's room after his months of confine-
ment among the cat-litter trays in Kilburn. His pathos made
Matthew regret his outburst over money. He shouldn't have
done it, he shouldn't have shouted at his father for asking for
money or his mother for not asking Lazlo for more. You
only had to look at Lazlo to be reminded of some student
character out of Dostoyevsky, all skin and bone and burning
passion, and not a penny to his name.

He shifted a little on his pillow. All those years of living a
wall away from Rosa meant that every creak and thump
from the other side was familiar, as was the fact that the
closer to the window you moved the more audible sounds
became. Rosa, of course, was something of a banger and
crasher, flinging drawers shut and slamming doors. Lazlo on
the other hand made no sound at all, as if elaborately
tiptoeing about, closing cupboards with stealth, inching
himself onto his bed with his breath held. It was, Matthew
supposed, rather like starting at boarding school, where he
had never been, but which must be plagued by the

consciousness of the nearness of strangers. He lifted his fist and held it up in the dusky late-spring dark. If he swung it sideways, he could thump the wall and imagine Lazlo starting up, gasping, dropping his book. It would be a childish thing to do, of course it would, but perhaps childishness was what descended on you when you found yourself back in your boyhood bedroom after years – yes, years – of living independently.

He lowered his fist and laid his hand across his chest.

"Come back," Ruth had said the other night. "Please. Come back."

She'd been in bed with him, or he with her, whichever, they'd been in her bed – their old joint bed – in her new bedroom, where he'd never intended to be, where he wasn't drunk enough or convinced enough to be, but where he somehow still was, holding her, with her head roughly where his hand now was, and her saying, almost into his skin, "Please come back. Please."

He'd stroked her hair back from her face, saying nothing. After a while, she raised herself on one elbow and said, "Don't you love me anymore?" and he said, truthfully, "Of course I do, but that doesn't solve everything," and she said, "It does, it *can*," and he said, tiredly, "We've been through this. We've been through all this, over and over."

"But you came tonight," Ruth said. "You've made love to me."

He couldn't say it didn't mean anything because that was neither true nor constructive. Of course going to bed with Ruth was significant, even important, but at the same time he hadn't meant it to happen, hadn't wanted it to happen, and now that it had, he was filled with a dreary desolation. He had only made things worse. He had only made Ruth hope again for something that couldn't happen because it was too messy and too insoluble and, above all, too late.

He'd kissed the top of Ruth's head and squeezed her bare shoulders and then began to disengage himself as gently as he could. He'd waited for her to start crying but she hadn't, merely remaining where he'd left her, crumpled and silent, a picture of misery and reproach. Once dressed, he stood in the doorway of the bedroom and wrestled with what he might say. Sorry was pathetic, thank you for dinner was ludicrous, I love you was unkind and dangerous. In the end he simply said, "Bye," and went out of the flat and into the lift, and leaned against the wall of it with his eyes closed. How was it possible to get, entirely without intending to, into a position where you kept somehow inflicting pain on someone you loved? When she had rung him and begged – awful, mortifying word, but accurate for how she'd sounded – him to come round for supper, it had seemed more difficult and elaborate to refuse her than to agree. And then he had ended up making things worse than he had ever intended, concluding by responding to some primitive urge to flee that had got him out of the flat and down to London Bridge Underground Station and then left him to trail back to North London cursing himself.

From next door came the sound of Lazlo opening his window. Matthew imagined him leaning out, breathing, marveling at where he found himself. Perhaps he was feeling as Matthew had felt before he met Ruth, both luxuriously free and equally luxuriously lonely. Matthew turned on his side, and punched his pillow up under his neck. If you couldn't just un-love someone, he thought, perhaps you could at least starve that love a bit, practice not allowing yourself to express it or react to its impulses. He shut his eyes. No calls from now on. No e-mails. No contact. Nothing.

"We have six days," Freddie Cass said, "until press night. And I am far from happy with this scene."

Edie did not look either at Lazlo or at Cheryl. Cheryl was probably, anyway, looking as if any imminent reprimand had nothing to do with her, and Lazlo would be expecting the worst.

"Don't strut, Cheryl," Freddie Cass said. There was a pause. Then he said, "Don't bleat, Lazlo." And then, after another silence, "Good, Edie."

"I'm supposed to strut," Cheryl said, boredly, "in this scene."

Freddie ignored her.

He said to Lazlo, "You'll be blind by the end of the scene. *Blind.* Who'll care about that if they've heard you whining for favors?"

Lazlo cleared his throat. Edie willed him not to apologize.

He said, "I am whining. I'm very unattractive by now. I'm completely self-centered because I'm dying."

Freddie Cass waited. Edie glanced at him. He wasn't looking at Lazlo, as was his wont when addressing someone, he was looking across the stage to where an electrician was dismantling a spotlight.

"I'm not getting that."

"I'll try again."

"Yes," Freddie said, "you will." He sighed. "And you, Cheryl, will stop playing the little tart. Even if you are one." He moved forward, toward the footlights, and touched Edie on the shoulder as he passed. "As you were."

Edie went past Lazlo, upstage to the spot where the door to the garden would be when the set was up. Lazlo caught her eye as she passed him and gave her the briefest of winks. She widened her eyes at him. He looked quite undismayed by what Freddie had said, quite unlike his usual easily wounded self. He looked, astonishingly, like someone prepared to stand his ground. Perhaps, she thought, picking up the shallow flower basket that Mrs. Alving was to bring in from the garden, this new energy and confidence could even be attributable to the simple fact that she had offered breakfast to Lazlo that morning and then overseen him while he ate it. He ate like Ben, with that peculiar combination of indifference and absorption that seemed to characterize hungry young men, consuming two bowls of cereal and a banana and four slices of toast as if they were simultaneously vital and of no consequence at all. She'd felt an extraordinary satisfaction, almost a relief, sitting opposite him with her coffee mug, and watching him eat. It had been so pleasurable that she had turned to Russell, to smile that pleasure at him, and found that he was reading the paper like someone in a pantomime, with the paper held up high, a screen against the outside world.

She reached across and banged the paper with a teaspoon. "Oy."

"One moment," Russell said, not lowering the paper.

"Rude," Edie said cheerfully. "Meals are for conversation."

Russell moved the paper sideways so that only Edie could see his face.

"Not breakfast."

Lazlo put his second piece of toast down.

"Sorry," he said contritely.

Edie smiled at him.

"Not you," she said, "him."

Russell moved the paper back to its original position.

"If you ever marry," he said, not addressing Lazlo by name, "you'll discover that all roads of fault and blame lead to 'him.'"

Edie put her coffee mug down. She looked at Lazlo.

"More toast?"

"No thank you," Russell said.

"I wasn't addressing you. You have only had one slice of toast since the dawn of time. Lazlo, more toast?"

He looked longingly at the sliced loaf on the counter.

"Could I . . ."

Edie stood up.

"Of course you could."

Russell shook the paper out like a bed sheet, and folded it with care.

"I'm off."

Edie, putting bread into the toaster, turned to glance at the clock.

"You're early."

"No."

"You never get in before ten."

Russell said nothing. He stood up and pushed the newspaper across the table to Lazlo.

"Have a good day."

"Thank you."

He looked briefly across the kitchen, at Edie's back.

"See you later."

She turned and gave him a wide smile. Then she blew him a kiss. He went out of the room, and they could hear him treading heavily up the stairs to the bathroom.

"If it would be easier," Lazlo said diffidently, "I could always take breakfast up to my room."

The toaster gave a small metallic clang and ejected two slices of toast on to the counter. Edie snatched them up and tossed them hastily on to Lazlo's plate.

"So overenthusiastic, that thing. And nonsense. About breakfast, I mean."

"I don't want to upset anyone –"

Edie looked straight at him.

"You aren't. Russell is fine. Eat your toast."

He began to butter it. She walked behind his chair, giving him a tiny pat on the shoulder as she did so, and went out of the room and up the stairs to the bathroom. Russell was bent over the basin, brushing his teeth. Edie leaned against the door jamb and crossed her arms.

"I suppose," she said, "I could always do breakfast in relays. Matthew at seven, you at eight to fit in with your new work schedule, and Lazlo at nine."

Russell stopped brushing and picked up a wet flannel from the edge of the bath and rubbed vigorously at his face with it.

"Very funny."

"There's no need," Edie said, "to be so unwelcoming. So *rude*. That poor boy is about as intrusive as wallpaper."

Russell tossed the flannel into the bath.

"It's not him," he said, "as well you know."

"So," Edie said, "things change. They don't go according to plan. What you picture as the future doesn't turn out to be the reality of the future. That's how it is, Russell, that's how it's always been. That's *life*."

He turned from the basin and walked past her into their bedroom to find his jacket. She detached herself from the bathroom doorway and went after him.

"Russell?"

"I am not complaining about life," Russell said, hunting in his jacket pockets for something. "I'm not objecting to the way things happen, the way things just turn out. What I find so difficult is when changes are made deliberately and obstructively."

"You mean me asking Lazlo here –"

Russell found his travel card and transferred it from one pocket to another.

"You could construe it like that –"

"You mean yes."

He sighed.

He said, "You seem to be finding every excuse not to be alone with me."

Edie gave a small bark of incredulous laughter.

"Really? And who urged me to audition for the Ibsen?"

"That's different."

"Is it?"

"That doesn't involve your personal emotions."

Edie let a small silence fall, and then she said witheringly, "How little you know. And you an actors' agent."

Russell took a step toward her. He looked down at her.

He said, "This is fruitless."

"If I can't even offer a lodger more toast without getting jumped on, it probably is."

He put his hands on her shoulders.

He said, "I had just hoped that we could move on from what we'd been doing for close on thirty years to something we've never had a chance to do." He took his hands away. "I suppose I was hoping to be married. Pure and simple. Just *married*."

Edie reached out and straightened his jacket collar.

She said, "Maybe we have different ideas about what being married means."

"Not always –"

She looked up at him.

"But this is now," she said. "We're not dealing with always, we're dealing with now. Which means me going downstairs now, and seeing what else I can stuff into that boy."

Russell made a huge effort.

"Well, he's certainly appreciative –"

"Yes," Edie said with emphasis, "he is," and then she left the room and went down to the kitchen where she found Lazlo putting plates in the dishwasher and Arsie on the table regarding the butter.

Lazlo straightened up as she came in. He was smiling.

"That was so great," he said. "I never eat breakfast. I never thought about it."

Now, looking at him across the stage, whether it was breakfast that was responsible or not, Edie could see that something had turned a corner in Lazlo. When he made his entrance, in five minutes or so, and stood by the table, fingering the books on it, and saying, " 'Everything'll burn, till there's nothing left to remind me of my father. Here I am, burning up too,' " they would all know, Freddie Cass included, that the whole production had moved into another gear.

Sitting on the grass in the park in her lunch hour, Rosa texted her brothers.

"Mum's 1st night. All go together?"

She was not quite sure what these texts would produce. Matthew would probably say they should leave it to Russell to organize, and Ben would probably say he was tied up, which meant that if he came he would want to bring Naomi, and he wasn't at all sure how he felt about exposing Naomi to his family. Whatever their response, however, Rosa had felt a powerful need to contact them over the opening of the play, a need to be included, or rather, in order not to look as if she wanted to be included to be the first to organize something in a way that looked responsible and concerned for family.

It was odd, but for the last week or ten days, Rosa had felt uncomfortably preoccupied by family. She had said carelessly to Kate that it was weird the way her family were all living at present, but her real feelings, she discovered, were far from careless, especially now that Vivien was distracted by her rekindled romance with Max. She was holding him off, she told Rosa, there was no question of him getting what he was asking for right now, but it had introduced an even stronger note of impermanence into Rosa's situation, a note that now resounded steadily in Rosa's head, like a drum beat. The thought of Matthew back in his bedroom and Lazlo now ensconced in hers was not exactly uncomfortable, but it did serve to remind her, in a way she didn't care for, that she too had reverted to a dependency that was hardly something to be proud of. And even if she had a job now and was proving competent at it – what she would have felt like if she hadn't been able to demonstrate that competency didn't even bear thinking about – and had made the first, tiny inroad upon her indebtedness, she still had the glum sensation of doing no more than bumping along the bottom. She could produce small bursts of fierce gaiety for Kate, or for Vivien, but she had no faith in them. Any more, really, than she had in the prospect of her family turning to her with relief and delight as the organizer of a happy, conventional family party to see their mother's first night.

She turned her phone off with a sigh, and dropped it back into her bag. It was better, she had learned in the last few months, not to be distracted by waiting for messages that never came. She could also tell herself, unconvincingly, that she was obeying office rules. She got to her feet. Rather to her manager's surprise, she would also perhaps obey another rule, and return to work ten minutes before the end of her lunch break, rather than five minutes after it. And she would apply herself to invoicing all afternoon and, at the end of it, if she hadn't heard from her brothers, she would ring them and establish herself as the prime mover in the suggestion that could only be applauded.

"Is this a bad moment?" Vivien said, into the telephone.

There was silence on the other end.

Then Edie said, "When have you ever considered such a thing?"

"Well, I thought you might have been rehearsing –"

"I have."

"And be tired –"

"I am."

"Well," Vivien said, "maybe I could ring a bit later."

"Where are you?"

"I'm at home," Vivien said, "in my hall, speaking on my landline telephone, sitting on the chair next to my telephone table."

"You sound really peculiar."

Vivien craned up so that she could see herself in the mirror on the opposite wall. She touched the back of her hair.

"I don't look it."

"Oh good. I look like the wrath of God. These last rehearsals are always completely exhausting. One minute you think you've got the play and the next minute you think you've lost it."

"That," Vivien said, "was really why I was ringing."

"My play?"

"Yes. I was thinking of coming for the first night."

There was another silence.

Then Edie said, "What's brought this on?"

"What on –"

"You've never been remotely interested in me and the theater. If I was more into victim-speak, I'd say you've never supported what I do. I suppose it's having Rosa there that makes you feel you've got to show willing."

Vivien said carefully, "Not exactly."

"What then?"

"I wondered," Vivien said, recrossing her legs and turning one foot to appreciate how her instep looked in a higher heel, "I wondered if I could bring Max. I thought Max and I might come together, and maybe bring Rosa."

"You're joking."

Vivien decided to keep her nerve.

"No, not at all. I'd like to come and so would he and we'd like to come together."

"But why?" Edie demanded.

"Why?"

"Max doesn't know a play from a puppet show and this, Vivi, is *Ibsen*."

Vivien leaned forward.

"This is different."

"What is?"

"Max. Max and me. It's all going to be different."

"Oh God," Edie said in a resigned voice.

"I want to reintroduce Max to everyone. I want you to stop sniping at him and give him a chance, and I want to remind him that I have a very interesting family."

There was a snort from Edie's end of the telephone.

"Russell, at least, has always been very civil to him."

"*Civil*," Edie said. "What kind of word is that?"

"I don't know why you're being so dismissive. We're not divorced, you know. He's still my husband. You've known him for twenty-five years."

"Exactly."

"All I want," Vivien said, threading a pencil into the coil

of the telephone cable, "is to be able to bring my husband to watch my sister as a leading lady next Tuesday in the company of my brother-in-law and my niece and nephews."

"Oh, all right," Edie said, "play happy families if you want to."

"You are so ungracious –"

"Not ungracious," Edie said, "just realistic."

"Edie," Vivien said, "this feels very real to me."

There was a further pause, and then Edie said, in an altered tone, "Are you sure?"

"About Max?"

"Yes."

"Yes," Vivien said, "I'm quite sure. He's never talked to me the way he's talked recently. He wants to do things my way, he wants to join my life, if I'll let him, rather than try to make me join his, the way he used to."

"So no more girls and flash cars and daring you to do things you don't want to do?"

"No," Vivien said.

Edie said, more thoughtfully, "D'you think anyone *can* change that much?"

"Oh yes," Vivien said, "I've changed, after all. I'm much stronger than I used to be."

"Um."

"I've told Max, Edie. I've told him he can only come back if there really is a change, if certain things just never happen again."

"Come back?" Edie said.

"Yes. He's asked to come back. I've made him wait, of course, but I'm going to say yes."

"Vivi," Edie said, her voice sharpening, "is Max suggesting coming back to the cottage?"

"I told you. I said he wanted to join my life, not the other way round, and I don't want to leave the cottage. I like it, and I like Richmond."

"So Max is moving back into your virgin bower –"

"My bedroom. Yes."

"And what happens to Rosa, may I ask?"

Vivien slid the pencil out of the telephone cable and began to draw a huge eye on her telephone pad, in profile, with absurdly lavish lashes.

"Actually, that's a bit difficult –"

"She can't stay there if Max is there!"

"No."

"So you're throwing her out –"

"Well," Vivien said, adding lower lashes to her eye, "I'm going to ask her to find somewhere else. I'm cooking a special supper for her tonight and I'll tell her then. I'm sure she'll understand."

"You are amazing –"

"I mean, she's seen it coming. She's been so sweet, waiting up for me and being so interested."

"Oh, good," Edie said faintly.

"To be honest, I think she's seen it coming."

"Well, not to would be like missing an elephant in your bathroom –"

"She's doing so well," Vivien said, ignoring her sister. "She's working hard and not going out and –"

"That's enough," Edie said. "Rosa is *my* daughter."

"I'll tell her very gently –"

"Frankly," Edie said, "you could do it on your knees, and in a whisper, and it still wouldn't alter the fact that you're telling her to go."

Everyone in the house, Edie was certain, was awake. There had been faint movements from the top floor for hours and, although Russell was very still, beside her, there was a kind of subdued alertness about his stillness that indicated he was not asleep. The clock radio beside their bed showed two-forty-five and the curtains glowed with the half-dark of summer city night-time. Only the cat, in a trim and resolute doughnut at the end of their bed, was asleep. Above and beside her, all the other occupants of the house were as restless as she was.

She turned her head on the pillow and looked at Russell. He was on his side, face turned toward her, eyes closed. His hair, worn rather long as it always had been, and thank goodness it wasn't thinning, was ruffled. He was breathing neatly and evenly through his nose. His mouth was closed. Even in the dim light, Edie could see that really Russell had worn very well, that he hadn't got wizened or paunchy, that he hadn't, despite a considerable nonchalance about looking after himself, let himself go. He looked, lying there, like a real person to Edie, like someone you could trust because what you saw you got. He looked, as a man, as a human being, as far away from Vivien's Max as if he'd come from another planet.

He'd always, in fact, been amused by Max. He'd been much kinder, if Edie was honest with herself, about Vivien's feelings for Max than her sister had ever been able to be. When Max had appeared once in a camel-hair overcoat, Russell had been much more good-natured about it than Edie had been. He let her make jokes about secondhand car dealers but he didn't join in. He was of the opinion that if this liaison had ever made Vivien happy then that was all that was necessary to know. Sometimes Edie had admired this forbearance; sometimes it had driven her nuts.

She reached out a hand and touched one of his.

"Russ."

He didn't open his eyes.

"Mmm," he said.

"Are you awake?"

"Mmm."

"I think the boys are —"

He said, "Nothing to do with us."

"Probably Matt's thinking about Ruth and Lazlo's thinking about Osvald."

"Probably."

She took hold of the hand she had touched.

"Vivien rang today."

"Mmm."

"She's started it all up again with Max."

Russell opened his eyes.

"Has she?"

"Yes. Big time. Dates and flowers and promises it'll all be different."

"Well, perhaps it will."

"You know Max –"

Russell gave a small yawn. He squeezed Edie's hand and then extracted his own and tucked it under his shoulder. He closed his eyes again.

He said, "Maybe he's changed."

"That's what she says."

"Maybe she's right."

"Well, I do hope so," Edie said, "because she's letting him move back in again."

Russell opened one eye.

"Good luck to her."

Edie moved her face an inch or two closer to Russell's.

"She's staying in her cottage. She says that's what she wants. Max is coming to live with her."

"Yes."

"Russell. *Listen.* Vivien's cottage is where Rosa is living. Rosa is living in Vivien's spare bedroom."

Russell opened both eyes and lifted his head from the pillow.

"Oh my God –"

"She's there now," Edie said. "She's had supper with Vivien because Vivien was cooking something special in a really weaselly Vivien-ish way before telling her she was throwing her out."

Russell gave a groan and turned over on to his back. Edie could see that he was staring straight up at the ceiling.

"I just keep thinking about her," Edie said. "I keep

picturing her lying in bed there, with Vivi all excited and starry-eyed through the wall, wondering what on earth she's going to do now, where she's going to go, how she's going to tell us that yet another thing has gone wrong."

Russell said nothing. He lifted an arm to scratch his head briefly, and then he lowered it again.

"Look," Edie said, "I know how you feel. I know it's difficult. I know it isn't what you want. But I can't bear thinking about what Rosa's feeling, I can't bear her thinking she's got nowhere to go. I just can't *bear* it." She paused, and then she said, "I want to make it a bit easier for her. I want to make a move before she feels she has to. I want to tell her she can come home."

CHAPTER THIRTEEN

"One seat in the back row, please," Ruth said, "and as far to one side as possible."

The young man in the box office, who had clearly been surprised to find Ruth waiting when he opened up, said that there were better seats in the center of the back, for the same price.

"I know," Ruth said. She had put on a black canvas bucket hat and sunglasses, and thought, glancing unhappily in the mirror as she left the flat, that she looked like a Japanese tourist. "I'm sure they're better, but the side is where I'd like to sit, please."

The young man sighed, and slid the ticket toward her. Behind him, on the back wall of the little foyer, was a blown-up grainy poster photograph of Edie and Lazlo, in profile, facing each other, and then, superimposed across their torsos, the shadowy faces of the other actors. Cheryl Smith had the looks and the air, Ruth thought, that made other women immediately feel unwomanly.

She picked up the ticket.

"Thank you –"

The young man nodded. This was not the kind of theater where the staff said banal, populist things like, "Enjoy the show." Behind her, other people were beginning to open the glass doors from the street, other people who might at any moment include Edie's family, and therefore Matthew, and although Ruth was there in order to catch sight of Matthew, she was not at all certain that she could handle his catching sight of her. She bent her head so that wings of hair swung forward under the brim of her hat, and went quickly into the auditorium.

It was completely empty. Admittedly, the show wouldn't start for half an hour, but the emptiness made Ruth feel vulnerable. She crept round the back of the stalls and took her seat in the far corner. If Matthew came, he would come with his family, naturally, and they would also, naturally, have seats in the center, toward the front, and Matthew would be preoccupied by being in company, and by his mother's big night, so it would not occur to him to look round the small auditorium and notice that, among the comfortably North London audience, there was a young woman masquerading – badly – as Yoko Ono, who was giving out elaborate signals of wishing strenuously not to be noticed. But if he did look round, and he did notice, there was then the miserable dilemma of how she would react to his reaction. If he didn't realize it was her, how would she feel? If he did realize, and chose to ignore her, how would she feel? If he did realize and didn't ignore her and did say something but not what she was longing to hear, how would she feel? The answer to all three questions was, of course, terrible.

It was no good, she thought, bending her head over the program and staring unseeingly at Edie's theatrical CV, telling herself she shouldn't have come. It wasn't a question of should or shouldn't. It was more a question of desire urgent enough to amount to need. She was sure that just the sight of the back of Matthew's head for two hours, just the knowledge that they were breathing the same air, would replenish the fuel in her emotional tank enough to get her through another few days, another week. To see him, simply to see him, might help reassure her that she had, in truth, done nothing wrong, that she was not the reason for his leaving, that she had not failed in some essential quality of womanliness, of femininity.

"I thought," Laura had e-mailed from Leeds, "that Matthew was always so supportive of your career."

Ruth hadn't replied. She could have said, "He was. He is," but then she could foresee the questions that would follow and she couldn't answer those, not the "But why, then?" questions. If she could, she thought now, scanning rapidly down Edie's numerous minor television appearances, she wouldn't be here now, skulking in the back row of the theater rather than sitting with Matthew's family in the secure, acknowledged place of approved-of girlfriend. She felt a prick of incipient tears. She swallowed. No self-pity, she told herself sternly, no poor little me. You've chosen to come here so you'll have to take the consequences. Whatever they are.

"In the seventeenth century," Russell told Rosa, "there weren't any theatrical foyers. In fact, I don't think there were any before Garrick. The audience came in off the street and made their way through narrow dark tunnels and then, wham, suddenly emerged into the candlelit glory of the auditorium. Can you imagine?"

Rosa wasn't listening. She was distracted by the fact that her Uncle Max had turned up wearing a double-breasted blazer with white jeans, and also that Ben, having said he'd come, and that he'd bring Naomi, was still not there and might have translated into action the doubtfulness in his voice about coming.

"I always liked this theater," Russell said.

He looked round. The auditorium was filling up and across the seats he could see several well-known newspaper theater critics in their usual places, right on the edge, so that they could spring up the moment the curtain came down – or even before – to file their copy. He waved in a general sort of way.

"There's Nathaniel. And Alistair. I wonder how many performances of this they've sat through."

"If Ben doesn't show up, I'll kill him," Rosa said.

"Ben?"

"Yes."

"Ben's coming?"

"Dad," Rosa said, "Mum is his mother too."

Russell waved to someone else.

He said, "So nice of people to come. Halfway to Watford, after all –"

Rosa said suddenly, "That must be Naomi."

Russell turned. Ben, in his beanie hat and a denim jacket, was steering a slender girl with spectacular primrose hair through the door from the foyer. She was wearing a tiny dress with sequinned straps and her legs and shoulders were bare.

"Barbie," Rosa said under her breath.

Russell pushed past her and made his way toward them.

He put a hand on Ben's shoulder.

"Old man –"

Ben looked awkward.

He said, "This is Naomi."

Russell smiled. He took his hand off Ben's shoulder and held it out to Naomi.

"How nice to meet you."

She transferred her doll-sized handbag from one hand to the other, and put the free hand into Russell's.

"Hi there," Naomi said. She gave a tiny smile, revealing gappy white teeth. Her skin was flawless.

"It's nice of you to come," Russell said. "I'm afraid this isn't a very cheerful play."

Ben grunted.

Naomi said, "We go to musicals at Christmas. My mum likes Elaine Paige."

"Fine voice," Russell said. "No singing this evening, though –"

Naomi said coolly, "I wasn't expecting it."

Rosa appeared at Russell's elbow. She loomed over Naomi like a Valkyrie.

"This is Rosa," Ben said, slightly desperately.

Naomi looked her up and down.

"Pleased to meet you."

"Me too," Rosa said. She glanced at Ben. "Glad you made it."

He shrugged.

He said, "Mum called me."

"Mum did? *I* called you."

Ben sighed. He rubbed his hand over his head, pushing his beanie lower over his brows.

He said, "She rang to ask if I minded you having my room."

Naomi was watching Rosa with brown eyes that were extremely sharp, despite their improbable size.

"Well," she said, "Ben doesn't need his bedroom now, does he?"

"Well, no –"

"So you can have it." Naomi looked up at Ben with quiet possessiveness. "Can't she?"

"Sure," Ben said.

Russell made a gesture for them to sit down.

"Five minutes to curtain-up –"

Rosa looked at Naomi.

"Won't you be cold?"

Naomi flicked a glance over Rosa's jacket.

"I don't feel the cold."

"Come on," Russell said, "seats time."

Ben put an arm round Naomi's smooth narrow shoulders.

He said to Rosa, "She can always have my jacket."

Rosa said nothing. She watched them turn away from her, Russell shepherding Naomi down the aisle toward her seat, bending toward her, talking, with Ben following behind with the bewildered air of someone trapped in an environment completely alien to him. Affectation, Rosa thought savagely, absolute affectation, all for Naomi's benefit, parading independence, parading detachment from background, parading the kind of cool anyone with half an eye could see was fake. She saw Matthew – suited, with a tie – half get up from his seat to greet Naomi, and then Max leap up and bend over her hand like some afternoon-television games-show host, and then she saw them all settle down into their seats, all in a row, couple by couple, and then Matthew, in a seat next to Russell, and then a space left for her, at the end, a space with nothing on her other side but more space. Her eyes moved back along the row and rested on Vivien.

"No hurry to go, darling," Vivien had said, putting the largest prawn from the seafood risotto on Rosa's plate, "absolutely no hurry. Max can just wait till you're ready to leave." She'd giggled, and added another mussel to the prawn. "He can wait."

Rosa began to walk slowly down the aisle toward her seat. There had been, really, nothing she could say but yes when Edie rang and said she'd heard about Vivien and Max and of course Rosa could come home, that day, if she needed to. But, if there had been nothing else to say, that didn't mean that she had said yes with any relief, any thankfulness. Being grateful for the offer didn't disguise, for a moment, the fact that the feelings of hopelessness and self-disgust, which she had, strangely, managed to escape from in Vivien's overstuffed spare bedroom, hadn't gone away but had merely been biding their time. I wanted this, she thought, looking at her family. A few months ago, I wanted this, I wanted to go back home. And now I am, all I feel is a failure.

She eased herself into the end seat, next to her father. He was looking straight ahead, at the drawn curtains of the stage, and she could tell, from the look on his face, that he was thinking of nothing but Edie.

Vivien thought that if only Eliot could have been there too – with or without Ro, who was somehow very hard to visualize – she would have been completely happy. As it was, sitting in a darkening theater with Max on one side of her – his pristine white knee lightly touching hers – and Ben on the other, and all the family beyond Ben, including Ben's girlfriend, who looked as if she'd be an excellent test case for Max's avowal of reformation, was a pretty good approximation to complete happiness. She had never, after all, envied Edie her acting talent, she had never wished she was Edie or wanted to live the way Edie did. She was, she told herself, very pleased for Edie that she'd got this part, just as she was very pleased for Edie that she'd managed to fill the house again, and that all the broken bridges were mended, and that she, Vivien, had played a part in sheltering Rosa until Russell came round to seeing that you couldn't turn the poor girl away a second time. In fact, Vivien thought, noticing that she could feel Max's shoulder as well as his knee, it had all turned out really well and everybody had got what they wanted, except that she wished Eliot was not in Australia, but even that was rather more bearable now knowing that Max not only felt the same, but had also suggested that they fly out for Christmas.

"Our son," Max had said, speaking of Eliot, the other day. "Our son."

Vivien smiled in the darkness. The curtains gave a small quiver and parted, slightly unsteadily, to reveal a large garden room with a view of a gloomy fjord visible through the back window. In the doorway to a conservatory beyond stood a working man with, apparently, a club foot. Opposite him, as if preventing him from coming any farther in, was a remarkable-looking girl in a maid's uniform, holding a large garden syringe.

"Good God," Max said, in an audible whisper, "that's never Edie?"

" 'Ah, but you see,' " Edie said, as Mrs. Alving, " 'here he has his mother. He's a dear good boy, and he still has a soft spot for his mother.' "

Matthew shifted a little in his seat. Edie looked impressive really, in a black dress with great full skirts and her hair drawn back under a white lace cap with black ribbons. She looked not just different, but distanced from her everyday self, and her voice was different too, and her gestures, and the way she spaced her words out. He'd seen her act before, of course, but really only on television and not, as far as he could remember, in anything where she wasn't still recognizably his mother. He had wondered how he would feel, seeing her on stage being someone so very separate from her real self, whether he would be excited, or even embarrassed. What he actually felt, sitting there in the dark between his father and his sister, was a surprising degree of interest, an interest that would intensify, he rather thought, when Lazlo made his entrance, when he saw his mother and Lazlo together on stage.

He could feel that Russell, on his left-hand side, was concentrating with the effort you use when you are willing someone to do well. That concentration, he thought, was typical of his father, typically generous, typically reasonable. Russell, after all, had had plenty to resent Edie for in the last few weeks, but for tonight had managed to put all grudges aside in order to focus on this production working, on Edie achieving something that had nothing to do with relationships or family or those tiny but telling shifts in power that meant you could go from light to dark in a matter of hours. One word was all it took, sometimes, one careless word. Or – Matthew tensed a little – the absence of words over a long, fatal period of illusory calm could result in the failure to stop a slide into something that couldn't be rescued by words any more.

He had kept his vow not to contact Ruth. He had joined a new – cheaper – gym near his parents' home and opened a savings account with his bank. Part of him was quite pleased about these manifestations of recovery, but part of him felt that they were pitiful, forlorn little plasters stuck on a still-gaping wound. And yet these efforts had to be maintained, even built on, because there could be no going back, even if he couldn't visualize – and he had tried – a woman who he would simply like to be with as much as he had liked being with Ruth. In the night, when he woke, and remembered everything with a weary renewal of suffering, he missed Ruth's just being there more than any other aspect of their relationship. For several years, after all, he had been wrapped in a companionship he had never had before and had never ceased to marvel at. He could discuss things with Ruth, confide things to Ruth, that it had never occurred to him as possible to articulate, and which were now bottling up again inside him despite his continued attempts to medicate himself by imagining what she might have counseled, how she might have responded.

He gave the briefest glance sideways, at his father. He was completely absorbed in what was going on, on stage, his elbows propped on the seat arms, his hands loosely clasped below his chin. Presumably, over all the decades he'd been married, his father had told his mother all kinds of things he hadn't told anyone else – in fact, didn't need to tell anyone else because he had Edie. Matthew looked back at the stage. Were all men like this? Were all men, if left to themselves, this lonely?

Abruptly on stage, Edie became extraordinarily illuminated. She flung out an arm, gesturing toward the open doorway.

"'Listen,'" she said, her voice full of sudden rapture, "'there's Osvald on the stairs! Now we'll think about nothing but him.'"

And then Lazlo, in a long pale coat, a hat in one hand and a pipe in the other, stepped dreamily onto the stage and the whole theater turned to look at him.

Up in the little balcony – only three rows deep and uncomfortably steeply raked – Kate and Barney Ferguson watched the Boyd family rise for the interval.

"I can't move," Kate said. "It was enough trouble getting me in here and I'm not trying to get out again until the end."

"Oughtn't you to go and see them?"

Kate looked down into the stalls.

"Well, you could find Rosa and ask her to come and see *me*."

Barney stood up.

"Who's the spiv?"

"That," Kate said, "is Rosa's Uncle Max. Married to Edie's sister Vivien, in fuchsia pink." She paused and then she said, "The color Rosa and I have always referred to as menopause pink."

Barney looked down, smiling.

He said tolerantly, "Nasty girls."

"That's us."

He turned in the narrow space between the seats and looked behind him.

"I'll just climb my way out and go and find her."

"Past an ice cream, perhaps?"

He smiled again.

"Not that kind of theater –"

"No," Kate said. "More's the pity."

Barney bent and dropped a kiss on her head.

"I like," he said, "knowing exactly where you are," and then he climbed over the seats behind him and made his way down to the foyer, which doubled as a bar during the interval.

Russell was standing at the bar lining up glasses.

Barney touched his arm.

"Evening, sir."

Russell looked round. He was glowing.

"You must be the last young man on the planet with manners. Isn't she wonderful?"

"Brilliant," Barney said.

"I mean," Russell said, starting to riffle through his wallet for notes, "I knew she could, I knew she had it in her, but she's bringing something else to this. I'm bowled over. And by the boy."

"Not surprised –"

Russell took his hand out of his wallet and gripped Barney's arm.

He said, almost conspiratorially, "Matt was in the Gents just now and overheard a couple of chaps saying there goes the next Hamlet and Gertrude and from his description of them, they're surely –"

"Barney," Rosa said, from behind them.

Barney turned.

He said, "She's wonderful."

Rosa nodded.

She said, "It's given me quite a turn –"

"Ignorant child," Russell said affectionately. He turned back to the bar and began to gather up glasses.

Rosa said, "Where's Kate?"

"Waiting for you. In what passes for the dress circle."

"Lovely of you to come," Russell said, over his shoulder. "Lovely of everyone. Lovely evening. Lovely everything. Wine?"

Rosa took a glass neatly from her father's grip and handed it to Barney.

"I'll go and find Kate."

"She'd like that. She's wedged."

Rosa slipped past him and vanished up the stairs. Barney took a sip of his wine. It tasted like the wine at student parties, the kind they'd bought in plastic bottles with screwtops and amateur labels. It was offering Kate a glass of something much superior that had first induced her to look at him, to see beyond – he hoped – the name and the voice and the manners. And now look at him, married to her, mortgage with her, baby on the way, parents all forgiveness after an educational career in which school reports had struggled to perceive potential. Barney smiled privately into his wine. Nothing except happiness and current idolatry would have induced him to entertain even the thought of going to see an Ibsen play, let alone finding himself rather absorbed in it. Rosa's mama was – well, really rather something.

He raised his eyes and looked across the group. Rosa's brother Matthew – pretty successful, from the cut of his suit – was talking to the kind of girl Barney's father would probably have referred to as a popsie. Barney made his way over to them and stared openly at Naomi. She was like something straight out of a sweetshop.

Matthew stopped what he was saying and said to Naomi, "This is Barney. He's married to my sister's best friend."

Naomi looked at him as one might regard something interesting but irrelevant from another species.

"Pleased to meet you," she said.

"Likewise –"

"Naomi," Matthew said, "is Ben's girlfriend."

"Lucky Ben."

Naomi didn't smile.

She said instead, "Your wife's pregnant, isn't she?"

"How did you know?"

"I listen," Naomi said, "I pay attention. I always did, even at school."

"More than I ever did –"

Matthew cleared his throat.

Barney switched his gaze from Naomi to Matthew and said, "Your mother is amazing."

Matthew nodded.

He looked a little bright-eyed, as if he was feverish. Now that Barney was paying attention, he thought Matthew also looked a bit gaunt, older, somehow.

He smiled and said, "I have to say, I wouldn't exactly have hurried here, without Kate, but I'm awfully glad I did."

"It's brilliant," Naomi said, "brilliant. I'm going to tell my mum. Does he die?"

"God," Barney said, "is this going to be like Shakespeare, stage littered with bodies at the end?"

"I don't know," Matthew said, "I've never seen it before, either. I've never –" He stopped.

"You must be so proud of her," Naomi said. "If that was my mum up there, I'd be so proud."

Matthew nodded.

"I just wish – everyone could see her –"

"*Everyone?*"

"Well," Matthew said, swirling the inch of wine left in his glass round and round, "everyone I know –"

"I'd feel like that," Naomi said. "I'd make them all come. I made Ben come."

Matthew looked sharply at her.

"Did you?"

"Course," she said. "Family is family, isn't it?"

"Yes," Matthew said.

Barney looked at Naomi's shoulders, and the sequins lying over them, like little trails of stars. Then he thought of Kate sitting upstairs with her hands resting on the mound that was their baby because there was nowhere else to put them. Amazing how different women could be, how different they could become, how – differently they could make you feel about them. He swallowed.

He put out a hand and gave Matthew's nearest shoulder a quick cuff.

"Better get back –"

"Okay," Matthew said.

Barney glanced at Naomi.

"Nice to meet you."

She nodded.

"All the best for the baby."

"Yes," Matthew said. "Give my love to Kate. Good of you to come."

Barney put his wineglass down on the nearest surface and made for the stairs. There was a girl standing a little way up them, staring down into the bar, a dark girl in black, with a hat on, and sunglasses. In Barney's father's now collectable vinyl record collection from the sixties, there was, Barney remembered, a 45 rpm record whose cover featured a woman he'd been much struck by, when he was about fourteen, a French woman, all in black, with symmetrically cut black hair and black glasses. Her name was Juliette Greco, and Barney's father, as an undergraduate as he called it, had hitchhiked to Paris to hear her sing live in some dive on the Left Bank. Barney hadn't thought about Juliette Greco for years, but this still, dark girl on the stairs, watching the crowd through the open doorway below her, had just the same cheekbones, just the same air of mystery.

"Penny for them," Barney said cheerfully, as he went up past her, back to Kate.

"I think," Edie said, "I'll just stay down here for a bit."

Russell, filling his nightly glass of water at the sink, turned round.

"Really?"

"Yes," she said, "I'm tired but not tired. I couldn't sleep yet. I'll just stay down here and revel."

Russell turned the tap off.

"Would you like me to stay with you?"

She shook her head.

"Sure?"

"Sure," Edie said.

He came across the room to where she was leaning against the cooker, and bent a little, to look into her face.

"You were quite, quite amazing."

She looked down.

"Thank you."

He put the hand not holding the tumbler under her chin.

"Look at me."

Edie raised her chin an inch.

"You were absolutely wonderful and I am unspeakably proud of you."

She looked at him, saying nothing.

"And I'm really sorry to have been such a grumpy sod about the children coming back and everything."

"Forget it –"

"I loved watching their faces," Russell said. He let go of Edie's chin and straightened up. "I loved seeing all that amazement and awe. If they'd had thought bubbles coming out of their thick heads, they'd have read: " 'This is Mum? My Mum?' ""

Edie laughed.

She said, "They're not thick."

"Only when it comes to seeing you as other than the provider of home comforts. Dear old room service."

"Not just them," Edie said, "guilty of that –"

"I know. I'm sorry. I'm truly sorry about –"

She put a hand up, across his mouth.

"Enough."

He nodded. She took her hand away.

She said, "I'll be twenty minutes. You go up."

He leaned forward and kissed her.

"See you in twenty minutes, fantastic Mrs. Alving."

She smiled.

She said, stretching against the cooker, "You can't imagine how it feels –"

"No," he said, "I can't, quite. But I can see," and then he turned and went humming out of the kitchen and Edie could hear him going up the stairs at a run, the way he had when they first had the house and everything seemed somehow an adventure.

She looked at the clock on the wall above the dresser. Twenty-past one. Arsie was curled up on the nearest kitchen chair, pretending, with great professionalism, that he wasn't waiting to accompany her to bed. She stepped forward and scooped him up into her arms, and went over to unlock the kitchen door to the garden. Arsie stiffened slightly, alert to the awful possibility of spending the night outside, like any other cat.

"Don't worry," Edie said, holding him. "I'm only taking you out for company."

The air outside was cool and sweet. It was only at night, Edie thought, that London somehow relaxed into its past, into the villages and huddles of huts it had once been, into a place that would quietly, un-urgently, outlive all its inhabitants. She walked slowly down the damp dark grass, holding Arsie against her neck and shoulder, admiring the way the white climbing rose whose name she could never remember shone in the gloom with an almost eerie luminousness, as if it had stored up energy in the daylight hours to use when darkness fell. There was a seat at the far end of the garden, beside Russell's shed, a basic wooden playground bench, that they'd ordered from an offer in a Sunday newspaper without realizing that Russell was going to have to assemble it, all one painful weekend, with the instruction sheets laid out on the grass, weighted with stones, and Russell crawling round them, cursing and saying he hadn't got the right screwdriver. Edie sat down on the bench, and settled Arsie, rather tensely, in her lap.

Down the far end of the garden, the house shone like some tableau of domestic contentment. Its black outline stood sharply against the reddish sky, and every single window was lit, oblong after oblong of clean yellow light, with a shape moving here and there, Matt perhaps, Lazlo in Rosa's bedroom, Rosa in Ben's, Russell in the bathroom. To look at that, to look at what she was shortly going to return to, and to remember Freddie Cass's arm briefly round her shoulders a couple of hours ago and his unengaged voice saying clearly in her ear, "Outstanding, Edie. Possibility of West End transfer not a fantasy," gave her a feeling of such hope and such pleasure and such energy that she could only suppose it was triumph.

CHAPTER FOURTEEN

"How would you like," Russell said, "a new computer?"

Maeve didn't look up from her screen.

"I don't care for that kind of joke."

Russell sat on the edge of her desk.

He said, "Haven't you noticed anything different lately?"

"In what way –"

"About me."

She shot him a glance.

"About *you* –"

"Yes."

"Well," Maeve said, taking her hands off the keyboard, "you're in a little earlier."

"Exactly."

"But," Maeve said, "I put that down to sulks. Your house is full again, Edie's making breakfast for the kids, or not making it at all because she's sleeping in a little these days, and you're sulking."

Russell gave a small sigh.

"I was a bit. But I stopped. I stopped when I saw how beautifully the next generation do it."

Maeve typed two words.

"Rosa," she said.

Russell took no notice.

He said, "But I haven't stopped my intention to galvanize myself. Inject some energy into the business. Buy a new computer."

"I may," Maeve said, "be beyond galvanizing. I am fifty-two years old."

"Nothing."

"You get so's you don't want to learn new tricks. You get immune to curiosity. Someone in *Who's Who* some time ago, maybe it was Elspeth Huxley, listed her main hobby as resting. I can identify with that. A new computer doesn't sound very restful."

Russell looked up.

"And perhaps some new paint." He looked down at the carpet. "And a new floor?"

"Stop right there," Maeve said.

Russell got off her desk.

"Perhaps –"

"The voice of good sense."

Russell took a step toward his own office.

"Maeve, even if you won't have a new computer and I never get around to redecoration, I do want to make some changes. I do want to revive a little *vigor* round here."

"Why?"

"Because otherwise," Russell said, "I shall feel everything is going backward."

Maeve said nothing. Russell disappeared into his office and, uncharacteristically, closed the dividing door behind him. Maeve looked at the door in some surprise. Having it closed suddenly made her own room seem much smaller, much more isolated, as if an energy supply had been shut off. After a moment or two she could hear, indistinctly, Russell speaking on the telephone and, even though she couldn't hear what he was saying, she could hear that he was talking animatedly, as if he were urging something, or proposing something. Then he laughed. Maeve looked at her screen. There was half a letter on it, asking why London Energy had abruptly canceled the direct-debit mandate for the firm's electricity bills. Would such a letter be any less tedious to compose or type on a new computer with a flat screen edged in silver? By the same token, was Russell's disappointment in his present personal circumstances going to be mitigated by tricking out his working life with a deliberate renewal of animation and commitment? You could only admire the man for trying, you could only commend him for attempting to fashion something he could live with out of something he really didn't want, but you couldn't let him fool himself, not if you'd worked for Russell as long as Maeve had. She looked again at the closed door. She couldn't – and she wouldn't – let him delude himself that a new computer would change a single thing.

Vivien laid three heavy books of fabric samples out on her white bed. The woman who ran the local interior-design shop had said pointedly that, while it was difficult to advise precisely on the changes Vivien was after without seeing the room, she herself thought that a strong neutral color, such as tobacco or anthracite, often helped to make an all-white room less, well, *bridal*. She suggested plain linen curtains and possibly a valance for the bed, with maybe a dark alpaca throw and a bedside rug with a masculine feel, edged, say, in leather. Vivien opened her mouth to say that she didn't want brown or gray in her bedroom, or a masculine feel for that matter, and then remembered why she was in the shop in the first place, and closed it again.

"It's not that I don't like it," Max had said, lying against a pile of her white broderie anglaise pillows. "It's just that I don't feel very comfortable in it. I feel like the lodger."

Vivien giggled. She was sitting at her dressing table – something she had only acquired after Max's departure – and was watching him watching her in the mirror, like someone in a movie.

"Well, you are."

Max immediately looked dejected.

He said in a small voice, "Am I?"

Vivien considered. She had already persuaded him out of the gold chain round his neck (on the grounds that she hadn't given it to him) and felt that possibly that was sufficient evidence of having the upper hand, for one day.

She smiled at him in the mirror.

"Just teasing."

Max said, "It's a beautiful room, doll. I mean it. You've done it beautifully. It's just that it makes me feel a bit out of place." He grinned at her. "A bit hairy."

She turned slowly on the dressing-table stool and crossed her legs.

"I'm not changing the bed –"

He winked.

"I'm not asking you to."

She waved a hand toward the curtains.

"Maybe those –"

Max looked at the curtains. They were heavy white voile, looped up with white cords. They reminded him of the day his sister got confirmed, and he managed – no, was allowed – to put his hand up the skirt of her friend Sheila's white confirmation dress.

He said, "That'd help, doll."

Vivien stood up. She was wearing satin backless mules he'd bought her and walking in them required concentration.

She said, "What do you suggest instead?"

Max looked at the curtains a bit longer, and then he said, "Velvet would be nice."

"*Velvet!*"

"Yes. Why not?"

"You," Vivien said, "are stuck in the seventies."

"I was young then –"

"I know."

"And in some ways," Max said, transferring his gaze from the curtains to Vivien's feet, "I haven't grown up at all." He grinned again and sat up a little straighter. "Luckily for you."

Now, looking at the blank squares of linen laid out on her bed, Vivien tried to recall the warm feeling of acquiescence that had induced her to think of changing her bedroom. Max hadn't actually called it "our" bedroom but, with his clothes in the cupboards and his aftershave on her bathroom shelf, she knew she had rather conceded exclusive possession. And sometimes – often even – that shared occupancy was wonderful, leaving her with a glow that lasted long enough to enable her to look with pity at women who came into the bookshop to buy novels to beguile solitary evenings. It was extraordinary not to be in that position anymore, the position of buying single salmon steaks and half-bottles of wine and four-roll packs of lavatory paper. But there was also some little reservation too, some small but unmistakable loss of freedom, the freedom to have gauzy white curtains instead of plain dark ones that wouldn't, as Max said while they were taking rather a riotous shower together, make a red-blooded man feel like a fairy.

Vivien turned her back on the fabric samples and went across the landing to her guest room. Even when Rosa occupied it, it felt like Vivien's guest room because although Rosa had a lot of possessions and was hardly tidy, she had managed, all the time she was there, to convey the sense that her living there was impermanent and therefore superficial. Max, however, had colonized the room. He had given up – "I only want to be with you, Vivi" – his large flat in Barnes and, despite the fact that all his furniture and a lot of his possessions had gone into store, he had still managed to arrive at the cottage in Richmond with an astonishing number of things. Vivien's guest room had vanished, almost completely, under piles of boxes and bags, sliding heaps of clothes on hangers, small mountains of shoes and sports kit. Some of it, Vivien thought, was familiar, but much of it, most of it really, was not. She took a little breath. The room now smelled of Max, of his aftershave. Close to her feet was a new tennis racket in a sleek black cover and a pair of tan suede driving loafers with studded backs. Vivien had never seen either of them before. She gave a little shiver of excitement. She had got Max back, certainly, and a lot of him was known of old. But there were other aspects that weren't so known, that were changed, new almost. She glanced down at the driving shoes. They looked Italian. It was, she thought with a little internal skip of pleasure, like having a *lover* in the house.

It had not occurred to Rosa that, in a household of five people, she would ever find herself alone. When pondering the implications of trailing home with all her worldly goods squashed, depressingly, into black bin bags, at the shameful age of twenty-six, she had consoled herself by thinking that there would always, at least, be company. She would not, as she had in the cottage in Richmond, spend evenings on the sofa eating the wrong things out of boredom while watching programs on television she had absolutely no recollection of next day.

Yet here she was, six days into being at home again, mooning round the kitchen by herself on a Tuesday evening, watched by Arsie from his position next to the fruit bowl, with a kind of knowing pity. Edie and Lazlo were at the theater, Russell had gone to a reception somewhere and Matthew was having dinner with a colleague from work. It wasn't simply that they were all out that was upsetting Rosa, but that no one had seemed to notice that she would be on her own. Of course, it wasn't reasonable to expect a family of working adults to behave like a family of school-aged children, but reasonableness, Rosa realized, was not top of her reaction list just now. It would have made all the difference – *all* the difference, she was sure – if Edie had left the briefest of notes about something in the fridge for Rosa's supper, or something she'd noticed that Rosa might like to read or watch. She couldn't help resentfully noticing, either, that Edie rather clucked round the boys at breakfast. Did you have to be a boy, then, to get maternal attention? Was there something extra abject about being a girl who hadn't coped with the outside world? Rosa made an angry lunge for an apple from the fruit bowl, and Arsie followed her movement with disapproval.

What added to the sense of disorientation, she decided, was that the kitchen itself was so very much the same. She could remember that blue paint going up on the walls and Edie madly machining the striped curtains on the kitchen table, so eager to see the effect of them hanging up that she had never finished the hems. The dresser was so much a fixture it had almost grown into the wall behind it, the table and chairs she'd known all her life, also the yellow pottery sugar bowl, the mismatched mugs, the Spanish ceramic jar of wooden spoons, the overzealous toaster, the little red-handled paring knife, which was the only one that really cut anything – oh, it was all so achingly, deeply familiar, but managed, simultaneously, to be disturbingly alien because the life lived in it had changed. Rosa had been away five years, and in five years the kitchen table had stopped being a family altar and reverted to being a kitchen table. This room, this house, this street had stopped, in essence, being her *home*, and turned itself, slightly chillingly, into merely the place where she grew up.

She took her apple and dawdled across the hall to the sitting room. Unlike Vivien, Edie was impervious to crushed cushions, just as she was impervious to piles of old newspapers and magazines. The sitting room looked as if several people had simply walked out and left it at the end of a day. Rosa leaned in the doorway, chewing, and wondered whether anyone would notice if she shook up the sofa cushions and removed discarded papers. If they did they would no doubt tease her and make her cross. If they didn't, she would have done it for nothing and that would equally make her cross. Was it, in any case, her sitting room anymore? If this was now her parents' house, what level of domestic responsibility would constitute interference? You could hardly, after all, as a rent-paying adult, see "helping" your mother the way you had when you were twelve. She and Edie would always be mother and daughter, but the relationship was no longer one of dependency and lunch boxes. Rosa threw her apple core accurately into the wicker wastepaper basket by the fireplace and took her shoulder away from the doorframe. Edie's sitting room was no longer automatically her daughter's affair.

She turned away and began to trudge up the stairs. She had anticipated a small feeling of triumph in occupying Ben's bedroom – the bedroom of the cherished baby, after all, right opposite his parents and significantly larger than either her or Matthew's bedroom on the top floor. But the reality had been rather a disappointment. Ben's room might be larger, but the view wasn't as good as from higher up, and it wasn't as private. The plumbing from the bathroom next door banged and gurgled and the door had a way of swinging quietly open as if she were stealthily being spied on. Also, the décor was dismal and the curtains ran off the rail with alacrity if drawn without the utmost delicacy. Three months ago, Rosa would have shocked herself if she'd confessed to liking the carefully considered feminine comforts of her aunt's spare bedroom, but now, secretly, she thought of them with a certain wistfulness. Ben's bedroom, even overlaid with her colorful and characterful possessions, remained resolutely Ben's bedroom. It wasn't home and it certainly wasn't hers.

She went on slowly up the stairs to the top floor. Matthew's bedroom door was closed. Rosa opened it a little and put her head inside. The room looked much as it had always looked, rather careless and impersonal. Matthew's suits, hanging on an extension rail, attached to his cupboard, looked like dressing-up clothes. There was a towel thrown over a chair back and an American thriller by his bed. Rosa closed the door again. Poor Matthew, poor Matt. She put her forehead against the door. The room had reeked of stoicism, of someone bearing something painful and inevitable. It had seemed to Rosa more like a cell than a room.

Lazlo's door was half open. Rosa gave the door a push and looked in. Then she moved forward, stepping across a new rug on the floor, noticing a *Ghosts* poster on the wall and a copy of Samuel Beckett's *Endgame* on the chest where she'd kept her china-shoe collection. Lazlo, she decided, was very tidy. The tracksuit on his chair was folded, the boots on the floor in a pair, the rug on his bed straight. Rosa went over to the *Ghosts* poster pinned to the wall and examined it. It was strange to see her mother photographed by someone who didn't see her as a mother, didn't know her as a person. The portrayal of Edie as Mrs. Alving gave Rosa a queer little rush of possessiveness, a desire to say loudly to all those people who simply saw her as an actress giving a fine performance, "Excuse me, but this is *my mother*." She wasn't used to feeling like this, it wasn't what she expected to feel, it was, in fact, as unbidden a feeling as the one of pure admiration that had overcome her when she saw Lazlo on stage, when she saw the way he and Edie could make her, for a while, utterly believe in something that bore no relation to the people they were in real life. Looking at their two profiles now, pinned up on the wall by Lazlo's bed so that she could get close enough to touch their faces with her own face if she chose, Rosa felt herself consumed by a desire to be part of whatever it was they had, whatever it was they could make between them.

She turned sideways and looked down at the bed. Then she bent and put a hand on it. His bed. *Her* bed. She stood on one leg and then the other and pushed her shoes off. Then she sat down on the side of the bed. It yielded just as it always had, just as she expected it to. She swung her legs up sideways and lowered her head carefully onto the pillow.

"Goldilocks," Rosa said, with a giggle, to the empty room.

*   *   *

218

Naomi said she didn't want a curry. It then transpired that she didn't want a pizza either, or pasta. Or Chinese. By then they were, for some reason, standing outside Walthamstow Town Hall, and Naomi was facing away from Ben, and staring at the fountain in front of it as if it was as absorbing as a television.

"What then," Ben said. He had his hand in his pockets.

Naomi raised her eyes from the fountain and gazed instead at the door to the Assembly Hall.

"I'm not really hungry."

Ben sighed. The quotation chiseled into the stone over the Assembly Hall door read: "Fellowship is life and lack of fellowship is death."

He said, "You mean you're pissed off with me."

Naomi didn't move.

"Course I am. Upsetting my mum like that."

Ben waited a moment, and then he said, "I didn't upset her. I didn't say anything to her. It was you that upset her."

"I had to tell her," Naomi said, "didn't I?"

Ben said nothing.

"I had to tell her you wanted me to move into a flat with you, didn't I?"

"But you hadn't said yes –"

"I had to tell her I was thinking about it. I had to." She gave Ben a brief, withering glance. "I tell her everything."

Ben gave a gusty sigh.

"You'll have to move out one day."

"Why?"

"Well, no one lives with their parents forever. They can't. It isn't normal."

"Are you," Naomi said sharply, "calling my mum and me not normal?"

"No, of course not, but you'll get married one day –"

"Not to *you*."

"And you'll want a gaff of your own. Everyone does. I do. I want a place with you."

Naomi lifted one bare arm and inspected its immaculate surface.

"I can't leave her."

"What, never?"

"Since Dad went off, it's just been me and her. We've done fine."

"I know."

"We've done fine having you there. She's done a lot for you. She's made you welcome."

Ben said, slightly shamefacedly, "I know."

"It's not like your family –"

"I know."

"We haven't got all that money, a big house –"

"I know."

"I'm all she's got, Ben."

Ben took off his beanie and scratched his head.

He said, "Don't you want to live with me?"

She gave a tiny shrug.

"Don't know."

He said, with some energy, "I thought you liked me."

"I do."

"Well, then."

Naomi put her arm down again and turned to face him for the first time.

"Liking someone isn't the same as living with them. I've never lived with anyone except Mum. How do I know what it'll be like, living with you?"

Ben opened his mouth to say, cheekily, "Suck it and see," and thought instantly better of it.

He said instead, "Come on, Naomi, you know what I'm like."

"I know what you're like in my place. I don't know what you'd be like in our own, without Mum there."

He gave an exasperated little laugh.

"Well, how will you ever know if you won't even try?"

"I haven't said I won't try –"

"Well, you haven't said you will."

Naomi looked down at her white miniskirt, at the toes of her sharp white shoes.

She said, "Why can't we go on as we are?"

"Because –"

"Well?"

"Because I'm getting a bit – cramped in there."

"Cramped?"

Ben rolled his beanie into a tube and beat lightly against his chest with it.

"I need – to live without parents. Without anyone's parents."

Naomi put her chin up.

"Mum's my best friend."

"She's still your mum."

Naomi suddenly looked acutely miserable.

"I can't imagine being without her –"

Ben said slowly, "Could you imagine being without me?"

She stared at him.

"What d'you mean?"

"I mean," he said, "that if you can't leave your mum, and I can't stay at yours anymore, would you choose your mum?"

"You're a bastard," Naomi said.

"No, I –"

"You're a selfish bastard. You're a typical man, selfish bastard –"

He took a step forward and put his arms round her.

She put her own arms up, elbows against his chest, and held him off.

"Get off me –"

"I didn't mean it," Ben said.

"Get off!"

"I didn't mean it. I shouldn't have said that. I shouldn't have asked you to choose –"

She relaxed a fraction.

"I'm sorry," Ben said.

She tipped her smooth fair head against him.

"I'm sorry," Ben said again. "It's only because I like you. It's only because I want to be alone with you."

Naomi snuffled faintly against his T-shirt.

"It's got nothing to do with not liking your mum –"

"Okay."

Ben bent his head so that he could see part of her profile. He said, "I expect I'm a bit jealous."

"Okay."

"I'm sorry I started this."

Naomi looked up. Ben looked at her mouth.

She said in a whisper, "I don't know what I'll do about Mum –"

He tightened his hold.

"Nothing for now."

"She'll go spare –"

Ben looked up and across the road. A burger van was trundling slowly along Forest Road toward the turning to Shernhall Street.

He said, looking after it, "Hungry?"

Naomi sighed.

"Starving."

"Burger then?"

She stirred in his arms, then began to straighten her clothes. He watched her brush imaginary specks off her tight little T-shirt.

"No," Naomi said, "I'd really fancy a curry."

It had been a bad audience. From the moment she stepped on stage, Edie could tell that the audience was going to be unhelpful, was going to hold itself at a distance and need to be wooed. By the end of the first act, she'd decided that it was not just unhelpful but obnoxious, laughing in all the wrong places, rustling and coughing. She'd wanted to lean over the footlights and suggest they all took themselves off to a nice easy musical instead.

"It's just as well," she said to Lazlo on the journey home, "that audiences don't know the power they have. I was rubbish tonight because *they* were rubbish."

Lazlo didn't argue. He sat hunched on the night bus beside her and stared at the painted metal ceiling.

"Are you tired?"

He nodded.

"That's what a bad audience does. Exhausts you, damn them, and all for nothing."

When they reached the house, Lazlo didn't go upstairs, as he often did, but trailed into the kitchen behind her and leaned against the cupboards.

There was a note from Russell on the table.

"Bed. Fuddled."

Edie gave a little exclamation and dropped the note in the bin. She went over to the sink to fill the kettle.

"Tea?"

"Actually," Lazlo said, "I'm a bit hungry."

There was a beat, and then Edie said, "You know where the bread bin is."

"Yes," Lazlo said. "Sorry."

"Bread in the bin, eggs in the fridge, fruit in the bowl."

"Yes," Lazlo said.

She turned to look at him over her shoulder.

"Well?"

He said sheepishly, "I don't know how to turn the cooker on."

"Goddamnit," Edie said, hunched theatrically over the kettle.

"Sorry –"

She turned round.

"*Can* you scramble eggs?"

"Sort of –"

She regarded him for a moment.

Then she said, sighing, "Well, I suppose there's nobody to blame but myself." She looked round the kitchen and waved an arm expansively. "Nobody's cleared up in here, I shouldn't think anybody's straightened the sitting room, I expect everybody has rolled upstairs and into bed –"

"Look," Lazlo said, "I'll just have bread and cheese."

Edie rubbed her eyes.

"I shouldn't take a bad evening out on you."

"I don't mind –"

"It's just," she said, looking round, "that there seems to be more of everything than there was. More of everyone. And less of me."

Lazlo began to move toward the fridge.

"Would you like a sandwich?"

"No thanks."

"I'll make a sandwich," Lazlo said, "and take it up to my room."

Edie waited for her customary sandwich-making impulse to take over. It didn't. She thought of Russell asleep upstairs, of Matthew, of Rosa in Ben's room with the door slightly, disconcertingly, open. All these images were, for some reason, only irritating.

She shook her head.

"Sorry, Lazlo. I've been really wrong-footed this evening."

He was laying slices of white bread out on the table in a long, even line.

He said, "It doesn't matter. They were horrible."

Edie moved two steps to give his shoulder a pat.

"I'm going to watch television. Add rubbish to rubbish."

"Okay –"

"Can you turn the lights out?"

"Of course."

"Sorry," Edie said again. Lazlo began to slice cheese. "Night, night."

He didn't look up.

"Night," he said.

Lazlo piled his sandwiches on a plate, filled a glass with milk, selected a banana and put it in his pocket. Then he dusted the crumbs off the table, put his spreading knife in the sink and looked around him. There were a number of things lying around that, had they been his, he would have arranged and ordered, but they were not his, they were Edie's and Russell's, and thus must be respectfully left where they were. As far as Lazlo could see, the first rule of etiquette about living in someone else's house was to live in it as tracklessly as possible. Gratitude expressed in improvements, however minor, could so easily be interpreted as criticism.

Lazlo turned out the kitchen lights and carried his plate and glass across the hall. Edie had not closed the sitting-room door, and he could hear the squawk of the television. Arsie was sitting on the stairs, waiting for Edie. He did not acknowledge Lazlo, by the merest flicker, as he went past. The first-floor landing was in dimness. Russell and Edie's bedroom door closed, Rosa's slightly ajar, giving on to a deeper darkness. Lazlo didn't even glance toward that blackness, didn't let his imagination stray for one second to the image of Rosa lying asleep eight feet away, her red hair tossed on the pillow.

Matthew had, as usual, considerately left the light on, on the top landing. Lazlo stopped at the foot of the stairs, put down his plate and glass, and took his boots off, setting them to one side of the bottom step. Then he picked up his plate and glass again and went silently up the stairs in his socks. Matthew's door, also as usual, was closed. His was open. He bent, in the doorway, to set his glass down and free up one hand for the light switch and, as he stooped, he caught sight of something unusual about his bed. He put the sandwiches down too, and tiptoed a little closer. Rosa, fully dressed in jeans and a T-shirt, which had ridden up to expose a few inches of pale skin, was lying on his bed, on her back, fast asleep.

Lazlo moved quietly over to the wooden chair in the corner where he had hung his bath towel, lifted the towel up, and carried it across to drape carefully down Rosa's torso. She didn't stir. Then Lazlo stepped elaborately back across the carpet to where he had left his supper, and transferred it to a spot beside the small armchair, close to the head of the bed. He returned to the door to close it until only a narrow line of light fell into the room, and then he sat down in the chair, next to the sleeping Rosa, and began, as noiselessly as possible, to eat.

CHAPTER FIFTEEN

B arney's parents sent so many lilies to the hospital after their grandson was born that Kate had to ask the nurse on duty to put them outside the door.

"I can't breathe with them in here –"

The nurse, who came from Belfast, said she quite agreed and anyway they reminded her of funerals.

"People get so overexcited about a baby. They just want to send the biggest thing they can find."

Kate leaned cautiously sideways – they'd given her a rubber ring to sit on, to ease the discomfort of the stitches – and peered into the Perspex crib moored beside her bed. The baby, swaddled as neatly and tightly as a chrysalis, slept with newborn absorption.

"I'm pretty overexcited myself."

The nurse paused, holding the lilies.

"You've every right to be. That's a lovely baby."

"I'm in love," Kate said, "I know I am. I've never felt like this before in my life."

"Give me babies for love anytime," the nurse said. "Babies don't let you down. *And* you know they're going to get smarter."

"You are amazing," Kate said to the baby. "You are the most amazing baby there ever was."

He slept on, wholly committed to his own fierce agenda of survival.

"Well," the nurse said, "I think you've a visitor."

Kate turned awkwardly and looked over her shoulder. Rosa was standing in the doorway, holding a pineapple.

She gestured at the great vase of lilies in the nurse's hands.

"I thought you might have enough of those –"

Kate abruptly felt rather tearful. She put an unsteady hand out.

"Rose –"

Rosa put the pineapple down on the end of Kate's bed.

"They're supposed to symbolize hospitality. So I thought that might stretch to welcome."

"Oh Rose," Kate said, sniffing, "he's so perfect –"

Rosa bent and kissed Kate. Then she moved round the bed and bent over the crib.

"Oh my God," she said, "he is *minute*."

"No he's not, he's huge. He was almost eight pounds."

Rosa flicked her a glance.

"You poor girl. You don't weigh much more yourself."

Kate put a finger out and touched the damp dark spikes of the baby's hair.

"Isn't he wonderful?"

"Yes."

"I can't believe it. When I'm not sniveling, I just hang over him and breathe him in."

Rosa reached down to touch his solid little mound of body.

"Does he cry?"

"Like anything," Kate said proudly.

"And – um, feeding him?"

"Getting better. It's not very easy but I am so determined to do it."

Rosa straightened up.

She said, "This is all a bit life-changing, isn't it?"

"Telling me."

"One minute you're a couple pleasing yourselves and the next minute –"

"Eleven hours, actually."

"Everything's changed for ever."

Kate was still gazing at the baby.

"I can't believe he wasn't ever not here."

"Is Barney moonstruck?"

"Completely," Kate said. "Bought me a ring –"

"A ring?"

"An eternity ring."

"Heavens," Rosa said, "how very – established." She sat down on the edge of Kate's bed and looked at her. "Are you okay?"

Kate pushed her hair behind one ear.

"Apart from crying and worrying about feeding and being in agony in the sitting department, I am ecstatic, thank you."

Rosa said seriously, "He's very lovely, you know."

Kate began to cry in earnest. She hunted about blindly behind her for a tissue.

"Here," Rosa said, holding one out.

"Sorry –"

"What d'you mean, *sorry*?"

"All this crying –"

"I thought you were supposed to cry."

Kate blew her nose.

"Talk to me."

"What about?"

"About the outside world. About something not to do with the baby, something that won't make me cry."

Rosa looked back at the baby.

"I thought one of the best things about a baby was that you didn't have to think about the outside world."

Kate blew again. She gave Rosa a nudge through the bedclothes.

"Do as you're told."

"Well," Rosa said, "Vivien and Max are playing *Blind Date* – she has very blonde new highlights – Dad has discovered work and I am – oh God, Kate, something so funny!"

Kate bent back toward the baby.

"What?"

"I went to sleep on Lazlo's bed."

Kate's head whipped round.

"You *what*?"

"Well, the house was empty and it is my bedroom after all, and I just lay on my bed for a second and next thing I knew it was three in the morning and I was still there and he was asleep beside me on the floor."

Kate sat bolt upright and winced.

"Ow. *Ow*! What did you *do*?"

"Got up," Rosa said, "really stealthily. He'd put a towel over me –"

"That was so sweet –"

"So I put it over him and tiptoed downstairs."

"And next morning?"

Rosa looked away.

She said, "I haven't seen him since."

"Have you told your mother?"

Rosa turned her head back.

"No. I haven't told anyone. Why should I?"

Kate screwed her tissue up and put it on her bedside locker.

"When you do see Lazlo again, what will you say?"

"Oh," Rosa said grandly, "I'll say don't get any ideas. What else would I say?"

Lazlo was in the bathroom. He had been in the bathroom, Matthew calculated, for twenty-eight minutes. What any man could find to do in a bathroom for twenty-eight minutes was beyond Matthew, especially a man whose life seemed dedicated, in a manner that was unfairly but unquestionably irritating, to being no trouble to anyone. If he was ill, there was a perfectly good second lavatory downstairs. If he was poncing himself up, he could do that all day while Matthew was at work and he, Lazlo, was doing whatever actors did or didn't do while waiting to go to work.

Matthew bent his head toward the hinge of the bathroom door. Silence. He raised his fist and thumped the panels.

"Hey there!"

There was a pause, and then a slight scuffle and then Lazlo opened the door. He was fully dressed and his eyes looked pink.

He said at once, "Sorry."

"You Okay?"

Lazlo nodded. He stepped aside so that Matthew could go past him. He didn't even seem to be holding a towel.

Matthew wondered, fleetingly and awkwardly, if he'd been crying.

He said gruffly, "Got to get to work –"

"Yes," Lazlo said, "of course."

He moved away from Matthew across the landing toward the stairs.

Matthew looked after him.

He called, "No big deal, you know!"

Lazlo turned briefly and gave a wan smile. Then he began to climb the stairs to the top floor. Matthew shut the bathroom door and locked it. Someone – Rosa probably – had left a towel on the floor and there were red hairs – Rosa definitely – plastered to the side of the basin. The shelf above the basin and the ledge around the bath were now crammed with bottles, so crammed that several had fallen into the bath and were lying there in the shallow pool of water left by the last person's shower. The shower curtain – was this the last bathroom in civilization to have a horrible plastic shower curtain still? – clung to the tiled wall in clammy folds, and the plug to the basin, which Matthew had attached to its chain a dozen times since returning home, had become detached again and was lying in the soap dish.

Matthew took off his bathrobe and attempted to hang it behind the door. The hook on the door, never large enough, now bore his father's bathrobe, his mother's cotton kimono – that must be fifteen or twenty years old now – some peculiar oriental garment of Rosa's and a large towel mounded on top. The cork-seated chair in the corner was piled with clean but unironed laundry, several newspapers and a telephone directory. The towel rail, never adequate for a family of five in the first place, was draped with a large, drying duvet cover.

Matthew let out an exasperated breath.

"Nowhere in this whole bloody house even to put down a *towel*."

He dropped his robe and towel on the floor and yanked the shower curtain rattling along the length of the bath. It was patterned with starfish. It had always been patterned with starfish but for some reason this morning, the starfish looked completely unbearable. He leaned down, turned the bath taps on and pressed the chrome button that would divert the water through the showerhead. The button sprang out again and ice-cold water deluged Matthew's feet. He swore and pressed again and ice-cold water cascaded on to his back.

Someone thumped on the door.

"Sod off!" Matthew shouted.

"I need a shower," Edie called.

Matthew turned the taps off and climbed out of the bath.

"There's no hot water –"

"Nonsense."

Matthew bent and retrieved his towel. He wound it round his waist and unlocked the door. Edie was standing outside in her nightgown and a long purple cardigan.

He said distinctly, "There is no hot water."

Edie looked at his towel.

"Why all this modesty? I'm your mother, for goodness sake. I've seen it all before, I've –"

"I can't have a shower," Matthew said. "You can't have a shower. No one can, unless they want it stone cold."

Edie pushed the sleeves of her cardigan up.

"Who's taken all the water?"

"I don't know," Matthew said. "Dad, Rosa, Lazlo –"

Edie peered past Matthew into the bathroom.

"Look at the state of it –"

"Yes."

"It's like living in a student flat."

Matthew said nothing. He was aware, suddenly, of how uncomfortable he was, standing there in nothing but a bath towel with his mother three feet away in nothing but a nightie.

He said, "Doesn't matter. I'll get a shower at the gym."

Edie stared at him.

"Why?"

"Because I want a shower and there's no hot water here and there is there."

Edie said loudly, "Are you intending to leave this bathroom looking like this?"

Matthew hesitated, then he said childishly, "It's not my mess."

"Really?"

"I keep all my things in my bedroom –"

"But you *use* the bathroom –"

"Of course."

"You all *use* the bathroom. But none of you seems prepared to pick up so much as a sock."

Matthew wondered if Lazlo could hear them.

"I pick up my socks, Mum. I'm sure Lazlo picks up his."

"Don't be so *idiotically* literal," Edie said crossly.

"Then don't be unfair."

"Unfair?"

"Yes," Matthew said.

Edie wrapped the edges of her cardigan tightly around her and took a step toward him.

"Matthew," she said, "I am working, in case it's escaped your notice. I am working six nights and two afternoons a week. If this play transfers, I shall be working like that for months. I am also, for some reason, expected to shop and cook and clean for five adults, never mind the laundry.

233

How dare you suggest that lending a hand isn't your responsibility?"

Matthew said, "It isn't like it used to be."

"What isn't?"

"Living here. Living as a family."

"Well of course it isn't," Edie said. "You're twice the size and paying taxes."

"Exactly."

"Exactly what?"

"Mum," Matthew said patiently, "we're paying to live here."

There was a short pause.

Then Edie said with incredulity, "You mean that absolves you from being obliged to contribute *any*thing except money?"

"No."

"What then?"

Matthew said desperately, "Oh get a *cleaner*, then. Get someone to do the ironing. Get the hot water fixed. Stop – stop being such a *martyr*."

Edie watched him for a moment.

Then she said sharply, "Go to your gym, then."

"It isn't easy," Matthew said. "None of this is. It isn't easy for anyone. We're all too old to live like this."

"Only if you want it to be like a five-star hotel."

Matthew looked back at the bathroom. His robe was still lying on the floor. He felt a wave of rage and hopelessness flood through him.

"I wish," he said bitterly.

Ruth chose a French sleep suit for Kate's baby. It was the only one she could find that wasn't an unsuitable color for a baby and that didn't have a plasticized cartoon character stuck to the front. Instead, it was white, with a small bear outlined in gray, positioned where a breast pocket might have been, crowned with a delicate galaxy of stars. She took a long time choosing it, mooning along a rack of tiny socks and garments labeled "0–3 *mois*" in a daze.

In addition to the sleep suit, she bought Kate a bottle of bath oil and a candle in a glass tumbler. She had seen in a magazine at the hairdresser's a photograph of a mother and a baby in a candlelit bath together, both, naturally, extremely beautiful and deeply contented, and the image had struck Ruth as so completely desirable that it had made her want to cry. She had taken all the presents back to her flat and wrapped them in tissue and ribbons with elaborate care and then sat looking at the package and wondering if she was, in fact, overdoing it for someone she knew as little as she knew Kate. The answer was that yes, she probably was overdoing it but the need to overdo it overshadowed even the possibility of embarrassment. The package sat on the table by the window of her sitting room for almost a week before she had the courage to take it to the hospital and, when she did finally get there, she was told that Mrs. Ferguson and the baby had gone home three days ago and hadn't the family let her know?

Ruth took the package back to her office and sat it on her desk where she could see it. It felt extremely important that she should get it to Kate, extremely important that she should see Kate, but she – she who was all boldness in her professional life – felt a disconcerting diffidence about telephoning. Supposing Kate was feeding the baby? Supposing Kate didn't immediately recognize her voice and said, "Oh – Ruth!" in that tone of voice people use when they are recovering their social balance? She looked at the baby package again. Then she looked back at her screen which, among all the work e-mails, showed three unanswered ones from Laura in Leeds. She hadn't even opened them. They would, she suspected, be about weddings and washing machines and she felt no desire to hear anything about either. She took a deep breath and dialed Kate's number.

It rang and rang and just as she was about to ring off Kate said breathlessly, "Hello?"

"Kate –"

"Yes."

"It's – Ruth."

There was a fraction of a pause.

Then Kate said, "Oh – Ruth!"

Ruth swallowed.

"Were you feeding the baby?"

"I wouldn't answer the phone if I was doing that," Kate said. "When I'm feeding him, the world goes away. It has to."

"I was wondering –"

"Yes?"

"Could I – could I come and see him?"

"Oh," Kate said, and then, in a different tone, "Of course –"

"If it isn't a bother –"

"No," Kate said, "of course not."

"After work perhaps –"

"Yes," Kate said, "yes. That'd be good. Come after work. What day is it?"

"Thursday."

"Come on Monday," Kate said. "Barney's back early." She paused and then she said, "It's nice of you to ring."

"I wanted to," Ruth said. She looked at the package again. "I really did."

Russell intercepted Rosa on the stairs, her arms full of the sheets she had just stripped from her bed.

"Rose –"

"Yes."

"I wonder," Russell said in the voice of one about to make a philosophical proposition, "if you could take those to the launderette?"

Rosa stared at him.

"What?"

"Well," Russell said, "I think you heard me. In case you didn't, I asked you, sensibly and courteously, if –"

"Dad," Rosa said, "I'm going to put these in the machine myself, and then I'm going to take them out of the machine and put them in the dryer and when they are dry I'm going to take them upstairs again and put them back on my bed so that *no* one but me – I repeat, no one – will be inconvenienced by my washing my sheets."

Russell sighed.

"It isn't that."

"What?" Rosa said again.

"It isn't your self-sufficiency. It's the number of loads going through the machine –"

"But it's Saturday."

"Exactly. Two performances for your mother on a Saturday and everybody's doing their washing and the kitchen is invisible under sheets and shirts."

"So Mum has sent you –"

"No," Russell said, "I just watched her for ten minutes."

"And listened to her –"

"And I thought she could do with a bit of a break on the laundry front at least."

Rosa considered.

"I see."

"Good."

"So have you told Matthew and Lazlo to take their sheets to the launderette too?"

"Unfortunately," Russell said, "Matthew has already put his sheets in, on what I gather is an unacceptably long cycle, and gone out. I am on my way to ask Lazlo the same favor as I'm asking you."

Rosa looked down at the sheets in her arms.

"I'll ask him," she said nonchalantly.

Russell looked relieved.

"Thank you."

"Dad?"

Russell, about to turn to descend the stairs, paused.

"Yes?"

"Why doesn't Mum send all our sheets to the laundry?"

Russell hesitated. For a moment, Rosa thought he was going to say something, but then he simply gave a little shrug and started off downward.

"Just ask her," Rosa called.

Russell reached the foot of the stairs and she heard his feet crossing the hall and then the sound of the sitting-room door being firmly closed. She dropped her sheets on the landing and looked upward. There was no sound from the top floor. She glanced at her watch. Eleven-fifteen. If Lazlo wasn't up he should be: he had a matinee at two-thirty.

She went firmly up the stairs and banged on Lazlo's door.

There was a small silence and then he said, "Yes?"

Rosa opened the door.

"Only me."

Lazlo was sitting in the small armchair, wearing jeans and a black shirt, with a book open on his lap. On the floor beside him was a bowl with a spoon in it and an empty mug.

Rose gestured at the bowl.

"Breakfast?"

Lazlo unfolded himself and stood up.

"I brought it up here –"

"Well," Rose said, "you're absolutely allowed."

"I thought I'd get myself out of the way."

Rosa came farther into the room and sat on the bed. She stretched her arms behind her, and leaned on her hands.

"You're hardly in it –"

Lazlo looked away. He put the book he'd been reading down on the bedside table. It was the Beckett play Rosa had noticed on the chest of drawers.

He said, quite firmly, "I don't know about that."

"What do you mean?"

Lazlo wandered slowly round behind the armchair and leaned his shoulders against the wall. He put his hands into the pockets of his jeans.

"I think it's all too much for your mother. I think it's too much for all of you. I think I'm literally the last straw."

"No, you're not –"

"It's wearing your mother out," Lazlo said. "She should be keeping her energy for acting, not for worrying about whether she's remembered to buy more milk. And I shouldn't be in your room. It's *your* bedroom."

Rosa looked at the ceiling.

"Oh," she said, "that."

Lazlo said nothing.

She turned her head, very slowly, to look at him.

"Why did you cover me up with a towel?"

He shrugged.

He said, without returning her look, "I didn't know what else to do with you."

Rosa gave a little shout of laughter.

She said, "I didn't come up here because I was missing my room. I came up here because it was trespassing. I came up for a bit of mischief."

Lazlo gave a quick smile.

"Really?"

"Really. I was fed up with being alone in the house and I was just prowling about." She sat up straighter and put her hands in her lap. "You're not displacing me. Promise."

He said awkwardly, "It's not just that. It's – well, you're a family –"

"Yes, we are, but we're all in transition, we're all in a rather temporary situation. We're not going to stay like this."

"I could easily go," Lazlo said.

"Where?"

He shrugged.

"I can find a room. I'm always finding rooms."

Rosa stood up.

"Don't go," she said.

He turned his head to look at her.

"I don't want you to go," Rosa said. "I like you being here. Don't go."

From the landing below there was the sound of some disturbance and then Edie's voice came clearly up the stair-well.

"Who left these bloody sheets here? I nearly broke my neck. Rosa? Rosa!"

Rosa put her finger to her lips.

"You'd better go," Lazlo whispered.

She shook her head.

"Rosa!" Edie yelled.

"I'm not going," Rosa whispered, "and nor are you," and then she stepped right up to him and kissed him on the mouth.

"I don't know why she's coming," Kate said irritably to Barney. "Do stop asking. I could hardly tell her not to, could I?"

"I don't know her –"

"Well, I hardly do. But she sounded rather urgent, poor thing, and I –"

"Why poor thing?"

"She is poor thing. Because of Matthew. I expect in her mind she somehow thinks coming to see us and the baby –"

"He's called George."

"I'm not sure about that. I'm not sure about that at *all*. He's just the baby to me because there *is* no other baby as far as I'm concerned so there's no confusion."

Barney pointed to the front of her T-shirt.

"You're leaking."

Kate looked down.

"Sometimes you are so like your father –"

"No I'm not," Barney said. "My father would never have gone shopping for nipple pads and a breast pump like I did. He didn't come near us until we were house-trained. I only said you were leaking in case you wanted to change before Ruth came."

"Or in case you're embarrassed by the contrast between my stained T-shirt and her business suit."

"No," Barney said patiently. "In case you are."

The doorbell rang. Kate began to dab at her chest with a tea towel.

"I'll go," Barney said.

She heard him go down the wooden floor of their small hallway, and then the click of the door being opened.

"Hello!" she heard Barney say, sounding just like his father. "You must be Ruth."

They materialized together in the kitchen doorway, Ruth in a black trouser suit carrying a pale-blue gift bag frothing with ribbons. She put the bag on the kitchen table.

"Hello, Kate."

Kate put the tea towel down.

"Nice of you to come –"

"I just brought you and the baby something –"

"Thank you."

Barney moved behind her and laid the flat of his hand against the fridge door.

"Drink?"

Ruth shook her head. Her hair, Kate observed, was as flawlessly cut as ever.

"Go on," Kate said.

"No. Really no. Thank you. I'd just love a glimpse of the baby, if I could. That's all –"

"He's called George," Barney said, taking a bottle of white wine out of the fridge. "After my father and grandfather."

Kate smiled at Ruth.

"He isn't," she said, "but that needn't trouble you. Come and see him."

"George," Barney said comfortably, pouring wine. "George Barnabas Maxwell Ferguson."

"All his family do that," Kate said. "They all have these great strings of names. Mental."

Ruth shot a glance at Barney. He looked perfectly composed.

He said happily, picking up his wineglass, "He's brilliant. You'll see."

Kate led Ruth across the hallway back towards the front door. The little room beside it was in darkness except for a night-light lamp shaped like a crouched rabbit. The room smelled of something sweet and new and innocent.

"Oh –" Ruth said.

Kate tiptoed across to a handsome cot that stood against the far wall. In it was a carry-cot, and in the carry-cot the baby slept on his side under a blue knitted blanket stitched with letters of the alphabet.

Ruth stooped forward.

"*Oh*," she said again.

"I know," Kate said.

Ruth put her hands on to the rail of the cot and bent down toward the baby.

"He's perfect –"

"Yes," Kate said, "he is." She looked at Ruth's tailored dark shoulders dipping into the cot.

"May I – may I kiss him?"

"Of course," Kate said, surprised. "Go ahead –"

Ruth's sleek dark head went down over the baby's for an instant, and then she raised it, but only a little. Kate looked at her hands on the cot rail. Even in the dimness of the room she could see that her knuckles were white with tension.

"Ruth?"

Ruth's head moved a little, as if she was trying to nod it.

"Ruth, are you okay?"

"Yes," Ruth said. Her voice sounded slightly strangled. "Yes, I'm fine."

She straightened up slowly, and then she put the back of one hand up against one cheekbone and then the other.

Kate peered.

"Ruth, you're not okay, you're crying –"

Ruth shook her head.

"I'm fine, really."

Kate waited.

Ruth looked back into the cot.

"He's so lovely –"

"Ruth –"

Ruth turned and looked straight at Kate. A strand of hair had glued itself lightly to her cheek. She gave Kate a small and hopeless smile.

"I'm pregnant," she said.

CHAPTER SIXTEEN

V ivien had decided that she would treat Edie to lunch. It would be on a Monday or a Friday so as to avoid her bookshop afternoons and Edie's theater ones, and she would take her to the rather nice restaurant in the basement of an upmarket clothes shop in Bond Street where they could, for once, Vivien told Max, lunch together like civilized sisters ought to do.

Max was reading a sports-car magazine.

"Bond Street?"

"Yes," Vivien said. "Bond Street."

Max shook the magazine slightly. He was still, Vivien noticed, wearing a bracelet.

"I don't quite see our Edie in Bond Street. Charlotte Street maybe, or Frith Street. But Bond Street –"

"I like Bond Street," Vivien said.

Max eyed her. She was stretching across the sink to open the window behind it, and he could see every minute contour under her thin white trousers.

"Whatever you say, doll."

When Vivien telephoned Edie later in the day, Edie said, "*Lunch?*" as if she'd never heard of it.

"We ought to catch up," Vivien said. "We ought to have time together to catch up face-to-face instead of always talking on the telephone."

"You're lucky to get that," Edie said. "I've hardly got time to brush my teeth at the moment."

Vivien, admiring the pillar-box-red roses Max had brought her in their tall glass vase on the hall table, said she had booked a table in Bond Street.

"Bond Street!"

"Yes."

"I don't know where that is."

"Edie," Vivien said, "this is my treat so please don't behave like a child."

"Oo-er," Edie said childishly, "I haven't got clothes for *Bond Street*."

Vivien leaned forward and tweaked a rose.

"Twelve-thirty Monday and no excuses."

She put the telephone down and went back into the kitchen. Max was on his mobile when she came in and, when he saw her, he whipped it away from his ear and snapped it shut.

He grinned at her.

"Caught red-handed –"

She affected not to notice.

"Oh yes?"

"A quick call to my bookie," Max said. "Thought I'd get away with it." He put an arm out and patted her bottom. "And I nearly did."

Edie arrived for lunch dressed entirely in black. She touched one earlobe as she sat down.

"Even diamond studs. How Bond Street is that?"

Vivien put her reading glasses on.

"Did Russell give you *diamonds*?"

"No. Cheryl lent them to me. And they're zircons."

"Zircons?"

"Posh glass, I gather." Edie looked round her. "*This* is very posh glass, isn't it?"

"Edie," Vivien said, "please don't play-act all over the place and spoil our lunch."

"I can't actually," Edie said, "I'm too tired."

Vivien looked sympathetic.

"Are you?"

Edie picked up the menu.

"What do you think?"

"I'll only think wrong," Vivien said, "so why don't you tell me?"

Edie said, staring at the menu, "I'm shattered. You'd think five adults living together would lead five fully adult lives."

Vivien said, with a small smile, thinking of Max, "People like to be looked after."

"Including me."

"What about," Vivien said, summoning a waiter, "some ground rules?"

"Like?"

"Like do your own washing, clean your own room –"

Edie put the menu down.

She said tiredly, "It's more than that, really. It's five people wanting five people's separate space."

The waiter paused by their table.

"Two glasses of champagne, please."

"Vivi –"

"Why not?"

Edie looked at her carefully.

"I suppose you do look – happy."

"I am."

"Good," Edie said. "Max behaving –"

"Oh yes."

"You're sure –"

"Flowers," Vivien said. "Treats, naughty shoes."

"Oh Lord."

"It's like being at the beginning again, only it's better because I know what I'm doing this time."

Edie folded her arms.

"Is he staying in?"

"Oh yes," Vivien said. "If we aren't out, it's candles on the kitchen table. Why don't you bring Russell down to supper?"

Edie sighed.

"Because I only have one evening a week free at the moment."

Vivien gave a stifled giggle.

"Oops! Silly me."

Edie said nothing. The waiter came back with two flutes of champagne.

Vivien picked hers up and held it out toward Edie.

"Happy days. Why don't you just throw some of them out?"

Edie stiffened.

"Oh no."

"Why not?"

"I love having them there. I love having the house full again. It's what I wanted."

"Even if it's killing you?"

Edie picked up her own glass and took a tiny swallow.

"It isn't killing me."

"But you said –"

"Oh," Edie said, picking up the menu again and leaning back in her chair, "you know me. Always saying things I don't mean for effect."

Vivien looked at her. Then she looked down at her own menu.

"What about the scallops?" she said.

Because they cost him nothing and simultaneously made him feel he was achieving something, Lazlo had begun taking long walks in the afternoon, accompanied by Russell's copy of *The Blue Guide to London*. He had walked to Noel Road, to look at the house Joe Orton had once lived in, and then to Duncan Terrace to imagine Charles Lamb going in and out with perhaps his sister Mary watching for him from an upstairs window. He had been several times to the Estorick Collection to gaze anxiously at the Italian Futurist paintings and wonder exactly what made them so alarming. He had walked round Aberdeen Park and Highbury Fields, he had looked at churches and chapels and libraries and prisons, he had followed rivers and canals and handsome Georgian and Victorian terraces. And when he returned, after two or three hours of walking and thinking, he was struck both by how glad he was to be home and by how painfully impermanent that home inevitably was.

What was particularly disconcerting about this state of affairs was that his life was, really, going better than it ever had. He might still be on close to Equity minimum wage because *Ghosts* was hardly a lavish production, but he had had excellent notices, two better-known agents were offering their services, and he was, thanks to Edie and her family, living in the least hand-to-mouth circumstances he had known. Even his student debt, incurred in order to go to drama school, was beginning to look less like an unwelcome, unavoidable companion for the next twenty years. Yet an anxiety possessed him about what would happen next, about whatever happened next being sure to be inferior to what was happening now, which made him despair of ever possessing the capacity to appreciate good things when they happened to turn up. He had never been consumed by this disquiet while living in Kilburn. Maybe it was because living in Kilburn, in those particular circumstances, had been so bad that there was comfort to be drawn from being very certain that nothing could ever be worse. And now, living as he was, he could remember and visualize the downward slide back to somewhere like Kilburn very easily, and that prospect could reduce him, to his shame, to clinging to the edge of the basin in Edie's bathroom, as he had the other morning, and panicking at the sight of his own frightened face in the mirror above it. What Matthew must have thought, Lazlo couldn't, and daren't, imagine. He had looked at Lazlo with the sort of look Lazlo remembered the older boys at school giving the younger ones when they hurt themselves playing rugby. Matthew was obviously the sort of guy who knew what to do with his inner demons.

Not knowing what to do with his own was one of the reasons, Lazlo was sure, that he was able to play Osvald. Maybe that was also what made him so certain that if he couldn't be an actor then he couldn't be anything. Freddie Cass had said to him that acting wasn't something you wanted to do, it was something you had to do. Lazlo had been very happy to hear that, had felt a relief and a gratitude at having his own need sanctioned, but it hadn't, oddly, assuaged the feeling of being an outsider in some way, a person who could only fully engage with other people if he was pretending to be someone else.

Which is why it was so very astonishing to have been kissed by Rosa. At first, he had simply thought she was teasing him, that kissing him was just a little more of the mischief that had led her to lie on his bed and fall asleep there. But although she had been flirtatious and light-hearted before she kissed him, she was quite different when she stepped back again. She had looked, fleetingly and amazingly, as if she was dreading that he might laugh at her. She had even almost said sorry.

"Typical Rosa –"

"What?"

She'd looked away, pushing her hair back.

She muttered, "Always blundering in where she's not wanted –"

He'd been in too much of a turmoil even to consider saying, "You are wanted." Anyway, at that moment, would such a statement have been true? Was it true now? What, in fact, did he feel about being kissed by her? What had he felt when he found her lying, quite unselfconsciously, on his bed? He couldn't believe how many walks were occupied in wondering about this. He couldn't believe the miles he seemed able to cover while asking himself if this girl, whom he'd rather dismissed as spoiled and careless and unappreciative of the solid support of her background, was actually and appealingly something of a fellow wanderer.

He'd shaken his head at Rosa. He'd meant her to infer that kissing him wasn't a blunder. She'd put the back of her hand up against her mouth, and then taken it away and said, with a slightly uncertain smile, "Better go and sort the sheet crisis."

He'd nodded. He hadn't moved from where he was standing by the wall. She went over to the door and hesitated for a moment. He waited for her to turn so that he could at least smile at her, but she didn't. She went out of the room and down the stairs to the landing below, and Lazlo heard Edie say, "I wonder, Rosa, if the sheets on the floor could *possibly* be yours?" He waited for Rosa to scream something in reply, but she didn't. Perhaps she was bundling the sheets up in her arms and taking them silently downstairs. Perhaps she had stepped over them and shut herself quietly in her room. Perhaps she was looking at herself in her bedroom mirror and wondering why anyone should want to return her kiss. Lazlo closed his eyes and slumped against the wall. Nil points, he told himself. Nil points to self.

"Look at this diary," Maeve said.

Russell looked up. Maeve was standing in the doorway between their offices holding up the large cloth-bound book she preferred to use instead of anything more up to date.

"You look at it," Russell said in a friendly voice. "It's one of the things I pay you for."

"You are out," Maeve said, in the tone of one reprimanding a student about an overdraft, "every single night this week."

"Yes."

"And last week. And four nights next week."

"Yes. So is Edie."

Maeve slapped her hand against the diary.

"These are invitations you wouldn't have countenanced accepting six months ago."

"Probably not."

"Why," Maeve said, "don't you do something worthwhile, like going to a lecture? Why don't you broaden your horizons?"

Russell reached across his desk for the telephone.

"You mean well," he said, "but I have enough to bear without you adding to it."

"I'm trying to alleviate it –"

Russell was pressing buttons.

"I'm trying," Maeve said, "to *help*."

"Hello?" Russell said into the telephone. "Hello? Russell Boyd here. I was hoping to speak to Gregory –"

Maeve backed out of Russell's office in time to hear the bell to the street door ring. She pressed the intercom, and on the tiny television screen that filmed whoever was standing outside she saw an unpromising-looking boy in a parka with a knitted hat.

"Yes?"

The knitted hat leaned nearer the mouthpiece.

"It's Ben."

"Is it?"

"Yes," Ben said without rancor. "It's me."

"Take your hat off."

Ben pulled off his beanie and pushed his face toward the camera. Maeve pressed the door-release buzzer to let him in. He came up the stairs at a slow and heavy trudge.

Maeve met him in the doorway.

"Sorry, dear. You looked like one of those posters for Brixton Academy."

Ben grinned at her.

"Good."

"I'm afraid your father's on the phone."

Ben shrugged.

"I thought we might go out for a beer –"

"Well," Maeve said, returning briskly behind her desk, "all he ever does at the moment is go out for beers, so I don't see why one of them shouldn't be with you."

"Okay," Ben said amiably. He wandered over to his father's office and gestured through the doorway. Russell waved and motioned to his son to sit down. Ben leaned against the door jamb and folded his arms and looked at all the photographs of Russell's clients slowly and consideringly.

"Come away," Maeve said behind him.

Ben took no notice.

Russell said, "Well, let's be in touch at the end of the week," and put the phone down. Then he looked at Ben. Ben was gazing at the picture of an actress who'd been photographed, for some reason, in a leopard-print fedora.

"Well," Russell said, loudly enough for Maeve to hear him quite clearly, "what brings you here?"

It was early still, so the bar was only occupied by a few people left blurrily over from lunch. Russell put his glass and Ben's beer bottle down on a table below a mirror engraved with art nouveau lilies.

"Is this an emergency?"

"Not really –"

"I mean, no phone call, no warning, you just turn up in the office, which I seem to recall you only ever doing once before when you were out all night after your A levels –"

"I just thought I would," Ben said. "It just occurred to me. Going home would have been such a big deal."

"What do you mean, going home?"

"I mean going to the house would have been such a big deal."

"Six stops down the line –"

Ben sighed.

"Not geography, Dad. Other stuff."

Russell picked up his glass and took a swallow.

"I don't know why it is, but when any of you children come and seek me out I feel instantly defensive. Have you come to tell me that you and Naomi have broken up?"

"Only sort of –"

"What d'you mean, sort of?"

Ben turned his beer bottle round as if he needed to read the label on the back.

"It's just," he said, "that we need a bit of space."

"You *have* broken up."

"No," Ben said patiently, "we haven't. We're going to live together."

"I thought you were living together."

"We're going to live together," Ben said, "in our own place."

"Good for you."

"Yeah. Well."

"So I suppose you need money for a deposit?"

Ben shook his head.

"We haven't found the place yet."

"Ah."

"We can't start looking until things are a bit calmer."

Russell closed his eyes briefly.

"What things?"

Ben said carefully, "Naomi and her mum have never been apart before."

Russell gave Ben a long look.

"I see."

"It might take her a bit of time to come round to the idea."

"Of Naomi leaving to live with you."

"Yeah."

"Sometimes," Russell said, "I get the feeling that I'm living in one of those unfunny family comedy series on television."

"Why?"

"Because you're going to ask me something to which I'm going to say no and I can write the scenario for both speeches in advance –"

"Dad –"

Russell sighed.

"Ask me anyway."

"It's hard for Naomi," Ben said.

"I'm sure it is."

"Her dad walked out years ago and it's just been her and her mum."

"Plus you."

"She's cool with it," Ben said. "It's more me. I want to live like I want to live. It's not her."

"But Naomi can't decide?"

Ben took a mouthful of beer.

"She's decided. It's doing it that's hard. So –" He paused.

"Yes?"

"I thought I'd give her some space. For a while."

"And come home."

"Yes."

"No," Russell said loudly. He looked down at the table. "It's appalling at home, already."

Ben said nothing.

"There are too many people and too much laundry and too many what you would call 'issues,' already. Mum is exhausted. I am – well, never mind what I am. But there is no room for you to come home, Ben, there is no more *energy*."

"I could," Ben said calmly, "sleep on the sofa."

"No!" Russell said, almost shouting. "No! The sofa is the last indoor space left."

"Okay, Dad."

"What?"

"I said," Ben said, just as calmly, "Okay, Dad. It's okay. I won't come home."

"What?"

"I thought it was worth asking. That's all. No big deal. I'll sleep on Andy's floor."

"You can't –"

"Why not?"

"Your mother will never forgive me."

Ben said kindly, "She won't know."

Russell stared at him.

"Won't you go straight to her?"

"No."

"Why not?"

"Why should I?"

"Good Lord," Russell said.

Ben looked at the lilies on the mirror.

"It's not a big deal, Dad."

"I thought it might be."

"Nope."

"But I wish you didn't have to sleep on Andy's floor."

Ben glanced from the lilies to his father.

"Done it before."

"Not for long. Not for possibly weeks."

"Doesn't bother me."

Russell gave a faint groan.

"Ben, I'm so sorry –"

"It's okay."

"No, I'm sorry. I'm really sorry. And I'm wrong, quite wrong. Mum will kill me. I'll kill myself. Have the sodding sofa. *Have* it."

Ben stirred uneasily in his chair.

"It's okay, Dad, honest –"

"No!" Russell said almost shouting again. "I can't turn you away to sleep on the floor, of course I can't. What am I thinking of?" He put a hand out and clasped Ben's arm firmly. "Come home, Ben, and have the sofa."

Ben looked at his father's hand, and then at his face. Then he smiled.

"Cool, Dad," he said.

Rosa telephoned Kate to say that she'd been made employee of the month. Her photograph had been put in a frame on the manager's desk and she had been given a metal badge, like an elaborate medallion on a pin, to wear on her uniform jacket.

"Brilliant!" Kate said. She had the telephone held to one ear and the baby was asleep on her other shoulder. As long as he was on her shoulder, he slept deeply; the moment she transferred him, however gingerly, to the carry-cot, he woke up and cried.

"Thank you," Rosa said.

"Rose," Kate said, summoning all the generous energy she could manage, "this is good! I mean this is progress, real progress. You'll be able to think about your own place again any minute."

There was a beat and then Rosa said, "Oh, I don't think so."

"Why not?"

"Oh," Rosa said again, "you know. The old reason."

"Debt?"

"Mmm."

"D'you mean you're intending to stay at home until you've paid off everything?"

There was another brief pause and then Rosa said, "Not – entirely just that," and then she said quickly, "How's the baby?"

"Asleep. As long as I hold him."

"Goodness –"

"It's amazing the things you can do with one hand. I even put my jeans on this morning, except the zip won't do up. Not by miles."

"Has he got a name yet?"

"No," Kate said, "he's called Baby. Barney calls him George."

"I'll be round soon," Rosa said, "or he'll be old enough for school and I'll have missed him."

"Rosa –"

"What?"

"Nothing," Kate said.

"What nothing? Are you okay?"

"Yes," Kate said, "I'm fine. I'm going to ring off now because my arm is aching. Bye-bye, star saleswoman."

"Bye," Rosa said.

Kate dropped the telephone on to the sofa and collapsed beside it, transferring the baby from her shoulder to her lap. He opened his eyes to check on his surroundings and then, satisfied, closed them again. It was so hard, so abidingly hard not to tell Rosa about Ruth's visit, but Ruth had been so fierce in making Kate promise to tell no one that she had had to agree.

"No one knows," Ruth had said. "No one. Only you. I only told you because you've just had a baby."

"But you must tell Matthew, if, that is, if it's –"

"Of course it's Matthew's," Ruth said, "of course it is. And I will tell him. I will. But nobody must know before he does. Nobody."

"But," Kate said pleadingly, "this is so lonely for you –"

"Yes," Ruth said.

She had left soon after. She had left before Kate could ask her what she planned to do after she had told Matthew, what she was going to do about her flat, her job, her future. She had left as abruptly as she had come, and after she had gone and Barney had said, in some surprise, "What was that all about?" Kate had had to go back and check on the baby as if some disruptive high wind had whirled through the flat and left chaos in its wake.

Very gradually, she eased the baby off her lap and on to the sofa. Then she lay down beside him and put her face as close to his as she could get it.

"You have no idea," she said, her mouth almost touching his cheek, "the difference you've made. You have no idea how hard you've made some things, how you've made me feel, how impossible it is to imagine what it was like before you were here."

The baby yawned in his sleep, unclenching one hand in the process.

"I said I'd go back to work," Kate told him, "I said I would. I want to. I don't want not to. But I can't. I can't do anything but be with you."

She put a finger into the baby's hand. He grasped it, never opening his eyes.

"Just don't grow up," Kate said. "Just don't get any bigger and then we won't have to do any of it. Either of us."

"Goodness," Edie said, "you still up?"

"Obviously," Russell said.

She dropped her bag on the kitchen table and took off her jacket. She didn't look at Russell.

"Good tonight?"

"Yes," she said.

He put his hand on the wine bottle in front of him. "Drink?"

She nodded. She went over to the sink and ran water into a mug and drank it. Then she came back to the table and sat down, at the opposite end to Russell.

He filled the wineglass for her and pushed it a foot along the table.

"Here."

She didn't move.

"Thanks."

"What," Russell said, "is the matter?"

Edie reached for the wineglass, failed to, and sat back.

"I'm just so dog tired."

"Um."

"It was a nice audience," Edie said. "Lovely, really. Not a bad house in numbers terms either. They were paying attention. It was – well, it was me."

"What was?"

"It was me," Edie said, "not paying attention."

Russell got up and moved Edie's wineglass so that she could reach it.

"There."

"Thank you."

"I think," Russell said, "that you know so clearly what

you are doing that, even when you aren't paying attention, it doesn't matter."

Edie sighed.

"It does."

Russell looked round the kitchen.

He said guardedly, "Well, I think you should go straight to bed now, and I'll do whatever needs to be done."

Edie took a gulp of her wine.

"Are they all in?"

"I have no idea."

"I can't go to bed unless they're all in."

"Edie –"

"I can't," Edie said idiotically. "I never could and I never will be able to."

Russell closed his eyes.

He said under his breath, "Mad and untrue."

"What?"

"Nothing."

"Don't *mutter* at me," Edie said. "Don't wait up for me just to *mutter*."

Russell took a breath.

"What needs doing?"

Edie let out a little yelp of sarcastic laughter.

"It would be quicker to make a list of what doesn't need doing –"

"Look," Russell said. "Look. This is worse than when they were at school. This is worse than when they were students. Just stop trying to do everything. Just *stop*. They'll all do more if they only know what you want!"

Edie turned her face aside.

"I can't let them."

"Why not?"

"Because they're poor and broken-hearted and in a mess of one kind or another and it's all my fault."

"Rubbish," Russell said vehemently. "Absolute rubbish

bloody *crap*. You're behaving like this because you need to justify not wanting to let go."

Edie put her face down sideways on the table.

"Give me strength –"

"Me too," Russell said.

Edie sniffed.

Russell ignored her.

She said, not moving from the table, "Why on earth did you stay up if you only want to bawl me out?"

There was a silence. Russell cleared his throat. Edie stared at the cooker and thought how the tiles on the wall behind it needed cleaning.

Then Russell said, "There's something I have to tell you."

CHAPTER SEVENTEEN

"She's in reception," Blaise said to Matthew.

Matthew was looking determinedly at his screen. He didn't reply.

"She's been there since nine."

"I know."

"She says you know she's here."

"Yes."

"Matt," Blaise said, bending down to try and interpose his head between Matthew and the computer screen, "you can't leave her sitting out there. You can't."

Matthew said, "The only way I've been coping with any of this is by not seeing her."

"It's no good, you know, just ducking out –"

Matthew transferred his gaze from the screen to Blaise.

"And d'you know what will happen if I go out to her? She'll ask if we can go and talk and because it'll be a public place and I can't make a scene, I'll say yes, and we'll go and have a coffee or something and then she'll start saying that it can work, that she'll do anything I want and I'll say it's too late, because it is, and then she'll cry and I'll feel a complete bastard and say I have to go and I'll get up and come back here and everything will be even worse, yet again, than if I hadn't gone in the first place."

Blaise straightened up a little. Then he sat on the edge of Matthew's desk and stretched his legs out.

He said, "She says she's just got one thing to tell you and it won't take long."

"It doesn't matter *what* it is –"

Blaise flung his head up and looked at the ceiling.

"Matt, you don't have a choice."

"Oh I do. It's the last thing I do have."

"Whatever you feel about her, you were in a relationship and you do have to listen to her, one more time. It's humiliating for her, sitting out there, with people like me, who knew about the two of you, tramping through. She can't be doing this because she *wants* to."

"Why not?"

"She isn't that kind of girl."

"She's *become* that kind of girl," Matthew said.

"Only because you're treating her like this."

Matthew flung his chair back and shouted, "Oh, for God's sake!"

Several people at nearby desks looked up.

One girl called, "Shut it!"

"Don't *lecture* me," Matthew hissed. "Don't *preach* at me."

Blaise shrugged.

"Leave you to it."

Matthew said nothing.

Blaise went back to his desk.

Matthew raised his eyes to the level of his screen and became aware that some of the people who had looked up when he shouted were still looking, in the unnervingly focused way of people waiting for the next development in a drama. Matthew shot his chair back in toward his desk and leaned to peer at his screen, his hand on the mouse. He counted to fifty and then he got up and walked, as slowly and nonchalantly as he could manage, across the office toward the reception area. He did not glance at Blaise as he passed him.

Ruth, wearing a business suit, was sitting in a black leather armchair, reading a copy of the *Financial Times*. Her hair was pulled back in a spiky knot behind her head and she had on the red-framed reading glasses Matthew remembered her telling him she hardly needed visually but found a useful psychological barrier in some meetings. Matthew paused. Ruth glanced up, on cue, and regarded him over her newspaper.

He walked across and stood awkwardly in front of her. She was wearing a completely inscrutable expression.

He said lamely, "Well, here I am."

She folded the newspaper without any particular hurry and laid it on the glass-topped table beside her. Then she stood up. Matthew suddenly felt a little shaky.

Ruth said, in a voice presumably intended for the receptionist behind her barricade of brushed steel and black acrylic, "This won't take long," then she bent and picked up her handbag and her briefcase.

Matthew put out an automatic hand to help her.

"No, thank you," Ruth said.

She moved past him and began to walk toward the bank of lifts. Her back seemed to Matthew to be emphatically straight. He turned to follow her, and as he did so it came to him, from some weird reservoir of sheer instinct, exactly what it was that she was going to tell him.

The contract cleaning company told Edie that a house the size of hers would occupy four people for a whole day and, if she wanted the windows included, would cost something in the region of three hundred and fifty pounds. Of course, that excluded any cleaning inside cupboards, and if she wanted –

"No, thank you," Edie said.

"Then I assume a basic surface clean –"

"No, thank you."

"Our quotations are extremely competitive –"

"I don't doubt it."

"Mrs. Boyd –"

"Thank you," Edie said loudly, "but no thank you. *No.*"

She threw the telephone into the armchair opposite. Ben had left a bath towel draped over the back of it. The rest of his possessions, including a duvet and a pillow, were piled behind the sofa, where Arsie had immediately found them and made a nest. It was a neat pile but it wasn't, however you looked at it, a small one. The mere knowledge that it was there made Edie feel rather tearful.

It was awful, really, that Ben should be reduced to sleeping on the sofa in the first place. But what was worse was that Edie's own feelings at having him home again were so confused, so unlike the rapture she had anticipated, that she hadn't known who to be furious with first. She had raged at Russell for being Ben's confidant before she was and then at Rosa for being in Ben's bedroom and had only been prevented from turning on Lazlo by Rosa's unexpected and forceful intervention. It had seemed to her, for a few days, intolerable that something she had longed for so intensely should be granted to her in a form that effectively stripped it of all its rightful satisfaction.

"Don't take it out on us!" Rosa had yelled. "Just because you've got what you wanted in the wrong way!"

Lazlo had come to find her in her cupboard of a dressing room, painting on Mrs. Alving's Norwegian pallor.

"I just wanted to say something –"

Edie went on blending makeup down over her jawline. She didn't glance at Lazlo's reflection, standing behind her and looking directly at her in the mirror.

"You know I don't like distracting conversations before a show."

Lazlo said tiredly, "There isn't a perfect moment. This hardly suits me either."

Edie flicked a glance upward. Lazlo's expression was one of weary determination, rather than anxiety.

She said, "So?"

"I'm moving out," Lazlo said. "You've been wonderfully kind and I am truly grateful, but it isn't working anymore."

Edie gave a little gasp and put her makeup stick down. "Please don't."

"If I go," Lazlo said patiently, "Rosa and Ben can have their rooms back. It's what you all need."

Edie swiveled round from the mirror.

"You mustn't."

"Mustn't?"

Edie said unsteadily, "I'd feel such a failure –"

There'd been a small silence and then Lazlo said gently, "I'm afraid I can't help that."

"I wanted it to work," Edie said. "I wanted everyone to feel they had a home." She looked away and then she said sadly, "I wanted to give you all a home."

"You did."

Edie turned back to the mirror and picked up her makeup again.

"But on my terms."

Lazlo said nothing.

"And of course," Edie said, "you're all too old for that. And so am I." She glanced up at Lazlo's reflection. "Please don't go just yet."

He smiled.

He said, "I'll let you know when I've found somewhere," and then he leaned forward and put a hand on Edie's shoulder and said in Osvald Alving's voice, "You've managed without me, Mother, all this time!"

Edie had nodded. She'd put her own hand up to touch his briefly and then he'd gone out of the room and she didn't see him again until they were on stage together, where their familiar dynamic seemed to have transformed itself into something altogether more fragile and fevered.

Now, sitting on the sofa among Ben's possessions, fragile was what Edie chiefly felt, fragile and vulnerable and un-certain.

She looked across at the armchair, where she had flung the telephone. Perhaps she would ring Vivien. Vivien wouldn't be any use of course and naturally Edie wouldn't confide to her the present turmoil of her feelings, but all the same, there seemed to be a most pressing need to talk to someone and, at the very least, Vivien would do.

"Is this too noisy for him?" Rosa said.

Kate peered into the baby car seat she had laid on the empty restaurant chair next to her.

"He's asleep."

"It's terribly clattery –"

"He's got to learn to sleep through it. He's got to learn to sleep through everything I do because he's coming with me everywhere I go. Forever."

"Even back to work?"

Kate closed her eyes briefly.

"Please don't talk about it."

"And you intend him to be the first grown man called Baby?"

Kate picked up a menu and studied it.

"He's called Finlay."

"But you aren't a Scot –"

"Barney is."

"No, he isn't. He's the most blah-blah English –"

"His family is Scottish," Kate said, "and this baby is called Finlay."

"And by Barney?"

"Barney calls him George. He tells everyone he's called George. He told Ruth –"

"Ruth?"

Kate gave a sharp little intake of breath.

Then she said, "What day is it?"

"What does that matter?"

"What day is it?"

"Thursday," Rosa said. "Kate –"

Kate said hurriedly, "That's okay then. She'll have told him by now."

Rosa twitched the menu out of Kate's hands.

"Tell me."

"Guess."

"I don't want to guess. Tell me."

Kate put her hands flat on the table.

"Ruth came to see us last week. To see the baby. Bringing presents and stuff, one of those incredibly expensive baby suits that babies are always immediately sick on –"

"Go *on*."

"And she seemed rather agitated and wound up and she cried when she saw Finlay and I asked her what the matter was and –"

"She's pregnant," Rosa said.

Kate regarded her.

"Yes."

"Why didn't you *tell* me?"

"I couldn't. She made me promise. Until she told Matthew."

"When was she telling Matthew?"

"Early this week."

Rosa looked away.

She said, "I haven't seen Matthew."

"Haven't you?"

"I never do. We live in the same house and, apart from hearing him thumping about over my head, we might as well not be. It's as if we're all steering round each other because if we don't we'll row." She stopped and then she said, in a different voice, "Poor Matt. He's been so down –"

Kate leaned forward.

"What'll this do?"

Rosa swung her head back to look at Kate.

"I don't know."

"Make or break?"

"I don't know."

"You'd think," Kate said, "in this day and age, we could at least get contraception right, wouldn't you? First me, now Ruth –"

Rosa leaned sideways and looked down at the baby.

"Ruth of all people –"

"Yes."

"I wonder if Mum knows?"

"What'll she say?"

Rosa put out a hand and laid it on the baby.

"Can't tell. She's all over the place at the moment. It's – well, it's a nightmare at home at the moment."

"Is it?"

"Yes," Rosa said. She straightened up, and then she said, with a small, private smile, "But rather interesting, too."

Kate waited.

Rosa went on smiling to herself.

Kate said crossly, "Well, go on."

"You can guess."

"Something happening? Between you and Lazlo?"

"Not – exactly."

"Well, then –"

"But," Rosa said, "I'd quite like it to."

"I'm surprised."

"So am I."

"I thought he was geeky."

"He is rather. But –" She stopped.

Kate looked at her.

"I see."

Rosa looked back.

"Kate, what about Matthew?"

"That's all about to be common knowledge, isn't it?"

"D'you know," Rosa said, moving about the knife and fork at her place, "once I'd have hit the telephone. Once I'd have immediately rushed round to Dad's office and rung Mum and texted Ben and generally gone into overdrive. But I don't want to now. I don't remotely feel like it."

"What do you feel then?"

"Sad," Rosa said.

"*Sad?*"

"Yes," Rosa said. She looked down at Finlay again. "Yes. Sad. Sad that if it's a baby, it had to be this way."

"Come *on*," Kate said vehemently. "The baby won't know!"

"No," Rosa said. She picked up the menu again and held it out toward Kate, "But we will. Won't we?"

The afternoon in the bookshop seemed to Vivien to be taking an unusually long time. It was the end of summer after all, so customers weren't coming in for those optimistic stacks of paperbacks to take on holiday but, all the same, the few people who did come in seemed to be passing time rather than buying a book and Vivien watched them with irritation as they drifted idly about, fingering books they would never buy and infecting her with their mild restlessness. She had taken advantage of Alison's absence to straighten things up a bit, sort the slew of scraps of paper by the cash register, realign the table of summer novels, but that was all that was possible really. Alison didn't like her actually doing house-work if she was the only person in the shop: she said it was off-putting for customers to be dusted round, made them feel that they were somehow an intrusion. She liked Vivien, if not actually helping a customer, to sit by the cash register lightly engaged in a task that could obviously be easily set aside. Alison herself was a knitter, great scarves and sweaters in the patterns and colors of the Andes, and she would have preferred Vivien to find herself some equally encouraging-looking, unthreatening occupation. Vivien's propensity for tidying, though undeniably useful, could too easily be inter-preted, by anyone sensitive to atmosphere, as taking pre-cedence over the mild disorder created by the necessary process of commerce.

Vivien had taken up her position next to the rack of birthday cards. These were haphazardly arranged with no particular thought given to sequences of price or size, and it was harmless enough, Vivien thought, to separate the reproductions of Jack Vettriano paintings from black-and-white art photographs of elephants or kittens. The card rack also gave her a good view of the shop, which contained, at that moment, a young mother with a toddler in a buggy looking at board books, and a man in a faded gingham shirt browsing in biography.

It was not the sort of shirt, Vivien reflected, that Max would wear. If Max wore gingham at all, it would be very new and either navy blue or pale pink. It was odd, really, to be so familiar, all over again, with Max's shirts, especially as – Max being Max and something of a shopper when it came to clothes – most of those shirts were new to her, and acquired in that peculiar space of time when she had been excluded from knowing any details of his personal life. And in those four years, Max had, sartorially speaking, started again. His taste might not have changed, but his wardrobe had and Vivien found it was very difficult sometimes to launder with equanimity garments that had plainly been to exotic places with women who were not her. A T-shirt printed with the logo of a luxurious hotel in Cyprus and a Malaysian sarong had already gone in the bin rather than the washing machine and Vivien couldn't decide whether it was a comfort to her or not that Max hadn't commented on their disappearance.

But then, Max was being very careful not to allude to his bachelor days unless it was to say something dismissive. He'd been to Jersey on business the week before, staying in a hotel he'd stayed at previously and, Vivien suspected, not alone, and had arrived home a night early, claiming that the whole place was depressing and all he wanted was to be home again.

"Bad memories," Vivien said, putting a glass of whiskey down in front of him.

He blew her a kiss.

"Horrible," he said.

The man in the gingham shirt approached the cash register and slowly laid down a large single-volume life of Napoleon.

"Please," he said, over his shoulder.

Vivien slipped the card she was holding into a slot and hurried across. The man, staring dreamily into the space behind the cash register, was holding out his credit card. As she reached to take it, her mobile phone, in her handbag under the counter, began to ring in an insistent crescendo.

"I'll ignore that," she said brightly.

The man nodded. He watched her slip the book into one of Alison's recycled bags, and run his card briskly through the machine. Then he bent and signed his name with the elaborate care of one who has just learned to do joined-up writing. Vivien watched him leave the shop, and then she seized her bag and rummaged in it for her telephone.

The caller had been Eliot. What was Eliot doing, ringing at five-thirty on an Australian morning? Was he ill? Vivien cast a glance at the mother and toddler. The toddler was now asleep in her buggy and her mother was grazing dispiritedly along the shelf of self-help books. Vivien rapidly dialed Eliot's number.

"Hi, Ma," Eliot said.

"Are you all right?"

There was a pause and then Eliot said, "I'm great, Ma. Why?"

"It's five-thirty in the morning. Why are you awake at five-thirty? Why are you calling me Ma?"

"It's a beaut morning," Eliot said reasonably. "We're going to the beach."

"So you rang to tell me it's a lovely day?"

"No," Eliot said, "I rang because Dad rang me and I'd forget otherwise. I'd forget if I left it."

The young mother pushed her buggy slowly past Vivien as if Vivien did not exist. Vivien watched her without pity, as she struggled with the door.

"What," Vivien said more loudly when the shop was empty, "what would you forget?"

"That it doesn't matter to Ro and me that you can't come for Christmas. We're going to Bali."

"What?"

"We're going to Bali for Christmas," Eliot said. "We've got cheap flights. So it doesn't matter."

Vivien pulled Alison's stool toward her and perched on it.

"You said Dad rang you?"

"Yeah."

"And Dad said we couldn't come for Christmas after all?"

"Yeah."

"Did – did he say why?"

"You should know," Eliot said. "Work or something."

"When did he ring?"

There was a silence, and then Eliot said uncertainly, "Yesterday?"

"Well," Vivien said, her voice not quite steady, "why are you ringing me?"

Eliot sounded surprised.

"To be polite."

"I'm sorry –"

"Dad said he thought you'd be a bit upset so I thought if I rang you and said we wouldn't be here anyway you'd feel better."

"But as I didn't know –"

There was another silence and to stop it becoming complicated Vivien said, with an effort, "How lovely. Going to Bali."

"Yeah," Eliot said, "we'd like a break." In the background, on a sunny blue morning in Cairns, a girl's voice said something Vivien couldn't hear. Eliot said, "Mum? Gotta go –"

"Yes, darling."

"You take care."

"Yes," Vivien said. "Yes."

The shop door opened and the man in the gingham shirt came in again holding the bag with the book in it.

"Thank you for ringing," Vivien said. "That was very – thoughtful."

The man came slowly up to the counter and laid the bag carefully on it.

"I'm afraid," he said, staring past Vivien, "I'm afraid I've changed my mind."

Leaving the stage after the final curtain call, Cheryl Smith said to Lazlo, "Like a drink?"

Lazlo hesitated. Edie, untying the ribbons of Mrs. Alving's lace cap, was just ahead of them.

Cheryl followed his gaze.

"You don't have to go everywhere she goes."

"I don't –"

"Beg *pardon*," Cheryl said, "but you've gone home with her every bloody *night*."

Lazlo said quickly, "I've been living in her house. It seemed polite."

"Break the habit of a lifetime," Cheryl said. "Come and have a drink with me."

Lazlo looked at her. She managed to make Regina's maid's clothes, dowdy though they were, look as if they barely contained her.

"I've got something to tell you," Cheryl said. "Something to your advantage."

"Well –"

"Go on," Cheryl said, daring him. "Mummy's boy."

Lazlo pushed past Cheryl in the narrow corridor behind the stage and put his hand on Edie's shoulder.

"Edie –"

She turned.

"I'll be a bit later tonight. I'm going to have a drink with Cheryl."

"Are you?"

"Yes. Will you get a taxi?"

"Probably," Edie said. "Doesn't matter. Don't worry." She gave him a faint smile. "Got to get used to different routines now anyway."

"Even if," Lazlo said, flattening himself against a wall for the stage manager to get by, "even if I wasn't moving out, there's only four weeks of the run to go, anyway."

"Unless we transfer."

Lazlo looked away.

"Not – much talk of a transfer lately –"

Edie glanced down at the cap in her hands.

"Funny. I've got rather used to this."

"Me too."

She lifted her head.

"You go and have a drink with Cheryl. You need to talk to actors your own age."

"It isn't that –"

"Well," Edie said bravely, "it should be."

Cheryl led the way at determined speed to the pub where Lazlo remembered almost breaking down after his first rehearsal. It was full and hot. Cheryl shouted at him that she wanted red wine and then disappeared to the ladies. When she came back, Lazlo had taken their glasses out on to the pavement and had found seats at the end of a picnic table dimly lit by a square yellow light falling from the window of the pub. Cheryl, in a denim miniskirt and her slouch boots, sat down on the bench attached to the table, and swung her legs over so that Lazlo and the two men already sitting at the table had a prolonged view of her knickers. Then she smiled graciously at them and picked up her wineglass.

She gestured with it toward Lazlo.

"Happy days."

"I hope so –"

"I'm in a film after this," Cheryl said, "on location in Norfolk, playing a single mother with a drug habit. I'll be perfect, won't I?"

Lazlo nodded.

She took a gulp of wine.

"What about you?"

"I don't know."

"Come on, Laz –"

Lazlo said cautiously, "Russell says I can read for a couple of his accounts –"

"Oh please," Cheryl said, "Ibsen to chicken nuggets?"

"I –"

"You," Cheryl said, "have a crap attitude. And a crap agent."

"He says he's trying. And two others have been in touch –"

Cheryl leaned forward, folding her arms underneath her bosom and creating an impressive cleavage.

"*My* agent wants to see you, sad boy."

Lazlo removed his gaze from Cheryl's breasts.

"What?"

"You heard me. He's seen you twice. He wants you to ring him. He's told me to tell you to ring him."

"The others –"

Cheryl leaned forward even further and jabbed at the table beside Lazlo's beer glass.

"No, Laz. Not a 'Come and see me sometime and maybe I'll think about it, but probably I won't' sort of agent. Stuart is for real. Stuart is a top agent. Stuart wants you to ring him tomorrow morning." She paused and leaned back a little and then she said, "Stuart has a casting for you."

"He can't –"

"He can. He has. He wouldn't be asking to see you if it wasn't for something specific."

"But my –"

"Ditch him," Cheryl said.

"He got me this part!"

"Ditch him," Cheryl said again, "if you've got any sense."

"But he's only seen me in this –"

"For God's sake," Cheryl said, "and when did showcases get better than bloody Ibsen?"

"I'm sorry," Lazlo said, "and thank you."

She stretched a hand out across the table and took one of his, firmly.

"You really are rather sweet."

The men at the other end of the table stopped talking.

"Now your hair's a bit longer," Cheryl said, "you're quite attractive. Very attractive really." She raised her eyebrows and smiled. "Very fanciable."

Lazlo attempted to pull his hand away.

"Sorry –"

"Oh come on," Cheryl said. "Live a little. Why d'you think I go to all this trouble?"

Lazlo pulled his hand free. One of the men at the table gave a little yelp of laughter.

"Sorry," Lazlo said again.

Cheryl gave him an amused glance. Then she shot a look up the table. She picked up her wineglass and struck an attitude with it.

"Suit yourself," she said. "Mummy's boy."

Maeve paused in the doorway to Russell's office. She was carrying a takeaway beaker of coffee and a complicated document from their accountant, flagged with little yellow stickers. Russell was standing in his dormer window, hands in pockets, staring out. Nothing was open on his desk: it looked as if he had not only not started work, but had also turned his back on the very idea of it.

"Room service," Maeve said.

Russell turned his head.

"You're a good girl."

Maeve put the coffee down carefully on his desk.

"The line in the play is 'You're a good little pudding, Mrs. King.'"

Russell sighed. Then he turned round completely and lowered himself into his desk chair as if he was convalescent.

Maeve laid the folder from the accountant down in front of him.

"Three signatures. I've marked where. Do you think you can manage that?"

Russell nodded.

"Shall I stay," Maeve said, "and guide your hand?"

Russell glanced at her, then he slowly reached to pick up his pen.

"After all these years," Maeve said, "do I still have to tell you that you should never sign anything you haven't read and understood?"

Russell put his pen down.

Maeve laid her hands on his desk and leaned on them.

"The fight's gone out of you," she said. "Hasn't it?"

He said, staring at the document in front of him, "I'm just tired –"

"You've been tired for weeks," Maeve said. "You've been out all hours at things a tinker wouldn't trouble himself with, and your house isn't your own, and nor is your wife and you can't get up the energy to lick a stamp. Can you?"

"It's only age –"

"It's not," Maeve said, "it's attitude. It's circumstances. Your present circumstances are not conducive to your health and well-being. What are you trying to prove?"

There was a pause and then Russell said, clearly and slowly without looking up, "I was trying to fill a gap."

"Well," Maeve said, "there you have it."

"And the gap is still there."

"Tell her."

"I can't," Russell said.

"Of course you can! She's a reasonable woman –"

"No," Russell said.

"Why not?"

He looked up at her, his face slightly sideways.

He said, "Because she's got a gap of her own. One she'd never thought she'd have."

"Oh," Maeve said, "those children –"

"No," Russell said. He picked his pen up again and pulled the folder toward him. "No, not the children. Work."

*　　*　　*

"I was going to tell you, doll," Max said. He drew imaginary intersecting lines on his chest. "Honestly I was. Cross my heart."

Vivien sighed. Max had been an hour later home than he had promised and she had spent that hour vowing that she would not, the moment he walked through the door, confront him about not going to Australia. And then she had heard the front door slam and Max's quick steps coming down the hall and the minute they were in the kitchen she'd spun round from the cooker and said, "Eliot rang today."

Max had taken a pace backward. He'd always done that, when attacked, as if physically retreating before gunfire, and it annoyed her quite as much as it always had done.

He then put his hands up, as if surrendering.

"How was he?"

"Don't," Vivien said. She was holding a wooden spoon coated with sauce.

"Don't what, honey?"

"Don't," Vivien shouted, "pretend you don't know!"

Max dropped his hands. He came forward and stood in front of her in an attitude of contrition.

"I was going to tell you, doll. Honestly I was. Cross my heart."

Vivien turned back to the cooker.

"Ringing Eliot about something that concerns *me* isn't just something that slips your mind. It's deliberate."

Behind her back, Max closed his eyes for a moment. Then he opened them and said, "The thing is, Vivi, I didn't know how to tell you."

Vivien didn't turn.

"Tell me what?"

"That – oh hell, this is so embarrassing."

"What is?"

Max came and stood beside Vivien. He touched her arm. She shook him off.

"It's money, doll."

She shot him a glance.

"What is?"

"I'm really sorry, but I'm afraid this isn't the year for going to Australia. I'm so ashamed. I'm so ashamed to tell you that there just isn't the money. Simple as that."

Vivien tasted her sauce and reached past Max for the salt. He seized her outstretched arm.

"I'm so sorry, Vivi. I shouldn't have got your hopes up."

Vivien removed her arm from Max's grasp.

She said, "You're not running the flat now. Your living expenses have halved. What d'you mean, there isn't the money?"

Max drooped.

"Sorry, sweetheart. Honor bright, it's not there."

Vivien said unsteadily, "You promised me."

"Oh, look now, doll, it wasn't a *promise*. It was a great idea, a lovely idea to go out and see our boy, but it was only an *idea*. Be fair!"

Vivien put the saucepan to the side of the cooker and turned out the gas.

She said again, not looking at him, "You promised me."

"Look here," Max said, "we'll go in the spring. I'm sure I'll see my way clear in the spring –"

Vivien looked at him.

"Where's the money gone?"

He spread his hands.

"Maybe it wasn't there, doll, maybe I didn't want you to think I couldn't give you everything you wanted." He tried a smile. "Maybe I was just being a bit overoptimistic. You know me."

"Yes," Vivien said. She took a step nearer and when her face was only a foot from his, she said loudly, "Liar!"

Max tried to hold her by the arms.

"Now wait a second, Vivi –"

She flailed her arms sideways to elude him.

"Liar!" she said. "Liar! Just like you always were!"

"Please, doll –"

"Promises!" Vivien shouted. "Promises, to get what you wanted! Promise me what you know I want! There never was the money to go and see Eliot, was there, or if there was, you've spent it, haven't you, you've gone into some stupid venture with some stupid shyster –"

"No!"

"Then you're paying off debts. Aren't you? Who is she? Who's the tart you're paying to keep quiet?"

Max reached out and firmly gripped her upper arms.

"Vivien darling, don't. Don't do this. Please don't! This is just like the bad old days –"

"Yes!"

"There's nothing to get steamed up about," Max said. "Nothing. It's just a muddle, a typical Max muddle –"

"Then why did you ring Eliot first?"

"Well, I –"

"You rang him first," Vivien said, "so that I couldn't talk you out of it. I bet you bought his flights to Bali, I bet you did that because you don't want to go to Australia with me. You don't want to spend all that money on me!"

"Nonsense –"

Vivien wrenched herself free.

"I sound like I used to," she screamed, "because you sound like you used to. Exactly like!"

"I didn't buy those flights to Bali –"

Vivien glared at him.

"Liar!"

"Don't keep calling me that –"

She took a step back and then she spun round and stormed across the kitchen. In the doorway, she paused, her hand on the knob, and then she said furiously, "I wouldn't have to, if you weren't!" and crashed the door shut behind her.

Matthew's computer case lay in the hall, as if he'd thrown it down carelessly on his way in. As far as Rosa could tell, he was the only one at home. The kitchen and sitting room were disordered but empty, and the doors to both first-floor bedrooms were open. Rosa stood in the dusky evening light on the landing and listened intently. There was no sound, no music. She looked upward for a minute, and then made her way back downstairs to the kitchen.

It didn't look as if anyone had had supper. It didn't look, in fact, as if anyone had done anything in the kitchen that day except have breakfast in a scattered sort of way and then leave in a hurry. Someone had propped an untidy bunch of envelopes against a cornflakes box, but no one had opened them. There was a banana skin blackening on a plate and two half-drunk mugs of cold coffee. The spoon Rosa had stuck in the honey twelve hours before was exactly where she had left it. If Matthew had come into the kitchen that evening, he'd plainly neither had the appetite to eat nor the heart to clear up.

Rosa ran water into the kettle and switched it on. Then she assembled, on the painted wooden tray with decoupage flowers she remembered making in a craft class when she was fourteen, a cafetière and two mugs and a packet of digestive biscuits. Then she added Edie's dusty bottle of cooking brandy and two pink Moroccan tea glasses. When the kettle boiled, she made coffee in the cafetière, took a plastic bottle of milk out of the fridge and carried the tray out of the kitchen and up the stairs.

There was complete silence on the top landing and no line of light under Matthew's door. Rosa stooped and set the tray down on the carpet.

Then she tapped.

"Matt?"

Silence. Rosa turned the handle very slowly and opened the door. Matthew hadn't pulled the curtains and the queer reddish glow from the night-city sky illuminated the room enough for Rosa to see that Matthew was sitting, fully dressed, in the small armchair that matched the one in her own room.

"Matt," Rosa said, "are you okay?"

He turned his head. In the dimness she couldn't make out if his eyes were shining or tearful.

"Yes," he said. "*Yes.*"

CHAPTER EIGHTEEN

"Why the silence?" Laura e-mailed from Leeds. "What's happening? Is it something I said?"

"No," Ruth typed rapidly. "Nothing to do with you, don't worry. But lots to tell you. Lots."

She took her hands off the keyboard and looked at what she had written. Then she deleted the last six words. She would tell Laura, she thought, of course she would, if Laura could be deflected from the choice between Cuba or Mexico for her honeymoon, but she wouldn't tell her yet. There was, after all, no need to tell Laura, no need until she had got a little further down her own path of thinking, of realizing, of unpicking, stitch by stitch, everything that had happened. And, more to the point, everything that was now going to happen.

Ruth took her hands right off her desk and laid them in her lap. It was that time of the day in the office when most people had gone home, taking the possibility of interruption and urgency with them. A colleague might come in for a chat or with the suggestion of a drink but finding Ruth dreaming at her desk would be something they expected, something they might even do themselves, to postpone the disconcerting business of going home. After six in the office was a time when being beholden to an obligation melted peacefully into a choice. She could, she thought, answer all the e-mails from America, or she could, if she chose, leave responding until the morning when the Americans would still be asleep, and concentrate instead, with tentative wonder, on the fact that the last thing Matthew had said to her when they parted was, "I'll ring you."

He hadn't, but she wasn't anxious that he wouldn't. She had, in almost a single second, shed the anxiety that had been such a burden for so long the moment she had realized he was crying. She'd been so tense about telling him about the baby, so poised for a rebuff, so braced for rejection that, when the words were out and he said nothing, it took her some little time to realize that he was saying nothing because he was crying. She'd put a tentative hand out toward him but he'd shaken his head and grabbed handfuls of tiny napkins out of the holder on the café table and scrubbed at his face with them while his shoulders shook.

Ruth said, immediately regretting it, "You're not angry?"

He moved his head again.

"Of course not –"

"I thought," she said diffidently, "that you might think you'd been very unlucky."

"No. No –"

She gave a little laugh.

"I did wonder if I'd been unlucky."

He stopped mopping his face and looked at her.

"Don't you want a baby?"

She stared down at the tabletop.

"I don't know. I think I do. I think I want – your baby. But it wasn't what I planned."

He said, a little more sharply, "Does it upset your plans?"

She looked up.

"Well, it upsets those ones. But those aren't the only ones."

"Aren't you pleased?"

She hesitated.

He said, more insistently, "Aren't you pleased, that you *can* be pregnant?"

"Yes, I suppose –"

"I think," Matthew said, leaning forward, sniffing, "I think it's wonderful to get pregnant. I think it's amazing to make a baby."

She said, "It wasn't very wonderful alone in the bathroom looking at that little blue line."

"No."

"And it still isn't very wonderful not knowing what will happen. Not – knowing how you feel."

Matthew pointed to his face.

"Look at me."

"Matt –"

He said quickly, "Don't hurry me, Ruth, don't push, don't want answers now this minute."

"Okay," she said reluctantly.

Matthew blew his nose into a clump of napkins.

"It's just knocked me out. This news."

"Yes."

He looked at her.

There was a pause and then he said, "It's wonderful, you – you're wonderful," and then he picked up her nearest hand and kissed it and returned it to her as if he was afraid of becoming responsible for it.

When she and Matthew first met, Ruth reflected now, staring unseeingly at her half-finished e-mail to Laura, Matthew had often told her she was wonderful. Her hair was wonderful, and her body, and her laugh and her driving and her taste in music. She was wonderful to him for what she was, for the package of a person that seemed to him desirable enough to warrant persistent and energetic pursuit. But, sitting at that café table with him and listening to him tell her she was wonderful, it had come to her, with a kind of glow, that she seemed wonderful to him at last for something she had done, rather than something she was. She felt, and had felt ever since, that Matthew had awarded her a recognition, that he had acknowledged an admiration and a pride at what she had *done*, in becoming pregnant. She couldn't remember if he had ever looked at her professional efforts and accomplishments with the respect and approval he seemed all too ready to accord her now. She was inclined to think that if he ever had she would indeed remember, recognition of achievement being about as basic to human need as food and drink, and thus this extraordinary glow of approval in which she was tentatively basking was not only unexpected, but was also probably a first.

She couldn't, of course, blame Matthew for withholding admiration in the past. For as long as she could remember she had, as so many of her girlfriends had, worked assiduously at relinquishing recognition. When she fell in love with Matthew, and the discrepancy in their earnings inevitably dictated the mechanisms of their life together, she had almost unconsciously played down her achievements, withdrawn all visible evidence of her paying power behind a barrier of standing orders and direct debits as well as ceding any available attention to Matthew whenever possible. It was only when this curiously primitive need to own her own flat expanded to become something she could not give up that she confronted him – no, both of them – with the bald fact that she did not want him to hold her back just because he couldn't do what she could do.

And the consequence of that determination to buy the flat was that she had been made to feel – or, she thought truthfully, just found herself feeling – that in behaving in a way that was not automatically self-deprecating and deferential she had surrendered the chief defining quality of femininity, that of being the giver. Essential womanliness, that warmth and tenderness and loyalty that makes girls conventionally desirable, was, apparently, something that Ruth had turned her back on, thrown down and stamped on. Never mind the unfairness of it, never mind the way that most cherished traits of femininity always seemed to be defined within a relationship, as if possessing no value unless to others, that was how it had seemed to her. She had acted with all the self-reliant, decisive independence that would have been so much applauded in a man, and felt her very sexuality had been assailed in consequence. She might be endorsed most heartily at work for what she was achieving, but what was that endorsement worth when spread thinly across the whole of her life outside work? Who would care, in ten years' time when all her contemporaries had families, that she was earning, at thirty-eight, more, annually, than her father had ever earned in all his working life? The Victorians had described women who were hell bent on higher education as agamic, asexual. How many people still, Ruth thought, including a shrinking part of her own out-wardly accomplished self, would have agreed with them?

And now, look at her. *Look* at her. Deflected into care-lessness about contraception by the urgency of her own need not to seem some unattractive freak, she was pregnant. She was in, by mistake, the most supremely female condition she possibly could be. And Matthew, not appalled as she feared he might be, not jubilant about his potency as men were supposed to be, had been, quite simply, moved. The news had touched him emotionally in a way she would never have predicted, a way she was not at all sure she felt herself. And that reaction meant that he would now certainly do what she had longed for him to do, and ring her.

What she would say when he did, however, she couldn't be sure. In the perverse way of human things, especially longings, she wasn't even sure how much she now wanted him to ring. When he did, he would ask questions, want to make plans and, as yet, she wasn't sure what she wanted, how she saw the way ahead. What was so extraordinary, especially given the fact that babies had not even featured near the bottom of her agenda up to now, was that the painful loneliness she had felt since she and Matthew parted seemed to have subsided. Telling Matthew she was pregnant had given her a sensation of independence, as surprising as it was welcome. To her amazement, the baby, even at this stage, was a fact, and not a choice of any kind. She laid a hand carefully across her flat stomach. Perhaps she had now regained everything she had lost. Perhaps she now, oddly enough, held all the cards, all the approval. She took her hand off her stomach and put both on the keyboard.

"I am," she wrote formally to Laura, "very well indeed."

Rosa thought she hadn't been to a matinee since she was small, and Edie and Russell used to take the three of them to matinee performances of musicals at Christmas. There had been something exotic about going into a theater in daylight and coming out in the dark, as if some time travel had happened in those few hours and the world was now a different place. Twenty years later, a matinee didn't seem so much exotic as out of step, a requirement to surrender and believe, against the evidence of all your senses, that almost amounted to a challenge.

The theater was only a quarter full. Such people as had come sat scattered about and the girl selling programs was yawning. Rosa went to the very back of the stalls in a belief that, even if Lazlo could see as far as that from the stage, he couldn't see in detail. But that afternoon, it would be unlikely he'd be looking at anyone but Edie's understudy. Edie was never ill, never missed performances, despised people who used health as an excuse for failing to fulfil obligations, but, all the same, Edie was in bed with a severe headache and a determination to perform that evening.

"Miss me," she'd said to Lazlo, silhouetted in her bedroom doorway. "Mind you miss me."

Rosa felt a twinge of disloyalty at seeing Edie's understudy rather than Edie. But then, it wasn't Edie she had come to see that afternoon, it was Lazlo, Lazlo with whom she'd made a plan, to meet in the interval between afternoon and evening performances. They were intervals he'd admitted were difficult to fill, as the need to conserve energy had to be balanced by an equal need not to relax down to a point from which it might be hard to rouse oneself up again. Rosa said she understood that, she could see that, and why didn't they just have a quiet something to eat somewhere, no big deal?

Lazlo looked doubtful.

"Usually I just read –"

"Well this time," Rosa said, "just talk."

"Okay," he said. He gave her his shy smile. "Thank you."

She smiled back, but she didn't tell him she would watch a performance first. She wanted to watch him in peace for a while, watch how he was without Edie, watch him, as it were, out of context. She wanted to see if she could discover why it was she found him so interesting and, even more, why she should want a man who was not in any way her type, and younger to boot, to think well of her. She settled back into her seat. There was a lot of the first act to get through – including the unwelcome sight of that awful Cheryl Smith acting so well – before the door on the left of the stage opened and Lazlo emerged, with his hat and his pipe, and said, with the hesitancy she had come to find so very appealing, " 'Oh, I'm sorry – I thought you were in the study.' " She glanced down at the program. He really had a very nice profile.

Vivien was lying on her bed when the telephone rang. She was lying there because she had planned to lie there anyway, to rest before Max took her to have dinner with a new client whom he said he wanted her to impress. So, when he rang and said that he was mortified but the client wanted to have dinner alone with Max because it was strictly business he wanted to discuss, Vivien had decided to go to bed anyway even if for different reasons.

"I don't know what to say, doll," Max had said. "I feel just terrible. And after promising you. But this one could be quite a big one, and you know how things are with me just now. A big one could make all the difference."

Vivien, sitting by her telephone table in the hall, said

nothing. She felt herself invaded, drawn back by the Vivien of the past, the Vivien who had stopped shrieking at Max and had taken instead to stonewalling him with silence.

"Vivi?" Max said. "Darling?"

"Bye," Vivien said. "Hope it works," and then she put the telephone down and went upstairs to her bedroom and kicked her shoes off. If she couldn't lie on her bed in anticipation, she would at least lie on it for consolation. She settled herself, with angry little twitches, and looked at the dress hanging on the cornice of her wardrobe. It was layered chiffon, printed in gray and white ("Love you in those cool colors, doll") and she had been going to wear it that evening.

The telephone on her bedside table began to ring. She looked at it thoughtfully.

"No," she would say to Max, "no, you can't change the plans again. I'm doing something else this evening now. I'm going to the cinema."

She let it ring six times and then she picked up the receiver and held it away from her ear and waited.

"Vivi?" Edie said.

Vivien shut her eyes tightly for a second, as if to squeeze back tears.

"Why aren't you at the theater? Don't you have matinees on Saturday afternoons?"

Edie said deliberately, spacing the words out, "I have a headache."

Vivien made a sympathetic noise.

Then she said, "You never have headaches."

"I have one now."

"You should take HRT. You should just admit your age and –"

"I'm tired," Edie said loudly.

"What?"

"I'm just tired."

"Of course you are. Working, the house so full –"

"I didn't ring up to be lectured!"

There was a short pause and then Vivien said, "Why did you ring up then?"

"I was lying on my bed," Edie said, "and there's no one in, not even Russell, and I, well, I wanted to talk to someone."

"So I'll do."

"Yes," Edie said, "you'll do. How are you?"

"Fine."

"Ironing Max's Jermyn Street shirts and concocting a seduction supper and planning your trip to Australia –"

"We aren't going to Australia."

"Vivi!"

Vivien put a hand up and blotted at the skin under one eye and then the other.

"Nope. Not going."

"Vivi, why *not*?"

"Max says," Vivien said staring toward the window, "that he can't afford it."

"Excuse me –"

"Please don't."

"Don't what?"

"Don't," Vivien said, "encourage me to think what I'm thinking."

"But he sold his flat!"

"I know."

"And it was a *big* flat –"

"I know, Edie. I know, don't go on about it, don't –"

"Oh Vivi," Edie said, in a different tone, "oh, I'm sorry."

"It's nothing. It's just a trip." She looked up again at the chiffon dress. "Nothing else," she said loudly, "to worry about."

"You sure?"

"Oh yes. He's very contrite. You can tell a really sorry man, can't you?"

From downstairs came the two-beat tone of the doorbell.

"Damn," Vivien said, sitting up. "Someone at the door."

"Ring me back, if you need to. I'm here till six –"

"I thought you had a headache?"

"It's going," Edie said, "it's really going. Vivi, what can I do –"

Vivien stood up and pushed her feet into her shoes.

"Nothing," she said. "Thanks, but nothing. Nothing needs doing. It's all fine."

Outside the front door, a man from the local florist's was waiting. In his arms he carried a bouquet of red roses, wrapped in cellophane, the size of a large baby.

He grinned at Vivien over the roses.

"Afternoon!" he said. "The lucky lady, I presume?"

Rosa had ordered a salad. It came with a ring of bread balls circling the rim of the plate, and Rosa had picked these off and piled them neatly on her side plate and pushed the plate away from her.

Lazlo paused in cutting up his pizza and eyed them.

"Aren't you going to eat those?"

Rosa shook her head. She had taken off whatever had been holding her hair back, and it was loose on her shoulders.

She glanced, smiling, at his pizza.

"Isn't that enough?"

He looked mournfully at his plate.

"It's never enough."

She pushed the bread balls toward him.

"Feel free."

He said, in a rush, helping himself, "You were in the theater this afternoon, weren't you?"

There was a tiny beat and then Rosa said, "Yes. I was."

Without looking at her, he said, "To see if I could cope without your mother there?"

She selected an olive from her salad and looked at it. Then she put it back.

"I didn't think of that."

"Didn't you?"

"No," she said, glancing at him, "I didn't. And you could."

He directed a small smile toward his plate.

"Yes," he said, "I could, couldn't I? I did wonder a bit. I hoped –" He paused.

"You hoped you could swim without your armbands."

"Yes," he said. He looked straight at her. "I did. Is that –" He stopped.

"No," Rosa said. "No. She'd want that, too. She'd want that for you."

Lazlo cleared his throat.

"The thing is," he said, "I've – well, I've got another part."

"Oh!"

"In television," he said. "A six-parter. I've got quite a big role. I'm – well, I'm sort of second lead."

Rosa leaned forward.

"This is wonderful."

"Do you think so?"

"Of course it is," she said. "Of *course* it is! And you deserve it."

"Well –"

Rosa put down her knife and laid a hand on Lazlo's wrist.

"Mum will say the same. Mum will be thrilled."

"Are you sure? It's Freddie Cass directing again. He – well, I hardly had to do a casting, it was just a formality. It seems a bit sneaky, it feels like I'm doing something behind her back, but I'm not really in a position to turn good work down."

"Stop it," Rosa said.

He gave a little intake of breath.

He said again, "Are you sure?"

"Sure, sure."

"It's just," he said, "that I owe her so much. Helping me, sheltering me –"

"She was there when you needed her." Rosa took her hand away and picked up her knife again. "And vice versa."

Lazlo said nothing. He put a mouthful of pizza into his mouth and chewed.

Then he said, "Why did you come this afternoon?"

"Oh," she said, "to look at you."

"You'd seen me."

"To look at you without any distractions."

"I'm not very good at this," Lazlo said, "but – but what did you see?"

She leaned back and folded her arms. Her hair was very preoccupying.

She said slowly, "Enough. I saw enough to give me courage."

Lazlo put down his knife and fork. He had the anxious, excited sensation he'd had several times recently, that some outside force was going to come bowling into his life and make changes for him, the kind of changes he knew he didn't have much capacity for making on his own.

Rosa said, leaning back, watching him, "You're moving out."

Lazlo nodded.

He said, "I must. There's no room. I feel awful, Ben sleeping on the sofa –"

"Where are you going?"

Lazlo looked at his plate.

"I've started looking for a flat. Just a small one. The money will be better in television –"

"I'll come with you," Rosa said.

He felt his face flame up.

"Come *with* me!"

"Yes."

He said clumsily, "I – I don't *know* you –"

Rosa unfolded her arms and leaned forward. She put her elbows on the table and propped her chin on her hands.

"Yes, you do."

"But I –"

"Lazlo," Rosa said, "you know me. You're just so much

in the habit of thinking of yourself as an outsider that you don't believe you know anyone."

He raised his eyes very slowly and looked at her.

"You are suggesting we live together?"

"Yes."

"But –"

"Live together," Rosa said, "as in *live* together. Not sleep together." She paused and then she said lightly, "Necessarily."

"I wasn't expecting this," Lazlo said. "I couldn't even have *imagined* this. You are offering to share a flat with me?"

"Yes."

"Why?"

Rosa said seriously, "Because I must move out and on too. Because I need the motivation to get a better job. Because I can't afford to live on my own yet. Because I don't want to live with another girl who's a sort of duplicate of me. Because I like you."

He felt his skin scorch again.

"Do you?"

"Yes," she said.

"I don't quite know what I –"

"Don't bother," Rosa said. "Don't try and say anything. Or feel it, for that matter. Just think about what I've said." She looked at his plate. "That pizza will be revolting cold."

Russell was half turned away from Edie in bed, half asleep, when she clutched him.

"Russell –"

Her fingers were digging into his shoulder, into his upper arm. His mind came dragging back from the soft dark place it was falling into.

"Edie? Edie, what is it?"

He twisted himself back toward her and she shoved her face against him.

She said, almost into his skin, "We're not going in."

He extracted his arms from the folds of the duvet and put them awkwardly round her.

"Edie love, you knew that –"

"We're not going in," Edie said again in a harsh, tearful whisper. "The play's not transferring. It's all over."

Russell adjusted his hold.

He said gently, "You knew that. You knew Freddie wasn't really trying to find a theater, you knew that was all talk. You've known that for weeks."

"I've only just *realized* it," Edie said. "I don't want this to end. I don't want this play to be over."

"There'll be other parts –"

"No, there won't. This was freak luck. Freddie's taking Lazlo with him to do this Italian detective thing and he never mentioned it to me."

"Perhaps there's no part in this cast for you –"

"I thought,' Edie said, "I'd be in the West End. I thought I'd have my name –" She stopped.

Russell said, "And I thought you were so tired and fed up you just wanted it all to stop."

Edie said nothing. She moved her face slightly so that her cheek lay against his chest.

He waited a few moments and then he said, "You've loved this run, haven't you? You've loved being on stage."

Edie nodded.

Then she said in a whisper, "I'm so afraid of it stopping."

"It's not the last."

"You don't *know* –"

"No, but I have a pretty good hunch."

He felt her face move as if she was looking up at him. "Do you?"

"Yes," Russell said.

"Do you really think I'm any good?"

"Yes," Russell said, "and so do other people."

"But not Freddie Cass."

"Yes, he does. But there's a part for Lazlo in his new project and not a part for you."

"Really?"

"Really."

"I don't think," Edie said, laying her cheek back against him, "I don't think I could bear it if I couldn't work again."

Russell let a small silence fall, and then he said comfortably, "And I'm sure you won't have to bear anything of the kind."

"I don't feel at all certain about that –"

He said nothing. He moved slightly, to free up an arm, and then he yawned into the dimness above Edie's head. From somewhere above them, the floorboards creaked.

Edie stiffened.

She said, in quite a different voice, "There's something going on between Rosa and Lazlo."

"Is there?"

"Yes, definitely."

He felt another yawn beginning.

He said, round it, "Does it matter?"

Edie said vigorously, "I don't like it, Russell. I really don't. Not here. Not in my house."

"Ah."

"I mean, if you take people in, take people back, it's only fair, isn't it, to expect a little –" She stopped and then she said sadly, "I don't mean that."

"I thought you didn't. I hoped you didn't."

"I didn't."

"What did you mean then?"

She said, in the same dejected voice, "It all feels so fragile."

"What does?"

"What they're doing, both of them so uncertain, so without a proper planned future –"

"Don't you think," Russell said sleepily, "that we looked just as fragile in our day? That dismal flat, all those babies, me earning three thousand a year if I was lucky?"

"Maybe –"

"I think we did. In fact I'm sure we did. I expect our parents – mine certainly – had a version of exactly this conversation."

"Russell?"

"Yes."

"I just wanted," Edie said, "to keep everything safe. I just wanted to make everything all right for all of them. I wanted to be back in control of things –"

"I know."

"And I can't."

Russell moved his head a little and gave Edie a brief kiss.

"I know," he said again.

CHAPTER NINETEEN

The trouble was, Ben reflected, that he hadn't thought things through. He had supposed, rather vaguely, that he would go back to a few weeks of his old life – unexciting but familiar and easy – and then he would take up, in an unspecified but attractive way, his new life with Naomi. It had not occurred to him, in trying to get what he wanted while causing as little upheaval as possible, that all the wrinkles wouldn't somehow just iron themselves out of their own accord. It had not really crossed his mind that Naomi meant exactly what she said when she told him she needed space to think, and that space included hardly being in touch with him at all beyond a few text messages of the kind you might send to any old common or garden friend. And it had certainly never struck him that ambling back home, even without his father's full blessing, would prove to be anything but easy or familiar.

He had thought, for the first few nights, that it didn't feel right because he was sleeping on the sofa. He told himself that there was just something pretty weird about being on the sofa when your sister was through the ceiling in your bedroom and your bed. But, as the days wore on, he suspected that, even if Rosa were to surrender his bedroom, it wouldn't now be the bedroom he had left only a few months before, and therefore the strangeness of the sofa didn't belong to the actual sofa: it belonged to the situation.

The situation was, as far as Ben could see, that his child-hood home had changed. He might know every corner and creak, but he knew them as he supposed he would know the similar characteristics of the secondary school where he had spent seven years of his educational life. You could know a thing, it seemed, you could feel a thing to be deeply, power-fully familiar, but at the same time you were keenly aware that this known and familiar thing was no longer in the least relevant to the place you were now at, never mind the place where you were going. When Ben put the key in the lock of the front door of the house, he knew precisely how to do it, but that was no comfort or pleasure because he didn't, fundamentally, want to be doing it anymore. It was as if the lock looked the same but had, in fact, changed its nature, just as the quirks of taps and light switches and cupboard doors had. It was like looking at a well-known face in a distorting mirror.

The same was true of his family. There were no surprises in any of them, except that they all seemed to him more shadowy. He initially supposed that this was because all of them were trying to deal with difficulties of one kind or another, which rendered them tired and preoccupied. Given everyone's work schedules, no one saw very much of anyone else, but all the same, the household had no coherence about it anymore and, instead of feeling in any way a unit, it felt like a collection of people living together without any real sense of binding unity. It was only after a few weeks, lying wakeful one night on the sofa and wishing for the hundredth time that it was even six inches longer, that it struck Ben that what was the matter with him was not really the sofa, or the accessibility of his family, but that he was missing Naomi.

Once he had considered this, he realized that he had never actually missed anyone before. He had never, all his growing up, been put in a situation of having to miss someone: no boarding school, no college years in the North of England, no opportunity to feel keenly the absence of someone important. And, once this painful and interesting revelation had broken over him, he could see that it was neither the house nor the family that had changed, it was him. He might only have been living with Naomi and her mother a short while, but it had been long enough to give him a taste of what it might – could – be like to live according to his own inclinations. Naomi's mother, for all her rules and regulations, had unconsciously allowed him to take the first tentative steps toward independence.

The feeling of missing Naomi was, once acknowledged, extremely acute. It rendered him at once impatient with living in a temporary way on his parents' sofa and, at the same time, eager to mend fences with Naomi and to set about achieving what he now clearly and urgently wanted, which was a place of their own. Such a place, he could now see, would bring with it responsibilities of a kind he had once shrugged off as the dull concern of generations older than his, but he was sure he would not be daunted by that. Indeed, if that kind of obligation was the price to be paid for living with Naomi, then he would gladly pay it.

The difficulty was, how. Naomi's texts had not suggested, in any way, that she was missing him as he was missing her. In fact, the brevity and scarcity of her communications might have led a fainter heart to think that she had definitively chosen an immediate future with her mother rather than her boyfriend. But Ben's heart, buoyed up with his new self-knowledge, did not feel faint. It felt that, even if it did not succeed, it was going to make stupendous efforts first, before acknowledging even the possibility of failure. He would shower and shave, he decided, put on clean clothes, buy flowers for both Naomi and her mother – a significantly larger bunch for her mother – and take the tube, that very day, to Walthamstow.

The water in the shower changed abruptly from tepid to gaspingly cold. Edie, her eyes tightly shut against the shampoo cascading down her face, gave a scream. Then she gave another, a scream of rage this time, rather than shock. They had all had showers, of course, they had all showered and gone out, even Lazlo, and left her to do battle with the aftermath of their leaving. Also, she thought, stumbling out of the shower and fumbling about for a towel, to deal with an elderly boiler and a water tank designed for the needs of a small nuclear family who bathed by a roster.

She found a damp towel and wrapped it tightly round her. Then she ran a basin of cold water and dipped her hair into it and rinsed her eyes. There was a perverse relief, somehow, in being able to cry because she had soap in her eyes, being able to blame some small, tangible element for the need to howl away to herself, wrapped in an already used towel, in the forlorn middle of a weekday morning. She straightened up a little and peered at herself in the mirror. Her hair hung in wet dark snakes. Her eyes looked as if they'd been buried. She looked, she decided, more like the embodiment of a state of mind than a human being. She reached out and pulled another dank towel off the pile on the chair and wound it round her head. Now she looked like a huge blue toweling thumb.

From downstairs, the doorbell rang.

"Go away!" Edie shouted.

It rang again, politely but firmly. Edie dropped the towel she had tucked round her armpits and clawed her way into Russell's ancient bathrobe that was hanging on the back of the door. Then she went cautiously out on to the landing and pressed her forehead against the glass to see down into the street.

On the step directly below her a young woman was standing. She wore a dark suit and was carrying a briefcase and there were sunglasses perched on top of her head. Edie looked at the briefcase. It seemed familiar, familiar enough to picture it propped against the wall inside the front door. It was Ruth's briefcase. Edie unscrewed the security bolt on the window and put her head out.

Ruth glanced up.

"Edie," she said uncertainly.

Edie put her hand up to her immense blue turban.

"Just – washing my hair –"

"I'm sorry," Ruth said, "not to tell you I was coming, but Matt said you'd be in, and I –"

"*Matt* did?"

"Yes," Ruth said. "Matt suggested I just come. When I said I wanted to."

"Wait," Edie said.

"Look, if it really –"

"*Wait*," Edie said. She slammed the window shut and tore off her turban. Then she ran downstairs. Arsie was sitting in the hall, affecting indifference to whoever had come. Edie picked him up and held him against her while she opened the door.

Ruth said at once, "I'm so sorry –"

"Don't be," Edie said. She stepped back. "It's – well, I'm very glad to see you."

"Are you?"

Edie looked at her.

"Why shouldn't I be?"

Ruth put out a hand to touch Arsie.

"Well, I thought you thought –"

A drip from Edie's hair slid on to Arsie's shoulder and he sprang from her arms.

"I *did* think."

"Yes –"

"But a lot's happened and I – well, my thinking has shifted a bit. You look very smart."

Ruth made a little self-deprecating gesture.

"You'll have to forgive me," Edie said. "I was in a temper as well as in the shower. Coffee?"

"Could – could I have tea?"

Edie looked at her.

"I didn't think you drank tea."

"I – didn't."

"Come into the kitchen. There's too much to apologize for in there so I won't even start."

Ruth said from the kitchen doorway, "It's nice to be back –"

"Is it? Have you been very unhappy?"

"Yes."

Edie picked up the kettle.

She said from the sink, her back turned toward Ruth, "So has Matthew."

"I know."

"Ruth," Edie said, "couldn't you just have made a compromise? Couldn't you just have made it possible for him to contribute *something*?"

Ruth went slowly across the room to the table and leaned against it. Then she put down her briefcase and took her sunglasses off her head and laid them on the table with precision.

"I came," she said, "to tell you that I was pregnant."

Edie froze for a moment. Then she turned off the tap and set the kettle down carefully in the sink.

"Pregnant?"

"Yes."

"I thought," Edie said with emphasis, "that you and Matthew hadn't seen each other since you – parted."

"He came for dinner," Ruth said. "He came to my flat. I asked him to. I was missing him so much."

Edie put her hands up to the collar of Russell's bathrobe and held it against her neck. Then she turned round.

"Does Matthew know?"

"Of course."

"How – long has he known?"

"About two weeks."

Edie shut her eyes.

"Two weeks –"

"Yes."

"And – forgive me – but are you going to keep it?"

There was a small pause and then Ruth said, with barely suppressed fury, "Yes."

"But if you and Matthew aren't –"

"We are," Ruth said. "That's why I've come. I've come to tell you what we're planning."

Edie put a hand out for a chair as if she was suddenly very old, and lowered herself into it. She didn't look at Ruth. Instead she looked at the box of Grapenuts someone had left on the table.

"But why come and tell me? Why not both of you? Why not tell Russell and me together? Why come like this, out of the blue –"

"Because I wanted to," Ruth said. "Because you needed to know. Because you were so angry with me."

"I wasn't –"

"Oh yes," Ruth said. "Women are always angrier with other women. I'd hurt your son. I'd achieved more than he had. In your view, I'd rubbed his nose in it."

Edie put her elbows on the table and her face in her hands. She said, muffled by her hands, "You'll learn."

"Oh," Ruth said, "I understood why you were angry. Of course I did. And I felt awful myself, awful at what I'd done and furious at being made to feel awful."

Edie took her hands away from her face.

"You'd better sit down."

"I'm fine –"

"Sit down," Edie said. "Sit down and I'll make you some tea."

She got up and retrieved the kettle from the sink.

She said, "Do your parents know?"

"Not yet."

"*What?*"

"I'll tell them next," Ruth said. "I'll tell them at the weekend."

"But why –"

"Because I wanted to see you first. Because I wanted to do something for Matthew."

Edie spun round.

"Matthew's not afraid of *me*!"

"It wasn't about that," Ruth said, "it's about saving him having to explain himself again. It's about me explaining to you how hard it is for women my age to deal with motherhood and work when both are so demanding and important, and how wonderful it would be if you could be on my side." She paused. And then she added, "Irrespective of Matthew."

Edie said nothing. She went back to her chair and sat down in it and pulled the belt of the bathrobe tighter. Then she looked at Ruth across the table, at her polished hair and her sharply cut suit.

"Do you think," she said, "that it's any easier for me?"

"Yes," Ruth said.

"Do you?"

"Yes," Ruth said, "I think that women after their families have gone are pretty unstoppable. That's what it looks like, from where I'm standing."

"Really?"

Ruth leaned forward.

"The classic reproach, the one about women promoting themselves at the expense of people who need their care, doesn't apply to you. Not anymore."

"Wait a moment –"

"I don't want to argue," Ruth said. "I didn't come to argue. I didn't even come to make comparisons. I came to tell you about the baby."

Edie looked up. She stared at Ruth as if she was seeing her properly for the first time.

"Oh, my God," Edie said. "A *baby*."

Russell looked at the glasses of wine Rosa had already carried to the table from the bar.

"No wish to be churlish," he said, "but this immediately makes me suspicious –"

"You like red wine."

"I do indeed. But usually I have to buy the red wine I like. In the case of my children, I invariably buy the red wine."

"Well," Rosa said, "things are changing."

Russell sighed.

"That's what I was afraid of."

"Dad –"

"You ask me to have a drink with you, you soften me up by getting the drinks in first and then you ask me for ten thousand pounds. That's the form."

"No," Rosa said.

Russell picked up his glass.

"Then I'll just have a quick swallow before I know what it really is."

Rosa said carelessly, "I'm being promoted."

Russell put his glass down again.

"I thought it was a crap job and only temporary and you hated it."

"I've been asked," Rosa said, "to run the branch in Holborn. I get a thirty percent rise in salary and my uniform will no longer have sunburst buttons."

Russell eyed her.

"So I congratulate you."

"Yes, please."

"And why couldn't you tell me this at home?"

"Home's difficult," Rosa said.

Russell looked away.

"I mean," Rosa said, "I probably help to make it difficult but it's not, well, it's not really working, is it, us all living together? It's not very successful."

Russell said, still looking away, "I never thought it would be."

"Well, you were right. You're right about lots of things."

He said tiredly, "Don't try to placate me, Rosa. I'm beyond all that."

"I mean it."

"Well, thank you –"

"And I don't mind going to Holborn and I don't mind working in a travel agency. I don't *mind*."

"Ah," Russell said. He turned to look at her. "Why don't you?"

"Because," Rosa said, spreading her fingers flat on the table and regarding them, "another avenue has opened up."

"Not a work avenue, I take it –"

"No."

Russell took a swallow.

"Lazlo?"

"Yes. I didn't know you knew."

"I didn't *know*," Russell said, "but I guessed. It would be hard to live in the same house and not guess."

Rosa smiled down at her hands.

"It's very early days."

"Yes –"

"And he's terribly shy. I'm not sure – he's ever had a real girlfriend before."

"He's a nice boy," Russell said. "An honest boy."

"So you don't mind –"

"Mind?"

"You don't mind if Lazlo and I move out to live together?"

Russell leaned forward.

"No, Rosa, I don't mind. I'm very pleased for you."

She eyed him.

"Will Mum be?"

"I should think so –"

"Will you tell her?"

Russell shook his head.

"No."

"Dad –"

"You must tell her. Lazlo must tell her."

Rosa made a little gesture.

"I really don't like to."

"What do you mean?" Russell demanded, sitting upright. "What do you *mean*, you don't *like* to? After all she's done for you –"

"It isn't that."

"Well, then –"

"It's just," Rosa said, "that I know how much she's done. I know how tired she is, I know how disappointed she is about the play not transferring, and I just don't want to add to everything, add to the feeling of losing things." She paused and then she said in a rush, "I mean I'm worried she'll really feel it, with Matt going and now us –"

"Matt?" Russell said sharply.

Rosa put her hand over her mouth.

"Oh, my God –"

"Rosa –"

"I didn't mean," Rosa said, "I didn't mean to say anything about –"

Russell leaned across the table and grasped Rosa's wrist.

"What," he said, "about Matthew?"

Vivien sat in her hall beside her telephone table. On it lay a list of all the people she was going to telephone, one after another, in a calm and orderly fashion, and when the list was completed she was going to go upstairs with a new roll of heavy-duty dustbin bags and begin, without hysteria, to fill them with Max's possessions.

The first person on the list was Edie. She had planned to ring Edie first and tell her what had happened and reassure her that she was, strangely and slightly light-headedly, perfectly all right. Then she intended to ring her solicitor and bank manager and Alison at the bookshop to tell her, in the phrase beloved of old-fashioned crime novels that didn't need to trouble themselves with too much inconvenient reality, that something had come up, something that would prevent her coming in to the shop tomorrow, but that she would be in as usual on Wednesday. However, on reflection, she thought she would ring Edie after she had spoken to her solicitor and bank manager, rather than before, so that she could sound reassuring about having everything in hand and being composed and controlled.

She had been extraordinarily composed when she discovered, by asking Max outright about the amount of money he had received for the flat in Barnes, that he had never actually sold it. She had been rather less composed when it became evident that, not only was the flat not sold, but it wasn't even on the market since it was still inhabited by Max's last girlfriend, who was both refusing to leave and refusing to pay the bills. And she had, to her subsequent regret, lost all control when Max fell on his knees on her bedroom floor and told her that only she could save him from the rapacious harpy who was bleeding him dry, and that was why he'd wanted to come home, to a real, warm, loving woman whose sole aim wasn't to castrate him as well as bleed him dry.

She had, of course, cried all night after that episode. She had expected to. What she hadn't expected was, despite the dispiriting sensation of having a tremendous hangover, to feel such a relief the next day. It was unmistakable, this relief, a feeling that she was at last emerging from something that had beguiled her for too long in a profoundly unsettling way, and obscured her sense of purpose into the bargain. When Max, haggard in his lavish velour dressing gown, had stared into his coffee the next morning and said, "I need you, doll. I want you, I love you. Please, please forgive me," she'd been able to say, to her amazement, "Of course I forgive you, but I'm afraid I don't want you anymore."

Sitting now on her telephone chair, she carefully tested her feelings as she had done a hundred times a day since Max's revelations. Did she still love him? Did she even still want or need him? No, quite decidedly. Could she face the thought of all the days and months and years ahead without him? Yes, not quite so decidedly, but that was more, she thought, the prospect of no man at all rather than no Max. And, even that possibility, the possibility of being on her own really meaning being on her own, was less unpalatable than seeing herself sliding back into being the person she seemed to be around Max, the anxious, appeasing, uncertain person who dealt with his unreliability with either silence or screams.

She looked again at her telephone list. She was going to rehearse very carefully what she was going to say to the solicitor because, although she obviously wasn't going to blurt it all out before she actually saw him, it was important, she felt, to give him an idea, in a dignified way, of what she wished to see him about. Perhaps she wasn't quite ready for that yet. Perhaps she wasn't quite ordered enough in her mind to talk about it as distantly as she wanted to. Perhaps it would be better to ring Edie first, after all, and ask her advice about how she should tell Eliot. It was only when she thought of Eliot, she told herself, that she felt remotely unsteady.

She picked up the receiver and dialed Edie's number. It would be an hour or two before Edie needed to go to the theater, a time when Edie could be expected to give even half her attention to her sister, a time when . . .

"Hello?" Edie said.

"It's me –"

"Vivi," Edie said, "you are just brilliant at picking the very moment when I really can't –"

"No," Vivien shouted. "No!"

"What?"

"Listen to me!" Vivien shouted. "Listen to me!" And burst into tears.

Now that he had switched off even the television, the house was eerily quiet. Even the perpetual hum of London seemed to have withdrawn itself to a distance. The only sound, really, was Arsie who, having leaped on him the moment he lay down on the sofa, was now extended up his chest with languorous purpose and purring loudly. He had his eyes closed, but in a way that indicated to Russell that he could remain, at the same time, exceedingly watchful.

Beside them, on a padded stool, lay the evening newspaper, an empty wineglass and the plate that had borne Russell's unsatisfactory supper. There had been nobody at home when Russell returned, and no indication as to where anybody was, or what they intended, except that the stack of Ben's possessions behind the sofa appeared, Russell thought, slightly diminished. He had cleared up the kitchen in a perfunctory way against Edie's return, made himself an unsuccessful omelette over too high a flame, finished the last third of a bottle of red wine, done the crossword in the paper and was now prone on the sofa wondering why an empty house should feel so peculiarly unrelaxing.

"Is it waiting?" he said to Arsie. "Is it just waiting for them all to come in?"

Arsie yawned. The inside of his mouth was as immaculate as the rest of him. He stretched one paw upward and laid it, claws only just sheathed, on the skin of Russell's neck, just above his shirt collar.

"Don't," Russell said.

Arsie took no notice.

"Please oblige me," Russell said. "Please take pity on how weary I am. Please don't behave like all the others."

Arsie unfolded his second paw and stretched it up to join the first one. Then he slowly curled his claws over the edge of Russell's shirt and into his skin.

"Get off!" Russell yelled, flinging himself upright.

Arsie flew in a neat semicircle and landed lightly on the rug. He composed himself at once into a tidy sitting position, with his back to Russell, and began to wash.

"I'm sorry," Russell said, "but that was the limit. You had been warned."

He swung his legs off the sofa to the floor, and put his elbows on his knees. In an hour, Edie would be home and, however tempting it was to think of going to bed, it was a temptation he must resist. He got stiffly to his feet and picked up the plate and glass. Part of the hour might be beguiled by making some very strong coffee.

"Aren't you in bed?" Edie said from the doorway.

Russell swam dizzily through half-sleep to consciousness.

"No, I –"

"Isn't Ben in?"

"No."

"Lazlo's having supper with Rosa, Matt's out somewhere with Ruth and I thought at least Ben –"

Russell began to struggle out of his armchair.

"I think some of his stuff's gone."

Edie looked sharply at the sofa.

"Has it?"

Russell went across to the doorway and bent to kiss her.

"Would you like a drink?"

She thought for a moment.

"Not much."

"Why don't you," Russell said, "why don't you just be accommodating for once and have a drink while we talk?"

Edie hesitated.

"Talk –"

"Yes," Russell said, "unless you'd like to make an appointment for the purpose on Sunday?"

He moved past her and went across the hall to the kitchen.

"Coffee? Wine? Whiskey?"

Edie went slowly after him.

"Wine perhaps –"

He glanced at her, then jerked his head toward one of the chairs by the table.

"Sit down."

"I'm going to –"

"White? Red?"

"Anything," Edie said, "anything. I feel too stunned after this week to make decisions that size." She pulled her arms out of her jacket and let it slump on the chair behind her. Then she leaned them on the table and let her head fall forward. "Matt, Rosa, Lazlo, Ruth, Vivi –" She paused and then she said, "Poor Vivi."

Russell put a glass of white wine on the table in front of her. She looked at it without enthusiasm.

"I thought you couldn't stand Max."

"I can't. It's not Max, it's the situation, Vivien's situation. Divorce and everything. She's going to have to sell the house."

There was a short pause and then Russell, standing at the other side of the table with the wine bottle in his hand, said with emphasis, "Yes."

Slowly, Edie raised her eyes to look at him.

He said, "May I say something?"

"Go on."

"Well," he said, "if the children are all branching out like this, if they really are going to do the things they seem to be doing, well, it would – it would be nice to help them, wouldn't it?"

Edie's gaze didn't waver from his face. He put the bottle down on the table, and leaned on his hands.

He said, in a different tone, "I know how hard this might be for you even to contemplate, heaven knows, it isn't very easy for me, but I've been thinking and the thought I've come up with, the thought that won't somehow go away, is that, in order to give the children a bit of help and rearrange our own lives, we ought, really, if you think about it, to – to sell up too. We ought to sell this house."

Edie went on looking at him.

There was a silence that seemed to go on for a disconcerting length of time, and then she said, "I know."

CHAPTER TWENTY

The estate agent had said that, on the plus side, it was very rare for a house of this size and quality, and still unconverted, to come up in this particular area. However, he said – and he was quite difficult to take seriously, Edie thought, because of looking rather younger than Matthew and wearing a childishly terrible tie – the minus side, which was quite a significant minus, was that the house was so very unconverted that most buyers with the kind of cash they were envisaging would find it difficult to visualize it in an improved and modernized state.

They had both looked at him when he finished speaking as if he must be about to say more.

After a silence, he'd said, "You get my drift?"

Edie had looked at Russell.

Russell said politely, "No. Actually."

The agent had taken a breath. Perhaps, Edie thought, we remind him of his own parents, and how he has to talk to them.

She said, to try and help him, "Are you saying it's good or bad?"

He took another breath, and then he said what he had already said, only more elaborately.

"I see," Russell said. "The house is in too bad a state to sell."

"No, no, it's a very desirable house in a good area. It's just that" – he glanced round the kitchen – "it's just that, the way it is, just now, the way it *looks*, because it looks so – very much of, um, well, its *time*, of course, it's family life and all that, that the kind of purchaser we have in mind, well, we would *like* to have in mind for this kind of property, might, you see, have difficulty in, well, in seeing the potential."

Edie had leaned forward.

She said, in a very kind voice, "You think we should tidy it up."

The agent had stared at her with something approaching violent relief.

"Yes."

"Well, that's easy –"

"No," he said, suddenly desperate again. "No. Not tidy up. *Empty.* Just – almost empty it." He waved his arms. "This room –" He gestured out of the window. "That shed –"

"Empty it –"

"Yes."

Edie said tolerantly, "You've watched too many television makeover programs."

He looked at her. He was almost glaring.

"It's not me," he said, "it's *them*."

And so, because of them, because of all those unknown, feared but longed-for people who would tramp round the house as if it belonged to no one but possibly to their futures, Edie was in Ben's bedroom on a Saturday afternoon, with a roll of black bags and a bucket of water in which floated a new green pot scourer. If she looked out of the window – which she did a great deal as if trying to imprint the view from it on her mind as a kind of talisman – she could see the piles of peculiar objects that were growing at the end of the garden as Russell emptied the shed. Sometimes he stopped and gazed at the house and, if she was looking out of the window, he waved at her. She waved back, but she didn't smile. This was, she felt, no moment, no time in their lives, for smiling.

She had expected to be taken over by emotion. She had relied upon the fact that every great event in her life so far had swept her up on a huge wave of blazing feeling, feeling so strong in essence and operatic in effect that she didn't have to decide how to behave, she just surrendered and was swept away. But, for some reason she couldn't fathom, this event, this business of moving house and thereby moving everything in their lives – except, Russell had pointed out, hopefully each other – wasn't knocking her out, bowling her over. It was instead presenting her with a whole range of reactions, some of which were painful in a way she had anticipated, and some of which were extremely surprising. She could feel something close to anguish at the thought of, perhaps, not going up and down those stairs in six months' time, but she could also feel that not having to go up and down the stairs might simultaneously spring her from years of habit which had, over time, quietly and insidiously become a prison.

"Not an *actual* prison," she said to Russell. "Of course not. Just a prison of me going on and on being me."

If she thought about people coming round the house and staring speculatively at the pale blotches on the walls that she was making by scrubbing the adhesive gum off so hard, she felt a dislike of them that almost amounted to loathing. But if, on the other hand, she turned that idea around and thought of nobody coming, nobody even wanting the house, she felt worse. She felt, she supposed, close to something Vivien had said, crying down the telephone one night after Edie had returned from her last but one night in *Ghosts*.

"When I think," Vivien had said between sniffs, "when I think of Max deceiving me again, leaving me again, I feel awful. But when I think of him coming back, what it would be like if I had to have him back, I feel really, *really* terrible."

Edie moved Ben's bed away from the wall in order to attack the gum marks left by his Kate Moss poster. There were several socks nesting furrily against the baseboard and a gold-colored earring like a flower and a sticky teaspoon. She picked them up gingerly and flung them across the bed onto the carpet. Ben was buying new socks now, new socks and bed linen and a screwdriver for this little flat he'd found in Walthamstow, two streets away from the flat Naomi shared with her mother. It wasn't much of a place, he said, but it had a sitting room and a bedroom and he was going to paint it with the help of another photographer's assistant and then he was going to lay siege to Naomi.

"What do you mean, lay siege?"

"I'm going to make it really nice and then I'm going to wait."

"Wait? For what?"

He'd been filling his rucksack with possessions from behind the sofa.

"Wait for her to see."

"Will she?"

Ben spread out a faded black T-shirt with a skull printed on the front and then he tossed it on the floor.

"Oh yes," he said.

"D'you mean," Edie said, "that you'll cook supper and light candles and buy *flowers*?"

Ben inspected another black T-shirt.

"Might do."

"And if it doesn't work?"

"Then," Ben said, chucking the second T-shirt after the first, "I'll still end up with my own gaff and I'll think again."

Edie began on the next batch of gum patches with her scourer. Ben wouldn't let her see this flat of his any more than Rosa and Lazlo would let her see the one they'd found in Barons Court.

"Barons Court!" Edie had said. "But that's the other side of London!"

"It's a very nice flat," Lazlo said seriously. He looked at Rosa. "Piccadilly Line."

Rosa looked at Edie.

"Good for work."

"Oh yes," Lazlo said, "very good for work."

"But why can't I see it?"

"You can," Rosa said, "in time. When we've – done something about the bathroom."

She looked at Lazlo. They both giggled.

He said, "And the kitchen."

They giggled again.

Edie said, "I really don't see why you have to be so secretive."

"Not secretive, Mum. Just private."

"They're paying two hundred pounds a week," Edie said to Russell, "and Ben's paying a hundred and twenty-five. How will they *manage*?"

"We don't ask them," Russell said, "and we don't worry. Certainly not until this fails to sell." He put a hand on the nearest wall. "Which it won't because I am going to paint the front door."

"I really think," Matthew had said, surveying the house from the street, "that you should at least paint the front door."

"It's always been that color."

"It isn't the color," Matthew said patiently, "it's the chips."

"But –"

"Do it, Dad," Matthew said. "Just bite the bullet and do it. Like the damp in the downstairs loo."

Matthew, Edie thought, aiming her scouring pad toward the bucket, and missing, was different. He was, in one way, back to the Matthew he had been when he first met Ruth, the Matthew who had kindly, if patronizingly, told his parents how much better their lives might be if only they followed his advice. But there were new elements now, as well, elements that were softer and more sympathetic, elements induced, it seemed, by his knowledge that he was going to be a father. He had, for example, gone, almost at once, to live with Ruth in the flat that had been such a bone of contention between them, in order, he said, to look after her.

"But she isn't ill," Edie said. "Pregnancy isn't an illness. It's a – well, it's a very natural state of being but she isn't an invalid."

Matthew was standing by the kitchen table, dressed for work and drinking orange juice.

"I want to look after her. I want to make sure she eats the right things and gets enough rest. I'm going to the doctor with her."

"Are you?"

Matthew drained his glass.

"I'm going for every ultrasound. I'm going whenever I need to know what Ruth knows."

He had left his room as if he had never been in it. In fact, he had left it so completely that in order to visualize him in it at all Edie had to remember all the way back to the serious-minded boy in gum boots who had so feared the leak in the roof that going up and down the staircase had been a real test of courage for him. That was the boy who was now proposing not only to devote himself to his girlfriend's pregnancy but also to put his own career on hold when Ruth's maternity leave was over in order to care for their child. He said it was his choice to do that, he said it was what he wanted.

"Is it – is it what Ruth wants?"

"Of course."

"But I thought you couldn't bear the flat –"

"What I couldn't bear," Matthew said, "was the situation. And then I could hardly bear what followed it. But now it's changed. Everything's changed. Everything."

Edie looked at him.

"Yes," she said faintly.

She sat down now, on the edge of Ben's bed, and then she lay back and contemplated the ceiling. When she and Vivien were growing up, she had always prided herself on being like their father, a restless man who found any kind of routine not so much anathema as impossible. Vivien, of course, was like their mother, the kind of person who sees change as some malevolent plot deliberately devised to distress her. But look at Vivien now, staring into the wreckage of the fragile edifice she'd spent so much of her life patching and mending, and not, repeat *not*, falling to pieces. It was Vivien who, in between looking for flats in Fulham for herself – "Why shouldn't I live farther in? Who's to stop me living exactly where I want?" – was urging Edie to think of where she and Russell might live after the house was sold. "Why don't you think about Clerkenwell? Or Little Venice? Why don't you have an adventure?" It was Vivien who had said to Edie, "Going on is hard, but going back would be a whole lot worse."

Going back. Edie stretched her eyes wide and focused on a long, wavering crack in the plaster above her head. To think now how she had longed to go back, how fiercely she had told herself that all she wanted, all she was truly able to do, lay in what she had already done, in the way she had lived her life since they had moved into the house. But if she was completely truthful with herself and somebody, some fairy godmother, materialized out of the battered walls of Ben's bedroom and offered her the chance to go back, she would have to make sure of where she was going back to. Not, now, to maternal supremacy, not, now, to that beguiling power of sustenance and control, that luxurious simplicity of society-approved choice: children first, everything else second. What she would have to say, slightly embarrassedly, to the fairy godmother, was that she would indeed like to go back, but not very far back, back in fact only as far as the first night of the production of *Ghosts*, when she had known that she had done something exceptionally well, and been applauded for it.

"How odd," she'd say to the fairy godmother, "to have one hunger almost replaced by one so very different."

"Not replaced," the fairy godmother would reply, adjusting her gauzy skirts, "merely augmented by, added to. Nothing, you see, stands still."

Russell had said that. He'd been shuffling through some property brochures that Vivien had zealously sent and he said, "I never thought we'd leave this house, I never thought I could, but now I wonder if I could stay. Nothing stands still, does it, and I suppose, if it did, we'd stop breathing. It's not change that's so painful, it's just getting used to it."

Edie sat up slowly. It actually wasn't getting used to change that hurt, it was getting used to the truth, or whatever that element was that wasn't the illusions you'd clung to and comforted yourself with for more years than you'd care to remember. And once you'd started doing without the illusions, you got braver, you could breathe the thinner air, take longer strides, allow yourself to make claims. And the claim I want to make, Edie thought, getting to her feet and moving toward the window again, is to work. I want to act again, I want to be on a stage or in front of a camera, and I mind very much indeed that nobody has asked me, since *Ghosts*.

She looked down the garden. Russell was standing outside the shed holding Rosa's old fairy cycle. Russell had said she must keep the faith, that there would be other parts, that he would help her to change agents if she thought that would make a difference. She leaned her forehead against the glass of the window and stared at him. He had put the bike down now and was pulling out of the shed yards and yards of crumpled green plastic netting that they had once used in an attempt to stop the boys' soccer balls flying over the fence into neighboring gardens. He looked purposeful and deter-mined and, at the same time, as if this task was far from easy. He looked like someone who was doing something he didn't want to do in order to be able to move on to something better. He looked like the kind of person Edie was going to have to be when she ate all the hard words and thoughts she had uttered and believed in the past about his agency, and asked him for work to tide her over until – until something better came up.

"I'll do anything," she planned to say to him, "and I'll do

it properly," and he would give her a long look back and say with emphasis, "Yes, you will."

She took her face away from the window and bent to pick up the bucket. She would go downstairs now, and make a mug of tea and carry the tea down the garden to Russell, and she would ask him, there and then – *humbly* and there and then – if he could help her. She looked back from the doorway, at Ben's room. It was his bedroom but it was also the past and there was, suddenly, excitingly, frighteningly, no time like the present. Not, that is, if you wanted a future. Edie closed the door behind her, and trod carefully down the stairs.

"'Perhaps,'" Lazlo constantly said to her as Osvald Alving, "'Perhaps there'll be lots of things for me to be glad about – and to live for . . .'"

Arsie was waiting at the foot of the stairs. He looked up as Edie passed him and made a small, interrogative remark.

Edie paused and bent to touch the top of his head with her free hand.

"'Yes,'" she said, as Mrs. Alving had always said. "'Yes, I'm sure there will.'"

A NOTE ON THE TYPE

The text of this book is set in Linotype Sabon, named after the type founder Jacques Sabon. It was designed by Jan Tschichold and jointly developed by Linotype, Monotype, and Stempel, in response to a need for a typeface to be available in identical form for mechanical hot metal composition and hand composition using foundry type.

Tschichold based his design for Sabon roman on a font engraved by Garamond, and Sabon italic on a font by Granjon. It was first used in 1966 and has proved an enduring modern classic.